Praise for
BEYOND

"A match made in heaven for readers wanting to immerse themselves in ghostly romance. All-consuming."

—NIKKI TRIONFO, award-winning author of *Shatter*

"A touching tale of young love that reaches beyond mortal limits."

—KATHERINE KING, award-winning author
of *The Other Side of the Stars*

"With heartbreakingly tough choices, this is a story that will hook you from the start."

—PEGGY EDDLEMAN, author of *Sky Jumpers*
and *The Forbidden Flats*

Praise for
BEFORE

"A sure-fire mix of romance and suspense. The perfect up-all-night book."

—LEEANNE H. ADAMS AND BRIAN J. ADAMS, creators of
Dwight in Shining Armor and writers of *Saving Zoë*

"Larkin and Haverlock deliver their signature style: swoon-worthy romance, nail-biting stakes and an ending that will both surprise and stick with you."

—CHRISTENE HOUSTON, Swoony Award-winning
author of *Cookie Girl Christmas*

Also by Catina Haverlock
and Angela Larkin

BEYOND

BEFORE

Catina Haverlock & Angela Larkin

SWEETWATER
BOOKS

An imprint of Cedar Fort, Inc.
Springville, Utah

To Scott, Adam, Zac, Ellie, and Crew.
You're my reason for everything.
—Catina Haverlock

For Nic and the kids.
—Angela Larkin

ISBN 13: 978-1-4621-2205-9

Published by Sweetwater Books, an imprint of Cedar Fort, Inc.
2373 W. 700 S., Springville, UT 84663
Distributed by Cedar Fort, Inc., www.cedarfort.com

LIBRARY OF CONGRESS CATALOGING-IN-PUBLICATION DATA

Names: Larkin, Angela, author. | Haverlock, Catina, author.
Title: Before / Angela Larkin and Catina Haverlock.
Description: Springville, Utah : Sweetwater Books, An imprint of Cedar Fort, Inc., [2018]
Identifiers: LCCN 2018025567 (print) | LCCN 2018026740 (ebook) | ISBN 9781462129294 (epub, pdf, mobi) | ISBN 9781462122059 | ISBN 9781462122059 q(perfect bound : qalk. paper)
Subjects: LCSH: Time travel--Fiction. | LCGFT: Novels. | Romance fiction. | Science fiction.
Classification: LCC PS3612.A64855 (ebook) | LCC PS3612.A64855 B44 2018 (print) | DDC 813/.6--dc23
LC record available at https://lccn.loc.gov/2018025567

Cover design by Shawnda T. Craig
Cover design © 2018 Cedar Fort, Inc.
Edited by Hali Bird and Melissa Caldwell
Typeset by Nicole Terry

Printed in the United States of America

10 9 8 7 6 5 4 3 2 1

Printed on acid-free paper

Contents

CONTENTS

Contents

April is the cruellest month.

—T. S. Eliot

Chapter One

HOMECOMING

(LANDON)

59 Days Before

In all my memory of living in this house, we've never once closed the shutters in the family room. You'd have to be crazy to block out the view of the forest and the lake beyond. Today every shutter in the house is locked down tight.

Violet is spying through a crack in the entryway shutter, letting out dramatic noises. My cousin Reese looks at me from his seat on the river-rock hearth and rolls his eyes. He turns his attention back to his phone and shakes his head, not bothering to hide his smile from Violet.

"Yep. Still there. All eight of them," Violet says.

"Any press is good press," Reese says, not taking his eyes from his phone.

Violet rounds on us, then stares at me, eyes wide, like I owe her something. It's not like I have any control over how many news vans decide to camp out in my front yard. Less than twenty-four hours after qualifying for the Olympics and my whole family is basically quarantined until my attorney and sponsors tell me what I can and can't say to the media about Presley.

The thing is, I don't even know what to say about Presley.

Violet stretches her neck with her hands on her hips. "Well?"

"What do you want from me, Violet? You know I'm not allowed to talk to them." She's really getting on my nerves, but there's no point in running from your twin.

Her eyes widen. "Yeah, but you're allowed to talk to us."

My mom slips into the room with a tray of steaming mugs and a large can of whipped cream. She offers a cup to my dad, who's pacing with a phone to his ear, biting at his thumbnail. He waves her away and mouths, "No, thank you." She crosses the room and sets it all on the hearth next to Reese.

"Drink it while it's hot," Mom says.

Reese nabs the can of whipped cream and squirts a Matterhorn-sized mountain into his mouth. Then he does the same thing on top of his hot chocolate.

"You disgust me." Violet scowls and then turns back to her peeping crack in the shutter. "There's got to be some trespassing law they're breaking here. I'm gonna Google it."

My dad hangs up and wipes the back of his hand across his forehead. "ActiveArmor is going to keep you. We haven't lost their sponsorship. For now, anyhow. It will all depend on how this pans out."

"That's good. Thanks, Dad," I say.

It seems like so far my sponsors believe that I have nothing to do with Presley's injuries, but public figures have been lynched for less. My eyes bounce to the flat screen, which plays the same eight-second clip. Every network and sports channel blabbering their own theory about the kiss on the mountain yesterday. Honestly though, losing a snowboarding gear sponsorship is the least of my worries. More troubling is the fact that I kissed a complete stranger on national TV.

Or is she? I knew her name, didn't I? And when I kissed her, it didn't feel like the first time. I knew the golden flecks in her green eyes and her smell and the exact way our lips would fit together before they even touched. So why can't I remember where I know her from?

I have no idea where she lives, what car she drives, where we met. I don't know her family or even her last name. All I know is that I knew what it would feel like to kiss her yesterday. I *needed* to kiss her. Maybe it was the adrenaline, but I didn't care who was watching. Standing on the side of a mountain with news cameras and half of Truckee there, I bent over her, spoke her name, touched her face, and kissed her. And when our lips touched, it felt like home. And that scares me more than the media vans on the lawn or losing a sponsorship.

My dad's eyes are tired. "Before we sit down with the lawyers tomorrow, we've got to have a straight story for them, son. And you saying 'I can't remember' or 'I don't know' isn't going to cut it. A girl's been hurt—pretty bad. And she was clawing her way up that mountain looking for you." He takes a seat on the couch opposite me and rests his elbows on his knees. "So I'm going to ask you again, what happened up there? I'm your dad. And you need to tell me the truth."

Violet abandons her spy post and marches over next to where my dad's seated. "Seriously, Landon. What were you thinking? Kissing some beat-up girl on a gurney?"

Without a word, my dad puts his arm around her waist, pulls her onto his lap, and wraps her in a tight bear hug. "Sweetie, I think this conversation is going to go better if you hustle up stairs." She struggles to break free, but he plants a huge kiss on her cheek.

"Dad!" she protests. He stands and nudges her towards the staircase.

"And you'll have a better view of all that nonsense outside from an upstairs window. I've got some binoculars in my desk drawer if you want." He smiles and winks at her.

Halfway up the stairs, she turns to look at us over her shoulder. Her eyes scan the group but narrow in on Reese. "Not sure why I'm being ejected, but that clown gets to stay."

"I'm just here for the hot chocolate," Reese counters.

My mom crosses the room, switches off the TV, then joins my dad on the couch. Her eyes are warm and calm.

"Why don't we just start from the beginning, bud," my mom says. "But before we do, I just want to say that your dad and I are worried that the pressure is getting to you. You've just come off the X Games. The Olympics are around the corner. Nobody would blame you if you need a break. You're more important to us than any of this."

My dad cuts in, "Son, we want you to be happy, so if you want out, we can pull the plug today."

A lump swells in my throat. I know how much my career has meant to my dad. He got me my first set of skis when I was two. All of the months and years we've spent on the slopes. All the places we've traveled. Sacrifices he's made to make my dreams happen. And now, just like that, he's willing to let it all go because he's worried about me.

Could it be the pressure? Could the stress be causing me to imagine things that aren't real or forget things that are? That doesn't feel right.

"I want to keep skiing."

My mom reaches across and gives my knee a squeeze. "Okay, then. But either way, we have to get to the bottom of this. Tell us everything you know about this girl."

I've been avoiding this moment—the time I would have to come up with something they'd believe about Presley. I've considered accusing her of being a crazy stalker. Violet would probably approve of that story. I could tell them she's just some girl I met at a party. But it didn't really matter what I made up, because if she said something different, no one, including the media, would know whom to believe. "Has anyone heard how she's doing?"

My parents look at each other and then back at me. "Not too hot, I'm afraid," Dad says. "She's been put into one of those medically induced comas. I guess she had a pretty bad head injury."

The news turns my stomach. I had no idea it was that serious. "I felt sorry for her," I say.

"We all did," my mom says.

"I felt sorry for her and it was just weird how she grabbed onto me like that. I felt bad just walking away." I planned on coming up with a better story, but this was at least partly the truth. "I mean, how would that have looked? You guys are all upset about how it went down, and I get it, but think about how it would have looked if I shook off some bleeding girl so I could go smile for the cameras?"

There's a quick knock at the door. "For the love of . . . when will those reporters take a hint? We aren't making a statement today," Dad says.

Reese is already at the door, looking out Violet's spy crack. "It's not the reporters." He turns to me with the same look in his eye he had that time we got caught tin foiling the principal's office. "It's the cops."

My dad faces me, all business now. "You've got to stop sidestepping the question. Do you know this girl or don't you?"

There's nothing I can do now but tell the truth. "No. I don't."

Chapter Two

WAKING UP

(PRESLEY)

45 Days Before

Presley?" The sound of my mother's voice is far away, but I feel her hand on my arm, squeezing and then smoothing the hair back from my forehead. "Your dad's here, sweetie. Can you open your eyes for him?"

My dad's here. I want to open my eyes. I really want to, but I'm sinking in blackness so heavy. I can't fight it off, so I drift down. Down so far I can't hear her anymore.

—

I don't know how much time has passed when I hear my mom's voice again.

"She's stirring," Gayle says. I hear footsteps, then feel something cold against my chest.

I want to see my mom, but my lids are heavy. My arms and my legs are heavy too.

"Her heart rate's rapid." Another woman's voice, but not Gayle's.

"Is that bad?" Gayle asks.

"It just means she's waking up."

My mother takes my hand and squeezes it.

"Presley, I'm just going to take a look at your eyes," the woman says.

Her voice is close now, and clear. I feel a cool thumb against my eyelid, and then I'm blinded. First one eye and then the other. I will my head to turn from the light and it obeys.

"Look at that," the woman says with a lightness in her voice.

I fight to keep my eyes open and my mother comes into view. She's leaning over me. Her face is tired, older.

"Hey, you. Welcome back." A strained smile stretches across her face.

"Mom," I whisper. My throat is raw and my lips nearly crack at the movement.

The doctor is at my bedside holding a Styrofoam cup with a bent straw inside. "I bet you're thirsty."

She leans in and holds the straw to my mouth, and I'm surprised at the effort it takes to close my lips around it.

"You've got a lot of medicine in your system right now. It's been helping you rest while your brain heals. It's perfectly natural for you to feel a bit foggy and confused. Probably very tired."

I struggle to pull the water through the straw, swallow, and listen to her words at the same time. The cool liquid slides down my throat, washing away a dry chemical taste.

"You've been asleep for nearly two weeks, so it's normal for your body to feel weak. I'm just going to do a little exam to see how things are coming along. I know it's hard for you to speak right now, so just do your best."

Two weeks. Two weeks from when? The last thing I could remember was waking up on the slope and Landon was miraculously alive. After eight months of lingering as a spirit, after falling in love with him, almost losing him, and then jumping through time, there he was. Standing on that slope—alive. And he's *been* alive for two whole weeks, and all I've been able to do is lie in this hospital bed the entire time.

A young male nurse I didn't notice before rolls a small table with a laptop on it to the right of my bed and begins typing. The doctor has me squeeze her fingers, push and pull against her hands. She asks me to follow her pen with my eyes from side to side, an action that feels harder than it should.

The doctor takes a seat on my left. "I'm going to raise your bed up a bit."

The motion of the bed rolls my stomach, and I'm grateful there's nothing in it.

"Can you tell me your full name?"

"Presley Hale," I manage. My throat is still so dry.

"How old are you?"

"Seventeen." My mom exchanges a look with the doctor.

"No, remember, honey? Your birthday isn't until August."

"I know you want to help her," the doctor says, "but it tells me more if we don't lead her." She turns back to me. "Do you remember what month it was when you had your accident?"

I'm still sixteen, which means it's before August. Landon is still alive, which means it's before April. I steal a glance out of the window and see a gray sky and bare branches. Snow on the mountains.

"It's winter," I whisper, mostly to myself.

The doctor smiles. "Yes. It's been a pretty intense one this year. Record breaking snowfall. Our ski resorts have loved that."

I can tell she's trying to put me at ease. Not make a big deal about my less-than-accurate answers.

"You had your accident at the beginning of February," she says. "You woke up just in time for Valentine's Day." She flourishes her hand pointing out the cheesy paper decorations hung about my room.

The doctor's fabricated smile fades and her eyes turn serious. "We're all still wondering how you ended up on that slope. Can you tell us anything you remember about that day? About what happened to you?"

6

"No," I say. They'll never let me out of this hospital if I tell them I was catapulted back in time with a guy who was dead but now lives. "I don't remember anything."

Gayle closes her eyes and speaks deliberately. "How do you end up on a snowy mountain in your summer pajamas and not know how you got there?"

The doctor places a hand on Gayle's knee. "She's had a brain injury. Some memory loss is expected at this point. You're going to have to be patient while she heals. In the majority of cases, it comes back with time."

The doctor stands up and signals to the nurse that he's not needed. "I have some more questions, a couple more tests, but I think that's enough for today. The priority now is that you get some rest." She shoots Gayle a weighted look. Then her smile returns. "It's a lot of work coming out of a coma."

My mother avoids the doctor's gaze and begins smoothing my blanket and rearranging my pillow. She resituates herself in her chair and says, "So, you've had a visitor."

"Dad?" Foggy recollections of hearing Gayle tell me he came float back into my mind. The letters we exchanged before would've never technically been sent. That means we really haven't communicated in years. I guess having a daughter in a coma brought him here anyway.

"He was here, but work called him back before you woke up. He's called to check on you every day since."

That's . . . sweet. Very dad-like. Unexpected. Though I'd been talking with my dad again, I never thought he'd show up this soon. I guess having a kid in a coma lit a fire.

"Maybe I should have said *visitors*," Gayle says. "The boy from the ski slope also stopped by."

A jolt of hope slams into me and fills my whole body. I do my best to hide this from Gayle and bite hard into my cheeks to stop the smile.

"Landon Blackwood. Sound familiar?"

Hearing my mom acknowledge his reality only adds to the thrill that he's alive. I prepare myself to utter the most traitorous lie I've ever spoken. "I don't know who that is."

Gayle's eyes narrow, and I feel like she's making a great effort to restrain what she's really thinking.

"You know there were witnesses at the slope who say you were calling out for him." She slides her chair closer to my bed and leans in. "So obviously, you do know him."

I don't feel accused. It's more like she's trying to unravel the clues.

"Please think, Presley. Honey, your injuries were life threatening. You've been in a coma for two weeks." She encloses my hand in both of hers. "What does this boy have to do with all of this?"

7

Chapter Three

Escape

(PRESLEY)

43 Days Before

The third nurse of the day removes the blood pressure cuff from my arm, jots something on my chart, and walks out, leaving the door to my hospital room open. This place is a prison.

I've been awake for two days, and it's been nothing but a constant stream of nurses, technicians, and everyone in between. And when the doctors aren't pumping me about what I remember, my mom is. The one bright spot in all of this is I'm getting stronger. I'm almost weaned from the pain meds (partly because I tell the doctors I'm feeling better than I am). I lie because thinking through pain is a lot easier than thinking through a narcotic haze. And right now, I need to think.

My mom won't let up with the Landon interrogations. She's not mad at me, but she's convinced that he hurt me. She keeps force-feeding me the humiliating news clips on her phone hoping some detail will jog my memory. The ironic thing is, I remember everything that happened in perfect detail. I'll just have to keep claiming amnesia. My mom seems to be buying it, at least for now. The police are a different story.

A pair of officers came this morning to question me about my injuries and Landon's possible involvement. They don't seem as convinced about my "amnesia" as my mom and my doctor are.

I feel horrible for Landon. He's likely being questioned about my injuries when the truth is he saved my life. But neither one of us can tell the true details. So what is he telling them? Maybe the reason he hasn't visited again is because he's been ordered to stay away by the police or my mom. I don't dare bring it up with Gayle because why would I be so anxious to see someone I supposedly don't know or remember?

I have to talk to Landon, but how? My mom brought a bag of my things, including my phone, but it's void of any numbers from my Truckee friends because technically I haven't met them yet. The phonebook in my room only has listings for Blackwood Ski Resort and Blackwood Auto, the family businesses. I have to get out of here.

They've had me up and walking. Today I stood through my whole shower and even made it down to the Coke machine and back without help. I think I'm strong enough now. I just need an opportunity, but getting out of here is like breaking out of Alcatraz with the round-the-clock nurse and Gayle surveillance.

On cue, Gayle comes in, frowning at her phone.

"Who are you texting?" I ask.

Gayle shakes her head. "A caregiver I found for Chase. She has a *lot* of questions."

I'm instantly sick with guilt. I knew Chase made it back to this time with me and my mom, but I can't believe I haven't asked a single thing about how Gayle's been managing him and his autism without me. "You hired a caregiver?"

"Just a temp for now, but I'm working on getting someone long term."

"A temp? Does she have autism training? Does Chase even like her?" My worries for myself and Landon take a quick back seat as I try to figure out what kind of person is taking care of my younger brother.

"She came highly recommended. Her references looked good. I didn't have a lot of time, honestly."

Of course she didn't. And it's not like she could keep Chase at the hospital with her.

"The doctors said there's no way to really predict how long your symptoms will last." A shadow passes over her face. "It could be as long as a year. I had to get somebody in place."

"A year? That seems extreme."

"No, it's a thing. Post-concussive disorder. I looked it up."

All of this talk about Chase makes me remember the thing that's been nagging at me. Boggling my mind, really. How did my mom and Chase end up back in time here with me? It's February, and my mom didn't start as Truckee High principal until August. I have to ask. "Have you already started your job?"

She lets out a flat laugh. "Well, I was supposed to start last week, but that wasn't possible. Obviously." She rubs her palms against her thighs. "We're not even unpacked at the house." She smiles weakly. "It is what it is."

"Remind me again why you're starting a job in the middle of the school year?" This fake amnesia has its benefits. It allows me to ask questions I couldn't get away with otherwise.

She looks worried. "Don't you remember? That scandal with the principal and the vice principal? They were both terminated immediately."

I nod, fake recollection dawning on my face. "Oh, right. I think I remember something about that now." I try to hide the fact that my brain is exploding when

I think about how the universe has reshuffled events to allow my existence in this time. And that other people's lives have been affected.

James could probably shed light on all of these questions, but last I saw him, he was being torn apart by Vigilum. I still remember how shocked I was to learn that the earth is crawling with dark spirits—desperate souls who use their abilities to manipulate the living and the dying. Some want revenge. But most want to find a way to get passage to the next life.

His gamble that the Vigilum would lose interest in me once Landon took his passage backfired. Once James realized they intended to kill me, he risked everything to save me. I can only hope someone like him can't die twice.

The throb in my head intensifies, and I feel a hot wave of nausea ripple through me.

My mom touches the back of her hand to my forehead. "You don't look so good. Should I call a nurse?"

"No. I'm just kind of nauseated."

"It's probably the wretched food in this joint."

"It's pretty much the worst," I say, wrinkling my nose.

"Slop," she says and then we smile at each other. "How about I walk down the street to this place I found? They have the best grilled cheese and tomato soup."

"My fave."

"I know." Gayle pumps her eyebrows a couple of times. It's weird that she's being so nice and accommodating. I can only guess her priorities have shifted a bit after almost losing me.

This softer side of her only enhances the guilt I'm feeling because the second she said she was going to walk down the street, I was already formulating how I was going to get her car keys and find Landon.

"Would you mind grabbing me a juice from the mini fridge before you go?" Every time my mom had passed the nurses' station, she'd raided the nurses' drink stash for me.

"You got it." She stands and leaves the room and I swipe her purse, reach in the pocket, grab her keys, and hide them under the blanket. I zip it up, hang it back on the armchair, and force myself to look natural when she returns.

She's holding two plastic cups with tin-foil seals in her hand. "Apple or grape?"

"Both. I'm not driving."

She sets them on my table, and I stifle the smile that's trying to take over my face because driving is exactly what I plan to do.

Chapter Four

HELLO AGAIN

(PRESLEY)

43 Days Before

It's funny how unnoticeable I was dressed in my normal clothes. I'm guessing the nurses didn't anticipate me to make a break for it, so when I walked past their station in jeans and a hoodie, they didn't even bat an eye. Even luckier, the hospital parking lot is small and Gayle's car was a piece of cake to find.

Gayle's sunglasses aren't my usual style, but the bright February sun is blinding, reflecting off the snow that covers the surrounding mountains. I've been quarantined indoors since I woke up and wasn't prepared for the intensity of broad daylight.

It takes me a minute to get my bearings because I was unconscious en route to the hospital. But the mountains with their distinct landmarks and silhouettes orient me and I drive toward Donner Lake. Soon everything looks familiar, and once I hop on I-80, I know I'm less than fifteen minutes from Landon's house.

I consider turning around. Most pressing, Gayle's going to kill me and probably call the cops when she gets back and realizes I'm gone with her car. Almost as bad though, I don't know how the Blackwoods are going to react to me. I don't think any of them except Landon remember me. I know I had a brain injury, but still clearly remember Frank referring to me as "someone" who was hurt that day on the slope. And not only did Violet seem to not remember me, she acted like she *hated* me. Will they even open the door?

And if they do let me in, what am I going to say? I probably should have thought this out a little better, but I had to take my chance when it presented. The only experience I've had with time travel is that it doesn't last. I can't afford that risk.

Sooner than I want, the turn to the Blackwood's driveway appears, and I follow the two parallel muddy trails through the snow. The drive is lined high on both sides with thick pine forest, and the image triggers nerves in my stomach, making me think back to the first time I came here. I was nervous then too, because I wasn't sure how to act around a family that had just lost someone. Now

I'm nervous because the family who so openly welcomed me before may very well slam the door on me. And even though none of this is my fault, I wouldn't really blame them.

The drive opens into a large snowy clearing, dominated by the sprawling Blackwood home. My heart squeezes. The memories I made in this house were overshadowed by the loss of Landon. Even as I built attachments to his family, there was always a darkness bleeding through the house, like ink in water.

Maybe this won't be that bad. They've shown themselves to be reasonable and kind, so something like a scandalous kiss wouldn't ruin everything. Would it?

The driveway is quiet, and I'm relieved at the absence of reporters. From the glimpses of footage my mom tried to show me, Landon's house had to have been the center of a media frenzy. After two weeks though, I guess the story is old news.

Walking up to the house, my face breaks into a smile when I read the license plate on a vehicle I don't remember: LBLCKWD. When I was with Landon before, I never thought about what he drove. But now I know. He drives a white Toyota Sequoia. Ski racks on the top, of course. I can't help myself. I flatten my palms against the driver side window and look inside. You can tell a lot about a person by their car and every detail seems like a gift. Like bonus content after a favorite movie.

A Dr Pepper sits in the cupholder and several empty bottles litter the passenger floor. His gym bag, half zipped, reveals a wad of workout clothes and a pair of black Nikes. Apparently he has a gum habit because dozens of silver wrappers are wadded up and strewn about the cab. I never knew he was so messy or that he loved Dr Pepper. I love knowing these things about him, but they make me wonder what else I don't I know. And how much will the things I don't know matter?

I turn toward the house and don't let myself linger in one place very long because I'm afraid if I do, I might change my mind. As I take the steps up to the front door, I wonder if my legs are weak because I've been in bed for two weeks or because of what I'm about to do. Deep breath in. Deep breath out. Whatever Landon's family thinks of me, he will be happy to see me. Nothing else matters right now.

I send up a silent prayer that it will be him that answers as I press the doorbell. It's not. It's Violet and she's not happy to see me. I should expect it, given how she treated me on the slope that day, but it's still crushing to have my best friend act this way. Her face is all hard lines except for one cocked eyebrow. She steps onto the deck and closes the door behind her.

"Why are you here?" Violet says. She looks different. Instead of the ponytail I'm used to, her hair hangs in perfect waves. She wears more makeup and her clothes look expensive. I never really noticed her clothes before, but now it'd be impossible not to.

Even though I know she doesn't remember me, I still have this foolish hope that somehow she might. "Hi, Vi," I say and I reach for her hand. She jerks back and slides her hands in her pockets, like I was a dog that tried to bite. Okay, definitely doesn't remember me. Still hates me. No point in lying so I answer her honestly. "I need to talk to Landon."

"It's Violet. And that's impossible." Her head shakes back and forth in a quick, decisive motion. "Do you have any idea what you've put him through?"

I haven't gotten in the door yet and this is worse than I thought. Not only that, in my brilliant breakout plan, I didn't think to factor in Truckee's freezing temps when I chose a thin hoodie instead of a coat. The wind picks up, and I hug myself—as does Violet, making us mirror images of stubborn resistance.

"I don't know what you're trying to do, but please just leave," Violet says.

It's killing me that I'm so close to Landon. If I could just get to him everything would be okay because he has to remember me the way I remember him. After that kiss, he has to. "I swear I'm not here to cause problems, and I know you don't understand, but . . ."

At that moment, the door opens and Violet and Landon's dad, Frank, steps out. "What are you two doing out here? It's freezing!" He moves aside and gestures for us to come in. That prayer I sent up is being answered after all. Violet shoots me a cold look before she turns and goes inside.

Through the door and I'm standing in the same Blackwood house, but right away it feels different. For starters, Landon's mess from his car seems to have followed him inside. His black backpack, Vans and Truckee High letterman jacket are all tossed on the floor in a heap, even though there's a coat rack by the front door. I can't identify the difference exactly, but the house seems more lived in. Music drifts in from somewhere and unfolded blankets sprawl over the couches in the main room. An opened bag of chips and a can of Dr Pepper sit on the coffee table. A little smile tugs at the edges of my mouth.

He's everywhere.

Frank's eyes are kind. "It's good to see you looking so well. We were worried about you." Behind Frank, Violet rolls her eyes.

"We were wondering when we might see you. Heard you took quite a hit to the head." He takes both of my hands in his, which are calloused and warm. I'm relieved and somewhat touched at the show of affection. He gives my hands a gentle squeeze and then freezes. I expect him to release my hands, but he doesn't. Instead, his eyes penetrate mine. Just as I start to feel alarmed at his scrutiny, he blinks, smiles, and releases my hands.

That was odd. He looked at me as if *I* was the one that came back from the dead.

"Yeah, I guess it was a pretty bad concussion." I flinch at my white lie, making him think my concussion is a thing of the past. The constant throb in my head calls me out.

Afton, Landon's mom, emerges from a side room. She has red reading glasses perched at the end of her nose, and her hands are full of paperwork. "Oh." She sets the papers on a small table and pushes the glasses onto her head.

"Hello, Mrs. Black—"

I'm cut off because at that second it sounds like a galloping herd of horses have been set loose upstairs. The next moment a flash of black hair attached to a muscular body leaps from the upper set of stairs and crashes onto the middle landing in a crouched position. Landon springs upright and bounds down the lower set of stairs. A football whizzes through the air and nails him square in the back. Maniacal laughter breaks out from upstairs and Reese appears on the upstairs landing.

Time stands still and a million details come into focus. First, Landon looks so good. He's poised at the bottom of the stairs, the football in his hand, ready to rocket it back at Reese. The muscles in his back flex against his snug T-shirt and his biceps work as he fakes like he's going to throw the ball at Reese. His hair, looking more wild than I'd ever seen it, is standing up as if at one point in the day it had been styled but had come undone with the rough-housing. The rise and fall of his chest and the flush of his skin from the exertion mesmerize me. So this is what Landon Blackwood in the flesh is like.

Landon lets the ball fly and it ricochets off the wall, knocking down a family photo. Reese doubles over pointing and laughing.

Afton raises her voice, "Are you two kidding me? How old are you?"

Laughing along with Reese, Landon turns his head toward his mother, but his eyes connect with mine. His brows push together as he makes a move toward me, but then seems to think better of it. I understand his restraint. I'm holding myself back too. We have an audience that can't know how we feel about each other. It would overwhelm them.

Finally, he speaks. "Presley. We need to talk."

Chapter Five

(LANDON)

43 Days Before

Finally some answers," Violet says.

"Yeah, finally," Reese jokes from his position on the upper landing.

There's no way we're having this conversation in front of my whole family. I don't care how suspicious or curious they are. I'm talking to this girl alone. My mom must sense the awkwardness because she suggests that the group join her in the kitchen.

Reese trots down the stairs and, as he passes, says, "Make sure you keep the door open." His face contorts into an exaggerated parental warning complete with waggling eyebrows.

Presley presses her lips together and tries to stifle a laugh. At least I think that's what she's doing. It feels like I know, but why would I? My family clears out, but Violet's the last to leave, clearly pouting.

"We can talk in my room." I motion for Presley to follow me, but she passes me and climbs the stairs like she's been here a hundred times. As we climb, she takes her time studying the collection of school portraits on the wall, smiling. She stops at the top of the staircase where the Blackwood school portraits hang. Her fingers graze the empty space on the wall next to my eleventh-grade photo. With a smile I can't decipher she reaches for my wrist and smoothes her fingertips over the woven leather bracelet Violet made for me.

"Landon Krew Blackwood," she says and slides the bracelet so the initials that were against the inside of my wrist are now facing out. "LKB."

She knew exactly where to find the initials on my bracelet. And even more surprising, she knows what they mean even though the whole thing is a private joke between only Violet and me. Then again, she *did* know my name on the slopes. It's not that hard to find me online. This bracelet though, it's personal. "Yeah, my sister . . ."

"I know. Made it for you as a joke."

"Yes," I say. She's smiling and suddenly I'm smiling. I can't help it. It feels like something that I didn't even know was broken is knitting back together.

Her lashes drop, hiding the knowing glint in her eye and she passes me by, leading the way to my bedroom. Without even pausing for permission, she turns the knob and lets herself in. I have no choice but to follow.

Circling, she takes in the room like a kid at Disneyland. Then, she's everywhere—trailing her fingers over my things, my trophies and photos, my bedding. She gathers my pillow next to her chest and breathes it in, then throws it back on the bed. Then in a few quick strides she's standing before me, toe-to-toe, knee-to-knee. So close I can feel her breath on my face. She smells so good. Clean and flowery—It's familiar and I find myself wanting to lean closer, but the space between us is already a sliver and I know I shouldn't close the gap.

"I can't believe we made it, Landon. We're actually here." Her eyes make a quick circuit around my room and then are back on mine. She lifts herself up on her toes and says, "Play for me."

"Play for you?"

"Yes. That song, what was it? 'Speed'? I want *you* to play it for *me* this time."

Before I have a chance to voice my confusion, she's made her way to my piano, sits at the bench, and pats the spot next to her. I've had to tell myself a lot of things to make sense of this girl. I travel a lot. I meet a lot of people. Maybe I don't remember meeting her. That could make sense. But there is no making sense of her knowing about "Speed." I know for a fact I haven't told anyone about this song.

By the time my zombie legs carry me over to the piano, she's already rifled through my sheet music and has "Speed" spread out and ready to play. She turns to me and hooks me again with those eyes.

"I know there's so much to say, so much to figure out, but I need to hear you play this. You don't know how sad it made me that I never had the chance to hear you play before."

Nothing she says makes sense. I don't know why I listen to her. Without overthinking it, I touch my fingers to the keys and the room fills up with the frenzied notes, the peaks and valleys of "Speed." I've always loved to play, but there's something about playing for Presley in this moment that makes my music feel important.

It must feel important to her too because when she looks up at me her eyes are rimmed in tears. They're spilling over, and even though she's smiling I still have the urge to wipe the tears from her cheeks.

Then, a flicker. A flash image of Presley sitting on a bed. But the weird thing is, I know it's her bed in her room. In this micro-vision, tears are also streaming down her face, over her lips, which are curved into a smile. In the wide-awake dream, all I want is to reach up and wipe her tears, but I can't. The vision evaporates like water on a flame, but the need to wipe her tears, to touch her stays with me. The logical part of my brain, the part that screams, "You don't even know this girl!" is put to bed and I switch off the light. Logic beats on the door, but I walk away from the sound—so far that I can't even hear it anymore.

I take her face in my hands, and I'm struck with an aching, unrelenting desire that weakens my resolve and sets me on a razor's edge so thin that I could tip either way. And I know once I decide it will be just like launching myself down a black diamond run; there's no skiing back uphill. The tension in my core vines through my body, making every tendon, fiber, and limb taught with a trembling constraint.

I can see in her eyes that she's aware of the line between us. Her breath and her body are still, controlled. Together, we breathe without movement, hovering on both sides of the line. Her lips part, drawing my gaze to the silky curves of her mouth and it's in that moment that I feel myself slipping. Inching closer to the point of launch. To the point where I decide.

I take a kiss from her and then retreat. But the absence of her lips on mine feels so wrong that I quickly come back for more. At once, we surrender to each other. We leap across the line clashing into one and then it's all warmth and pressure and perfect rhythm. A kiss so intentional that it's more than pleasure. It feels like medicine traveling through my body, sealing up what was torn, putting back the pieces that were out of place.

But as good as this feels something shifts in me, telling me to pull back. Logic cracks the door and flips on the light—demands an audience. As much as I want to keep kissing her I know I have to tell the truth. I tear my lips from hers, immediately hating the feeling that follows. Our eyes are locked, hers still burning with intensity.

Without warning, more images flip through my mind, like someone is changing the TV channels on hyperspeed. The pictures are gone before I can grab hold of them. A few details linger, though. Presley standing at the foot of my bed, wearing my letterman jacket. Me standing behind her while she played the piano, my hands on hers, guiding them through the notes. But that's impossible. She's never been in my room before today.

So what is it then? If they aren't memories, are they some form of déjà vu? Wishful thinking? There's just too much that's unexplained. She acts like she's been here before. She knew about the song. She let me kiss her and what kind of girl would go to such lengths to seek out a complete stranger? She definitely doesn't look at me like I'm a complete stranger.

I can't do this. I tear my eyes from hers and study my hands. Without looking, I reach over and close the keyboard cover. "This isn't right." I hazard a glance up. Her face is a mixture of hurt and confusion. I choose my words carefully because I know what I'm about to say is going to cut even deeper. "I can't deny there's something about you. But I can't let this happen when I don't know you. I don't remember you."

Chapter Six

Bomb

(PRESLEY)

43 Days Before

I hear the words, but they can't be right. "What do you mean, you don't remember me?" I look for some hint that he's teasing me but his eyes only show apologies.

"I don't even know how we met," he says.

My heart jolts. "You're serious," I say.

"Completely," he says. His eyes are clear and honest.

My throat tightens but I push back the prickling of tears that threaten to erupt.

My instincts tell me to tread very carefully. As I think of what to say next, I'm picking through a tangle of colored wires, praying I don't cut the wrong one. I choose one and snip.

"Do you remember the accident?" I'm almost positive he doesn't remember his drowning, but I have to be sure.

"You mean *your* accident?" he asks. "Are you saying we met the day you were hurt?"

He really doesn't remember anything. My heart picks up pace. "No, that's not what I'm saying." I know I'm being cryptic, but I have a bad feeling about telling him mind-bending things like, "you died," because I don't know what chain of events that could set off. What if there are terms and conditions to his second chance? What if there's a reason he doesn't remember dying? Could my telling him send us back? Could his forgetting be part of the reason we've been able to be here for two weeks without slipping back? I lay that wire down. I can't risk it. "I knew you before that."

He scrubs at his face with both palms. "You have to give me more than that."

"I know." More than being cautious, I know I'm being selfish too. If I tell the truth, he'll think I'm a mental case. That would only take me further from him. I can tell his feelings for me are so fragile right now, I can't clip that wire. "You deserve more of an explanation, but you have to trust that I have my reasons."

"Come on." He slides back a few inches from me on the piano bench, but it feels like ten miles.

"No, listen. It's important that you remember on your own. I don't want to spoon-feed you memories like some relative with a photo album." I know the memories are in him, somewhere. He's fighting them, but I can tell because there are moments when he looks at me like he did before. Like he sees me for who I am and what we have.

"This isn't some game, Pres." I immediately smile at the use of the nickname he used to call me, but he's quick to correct himself. "Presley, I meant Presley." He grabs at his hair and growls. "I don't think you understand what this has done. Did you know the cops actually brought me to the police station and questioned me in front of my parents? They thought I could have been the one to hurt you. I was lucky I had a rock-solid alibi, but still."

I cringe that my assumptions about the police were right.

He curses. "My sponsors weren't thrilled with the rumors and suspicion this threw on me. But I think the worst part of it is that everyone close to me thinks I'm hiding something. Do you know how that feels?"

I suppress a humorless laugh. I happen to know a little something about hiding things. "I can imagine."

"So, yeah. I'm okay with a little spoon-feeding." His blue eyes are perfectly flat.

The door swings wide and Violet steps in followed by another girl. The girl's face is soft and heart-shaped, and her cupid bow lips part in surprise when she sees me. Her dark, almond eyes bounce between Landon and me.

"Look who stopped by," Violet says, one eyebrow raised.

Landon shoots up from the bench and takes a few steps toward the girl. "Ivy . . . I tried to come talk to you, but your dad . . ."

Ivy's voice comes out shaky. "Yeah, I wasn't ready to talk." She turns her gaze to meet mine. "I thought maybe we could try to figure things out today, but I see that you're busy." She quickly brushes a tear away before it can fall. "I'm gonna go." She turns her back on us and her sleek black hair disappears around the corner.

Landon doesn't even glance my way before he calls after Ivy and runs to catch her. Violet leans against the doorjamb, slender arms folded across her chest. She studies me, one side of her mouth curled. "It's a shame she had to take off. I thought you'd like to meet Landon's girlfriend."

I say nothing to Violet as I slip past her and make my way down the stairs. Outside in her car, Ivy is seated in the driver's spot and Landon's body is blocking her from closing the door. He's stooped low, resting his arm on the roof. His gaze catches mine as I walk past them and his eyes apologize. He watches me until I reach my car, but then turns back to Ivy.

The euphoric adrenaline I had felt in Landon's presence drains away—every drop—and leaves me feeling weak and sick. It's impossible to tell how much of what I'm feeling is head injury and how much is heartbreak.

Numbly, I drive away without looking back. I try to think through the persistent throb in my head and tell myself I shouldn't be completely surprised or offended. He is an incredible catch. Magnetic, funny, athletic, and obviously stop-you-in-your-tracks handsome. Why wouldn't he have a girlfriend? He never divulged that to me, but I never asked either.

I do my best to keep it together, but I think I would absorb this blow a lot better if he hadn't just kissed me. I thought we were getting back to where we left off. Now everything just feels impossible. He doesn't remember me *and* he has a girlfriend.

I drive aimlessly for a few minutes, ignoring the constant chirp of my phone. Gayle has to be out of her mind by now, and I feel bad about that, but I can't walk back through those hospital doors. Not yet. I send her a text letting her know I'm okay and nothing more. I'm grateful the sun is sinking behind the mountains giving me a rest from the blinding Tahoe sun. All I can think of now is getting home and crawling into bed.

Rounding the corner to my house, I'm surprised that my Jeep's not in the driveway and there's no sign of a vehicle for Chase's caregiver. When I get out of Gayle's car, I realize I've made the only tracks in the virgin snow. No tire tracks before me, no footprints. Even the walkway and porch are covered in a flawless white blanket. Weird. I know it hasn't snowed in the two days since I've been awake and I know Gayle's been home off and on, so where are the signs that she's been here? The sunlight is swallowed up making the whole world a washed-out blue.

Something's not right.

The front door is locked, but where is the Chase-proof keypad? Electronic locks are always priority one. I'm freezing by now so I jog around the side of the house to the hose hanger, searching for the small magnetic box that's always held the landlord's hide-a-key. It's cold in my hands and the lock protests, but I get the door open and I step into the dim entryway, lit only by the fading light from outside. I feel for the switch and flip it, but no light comes on. In frustration, I flip the switch several times to no avail.

Even though I'm indoors, I can see my breath. The house feels like a huge walk-in refrigerator. An empty refrigerator. Not a stick of furniture anywhere. This isn't my house anymore. On top of that, I am alone. At least, I hope I am. There is something in the air, like a buzz of energy. A pull of tension. Something that makes me want to stand where I am, but I slowly circle, scanning the room to ensure I am the only person in it. As much as I try to ignore it, I feel like I'm being watched.

The chill from outside snakes its way inside of me. Goosebumps needle over my skin and up the back of my neck.

I turn to run to the door but it slams shut in front of me, ripping a scream from my throat. I claw at the knob, but my hands are shaking so much that I can't grip it properly.

A deep voice from behind instructs, "Leave it shut."

Chapter Seven

IT'S ABOUT TIME

(PRESLEY)

43 Days Before

I recognize James's voice immediately and run to him, crashing into his arms. He holds me tight, squeezing me to him.

"I didn't mean to scare you." He steps away, still gripping me at arm's length and looks me over. His sandy hair is out of place and the usual calm that holds his features is gone, leaving his brow pushed into a broken line I'm not used to. He shakes his head. "How are you still alive?"

"Me? What about you? Last time I saw you, you were . . ." I swallow a lump as a flashback slideshow flips through my mind, pulling my consciousness back to that snow-blanketed day Landon almost left me. The hungry stares of the hoard of Vigilum. The revenge boiling inside their leader, Liam, draining all traces of mercy from his eyes just before he tortured me. The helplessness in Landon's face when he realized the dark spirits were more powerful than him and James. And then the final convergence of that terrible dogpile. The sound of gnashing teeth and the shrieks of triumph as the Vigilum did their worst to James.

"I thought they'd killed you."

James shakes his head. "No. I was brought to this time with you and Landon." A shadow passes over his face. "Just in time."

"Will they find us? Liam and his followers?"

"No, no. You don't have to worry about that. Vigilum don't have the ability to travel in time.

Muscles that feel clenched around every bone in my body relax at his words, and I'm grateful for the pardon that our leap through time affords us.

"Well, how is it that we're all still here after so much time? When I time jumped with Landon before, it only lasted a few minutes and we were taken back. Why didn't the same thing happen here?"

James's shoulders come up in a shrug. "We are anchored it seems. I think Landon's time of death was some kind of checkpoint or portal. When he crossed it with whatever power he was able to muster, it brought us into a different realm. The realm of the living. Whatever gate that opened to let us through, is now shut."

James's explanation doesn't make total sense, but I'm relieved and amazed that Landon was somehow able to break through the barrier.

I have so many questions for James. Enough questions to keep us in the frigid house for the rest of the night. But there's one question I can't wait any longer to ask. "Why doesn't Landon remember me?"

James steps closer, his voice low. "My best guess is that when Landon passed through from the realm of death back into the realm of life, he must have forgotten everything," James says.

"He forgot." My voice is emotionless, but it's hard to ignore the flippant way James said those words. How could Landon forget that he knew me? Laid down his passage for me? Loved me? I certainly hadn't forgotten.

"For Landon, passing from death back into life was like passing through a curtain. A curtain that wiped things clean and caused a forgetting," James says.

"So the reason I haven't forgotten him is because I've been alive this whole time?"

"That's right. You were and still are in the living estate. There was no passing through for you."

James jerks his head to the side like he's listening for something. His eyes rove around the dusky lit room and a crease appears between his brows.

"What is it?" I ask, my heart instinctually picking up pace. Even though James said Liam can't find us, visions of him and his followers darken the corners of my mind.

James motions for me to be quiet by holding up one still hand. He listens for a few moments more before he lets down a bit and meets my eyes.

His voice is more hushed than before. "You cannot be seen talking to me. It would reveal you as one who can see the dead. And we know how that worked out for you last time."

I look around the empty house, confused at his jumpiness. "Okay, but we're alone."

James's voice is grave. "*Never* assume you're alone."

Unbidden, the hairs raise on my arms with a prickling wave and my eyes sweep the room again, this time looking deeper into the shadows.

"Look," he says, "I came to tell you to stay away from Landon. I know how difficult this must be for you, but it's imperative that you respect the choice he made that day to move on without you."

My face crumples into confusion. "What's that supposed to mean? He's not dead anymore, so him moving on to the next life without me is a bit moot, wouldn't you say?"

The line along James's jaw tightens. He looks at me for a few heartbeats, his eyes penetrating mine.

Finally, his back straightens. "I can imagine that you have formulated some kind of plan to prevent Landon's death from happening a second time. Some sort of intervention. And I'm here to tell you that you shouldn't."

I'm hit with a solid wall of hurt. A sudden, disorienting force I didn't see coming.

"How can you say that?" My voice shakes and my breath comes in uneven swells.

The crazy part is that I hadn't as yet made any such plan. All I've cared about since I was able to open my eyes and sit up was getting to Landon. Holding him. Telling him I loved him and celebrating together the fact that we made it. I had just imagined that because he's okay and that I'm here, everything would be different. I had imagined he would remember his death and remember me, so why would I need a plan to prevent it? Of *course* he wouldn't make the same choices that lead to it.

Now, realizing the ramifications of his *not* remembering me, my mind starts to reel with what-ifs. What if he *does* make the same choices that led to his death? Would I even be able to stop him if I wanted to? Would James try to stand in my way?

I lift my eyes to James's. I see him differently now and feel a need to protect my thoughts.

"I can imagine how hurtful it is to hear me say you shouldn't try to keep Landon from his death, but you have to know it's inevitable."

The more he speaks, the more panic rises in my throat. James's eyes are so serene. Rooted. And that makes me even more scared. And angry.

He continues, "Deaths are not some insignificant hiccup in time that can be easily erased. They are markers of time. Imprints. Anchors. Landon's death will occur as it should at the same appointed time. It may happen differently, but it will happen. It will find a way."

I take a couple shaky steps back. "You're lying!" I want to run, but as I turn from James, he takes hold of my arm and makes shushing noises. Noises that make me feel even more betrayed. Because if what James was saying was the truth, he should be as outraged as I am.

"Please lower your voice." His eyes make a circular patrol of the room again and then, seeming satisfied, he lets go of my arm.

"I don't understand how you could give up on Landon like that. Don't you care for him at all? How could you let him go through that again after all of the time you've spent with him? And his family? How could you put them through that another time?"

"Remember, as far as Landon or his family know, none of it has happened yet. It's not as if they'd have to endure it twice," he says.

"Suffering is suffering, James. And even if they don't remember it, why not prevent it from happening again? How cold-hearted can you be?"

Finally, a wrinkle of feeling slashes across his forehead. "I know my stance seems . . . heartless to you. But you have to understand that those of us who have passed through and seen the other side, don't view death in the same way as mortals do. Landon's death isn't an ending. It's just the beginning. And though I know you prefer to be with Landon and your parting will cause pain, any interference of the inevitable will cause you more pain. In my opinion, there's nothing worse than crushed hope. And your hopes for his escape from death are misplaced."

"You're insane if you think I'm just going to walk away. Quietly let him go straight to the slaughterhouse so all of your theories can prove correct. In case you haven't noticed, James, I don't, nor have I ever, cared a single thing about the rules. Not when it comes to Landon. And if you recall, you've broken a few rules yourself."

James considers me. "I think you misunderstand my motives. I don't wish for Landon to die. I don't wish for your pain or for his. It's just a matter of me performing my duty."

It's then I start to feel a sick dread inside.

"What are you talking about?"

His eyes warm to kindness. No, pity. "Think about it. I've been brought to this time along with Landon." He pauses, seeming to hesitate before what he says next. "I can't travel to any other time. I'm stuck here."

My skin is prickling and my face feels hot. With concentration, I keep the waves of panic in my stomach from rushing up my throat.

James continues, "Why do you think these things are so?" He blinks, giving me a moment to ponder his question. "I'm a guide. At this point in my existence I have only one task. *One* task, Presley."

I know what he's going to say, but my mind still begs for something else. Begs for an alternative.

"My only purpose in this place and in this time is to guide my assignment, Landon, from death into the beyond."

The tears quietly drip from my face and though I don't want James to touch me, he reaches and catches them with the backs of his fingers.

"That's my job. To guide him safely through. Now your job is to try to accept it."

I feel like there are miles between me and James. Because he sees Landon's death as set, meant to be, and natural. I see his death as conditional, possibly preventable, and the worst thing that could happen.

"I want you to let events take their course without interruption," James says, his voice firmer now.

I let out a single joyless laugh. "So, what? You're here to bully me into compliance?"

His eyebrows lower. "Have I ever bullied you into anything?"

I can tell what I said cuts him. And I feel bad about it. In truth, James has always done what he thought was best. I have to give him that. Most of the time, that included protecting Landon and me at his own risk.

"I'm sorry. I know you mean well. But I won't lie to you. I can't just stand by and watch Landon die."

James's face pales and somehow that bleeds more strength and resolve into me. "I don't agree that Landon would want to die again," I say. "I think if he remembered everything—he would choose to live."

"Even if life were his choice, that doesn't make it right," James says.

"Who are you to decide what's right for someone else?" I make sure my tone is softer, because I mean no disrespect. It's just an honest question.

"I understand things that you don't, Presley. You'll just have to trust me."

"I guess I can say the same." Our eyes are locked, and I can tell James is troubled with my response. I hate that we are so divided. I want nothing more than for him to counsel me, help me. Be *my* guide. James's eyes are steady. "I also came to warn you. If you speak to Landon about his death, you might as well send up a flare to the Vigilum."

"I thought you said they can't find us here because they can't travel through time."

James's eyes widen. "I'm not just talking about Liam and his followers. I'm talking about all Vigilum in all times." He seems to think better of letting his voice rise so he lowers it to a near whisper. "Do you really think that the only Vigilum you'll ever have to worry about are the handful you've encountered so far? Presley, perhaps you underestimate the sheer number of them that are out there."

My eyes narrow and I scour James's face for signs of deception. He isn't a liar, but he has been known to withhold important information to suit his purposes. "That sounds . . . convenient."

"You think I'm manipulating you?"

I shrug. I see the disappointment in James's eyes. He's probably thinking the same thing that I am. That this new wall between us is so depressing.

James lowers his chin and levels his gaze at mine. "I'm not exaggerating. I'm only trying to keep you safe."

"So, you're telling me if I say anything about Landon's death—anything to jog his memory—that I might as well tell the Vigilum where I am?"

"In essence."

"Oh, come on. Really?"

I try to brush off the fear that's threatening to erupt. "The only reason the other Vigilum found out about me before was because they were watching Landon, *who was dead*. It was his lingering that drew their attention. The Vigilum in this time have no special interest in him—he's alive. So they would have no reason to watch us. I don't see why you're being so paranoid."

I feel quite proud of my logic for a moment until I see the look on James's face. "Paranoid, huh?"

I hold my ground. "Yeah. Paranoid."

James shakes his head in a painfully slow manner. "You have no idea. I suppose it's my fault for expecting too much from you. After all, you've only dealt with Vigilum for how long now? A few months?"

I count in my head how long I've known Landon. "Six months."

James's eyebrows raise in mock astonishment. "Oh, six months! Well, then."

"James—"

His nostrils flare and he lowers his brows at me. His countenance begins to radiate some kind of power that I can't see, but I can feel. It scares me.

"How about you take some advice from someone who's dealt with Vigilum for nearly two centuries?"

I can't help but to shrink back a little. His words sting. Not because he's angry, but because I can sense that he's right and I need to listen to him. I'm suddenly ashamed of my ignorance and stubbornness.

"Vigilum are everywhere, Presley. They're incredibly hard to detect. They blend in with any crowd. They can be any age." James lowers his voice. "They can hear through walls . . ." He shakes his head vigorously. "What am I saying? They can *walk* through walls. They have nothing, and I mean *nothing*, to do with their time but to scour the earth, watching and listening, hoping to pick up on any small scrap of information that could lead them to a death.

"If someone is depressed? They'll find out. Eating disorder? They'll notice. Drank too much? They'll know. Nodding off while driving? You better watch the backseat because you might have company. Truly, Presley they will take *any* hint of impending death and will study it, monitor it, and analyze it with the most unflagging patience you could imagine. Don't you see? They have nothing but time."

My breath feels shallow and I lean against the wall to steady myself. "I won't do any of those things. I'll stay under the radar."

James gives a hint of a smile. "What you are trying to pull off, Presley? Stop the march of death on its appointed day—that will never go under the radar."

A single tear runs down my cheek. "Even if that's true, I have to try. For Landon."

The half smile on James's face disappears. "Have I ever told you where the name 'Vigilum' comes from?"

"No."

"It means wakefulness. It means to guard. It means they will always be watching and they never sleep."

This understanding hangs between us like a palpable mist. I know that my decision to help Landon remember carries danger. It's dangerous for me, because of what I am—a person who can see the dead.

Dangerous for my family because they are associated with me.

And dangerous for Landon because if the Vigilum somehow found out that I was going to stop a forthcoming death, they'd find a way to stop me and Landon would die.

"If they're always watching, then I'll have to be more careful," I say.

"Yes. You will. May I suggest that you start by not speaking to anyone that you do not know for absolute certain is alive?"

I nod in understanding. Accidentally speaking to a Vigilum could be bad. Real bad.

I take a step toward him and rest my hand on his arm. "I know you want what's best for me and Landon. We just happen to think what's best is two different things." I squeeze his arm lightly and let my hand drop. "So, you're really not going to help me save him, are you?"

"I'll be nearby, if you need me. What else can I do since I'm trapped in this time? But no. I won't intervene with Landon's death." Do his eyes register apology or just sadness? I can't tell. His shoulders droop a bit. "I wish you'd believe me that trying to save him is a fool's errand," he says. "Even for me."

His words threaten to drag me down, but I can't allow that to happen. "I have to try."

James considers me for a moment and then drops his eyes and nods. "And, please, remember everything I've told you tonight. The danger is real."

I know he means well, but I'm going to do everything I can to forget what he said about the impossibility of my task.

I will find a way to save Landon.

Chapter Eight

GUILTY

(PRESLEY)

43 Days Before

James was going to be no help. But I did have to ask one favor from him—to tell me where I live *now*.

I pull into the driveway, which is lit up like a Disneyland parade. There are two police cars with red and blue lights swirling, creating a dizzy psychedelic light show on the lawn and house. Gayle is standing on the front porch, wrapped in a blanket and speaking with a police officer. At the sound of my tires pulling up the drive, she drops the blanket, bounds down the steps, and has her palms against my window before I have a chance to come to a stop. I'm going to be in so. Much. Trouble.

I brace myself for the worst but then notice she's crying. She opens the door and pulls me into her arms. With her face buried in my hair, her breath is interrupted by hiccups that always follow an intense cry. Just when I think she'll never let go, she takes a step back and examines me with her eyes and hands in the way that only worried mothers can.

"Are you all right?" she asks through trembling lips.

I tell her that I'm fine, even though "fine" could be no further from the truth. In the last thirty minutes, I've learned that Landon doesn't remember me, that apparently has a girlfriend, and that according to James, he will die all over again and there's nothing I can do to stop it. Oh, and I need to watch my back because Vigilum could find me. So yeah, I'm not fine.

"First things first, let's get you inside." Gayle guides me toward the house and invites the officers to follow. She settles me on the couch, covering me with one of Chase's heavy quilts and returns to the entryway and converses with the officers in low tones.

I take a quick look around, noticing the ceiling, walls, and floors are all the same—knotty pine with exposed beams and peaked ceilings, giving the house a cabin feel. Thick braided rugs and plaid curtains that must've come with this place, add a cozy touch. Signs of Chase are everywhere: a half-completed puzzle and an open jar of dill pickles clutter the coffee table. His favorite condiments stand next to several soiled paper plates on the kitchen table. I call out to him, hoping that he's home.

"Chase? Hey bud!"

The answering sound of his feet stomp from upstairs, then his tousled hair and brown eyes appear over the pony wall from the loft above. He hums and flaps his hands, then thumps down the stairs and over to me. Has he grown since I've been away, or has he always been this tall? He holds his iPad in one hand and tries to pull me up with the other. My chest aches when I think about what must have been going through his head during my two-week absence. For all he knew, I was gone for good. I doubt Gayle brought him to the hospital, given how stressful the situation was. There's nothing I want more than to get off this couch and follow him wherever he wants to take me, but I've overdone it today. The returning nausea and dizziness signal that my body's reached its limit.

"How about you sit by me for a minute?" I encourage, patting the couch. It takes no coaxing. He drops his iPad on the coffee table, and flops his sturdy body on the couch next to mine. Scooting in closer, he squishes me between himself and the back of the couch. His brown eyes hold mine for a moment, then he hunches over until his forehead rests on my shoulder. I tilt my head down a little and his stubbled cheek brushes against mine. Sandpaper against soft. I wrap one arm around his neck and stroke his curly hair with my free hand. "It's okay, bud," I whisper to him. "I'm home now. Presley's home."

Hot tears pool in the spot where our cheeks touch. They aren't mine. My instinct was right. Chase was surely confused and afraid that I wasn't coming home. Or he just missed me. Or both. One thing I've learned by loving this boy is just because someone can't fully express their emotions and fears with words, it doesn't mean they don't have them.

Guilt, hot and thick, boils in my stomach and slithers up until it finds purchase in my throat. Messing things up for myself is one thing, but pulling my family into the middle of this is too much. I try to swallow the sob that's fighting to break free, but let it go instead. And crying is liberating. It's something I've not let myself do since waking up. But this is not a cry for Landon, or my injuries or any of the events that have transpired tonight. Not now. This is not a cry for me. It's for Chase. For us. And for just a moment, we are not an older sister who takes care of a brother with autism. We are simply siblings, who above all, love each other.

We hold each other this way for several long moments, when at last our reunion is interrupted by a deep, but hesitant voice. "Excuse me. Ms. Hale." I open my eyes to find one of the policemen seated on the edge of the armchair in the corner of the small living room. His elbows rest on his knees and his chin is perched on steepled fingers. His face wears an apology, but he studies me too.

"Sorry to disturb your rest, kiddo. Are you feeling well enough to answer a few questions for me?"

He asks me how and why I left the hospital. Was I alone or with someone? Where was I headed? Lucky for me, my unique experiences have made me into a better liar than I like to admit. So, I tell him that I was indeed alone and the lie flows like honey. Sweet and smooth. I explain that I left because I was feeling panicky and claustrophobic.

The officer eyes me skeptically. *Come on, kid*, I can almost hear him thinking. *Quit dishing this crap so I can go home.*

"Ms. Hale, are you sure you didn't go see anyone?"

"Why would you think that?" I ask.

"Well, dispatch just radioed in that one of our locals, Frank Blackwood, made a call to the station a few minutes ago. He informed our gal that one Presley Hale had made a visit to see his boy, Landon. Said he wanted to stay ahead of it. Be proactive and let us know, since Landon's been questioned about your injuries." He stares me down with that same expectant expression.

I don't mean to, but I worry my bottom lip between my teeth. I don't know what I was expecting him to say, but it wasn't this. "Okay. Yes," I say. "I did go to see Landon."

"That boy have anything to do with your injuries?"

"No!" I cannot be clear enough about that. If Landon were to get in any kind of trouble for this . . .

"Let's just start from the beginning then," he says and pulls a small notepad from his shirt pocket. He sits poised with a pen and asks, "When did you first meet Landon?"

I send up a silent prayer of gratitude that I've got a good answer for this. "I can't remember anything before my accident. I don't remember Landon at all. I only went to see him because my mom told me he'd been to check on me at the hospital. I thought maybe he could help me remember. But he didn't. That's it."

"That's it, huh?" The officer scribbles a couple of notes on his pad.

"You can talk to my doctor about it," I offer. "She says it's normal to have memory loss with serious concussions." Chase grabs at my arm and tries to pull me from the couch again. "My head is killing me. Any way we can pick this up later?" Chase whines and tugs on me again.

Gayle appears at the end of the sofa with her cell phone clamped between her ear and shoulder. "Okay. Of course. Yes, I understand. I get it. We'll be there within the hour." She ends her call and crosses the room to the officer, whose name badge I can now see says, "PERKINS."

"Thank you for coming so quickly tonight," she says, extending her hand to shake his. "That was Presley's doctor. She wants Presley back in the hospital immediately." Gayle raises one eyebrow and shoots me a sideways glance.

Perkins nods, rises from his chair, and shoves the notepad and pen back in his pocket. "We'll check in with you in a day or two. In the meantime, I think we can be sure of one thing." He tugs upward on his pants, even though they aren't sagging. "Landon Blackwood had nothing to do with Presley's injuries. His alibi is airtight. He was training with his coaches nearly every minute leading up to the qualifying events, and was at home with his family when he wasn't on the slopes."

My head still throbs and my nausea threatens to consume me, but a surge of relief snakes through my body. Landon is cleared.

Chapter Nine

Baby Bird

(Presley)

43 Days Before

"Please, Mom." It's shameless pleading. And I'm fine with that. I prop myself up on the couch. "Just let me rest at home. I'm sorry I left the hospital. I promise to stay put here. I won't even go outside. Put Friend Finder on your phone and track me anytime you want. I swear, you will only find me here."

Gayle sits at the foot of the couch, so that the three of us now share the small space. She rubs my legs through the quilt. "Sweetie, don't you think I'm sick of that hospital too? The arrangements aren't exactly five-star. The meatloaf alone . . ." She makes a funny face and gives my legs an affectionate squeeze. "But you need more care than I can provide you here. Another MRI, according to your doctor, impact testing and all kinds of other things that simply can't be done from home."

My bottom lip trembles. "Did the doctor say how much longer I'd need to stay?"

"A week. At least," she tells me.

I moan.

"I know. It feels like a long time."

"What about Chase?" I ask.

"Chase is managing. I don't want you to worry too much about him right now. He's started school and seems to like his teacher. And his caregiver is here every minute that I'm not."

Every minute that she's at the hospital because of me. The guilt boils again.

"Mom, you can spend more time at home. I won't need you at the hospital every minute."

"You're probably right. You're getting a lot better." Gayle's lips tremble and she clamps them together and shifts her gaze down. When her eyes meet mine again, they are rimmed with moisture. She looks through me—her mind in a different place.

"Do you remember that baby bird?" she asks.

"Baby bird?" I'm a little confused at the abrupt change of topic.

"You were only four or five, so you might not." Her gaze returns from wherever she was and her eyes, bright with tears, hold mine. "The one that fell from the tree in our backyard in Vegas?"

I do remember. Both Gayle and I were so upset about that bird. But especially Gayle.

Chase must be getting bored with this conversation, because he grabs his iPad and pulls up one of his favorite spelling games.

"Man, I remember that day like it was yesterday. You had all those neighbor kids over to play. I remember spying on you and your friends through the kitchen window. You were a tight little group. Squishing ants, picking all the flowers from my flower beds, attempting stunts of all sorts on the trampoline." She laughs at the memory, then her expression turns tender.

"Every now and then you'd pull Chase from playing by himself, right into the middle of your group. You'd hand him toys, show him how to do somersaults on the trampoline, tickle him, and all kinds of other things to get him to engage with you." She closes her eyes and shakes her head. "I was so proud of you. Who you were becoming so early in life. But sad too, that you had to work so hard to pull Chase into your world. It was bittersweet, you know?"

With Chase it's always bittersweet. Emotions that should be separate, like water and oil. They naturally want to remain distinct, but when things get shaken up, they're forced to mix.

"Anyway, I'd left the kitchen for a minute when I heard you scream for me all the way from upstairs. I rushed outside to see what was going on. I was sure one of you had broken your neck on the trampoline. Been bit by a black widow, I don't know."

"'Look, Mom!' you told me. You were holding that little baby bird. He was covered in that fuzz and you could see his pink skin underneath. He couldn't have been more than a couple of days old."

I remember watching that bird fall. I'd been lying on my back on the trampoline, finding pictures in the clouds with my friends when he fell.

"Yes," I say. "He fell so far. From one of those tall, skinny trees." The nest was too high to put him back.

She dabs at a tear, then says, "I remember the way he arched his head and thrashed about. Poor thing."

I wonder at Gayle's story. It's not like her to be so tender with me. To spend this much time. I'm confused how this story has anything to do with me going back to the hospital. But this new side of her is a nice change. I squeeze her hands.

"That mama bird was frantic. She swooped and shrieked back and forth between our little group and her other babies. It seemed like maybe we were upsetting her, so we found a box and—"

"I put grass in it," I cut in. "I wanted to make a soft bed. I thought maybe that would help his bones feel better." I laugh, though it's not a happy one.

Gayle nods. "Yep. You took extra care, for sure. We put the box at the bottom of the tree and went inside. I thought maybe mama bird would calm down a bit if we were out of her space. But she didn't. She grieved, Presley. She grieved. Her screeching. It was unlike anything I'd heard. I watched from the window and saw that she was trying to feed the little guy, but he couldn't even lift his head.

"And I remember thinking how quickly that mama's life had been turned inside out. Just minutes before, she'd had all her babies safe in her nest, so high in that tree. And now one lay in a box . . . dying." Gayle is suddenly overwhelmed with emotion. She wipes at her eyes but several tears escape and fall from her face, landing with hot splashes on our clasped hands.

"I called the vet and asked if there was anything he could do," she continues. "But there wasn't. So I watched from the window. She tended to that baby for hours. Back and forth between the box and her nest. I remember thinking, if she could only pick it up and put it back in the nest. Maybe it could heal there. How frustrating that must've been for her."

There's a lump in my throat that wasn't there before. A familiarity to this story that I can't quite place, but Gayle's words pierce me and my heart feels tight.

"When it started to get dark," Gayle says, "we moved the baby's box into our little casita so none of the neighborhood cats would get it. And that mama screamed all night. Such desperation in her calls. I could feel it. I stayed awake and mourned with her. It sounds so silly, doesn't it?"

I shake my head. It doesn't sound silly at all.

"The vet was right. In the morning when I went to the casita, I found him in his box of grass and flowers; his little body all stiff and cold. I sat by that box, and I cried and cried and cried. I so badly wanted to get that baby bird back to safety. But I was helpless to do anything.

"So I moved his box back to the bottom of that ugly tree. I thought maybe it would give his mama some closure. And it did. She inspected the box and her baby. And then she stopped crying.

"But I didn't. I cried for most of the day. I remember feeling so irresponsible because moms shouldn't come undone like that in front of their kids."

"I don't think there's any such rule, Mom," I say and rub her arms.

"I tried to go over all the reasons I was *so* upset. Then I realized, it wasn't just that the baby bird had died and his mama couldn't help him. It's that they were painful reminders, Pres. Because just two years before that, *my* baby bird

34

had fallen from his nest. Chase. He was so perfect and new just like that bird." Gayle stares off. "And then he wasn't. He was gone."

Gayle pulls her hands from mine and presses her palms against her eyes. It seems like she's trying not to cry—like placing her hands there will stop the tears. But she cries. It's a quiet cry, barely audible, but it's strong. I sit up straight and pull her into me. "It's all right, Mom. It's okay. He's doing better now. So much better."

"He's my baby bird, Presley. He was that baby bird, and I was that mama. And no matter how loudly I screamed or how frantic I was, nothing was going to bring him back. No amount of love and attention, no amount of doctor's visits, no amount of early intervention. Nothing could restore what we lost."

She pulls back from my embrace and holds my face in her hands. "And these last few weeks, I lived it all over again with you. Did you know the doctors couldn't guarantee that you would ever be the same when you woke up?"

"Mom . . ." I didn't know that. *I had no idea.*

"They had no answers for me other than your brain scans didn't look especially great. They hoped time and rest would help the swelling go down, but there were no promises made." Her shoulders and chest shake as she fights through the sobs.

"So I sat by your bed every minute. And I read you your favorite books while you slept. And I rubbed your feet and brushed your hair. I moved your legs and arms, back and forth, up and down, even though the physical therapist assured me his work with you was enough. But nothing could be enough. Nothing could be enough until you woke up. This time you were my baby bird."

Then Gayle sits a little straighter and places her hands on my cheeks once more, but this time she holds me firmly. The sadness in her eyes has dissolved. It's replaced with determination.

"And that is why you are going back to the hospital right now. You will follow every instruction from every doctor, and will never again pull what you pulled tonight. Do you understand me?"

I understand. I understand Gayle better than I have my entire life.

Chapter Ten

THE RULES

(LANDON)

42 Days Before

1. I will not initiate conversation with Presley. If she talks to me, I'll respond as needed, but I won't start anything.
2. I will not look for her on social media.
3. I will not try to find out where she lives.
4. If she comes to my house again, I will respect Ivy's wishes and ask her to leave.
5. If thoughts of Presley are bothering me, I'll text or call Ivy.
6. From now on, I'll always tell the truth to Ivy.
7. I will burn the sheet music for "Speed."
8. I will not rewatch any of the news clips of our kiss on the slope or look for pictures of her in news stories.
9. I will never be alone in a room with her.
10. I will not ever kiss her again.

Chapter Eleven

TRUCKEE: TAKE TWO

(PRESLEY)

36 Days Before

I check the back seat before I get into my Civic. Part of me wonders if James was exaggerating when he described the sheer number of Vigilum on the loose. But the other part of me has seen enough that I'd be stupid to completely ignore his warnings. Between that and knowing I'll see Landon today, my stomach was so nervous this morning, I skipped breakfast.

I'm missing my Jeep already, but from what I could piece together, our move this time happened so quickly there was no time to buy me a Truckee-appropriate vehicle. The phone GPS recites directions from my house to Truckee High in a robotic tone. It feels bizarre not knowing the way to my own school, but since I've basically been quarantined, I've had no time to get to know this part of town. After a nervous check in my rearview mirror, I back out of the driveway, glancing in it a dozen times as I drive to school.

I lucked out and only ended up staying four days at the hospital. My doctor was comfortable with how my test scores improved and let me out on the condition that I rest another three days at home. When she finally cleared me to return to school, it was only for a half-day schedule. On Monday, Wednesday, and Friday, I'll go to school for four hours starting in the morning. Then, on Tuesdays and Thursdays, my day starts at lunch.

She also encouraged me to stay active with all of this new downtime, as long as I avoided activities that required strenuous mental exercise. So Gayle has arranged a job for me. The new vice principal's wife runs a small bakery in downtown Truckee and needs help in the afternoons. Gayle cleared it with the doc. Apparently pouring coffee and wiping down tables don't count as mental exertion. I wish I could say the same about going back to school.

The lot is half full when I arrive, and out of habit I take the spot I used to park in. I keep the engine running and the heater on. My knee is bouncing up and down as I consider how unreasonable James is being. How does he expect me to know for sure if every single person at Truckee High is living or not? I had only attended for a couple of months before, and as I look around at the students making their way to the front doors, there are several faces I don't recognize.

Feeling a little paranoid, I find myself drawn to people who seem quiet or who aren't carrying a backpack. I think back to when the Vigilum started shadowing Reese. They seemed more determined and serious than the general student body and always wore stuff that wasn't necessarily goth, but that stood out as different and dark. Knowing there's little more I can do than just be careful, I force myself to stop worrying about who might be a Vigilum. Instead, I give myself a moment to look around and take everything in.

My first day at Truckee High—for the second time. Same forest-lined parking lot where my Jeep was egged, same clock tower out front, same twelve steps leading to the glass doors. Everything looks the same, but feels so different. I pull my schedule up on my phone, gather my belongings, and double check that I locked my car.

Inside the school, the trophy case down the hall still holds the championship alpine team photo. "J" with his sunburned nose, Reese's hand raised in a hang loose sign, and Landon kneeling front and center, grasping the golden trophy. Missing from the top of the case though, is Landon's 8 x 10 memorial photo. Nothing there but a thin layer of dust.

My eyes sweep over my surroundings. Somewhere in this hall is a locker that belongs to him. Somewhere in this swarm of people racing against the tardy bell, Landon breathes. Walks. Speaks. His heart beats. It's like I can feel him without seeing him.

Is it my imagination or is there a thrum of energy vibrating through this place that wasn't here before? My blood hums with adrenaline and anticipation. Despite the obvious obstacles in my path, I still feel like anything is possible. I start to think maybe I'm crazy, until I see them.

Reese is first, rounding the corner into the hall with his carefree swagger. He tosses his head back and laughs at something I can't hear, Sam trailing close behind. Then Violet runs around the corner and surprises Reese by jabbing her fingers in his ribs from behind. He jumps then points a playful finger in her face. I lean against the trophy case and lower my head. They pass without noticing me.

The lightness I felt just a moment ago pops like a balloon. I remind myself that none of these people remember me for the relationships we built before. It was painfully clear at the Blackwood home that they only know my name because of the spectacle I caused on the slopes a few weeks ago. Still, my urge to call out to them, to join them, and just be one of them overpowers me. It takes all I have to stay put. To just stand in this place and let them be them. Without me.

My heart picks up tempo. Landon can't be far behind. The seconds stretch out, my breath stalls, and I fasten my eyes to the corner from where eventually he'll have to emerge.

And then he's there.

His face is turned away, as he calls back to someone I can't see.

"Landon." It's just a whisper, but I can't keep from saying his name. There's no way he heard me, but he turns and meets my eyes. I'm still taken aback at his magnetism that's so powerful in the flesh.

He's shocked to see me. The rhythm of his walk is disrupted for a moment. I want to be the first to look away but I can't. I feel hopeful because when he passes, it seems like it takes some effort for him to pull his eyes away. But he does. He catches up to Reese and Violet, and they disappear into the crowd, leaving me alone.

Nothing's like it was before.

———

With a junior class of over a hundred kids, odds are I won't have the same U.S. History class as any of the Blackwoods. So I'm happily surprised when at the sound of the tardy bell, I step into Mr. Nissila's class and see them all there. Taking up half of the back row, Reese, Violet, and Landon are talking and joking with each other while they shed their coats and retrieve supplies from their bags. I'm relieved that Ivy isn't present and glad that Garrett, my old friend, is. But it's not like I'm holding my breath that he'll remember me.

None of them have noticed me yet, and as I approach the teacher's desk to get a seat assignment, Mr. Nisilla gets out of his chair and meets me before I can get to him.

"Miss Hale," he says with a funny little formality that reminds me of a character in a Dickens novel. "We've been expecting you." I wasn't surprised he knew my name. It's no secret that the new principal has a daughter. He puts a stiff arm around my shoulder and turns me toward the rows of desks. "Class, meet Presley Hale. Presley Hale," he waggles his fingers at the rows of curious faces, "Class."

I nod and force a small smile. All of my brainpower is focused on not looking Landon's way. In my peripheral vision, it seems like he could be looking at me, but I'm not brave enough to check. "Is there somewhere you'd like me to sit?" I ask, seeing a few available desks.

"Yes!" He answers with an unexpected volume that startles me. I follow him toward the back of the class. I can see that he's heading straight for the Blackwoods, and I'm both thrilled and terrified about this. "Up." Mr. Nissila gestures for Violet to vacate the seat that's positioned between Landon and Reese. "Ms. Blackwood, I need you to relocate. I have an experiment in mind."

Violet glares at me as she answers the teacher, "Of course." I match her gaze. I don't need to be scared of her. She's my best friend; she just doesn't remember it.

Mr. Nissila jabs his finger back and forth between Landon and Reese. I hazard a glance at Landon and his mouth is pressed into a thin line. "You two behave and make Miss Hale welcome." The teacher leans in toward me and raises his bushy eyebrows. "I'm hoping you'll be a good influence on these knuckle-heads. You know what I mean?"

I slip into my seat. Landon is staring straight ahead, and Reese is leaning over, scribbling something on a scrap of paper. He folds it in half and then slides it across my desk, grinning. I open the paper and read his writing, which is slanted and in all caps.

I PROMISE TO BE NICE TO YOU EVEN THOUGH YOUR MOM IS THE PRINCIPAL. COME SIT WITH US AT LUNCH. I'LL SHARE MY TOTS.

I can't help but to let out a little laugh at that last part. He's quoting *Napoleon Dynamite*, one of my favorite movies I'd watch over and over with my friends back in Vegas. Reese is smiling at me with that undeniable charm that I remember. An open smile that makes me feel like I don't even have to try with him. Like our friendship could almost pick up where we left off. I smile back, shaking my head, and tucking the note into my folder. I turn away from Reese and catch Landon looking at me. He whips his head around toward the front of the class. His hand grips the side of the desk and for the first time I notice his red-stoned class ring on his finger. Personal details like this still feel so surreal.

I wonder if I should accept Reese's invitation to join the Blackwoods for lunch. With my half-day schedule, I will only have three lunches a week. Such a limited amount of time to be around Landon. But with Violet and Ivy in the picture, I consider the hostility I'll most likely have to deal with.

Over the last week while I've been home and in the hospital, I've had plenty of time to think. Think about how my primary goal is to keep Landon from going to that bridge and swinging from that rope. Yes, I want him to remember me. Yes, I want him to love me again. But I have to be realistic. He's in love with another girl. He has to be. He chose Ivy over me that day at his house. My lips were still warm from his kiss and he still chose her. As much as it hurt, part of me admired him for it. For his loyalty to her.

It sucks to think it, but there's a possibility Landon will never remember us together—how we were before. But even if he doesn't remember he loves me, I can never forget. And because of that, I'll do everything in my power to keep him safe from the Vigilum and from himself. I've been telling myself that accomplishing this might mean doing things that are very uncomfortable. That require me to swallow my pride. Things like sitting at a lunch table where every-one but Reese pretty much hates me.

I have to find a way to keep close to Landon. No matter what.

I retrieve Reese's note from my folder and flip it over so I can write on the blank side, scratching my response down before I change my mind:

I'll be there.

Chapter Twelve

DISTRACTION

(PRESLEY)

36 Days Before

My Wednesday-afternoon training at Wild Cherries Coffee Shop went well. Sara, who happens to be the wife of Mr. Nissila, runs the place. She's so organized and efficient, that after shadowing her for a few hours, I was ready to run the counter while she worked on the books in the back office.

Gayle made good on her promise and hired a permanent caregiver for Chase. Her name is Janet and I have to admit that I like her. She has a twenty-year-old nephew with autism who she helps care for, so Chase's size and strength don't appear to faze her. She seems trustworthy, but I did spend a few hours last night shopping Amazon for nanny cams. Gayle just rolled her eyes, but I got my way, and she agreed to have cameras installed in every room. I thought having help with Chase would be a nice break for me, but I already miss his shadow.

Today, Wild Cherries is pretty dead, which just gives me *more* time to focus on missing Chase. I guess four o'clock on a Tuesday afternoon isn't prime coffee time. When I came in, there was just one redheaded girl with blunt bangs and her nose in a book.

I never feel comfortable loafing while on the clock so I try to pass the time studying the chalkboard menu specials and refamiliarizing myself with all the ingredients. Sara left me a small to-do list of prep-work: changing out the strawberries for the parfaits and smoothies, refilling the ice cream machine and taking down all of the outdated flyers and advertisements people pinned up on the message board. I sweep the outside walk and wipe the tables down again because there seems to be some kind of blackbird situation. I've taken the broom to them a couple of times, but they keep coming back.

As far as places to work go, this shop is pretty cute. I like the black-and-white checkered floor, the pub tables, and the red painted corrugated metal accents. It smells great in here too. Sara had been baking all morning and the mixture of fresh brownies and coffee makes my stomach grumble. The picnic tables outside are empty with a crust of snow on them, but I can imagine what a great space the patio must be in nicer weather.

A flash of black and white skitters under the table outside. It's some kind of Chihuahua mutt. He sniffs around frantically, and I can hear him whimpering from inside. As if he noticed my attention, he runs over to the door and starts hopping around on his hind legs like some kind of ill-trained circus act. His incessant scratching and whining even makes the red-haired book loner look up and take notice.

It's clear he's disturbing our only customer, so I cross the dining room, intent on chasing him off, even though he's kind of cute. I swing the door open to tell him, "Shoo! Go on!"

He somehow slithers through the crack in the door and circles the dining room, his nails making a chit-chit sound against the floor. He's still making that crazy sound, which is a mix of growling and whimpering and the more I try to catch him, the more elusive he becomes—ducking and darting like some canine bullfight. The customer has set her book down by now and stares at this ridiculous face-off. I know that animals aren't allowed in dining establishments and the last thing I want is to have someone leave a complaint with my boss, so I apologize to the girl and hurry behind the counter to find some kind of food to lure him out with.

I grab a few slices of smoked turkey and make my way back to the door, dangling the meat at the dog. He immediately trots over to me like he was my best friend. Wagging his tail wildly, he inhales the meat, runs his pink tongue over his whiskers a couple of times, and then scratches to be let out. I laugh at him, give a little scratch to his domed head, and open the door. He darts across the street and out of sight.

The girl is still looking at me.

"I'm sorry about that," I say.

"I won't tell if you don't."

"Thanks. Can I get you anything? Coffee? We have these really great snickerdoodles—"

"Thanks. No." I'm expecting her to look sheepish since she's taking up a table in the shop, but not buying any food. She doesn't though. "I'm just here for the sunny window and the people watching." With her head, she gestures out the window to the people passing on the sidewalk. "And the smell of coffee, of course. I don't drink it, but I love the smell of it."

"Same," I say. "The place is kind of dead today." My eyes make a circuit around the empty dining room.

"Oh, it'll fill up. It usually does around this time. The high school kids. They're all caffeine addicts."

"So I take it, you're done with high school, then?"

She gives a single laugh. "Yeah. I'm just taking some time off to figure out my next move."

"Right. Well, let me know if you change your mind and if there's anything I can do for you."

"I will. Thanks."

At that moment the door swings open, and Reese and Landon, joined by my previous group of friends—Sam, Violet, and Garett—step inside but with a new addition—Ivy. Reese's mouth stretches wide in a grin. "Presley! What are you doing here?"

I return his smile, even though I'm feeling taken aback by their unexpected appearance. "I work here." Violet and Ivy exchange a weighted look.

"I thought you were supposed to be resting," Reese says.

I know he's just trying to tease me, but his comment dredges up the obvious. I have a concussion because I was injured that day on the slope. The day I chased down Landon in a pair of pajamas while bleeding. The day Landon kissed me on national TV. I grit my teeth knowing there's no way I'll ever live any of that down.

"Yeah, well, the doctor says it's good to keep busy." I hate mentioning the doctor. It makes me feel like a freak. Before the conversation can go any further down that road, I move behind the counter and quickly change the subject. "What can I get for you guys? I hear your caffeine cravings must be fed on a regular basis." I look over to the red-haired girl for comedic confirmation, but she's gone. She must have slipped out when these guys came in. She forgot her book, but since she seems like a regular, I'm not worried.

Violet pushes through the group, casually calling over her shoulder, "We'll take the usual."

Reese rolls his eyes and calls after her, "Like she'd know what that is, Vi. She's worked here for all of three minutes."

Vi looks back at me, sniffs, and shrugs before she takes her seat. Chairs scrape against the floor and the rest of the group joins her.

Reese looks back to me. "She acts like it's something special. Just bring us six larges. Three with cream, three black. Oh, and a turkey trio bagel sandwich. I'm starving."

"You're always starving," Violet says.

"I'm a growing boy."

"I think that bagel sandwich is only on the breakfast menu," I say. "Is there something else you'd like?"

Violet cuts in again, "The other girl always made one for him even though it was a breakfast thing." She touches a red painted nail to her chin and taps a few times. "As a matter of fact, I think I recall that girl doing just about anything Reese asked her to." She smiles devilishly at Reese.

He narrows his eyes at her. "You are the worst, you know that? The worst."

He says to me, "It wasn't like that. She was just nice. You totally don't have to make a special thing. Whatever meaty sandwich thing you guys have is fine."

"No worries. It's not a big deal. I can make you a turkey trio," I say. Violet raises her eyebrows at me like she's not surprised, and I remind myself once again that she's not a beast, she's my best friend.

I begin filling coffee cups and setting them on a tray. When I'm finished, I turn around with the tray in hand, and Reese says, "I can take them."

I'm already walking to the table, so I shake my head. "I got it. Thanks though." I set the tray down on the table and ask, "Cream?"

Landon raises a finger and says, "Here." My eyes meet his and I'm completely surprised by how much emotion I'm suddenly feeling. I never knew Landon drank coffee or that he took it with cream. It feels like the most interesting thing in the world. And it makes me hungry to learn every little detail about him. What kind of music he likes. Where he wants to travel. His favorite holiday. Everything. It hurts to admit that the Landon I knew isn't the same as this Landon.

I slide his cup toward him. He lowers his eyes and takes it from me, his finger brushing against mine. "Thank you," he says.

"You're welcome." My voice is quiet and I will my chest to stop squeezing at the little trail of fire his finger left behind when it grazed mine.

Ivy clears her throat and brings me out of my thoughts. They all reach in and retrieve their cups, and I take the empty tray back behind the counter and start making Reese's food. He comes back and rests his arms atop the glass display case. "So, a bunch of us are going skiing this weekend. You wanna come with?"

I tear away a clump of alfalfa sprouts from a canister and begin arranging them on the sandwich, smiling. "Who is 'a bunch of us'?"

Reese drops his eyes and grins. "These lame-os."

"That's what I thought," I say." And you know, you don't have to apologize for them. I get that they aren't super excited to hang out with me."

I think back to joining Reese for lunch yesterday. It was one of the most awkward experiences of my life. I felt like a child with Reese trying to facilitate a conversation between me and the group. The only time they spoke to me was to ask if amnesia was a real thing and if I really couldn't remember anything about my accident. Sam and Garett eventually made an attempt to be welcoming, but Violet, Ivy, and Landon made their own conversation and ignored the rest of us. My stomach had been so nervous, I hardly ate.

"Even if these guys aren't excited to hang out, I am." He looks straight into my eyes with that happy confidence that has always felt unshakable. "And I want you to come. Those losers can pout about it on their own time."

"Don't, Reese," I say sounding more whiny than I meant.

His face looks puzzled. "What? They are acting like losers."

"But, even if that's true, I don't want to come between you and your friends. You and your *family*." I hazard a glance at the group and see that Landon is watching us. He looks away and takes a sip of his coffee. Ivy is telling some kind of story to the group with exaggerated looks on her face and laughing too loudly.

"They'll get over it. Trust me. Violet is always finding something to be upset about. You're just the target of the week. She'll move on. And Landon has Ivy. He'll be fine."

I glance once more at Landon. Ivy reaches under the table and rubs his knee while she talks. I feel my stomach turn. "I'll go," I say before I have a chance to take it back.

"You will?" Reese's face lights up.

"Yeah, I'll go." My heart is pumping because firstly, I hate skiing. At least I think I will. It sounds like another trip to the hospital waiting to happen. Also, my doctor hasn't cleared me for sports yet, so I'll have to do a fair amount of lying to Gayle and possibly Reese. But most of all, I think about James's warnings. How I can't talk to Landon about his death—about why I'm really here. And I wonder how in the world I'll spend that much time with him and not breathe a word about it.

And there's Reese. I can see in his face how happy he is that I'm coming. I care too much for him to lead him on, but I feel like it's impossible not to. I tell myself that if Reese really knew what I was trying to do—save his cousin's life—he'd somehow forgive me.

Chapter Thirteen

CROSSING LINES

(PRESLEY)

34 Days Before

It's nearly 8:00 a.m. but looks like evening outside. The sky is dark and heavy with iron clouds, which canvas the entire sky. The last two weeks the sun has done nothing but shine, but today of all days the forecast calls for snow.

I pull into the parking lot at Mount Rose Ski Resort and scan the imposing snow-covered mountains. I want to flip a U and go right back home, curl up on the couch with a blanket, and break my "no-screen" rules by binge-watching some Netflix. Because Reese is a liar.

He described this place as having tons of small "bunny hills perfect for beginner pansies," but I see nothing but massive, jagged mountains looming like giants behind the log cabin-style ski lodge. I pull into a spot and shove the shifter into park, intending to send Reese a text. I'll tell him I have the flu or that Chase's caregiver called in sick. I'm a little early and with any luck he's not here yet. But as I'm digging through my bag for my phone, a knock thuds against my driver's window.

It's Reese. He's wearing gloves, a stylish navy blue ski coat, and a matching beanie. A pair of expensive looking goggles rest on his forehead. He motions for me to get out with an enthusiastic grin. I curse under my breath, then grab my backpack and do as I'm told.

"Hey," I say. "Are we really going to be able to ski if it snows?" I gesture to the clouds. I'm hopeful that they'll shut the resort down if the storm comes in strong.

Reese throws his head back and laughs out loud. "You are *such* a chicken." He grabs my hand and pulls me across the lot toward the group, which is huddled in a loose knot near Landon's SUV. They're all dressed similarly to Reese—ski jackets and pants, beanies, gloves.

We reach the group and Landon and Garett busy themselves at the other side of the vehicle, hands twisting and tugging at the ski rack on the roof. One by one they pass down sets of skis to Violet, Ivy, and Sam.

Landon doesn't acknowledge me but Garett greets me with, "Hey Presley," and there's a genuine smile on his face and in his voice. He motions me to the car with a gloved hand. Sam turns and waves too, but Ivy and Violet don't break from their conversation or even glance my way.

"We've found the perfect set for you," Garett says. He pulls down another pair of skis from the rack and stands them up. They are considerably shorter than the skis the other girls are holding. Violet looks from the skis to me and covers her mouth with one hand, but I can tell by the way her shoulders twitch that she's laughing at me. I get it. The rookie gets the baby skis, and she's loving this.

Man, I miss the old Violet. The one who would put an arm around me and say something like, "Don't even worry. You'll be graduated from these skis by noon. You've got this." I have to wonder if she's still holding a grudge over the incident on the slope, or if this is just how she was before Landon's death. Tragedy has a way of shaping people, and maybe that's why Violet was so kind before. I think of how my injury has softened Gayle.

I feel vindicated when Reese says, "Knock it off, Violet."

Her eyes widen. "What?" she asks innocently.

Reese takes the skis from Garett and gives me a quick lesson on how to carry them. "Here, like this." He props the skis over my shoulder and helps me secure them with my right hand. "Hold on here," he instructs. "Now this hand is free to carry your poles."

I hazard a glance at the group. Violet and Ivy are already several feet ahead, skis slung over their shoulders and making their way toward the lodge. Sam isn't far behind them, but looks over her shoulder at me with an apology in her eyes. Landon hangs out by the car and watches as Reese takes my goggles and adjusts them. I startle a little when Landon's eyes catch mine.

Unlike the other times in class and at lunch when I've caught him looking at me, he makes no effort this time to look away. His eyes narrow a bit making a line between his brows and a tenseness in his jaw. I mean to be the one to break our gaze, but he's first. He shakes his head slightly, then turns his focus to the rack, hands working quickly to secure it.

When we reach the ticket booth, I prop my skis against the building and slide my backpack from my shoulders. Reese must read me because he says, "Nah. Put that back. I've already got your lift ticket."

"Reese, no!" I protest. I looked online and these things are like a week's wages. "You can't. Let me pay you back."

"Hush, little padawan." He places one gloved finger over my lips. "Still an apprentice you are. Bunny hills you need. When a Jedi skier you become, ski at Blackwood Resort for free you will." He winks at me.

I should be laughing at his stellar Yoda impression, but I'm so embarrassed. If it weren't for my lack of skills, these guys would be skiing gratis at their family resort instead of paying to ski at a place for rookies. I'm surprised Violet and Ivy agreed to this.

Heat bleeds through my cheeks. "Fine, then I'm buying you dinner at some snazzy little lake-front joint. Or school lunch for like a month."

He smiles warmly. "You better never reach for your wallet when you're with me."

The heat in my cheeks morphs into a different kind of burn, spreads down my neck, and ignites in my chest. I think back to the new tires Reese bought me when mine were slashed. His compassion towards Chase. To the night he told me he loved me and would wait for me. How I knew at that moment that I loved him too, and if Landon weren't in the picture, I might have chosen him. I can only imagine how my cheeks must blush at the memory.

And now I want to save the boy who no longer wants me. He's in love with another girl and at some point, I'll have to consider accepting that. His life is still at stake. And I will not let him die again. Despite our disconnect, I want him to live.

I can't let anything pull me from this path. No distractions. I resolve to keep Reese inside a friendship-only circle. Anything more could put me off course. Wouldn't it?

I haven't put my gloves on yet and the icy temps make them ache. Reese removes his gloves and takes my hands in his. They send warmth through me in more than one way.

This is going to be harder than I thought.

Chapter Fourteen

STUCK

(LANDON)

34 Days Before

Hey guys," Reese calls out. He and Presley crunch through the snow toward the row of outdoor lockers where our group is stowing our shoes and backpacks. Reese picks the locker next to mine.

"Give me your backpack," he says to Presley, shoving it inside his locker and glancing my way. "Don't wait for us. We're headed to the lodge to rent some boots for Pres. You guys should have time for a couple runs before we're done."

I flinch at the way he calls her "Pres," but then force my face into "whatever" mode. It's not like I have any right to care what they do. And of course she'll need ski boots. It's her first time. Reese invited her—he *should* be the one to help her.

Ivy shuts our locker and laces her arm with mine. She aims her words at Reese. "I don't think we'll be spending a lot of time on the bunny hill today."

Presley blushes, making the freckles on her cheeks and nose stand out. I want to tell Ivy to shut up. I know Presley must think I'm just as rude as Violet and Ivy. And that turns my stomach. I'm just trying to do the right thing. Play by the rules.

"Maybe we just do our own thing and meet up for lunch?" Ivy suggests, shrugging her shoulders.

"Good by me," Reese says over his shoulder, already leading Presley toward the lodge. He takes her skis from her and rests them on his shoulder with his own. They climb the few steps to the lodge and disappear through the entrance.

"Why don't you guys catch the first one without me," I motion to the black diamond chair lift where a line is starting to form. "These need some wax," I say, tapping my skis. "I forgot to do it this morning."

"Are you sure?" Ivy asks. "I'll wait."

I kiss her cheek. "Go kick Violet's can. I'll be ready when you get back."

Ivy, Violet, Garett, and Sam finish tightening their boots and get snapped into their skis. The girls push off toward the lift, but Garett hangs behind and slaps me on the back. "Don't think I don't know what's really going on here." He winks before wiggling his goggles into place, then digs his poles in and pushes off before I can respond.

What's that supposed to mean?

I make my way to the lodge and to the repair counter. My skis will be ready in fifteen minutes, so I take a seat and scan the shop. I'm surprised that Reese and Presley aren't in line at the rental counter. A quick scan reveals that Presley's seated on a bench in the new equipment section. She's laughing and Reese is kneeling in front of her, a boot in one hand, her foot in the other. He pushes her snow pants up, then pulls her socks up until they cover her entire lower leg.

I think back to lunchtime this week. Presley brought her brother to eat with her. She had to have arranged it because he has a different lunch time than we do. The first time I saw her with him, she was kneeling in front of him tying his shoes, much like Reese kneels now. I'm sure she heard the snickers and whispering. But she tied one shoe, then the other. When she was done, she planted a kiss on his forehead, sat back at the table, and took a bite of her sandwich, encouraging Chase to finish his apple.

"They're not *that* small," Presley giggles.

"You wear a size five, Pres," Reese says. "These are elf feet."

She covers her face with both hands.

"Small feet are cute," Reese cheeses. "You should see Violet's boats." He smirks.

Violet had that coming. I shove my hands in my pockets and walk over to them. "Hey. You guys buying boots today?" It's not technically breaking the rules if I address my comment to Reese, is it? "I thought you were renting."

Presley drops her hands from her face and looks at me with wide eyes. Then to Reese.

He stays focused on maneuvering Presley's foot into the boot but answers, "Nah. This is definitely not going to be her last time, so we're just getting her set up with a new pair."

"Huh," I say.

Reese asks why I'm not with the rest of our group, and I tell him I'm having my skis waxed. He raises an eyebrow but doesn't say anything. I know he remembers that we waxed our skis together just last week. I suck at this.

I circle back to my chair at the repair counter and vow not to look at them again. All of sixty seconds pass and I fail. Presley shrieks, then falls into laughter. I haven't heard her carry on like this since I met her. Why does it sound so familiar?

Reese is laughing as hard as she is. I shouldn't care why it's so easy for them to be happy like this. I steal a sideways glance and my stomach tightens. Reese stands behind Presley in front of a full-length mirror. His arms are wrapped around her waist, helping her to balance. Walking in ski boots for the first time takes some practice.

"Okay, take a few steps," he encourages. "How does that feel? Are your feet slipping at all? They should be nice and snug, but not too tight." She wobbles a little and grabs at his arms for balance. "Believe it or not, it will feel much easier once you're snapped into your skis," he assures.

I regret having my skis waxed. I should've never come in here. I decide to wait for my skis outside. I rest my elbows on the railing and drop my head to rest it in my hands, trying to distract myself with any thoughts that don't involve my cousin or Presley. The resort has gotten busier since we got here. People shout to one another, and lift attendants call out instructions to keep the lines moving. Several happy groups packing skis and snowboards make their way from the parking lot to the runs. They laugh and roughhouse with one another. I'm envious of how carefree they all seem.

When my skis are done, I take a bench near the lodge and snap in. I head toward the black diamond lift but stop when I hear Reese call out to me. I turn to find him and Presley snapped in and looking ready for a run as well. At least Reese seems ready. He smiles at me, then knocks on Presley's helmet. "What d'ya think of her new brain bucket?"

A new helmet too. Nice. He's really pampering her.

Overly hyper, Reese beats on his chest with one fist. "Okay, let's do this!"

Presley chews a little on her bottom lip, eyeing the pairs of skiers boarding the chairlift. "Hey," she says to the two of us. "Why don't you guys go first, and I'll wait here until you get back. I think I'll get the hang of this if I can just watch for a bit."

Reese and I both laugh at that. If I allowed myself to initiate conversation with her, I would tell her that the only way to learn to ski is by getting on the slope. You can't learn to swim without jumping into the water.

Reese loops his arm around her waist and pulls her into a sideways hug. "You've got this, Pres. You nailed your stops over there." He motions back to a miniature slope where beginners practice the basics. "If you can stop, you can ski. Let's go."

Ignoring her protests, he keeps his arm around her waist and ushers her to the line. I should be on my way to the black diamond lift, but I wait, watching. When it's finally their turn, Presley wrenches herself from Reese's arm and like someone dodging an oncoming car, launches her entire body to the right, out of reach of the swinging, suspended chairs. The chair scoops Reese up and carries him up the mountain. I can tell he's trying not to laugh. I think it's safe to say this is the first time we've both seen someone take cover from a chairlift.

Then he calls to her from his ascending chair. "It's okay! I'll jump off at the first stop and come back for you. Just stay where you are."

But she looks determined in the way she hoists herself back to standing. Digging her poles into the snow, she inches back into the queue, which is shorter now. Her lips pressed into a stubborn line, she grips both poles in one hand and waits purposefully at the front. Her face is craned over her shoulder, arm extended, and ready to grab the chairlift. Just like a pro. Then right before the chair catches her, she throws herself to the side again.

I try to put myself in her shoes. For someone who's been skiing since he could stand, catching a lift is as easy as walking. But this is her first time, and judging by her acrobatics to avoid it, it all must feel like jumping from a moving train. Without overanalyzing it, I push over to her, grab her hand, and pull her up. She doesn't fight me. Her poles are splayed in the snow, so I gather those up too, and with my free hand take hers and lead her once again into the line.

"Don't do that again," I tell her, my hand at her back and nudging her toward the front. "People are staring at you." I nod toward the liftie, who has his hand poised near the brake lever. He raises an expectant eyebrow, so I give him a thumbs-up. The chair swoops underneath the two of us, our feet leave the ground, and we're airborne.

I pull the safety bar down over our laps. Presley grabs it with both hands and cranes her head back toward the boarding area, panic defining her every feature.

I can't help it. I double over and let myself laugh. It comes hard and constant, and I feel slightly ruthless because she's scared. Like skydiving-for-the-first-time scared. But she's totally safe. She just doesn't know it.

"Will Ferrell," I say, trying to force the laughter down. "That scene on *Elf* . . ." I have to stop and catch a breath. "When he's trying to get on the escalator . . ." Laughter erupts again, so I put a gloved fist over my mouth and hold my breath to make it stop.

Presley turns on me with wide eyes. The panic in them seems to ease into annoyance or exasperation. "That's who you looked like back there," I say, pointing to the bottom of the mountain. "*Elf.*"

The lift grinds to a choppy halt and she grabs my arm. "What was that?" She jerks her head toward the boarding platform, then back to me. "What's wrong with this thing?" Her eyes implore mine. "Why are we stopped?"

We're halfway to the first stop and at least forty feet high, our skis dangling below us. She looks to the ground, then back to me again. The color has drained from her face. "Oh my gosh, we're so high. This is not happening."

Instinct urges me to pull her to me. Hold her head against my chest. Calm her. I inch away from her instead.

"No worries. This happens all the time. Probably some gaper."

"Gaper?"

"Yeah, you know. Some newbie who . . ."

"Someone like me," she cuts in.

"I didn't mean it that way." An awkward silence rests between us. I rub the back of my neck. "Actually, yeah. I'm pretty surprised they didn't stop the lift with all those shenanigans you pulled down there." I laugh out loud. "Admit it. It was a little bit funny."

"Maybe a little." She surrenders a grin.

"You were laughing at me down there," she says. She considers me for a moment, then shakes her head. "I haven't heard you laugh like that since . . ."

She stops herself and turns away.

"Presley." I urge her to face me with a gentle hand on her arm. She responds to my touch and when her eyes meet mine, they are shining.

"Presley, come on. You haven't heard me laugh like that since *when?*"

She's quiet for a moment and I realize that I shouldn't be touching her like this. I take my hand back, ashamed at my lack of willpower to follow the simple rules I set. Even so, I find myself wishing that everything could just stop for a while. That we could hang here suspended, alone.

"Why did you kiss me? That day on the slope?" she asks. Her cheeks have warmed to an irresistible pink that matches her full lips perfectly. "You knew my name. You said it right before you kissed me."

My heart is thudding inside my chest because I'm frustrated that I can't answer the simple question. I'm even more frustrated because I feel like she can. "You tell me." My voice is sharper than I meant it to be.

Her eyes don't leave mine. They're pleading. Asking me for something I don't know how to give, but I want to.

The pull of her eyes must have distracted me because I didn't notice the lift had started moving again. In a few moments it will be our turn. I bury the emotions her question exposed. What choice do I have?

"Time to get off," I tell her, trying to ignore the disappointment in her face. "Don't worry about your poles. I've got 'em. Just hang on to me." I loop my arm under hers and squeeze. "It's easy. Don't stress."

We get off without a hitch. I keep my arm linked with hers and escort her down the small grade to the top of the bunny hill.

Reese is waiting for us there, his eyes hard and his arms crossed over his chest. "What was all that?"

Chapter Fifteen

Friction

(Presley)

34 Days Before

Y ou saw her," Landon says, gesturing to the bottom of the lift. He hands me my poles without a look, then glides past me toward Reese. Washing his hands of all that talk about kissing me, apparently.

Landon props his poles against his hip and adjusts his goggles over his eyes, laughing. "Dude, she was going to get kicked out if she kept it up."

Something about Landon's manner tells me he's trying a little too hard.

Reese isn't laughing though. "I said I was coming back for her."

"Well, she didn't listen. I'm not sure if you could see from up here, but she was a disaster down there," Landon says.

The volume in Reese's voice climbs slightly. "Why weren't you at the black diamond, anyway?" Something about his tone makes my stomach tighten. I don't like where this is going.

"You should be thanking me. I helped out your girl, man."

"The lifties would have helped her," Reese counters.

"I took care of it. It's cool. You weren't there," Landon says. Even through his gloves, I can see his fingers tighten around the poles.

"Really? I couldn't exactly jump from the chair. I was coming for her," he repeats.

Landon points a finger at Reese. "Bro, I was doing both Presley and you a favor. Just wanted to help her get up here without having her head knocked off by the lift, okay? That's it."

I break in because this is one hundred percent my fault. "Guys. Please." A toxic mixture of guilt and adrenaline send sickening waves though my chest. "I shouldn't have come. Skiing. This is your thing. A Blackwood thing. I shouldn't be here."

"The hell you shouldn't," Reese says, sliding over to me and wrapping his arm protectively around my shoulders.

"Really, I shouldn't. You guys can't be arguing about this. About me. It's lame." I feel hot tears welling up.

"Just so I'm clear," Landon says. "Presley's your girlfriend now and no one else can ride next to her. Is that the problem?"

"Presley is not my girlfriend, but the last time I checked *you* have one."

Reese takes me by the shoulders and ushers me to the side, not taking his eyes from Landon. "How long have you and Ivy been made up now?" he demands. "Like a week?"

From behind, Violet's voice calls out. "Guys!"

She sweeps to a stop in a quick arc, spraying snow on the three of us. The others aren't far behind. The attendant ushers us away from the lift and soon we have five sets of eyes studying us.

"Are you guys *fighting?*" Ivy asks. "What happened?" She shoots me an accusatory glare.

Violet takes turns studying her brother and cousin. I cringe when her eyes settle on Reese's clenched jaw, then Landon's defensive expression. "Who's going to tell me what's going on?" Her eyes swing from Landon's to meet mine.

Reese waves her off. "It's nothing. We're all good." He takes my hand and pulls me away.

I risk a look over my shoulder at the bewildered group and Violet calls to me, "This is messed up. These two never fight. Ever."

Chapter Sixteen

NICE TO MEET YOU

(PRESLEY)

32 Days Before

After the weekend drama on the slopes, I'm glad when the red-headed girl comes back to Wild Cherries on Monday afternoon. After she'd forgotten her book that day, I'd been keeping it aside for her. It's a smallish white book about a brilliant neurosurgeon who, after ten years of training, gets terminal lung cancer. It didn't seem like the kind of book a young girl would read in a coffee shop. But then again, you never know what's going on in people's heads. I'm sure she'd be shocked to know my current thoughts on death and dying.

"You left this here." I set the book on the table in front of her and I'm struck again at the shade of her amber eyes. They're bright, like they're lit from the inside.

"Thanks," she says. Her pale hand rests on the book and she slides it toward her.

"So, I feel like since you're a regular around here, I should at least learn your name. I'm Presley." A few beats of awkward silence pass between us.

"Erin." She seems kind of cagey and I can't tell if it's because she just wants to be left alone or if she's just shy. "I haven't been here long, so I don't know many people."

Just shy, then.

"Where are you from?" I ask.

She smiles and drops her eyes. "I guarantee you've never heard of it."

I shrug. "Try me."

"A little place called Blue Diamond. It's sort of like the wart on the butt of Las Vegas."

I know the place she's speaking of. My mom used to drive Chase and me to the tiny little foothill town about twenty minutes outside of Vegas when she was feeling claustrophobic. Blue Diamond had one small school, a park, a post office, and an itty-bitty store. We built the only snowman of our childhood in that little park.

"You're joking. I'm from Vegas. I've been there a ton of times," I say as I lean against the wall.

Erin's eyes widen. "No freaking way. That is crazy!"

"So, what brought you to Truckee, then? Did your family move here?"

Again, she drops her eyes and I wonder if I'm being too nosy or pushy. It just feels so nice to talk to someone who I don't have any "before" memories of. Someone who isn't treating me differently or who has forgotten they ever knew me.

"No. My family's still in Blue Diamond. I just had to get out of there, you know? Get a change of scenery. Think about what I really want to do."

"Right. Well, the good thing is, it's only a day's drive if you ever want to go back and visit."

"No." Erin says it so abruptly that I think for sure she's wishing I'd just stop talking and go away, but then she looks me in the eye. "Sometimes relationships are so one-sided that it's better to end them altogether." Her eyes hold mine, like she's sizing me up. Trying to see if I'll flinch at her openness. I don't.

"I get it. I've gone most of my life without speaking to my dad."

Erin's eyebrows go up. "Rough."

I slide into the seat opposite her and drop my arms at my sides. "Yeah. The really messed up part is that for most of my life I was angry at him for the wrong thing. I recently found out my mom wasn't exactly telling me the truth about him. About the reasons why he left. This whole time I just thought he was this loser, but in reality, my mom had done some stuff that basically made it pretty hard for him to be in my life."

"That *is* messed up. So what are you going to do? Have you talked to him about it?" Erin asks.

"We've written a couple of emails. Nothing too deep. I'm kind of waiting to see if my mom is going to own up to it."

Erin thinks for a moment and then leans back in her seat. "She might never admit it. Kind of seems like a waste of time—all that waiting. You could be talking to your dad, you know? I wouldn't wait if I were you. You just never know—"

At that moment, we're interrupted by the scratching nails of that little black and white dog. He's frantically whining and hopping against the glass doors again.

"He's baaaaack," Erin says in a singsong voice.

In a way, I'm kind of grateful for the interruption. I feel like I've shared too much too soon with Erin.

I let out a big sigh. "I don't know what to do with this dog. He keeps coming back. I'm afraid my boss will get mad if she sees me feeding him, but he won't go away unless I do."

Erin laughs. "You've trained him. Now he's never going to leave. He knows where the good stuff is. What's his name?"

"I don't know. He doesn't have a collar."

"You should name him after your dad. Then every time he comes you'll be reminded to call him up." Erin gives me an impish smile. If she's still talking about my dad, maybe she doesn't think I'm strange for emotionally dumping on her the first time we met.

"Russell would be a weird name for a dog. It's like Clark or Gene." I make a face at the dog and wonder what name would suit him.

Erin shrugs her shoulders. "I say you go with it. You could always call him Russ for short."

I laugh. "That's even worse! That's . . . that's like calling him Chuck or Merve."

"All fantastic dog names," Erin counters casually.

"You are very bad at naming dogs." I smile and shake my head at her. "He should have a name like Bandit or Ziggy."

"Pff. Those are the worst dog names I've ever heard. Like, if I tried all day I could not come up with worse names."

"Erin, I am not naming that dog Russ. Or Russell or anything else that sounds like a fifty-year-old accountant."

Erin ignores me. "Russ!" she calls and the dog perks up his ears at the sound of her voice, even through the door.

In resignation, I open the glass door and he trots in like he owns the place. Erin smiles and calls to him again. "Good boy, Russy, Russ. You know your name, don't you?" The dog skitters across the floor and dances around at Erin's feet. She reaches down and scratches his chin. "I like his white whiskers. They're like a cat's. Aren't they, Russ? Just like a cat's."

I roll my eyes and go to retrieve the standard three slices of smoked turkey. Russ knows what's up and like usual, he follows me over, gobbles the meat down without chewing it, and then runs back to the door to be let out. He shimmies through the crack in the door before I even have it open all of the way and then scampers off across the street, dodging traffic like some Chihuahua ninja.

Erin shakes her head as she watches him weave between the oncoming cars. "Russ has a death wish, man."

I consider this girl for a moment. She's funny. She lets me moan about my family drama without judgment. And she just talked me into naming that dog after my father. She's not Violet or Reese or Landon. Of course I wish they were the ones I was spending time with. But she's someone.

I think I just made my first new friend.

Chapter Seventeen

Missed

(PRESLEY)

30 Days Before

I'm sitting in U.S. History on a Wednesday morning, and as usual, Landon is focused in on Mr. Nissila like he's the first man on Mars. To make matters even more awesome, Reese and Landon aren't speaking to each other. Reese, who never pays attention in class no matter what is going on, is suddenly studious as well. So sitting in the middle of these two is pretty much the pinnacle of awkwardness.

Honestly, I want to knock their heads together. Two cousins who are this close should not be fighting over a girl, any girl. But in some ways, their conflict gives me a little hope. Because why would Landon care so much about what I do with Reese if he didn't feel something? And if he feels something, that has to mean he remembers something, doesn't it?

Also, I have to wonder if Reese has any memory of me. If the time we spent before has cast any shadows, or if all the affection he's shown thus far is how he would have reacted toward me anyway.

I take a sideways look at both of them in turn. Reese's jaw is tight and he's bouncing the edge of his Nike against the leg of his chair. Landon, on the other hand, is calm as deep water. His dark lashes blink slowly and his breath comes in even pulls. I forego my normal guardedness and let myself look at him longer than usual.

My goal is to keep him safe. To prevent the worst. But when I'm only a couple feet away from him—close enough to pick up his familiar smell, close enough to see the white moons of his fingernails, or the hint of textured growth along his jaw—it's hard to be the savior. Sometimes, I just want to be Presley. Sometimes I just want to love him and have him love me back.

I skip lunch altogether, just needing a minute to myself. To be away from Gayle and Chase and everyone at school. I'm still surprised at how hard it is to pretend all the time. Pretend the time before with the Blackwoods never happened. Pretend there aren't any dark spirits looking for someone like me. Pretend my heart isn't broken. Pretend I'm not scared most of the time that I might fail Landon or that James is right and there's no point in me trying to save him.

There's still a couple of hours before my shift begins at Wild Cherries, so I get in my Civic and just drive. I crank the radio to drown out the thoughts wrestling in my head. Before long, I'm in my old neighborhood and against better judgment, turn down my old street.

The house is still empty. It looks older than I remember—the yellow paint faded to more of a dirty cream color and the windows like dead eyes. I pull in the driveway, but instead of going toward the house, I take the trail toward my old running route. The path that used to be tramped down to a well-beaten track is now grown over with tangles of bleached dead grass and half-melted snow. I shiver against the cold and trudge forward, itching to run like I used to, but knowing I should walk instead.

As I follow the familiar trail, predicting the curves and hills, remembering a specific fallen log and other trail markers, I can't help but think back to the time I spent with Landon here. This private forest had become our own hideaway. A place we could speak freely. The place we grew close on the many runs we took together.

But most significant to me at the moment, it's the place we first spoke.

The urgent pull in my body recedes and I take in the clearing before me. This is the only spot on the path where the trees thin out and the skyline and mountain peaks are visible. The small meadow is void of the usual wildlife except for a couple of ravens, which seem to find a way to survive in any condition.

This is the exact spot I met Landon for the first time. The energy and life in his eyes had caught me off guard, and though I was at first angry and scared, I was also intrigued. I'd never felt that way upon meeting someone. And though I've never been a big believer in fate or anything like it, I can't deny there was an extra something . . . a gravity and importance to the meeting.

I have to wonder, if I had known then what I know now—if I could have seen all that would happen—the danger, the Vigilum, the hurtling through time and space, the forgetting. Would I have made the same choices? Or would I have walked away that day and never looked back?

I'm torn from my thoughts by the rattle of a train in the distance and then the forlorn howl of the whistle as it travels through the town limits. Taking a few steps forward, I make my best judgment of the exact place Landon and I first spoke. Crouching down, I flatten my palms against the frozen earth, almost feeling the memories through my hands. I close my eyes and let them come. His face appears, and I drink in the warmth in his eyes and the curve of his mouth when he smiles at me. He speaks my name with affection and my mind melts into the memory of his arms encircling me. And finally, his kiss.

I shouldn't be doing this. There's no guarantee that I will ever have him like that again. In fact, the odds are decidedly against me. But at least letting myself remember him in this place with that much clarity teaches me one thing. I would do it all again. A thousand times again.

I reach over and close my fingers around a sharp stone, and slowly and deliberately carve a word into the dampened soil. A word that means something to me ever since I saw it engraved inside Landon's class ring. I straighten and toss the stone aside, looking down at the word one more time, etching it into my heart. Then I turn and walk away.

(Landon)

It's not like I haven't skipped school before. I've done it dozens of times with Reese. This time isn't the same though, and I know it. First of all, I walked out of the middle of class while Ms. Lopez was speaking. No explanation. Nothing. Just walked straight out the front doors, got in my car, and drove away.

Presley didn't come to lunch. It's the first time she hasn't, and nobody knew where she was. I started feeling . . . anxious. I tried to hide it. Violet noticed something was off and asked me if I was okay. I lied, and I'm pretty sure she knew it. She always knows when I'm lying.

I'm chewing on the inside of my cheek because I'm not sure why I pulled off and parked at some random trailhead. It's not my usual side of town. I've never been to this spot. But it's like I was led here by some demanding sort of internal GPS. I knew the way—that there would be an old chipped sign that someone had shot up marking the turnoff to the trail. It feels like I've been here before, but I know I haven't.

It's like an itch that I can't reach. It wants me to get out of the car so I rip the keys out of the ignition and throw open the door but hesitate, standing with the car door hanging open. Angry at myself that I don't seem to know my own mind, I slam the door and traipse toward the trail, meeting the head in a few long strides. Already feeling a small measure of relief, I tramp past the signs and maps, like somehow my body knows I'm on the right track.

Traveling the path, I scan the landscape for familiarity. It all seems familiar. And it all seems foreign. I walk for what has to be a couple of miles until I hear the rush of the river in the distance. Though the trail is hooded by thick trees, the placement of the river orients me and I guess that I must be in the general area of the train bridge. The distant rumble of a locomotive confirms my thoughts. As it draws nearer, the thunderous rattle feels wrong as it disturbs my insides and I steel myself against the blow of the whistle. *Since when do trains freak me out?*

I push forward, my feet eager to get somewhere my mind can't name. My breath is coming faster and I break into a jog and then a run. The trees flash by on either side as I leap over occasional puddles and fallen branches. The squeezing of my chest starts to loosen and I slow the pounding of my feet against the earth.

This is the place. Somehow I know this is the place. There's nothing extra special about this little clearing on the trail other than the bright blue sky and the rugged snow-covered peaks that are now visible. I approach the little meadow slowly, my heart still thudding against my ribs. I take it in, but then turn from it, some force I can't explain telling me to look around. Look more closely. Each step feels important. Each swath I cut with my eyes, back and forth seems critical.

Then, in the middle of the trail, I pick up on an anomaly. Where the dirt is somewhat smooth, damp and packed down, there are some harrowed marks. Like some crude instrument has snagged through the mud, turning up broken soil on either side of the lines. They make a word.

FORTIS

Of course I know this word. It's the one-word motto for the Blackwood family. My great grandfather, Ambrose Blackwood, first had it tattooed on his forearm in World War II to help him remember his inner strength given to him by God. My dad still tells the stories of when Grandpa was lying in a rotting prison camp and how that motto helped get him through some of his darkest moments. So when my parents had that word inscribed inside my class ring, I was touched.

I kneel down to run my fingers over the fresh, rough letters, not caring that my pants are getting wet at the knees. I'm reading the word over and over again. *Fortis. Fortis.* But like some kind of emotional dyslexia, my mind is saying *Presley. Presley.*

I close my eyes against the intrusion, but it only makes her face appear in the blackness. Her eyes are unsure, scared even, her brows pushed into a distrustful line. Her face then slides into an expression of anger and for some reason this makes me want to laugh. I don't know why, but her being angry at me feels amusing . . .

My eyes fly open at the sensation of my phone buzzing in my pocket. I fish it out, getting mud on the glass display screen. It's Ivy.

I answer. "Hi."

"Hey," she says. "I was worried about you. What's going on?"

My face is pinched, knowing I'm going to have to explain my behavior to everyone at some point.

"Sorry. I wasn't feeling well."

There's a pause on the line and I wonder if she believes me.

"Oh. I'm sorry. Can I bring you something? I mean, I know you have an awesome mom and she's probably got it covered, but I like taking care of you."

"I know," I say.

Another pause. "You didn't answer my question."

"I'll be fine. Don't go to any trouble. Thank you though. That's really nice of you."

She sighs through the phone. "Okay then. But you better promise to rest. This is the last week before you're back to that crazy training schedule and you need to be in top form. You are in bed, right? Not playing that lame video game you and Reese are addicted to?"

"I'm in bed." The lie falls off my tongue effortlessly.

"Okay then. I'll let you rest. The bell's about to ring anyway. Bye, babe."

"Bye, Ivy." I swallow back the guilt. I didn't mean to lie to her, I just didn't want to have to explain something I don't understand myself.

I slide the phone back into my pocket, taking one more look at the word scrawled in the dirt. I don't understand the coincidence of this being here. I don't understand why I was drawn to it in the first place. And I for sure don't understand why this word and this place are conjuring up so many thoughts and visions of Presley. Coming here, for whatever reason, is good though because my body feels markedly relieved. Like the first few minutes after you get sick. That anxious feeling seems gone for good, and I can now stand up and walk back into my life without this nagging sensation.

In truth, I'm looking forward to my training schedule picking up in intensity. I can't wait for longer days of sunlight. To welcome the consuming distraction and the clarity I always feel when I'm riding the razor's edge of speed and danger. Once I'm up on the mountain in the clean air, under the sun every day, I'll feel better. That's where people go to find their center again, right? People all over the world have climbed summits to find peace and direction. I'll find those things too.

I *will* be able to move on without Presley.

Chapter Eighteen

Melt

(Presley)

28 Days Before

Things with Landon aren't getting any better other than he's talking to Reese again. He's still ignoring me, though. The more time that stretches between us speaking, the more anxious I get. Because how can I save someone who's pushed me away? I felt so hopeful that day on the ski lift. I could tell he wanted to talk to me. Now, I'm just wondering what has changed.

I've been wishing there was something I could do to help Landon remember me. Over the last couple of days I've gotten a little desperate, researching memory loss and what can be done to restore it. Outside of any bona fide medical procedures and therapies, there's really only anecdotal theories. And with many of them, I can't see how I'd get Landon to cooperate. But, in my digging, I've found these suggestions:

1. Have the person close their eyes and visualize. (Not going to work. He'd think I'm a weirdo if I asked him to do that.)
2. Build a rapport with the person. The familiarity may jog their memory. (That's going worse than ever.)
3. Get a tattoo. (A big heart on his arm with my name on it ought to do the trick.)
4. Hypnosis. (I'm ashamed to admit how much time I took strategizing how I could make this happen. I kept hitting the same dead end though; subjects need to be willing to be hypnotized for it to work. I could never convince him to try and even if I could, I don't know how to do it and I'd sound crazy trying to explain our history to someone "trained" to hypnotize.)
5. Image recognition. (This is a concept I want to spend more time thinking about. I know Landon has had some whispers of memory. He had to have if he kissed me. There is something that is triggering him. Maybe it was the image of my face. Maybe it was a déjà vu feeling because we were in similar situations or surroundings. Could image

recognition have anything to do with him remembering me—even a little? If so, could I re-create that somehow?)

6. Smell and taste. (I learned that the olfactory bulb, the small organ responsible for detecting smells, is connected to the amygdala and the hippocampus, which handle memory and emotion. This all made a lot of sense to me.)

The smell/memory connection is the reason I feel happy every time I walk into a library or bookstore. It's the reason I can't eat a Taco Bell taco even ten years after I got food poisoning. Sadly, the smell of fresh snow and woodsmoke in the air, a smell I used to love, now makes me anxious and scared because it reminds me of the day Landon left me. The day Liam tortured me. That mix of smells reminds me of the moment I thought all was lost.

I've been jotting down experiences Landon and I had in which a smell or taste is connected. And I think I may have found a way to jog his memory.

Landon showed me how to make the Blackwood peanut butter truffles that night in my kitchen. I still remember rolling the buttery mix between my hands, melting the chocolate, and how good they tasted. More than the memory of the tastes and smells though, I perfectly recall how the air was charged between us. Electric attraction, buzzing with energy. After all, we had been talking to each other over weeks—learning about one another, laughing, teasing, confiding. Growing closer and closer by the day.

But most of all, restraining.

I had never wanted to touch or kiss someone so badly in my life. And I know that feeling had to be magnified for Landon since he hadn't been in his body for months. He had shared with me that night how his desires were stronger than ever even though he had no way to act on them. I remember the ache I felt, wanting to help him, but I couldn't.

So when our spirits yearned so deeply to connect with each other and finally broke through the boundaries of our bodies uniting in that first kiss, it was mental, emotional, and physical dynamite. Easily the most powerful feeling I've ever had.

It wasn't one sided. That memory is somewhere in Landon's mind, body, or spirit. And I'm going to draw it out.

Once I let my boss, Sara, try a sample of Landon's peanut butter truffles, it didn't take much to convince her to let me add them to the menu. They were the perfect snack-sized, homemade impulse item to compliment the bitterness of coffee. She was convinced if packaged properly and if we gave samples to customers, people would become addicted. Sara thanked me for the idea and sent me around the corner to Safeway to pick up ingredients for a triple batch.

Back at Wild Cherries, I mix and roll dozens of truffles. At first I'm not sure I have the right ratio of ingredients. I never wrote the recipe down. I decide to take a small bite of the mix to see how I'm doing. The flavor hits my taste buds, and I know right away I'm pretty close, if not right on. The creaminess mixed with the sweet and saltiness and that little bit of crunch from the Rice Krispies brings back the memory of that night in even clearer focus.

Suddenly, the work of rolling and placing the truffles on the pan to get them ready for their chocolate dip feels serious. Important. Like every one of them needs to be perfect because any one of them could be the magic pill that makes Landon remember. Part of me feels silly for attaching my hopes to such a simple thing, but I'm determined to try everything.

The chocolate is melted to a silky sheen in the fondue pot, and as I concentrate on dipping the first truffle with the perfect coating, the doors open and the Blackwoods, along with Garett, Ivy, and Sam step inside.

The beat of awkwardness is immediately overshadowed by Reese's loud exclamation, "Dude! It smells good in here." He elbows past Landon and Violet and trots over to see what I'm doing.

"Oh, no way! My aunt Afton makes these things. They're like little pellets of heaven." He reaches over and takes an undipped truffle. It quickly disappears into his mouth.

He's sucking the remnants off of his thumb in a way I'm trying not to find adorable, when Violet and Landon appear over each of his shoulders. Violet looks at my truffles and then levels her eyes at me. "Huh," she says. "These are just like Mom's. May I?"

My heart is pounding because this is all happening so much more easily than I thought it would. I'd been having awful visions of ding dong ditching Landon's house with a plate of truffles, or stealing his locker combination, or some crazy situation in which I tackle him, sit on his chest, and force feed one to him. And now here he is. A few feet away, looking right at them. Ready to taste the memory of our first kiss. He doesn't meet my eyes, but concentrates on the rows of truffles before him.

Come on, Landon . . . ask me for one.

Violet clears her throat, and I realize I never answered her when she asked for a truffle. I step back a little and say, "Of course. Be my guest. On the house."

She hesitates for a moment, and then selects a smallish one. Her teeth sink into the ball and then she chews, taking her time. "Weird."

My stomach drops for a second because I need these things to be perfect and the daughter of the person who invented the recipe just called them weird. "Did I forget something? Not enough butter?"

Please let there be enough butter.

Violet swallows and rubs her full lips together. "No. They're perfect. It's just weird because I've had a lot of versions of Buckeyes, and they're never as good as my mom's. Usually too sweet or too dry. And nobody ever puts the rice cereal in." She plucks a napkin from the dispenser and rubs the paper against her fingertips. "They're a dead ringer for the Blackwood recipe. Where'd you get yours?"

My throat feels dry and swollen, but I'm so happy that they passed Violet's inspection that I just blurt out the truth, "An old boyfriend showed me how to make them."

Landon's eyes flicker to mine for the first time in almost a week, and a surge of triumph and joy balloon inside me, filling up my whole chest. Though I can't speak openly and specifically about our experiences, I can still communicate our shared memories in my own way. I seize the opportunity, holding his eyes.

Landon's brows push together and he quickly looks away, breaking the connection. I see Ivy and the others watching us from their seats across the dining room, and I know I only have seconds before Landon turns and walks away.

"Anyway," I say, "it's funny how such a little thing can hold so much memory." I lean a hip against the counter. "I'm curious what you think, Landon." He lifts his eyes to mine again and I feel the remnants of that familiar thrum of energy we had before that night in my kitchen. It's vibrating between us again and I can tell he's opened the gates behind his eyes and he's letting me in.

I pick up a truffle and hold it out to him, and he takes a step toward me, but then stops. He seems to be concentrating. And by the way the muscle flexes in his jaw, I can tell he's struggling with something. His eyes hold mine for a few beats of time. Long enough that my confidence grows by the second.

He swallows and shakes his head and at that moment I see the gates slam behind his eyes. "No thanks. I'm training." Then he turns and crosses over to the others, sitting next to Ivy.

My heart falls and lands like a stone in a dry well.

Reese gives a short laugh. "Like that's ever kept him from eating total crap." He calls over to Landon, "Dr Pepper and gas station burritos aren't exactly super fuel, you know."

Landon waves him off without looking over.

Reese rolls his eyes and turns back to me. "So tonight we're all doing Kings Beach. I want you to come."

I set the truffle meant for Landon back on the counter. "Isn't it a little cold for the beach?"

"Not if you're going to build a giant bonfire." Reese flashes a smile and snatches another truffle before I can scold him. "Come on. It'll be fun. You and me."

I glance over at the group at the table. "And them, I'm guessing."

"Yeah, but who cares? You'll be with me, not them. Unless Landon pulls another stunt like he did at the lift." Reese raises one crooked eyebrow and I laugh at his crazy expression.

"Are you guys okay now?"

Reese waves a casual hand. "We're fine. It was just a misunderstanding. I should have known that. He's super tight with Ivy; it's not like he was trying to . . . I don't know, make some kind of move on you."

I feel my face fall a bit at his comment, but do my best to hide my disappointment. "Right. Totally. So, everything's okay then? What about Ivy? She looked pretty mad that day too."

Reese shrugs. "I dunno. I don't really care that much honestly. I mean, she's a nice girl, but man, the girl is clingy. You know what I mean?"

I smile at that, hoping maybe Landon might feel the same way. "What's the matter, is she interfering with your Landon-Reese bromance?"

"Demolishing it." He smiles, but then his face turns serious. "I think the main thing is that Landon is getting ready to start up training again full time, and his family doesn't want him distracted. His fight with me was pretty out of character, and they were kind of surprised by how much it shook him up." Reese leans his arms on the counter and shifts his weight to one leg. "I mean, I was pretty messed up over it too, but I'm just a grease monkey at my dad's garage, not an Olympic golden boy." He smirks in such a way that I can tell he's not pouting about their respective roles. Just stating the obvious.

I shift my gaze to the group again. Landon is quiet, looking out the window. Sam and Garett are playing some hand slapping game and when Garett slams his hands down too hard on Sam's, she stands up and whacks him across the head, sending Ivy into peals of laughter. Violet, I then notice is watching me. I look away and back at Reese. "Will Landon's parents be mad if I go to Kings Beach, then?"

Reese's mouth pulls up on one side. "Like they'd know you're there."

"Yeah, but if they want him to stay away from me . . ."

Reese's eyebrows push down. "I never said that."

My cheeks warm in embarrassment and thankfully Reese finishes his thought.

"They just don't want us fighting is all. And now that we have the misunderstanding worked out, I can't see that happening again." Reese reaches forward and grabs hold of one of my fingers and tugs playfully. "Besides, I plan on keeping you all to myself."

Even under the crazy circumstances, Reese's smile is intoxicating. It's hard to forget why I liked him before.

Chapter Nineteen

Sparks

(Landon)

28 Days Before

The bonfire is warm on my face, and Ivy is chatting with Sam at my side. She seems happy and that's good. I want it to stay that way.

I almost didn't come tonight. When Reese told me he was bringing Presley to Kings Beach, I knew it would be a bad idea if I did. It's not like I don't trust myself around her; it's just that my parents are so adamant that I keep my focus on Alpine. And truthfully, they're right. They helped me see that now is not the time for typical teenage dramas. I have a bigger responsibility than most kids my age, and simply can't afford to be getting into fights over girls. Especially with Reese.

My plan is to just keep my cool whenever I get these weird feelings about Presley. Hold tight and ride it out. Earlier at Wild Cherries, though, that was easier said than done. I was drawn to her, and it was hard to shake it off. Walk away.

My mom studied psychology, and she mentioned that it's normal to have unusual preoccupations when under a lot of stress. It's kind of like a coping mechanism or a way of self-soothing. She explained that fixating on an issue in my life—unrelated to skiing—helps my brain take a break from the pressure.

So that's what I think I've been doing. I think Presley is just some distraction that I've let get out of control. These visions I have are a figment of my imagination to help me take my mind off of the pressure of training and everything else related to the Olympics. I've created these images of her in my mind. They aren't real. It's just my body and my brain trying to deal. Now that I know what's really happening, I'll be fine.

I wrap an arm around Ivy's back and pull her closer to me. She turns from her conversation for a moment, firelight dancing in her dark eyes, then plants a kiss on the side of my mouth before turning back to Sam. The kiss felt like she'd put a stamp on a letter. And I argued with the thoughts that immediately tried to surface. That Presley's kisses didn't feel like a stamp on a letter. They felt like—no. I'm not going there. It doesn't matter what they felt like because they weren't real. Even the feelings I had when I kissed her in real life, were not real. So I have to stop comparing what I felt with her to what I feel with Ivy.

Ivy is real. Ivy is here. Ivy knows me.

Reese and Presley are settling in across the fire. He unfolds a low sand chair for her and takes her hands while she lowers herself into it. Her hair is wild tonight. Full of curls that occasionally get taken up in the breeze and snake around her face until she smoothes them back with turquoise-blue polished fingernails. She's not dressed as warmly as she ought to be, but she still looks cute in a silky bomber jacket, jeans, and lace-up ankle boots. She wraps her arms around her knees and shivers a bit. I realize I'm staring, so I look away.

Even with my new understanding that Presley is a psychological distraction, I'm still not looking forward to avoiding her eyes for the next three hours around the fire, so I tell Ivy I'll be back soon and grab my light-up frisbee from my car. But when I get back, everyone has deserted the fire and is already playing a game of football.

It appears that Reese has forced Presley into being the quarterback and he's the center. She's laughing hysterically at having to catch the snap so near to his gyrating butt. It's clear he's trying to make her laugh, and it's working. He snaps the ball, stands, and blocks Garett from tackling Presley and then breaks free holding one arm out to catch.

"I'm open. Throw it here, Pres!"

Presley is dancing around frantically, trying to see around Garett's giant frame. She finally hops up with a squeal, throws a wobbly pass, and Reese dives to catch it. Then, out of nowhere, Ivy leaps onto his back, sending him toppling to the sand. Presley is jumping up and down cheering, and Reese is scolding her for cheering for the wrong team.

"I know what team I'm on, Reese. That was just hilarious that little Ivy took you down, son!" Presley is still laughing at him so he rolls over and pushes Ivy off him and then takes a full run at Presley.

She pauses for a moment like a deer in headlights and then turns and runs down the beach, close to the packed wet sand of the waterline. I'm amazed at how fast she is and how her small feet turn up the sand like rapid bullet fire. Garett follows like a Labrador who can't resist chasing after a startled duck launching into flight. Soon, his long legs catch up just as Reese is about to snatch Presley off her feet. The boys tussle in a big tangle of arms and legs and in the confusion, Garett gets pushed and lands seat first in the lake.

He's up in an instant and hollering at the icy water dripping from his pants. Violet is already marching to the scene like a playground monitor.

"You guys! That's not funny! You know how cold that water is." She's gesturing wildly with her hands. "People drown in this lake in the middle of *summer*, you dorks."

Garett's hands are up in surrender. "Sorry, Vi. Jeez. It's not like I meant to fall in." He kicks a spray of sand toward Reese. "Reese is the idiot that pushed me anyway."

Reese kicks sand back at Garett and then they're both in headlocks before Violet can do anything about it. She looks at Presley for female backup. Presley shakes her head and says, "Cabbages."

Violet laughs and then suddenly stops herself. I know why she thought it was funny and then all of the sudden didn't. "Cabbages" is what she calls me and Reese when we're being idiots. My mom would get after her when she'd call us mean names when we were little, so she invented "cabbage" as a name she could use to insult us without getting into trouble. It's an inside joke that nobody really gets, but us three.

The knot in my stomach begins to twist again. I force myself to breathe through it and reason with myself. Yes, it's weird that Presley knew that name. Yes, it's hard to explain. But it could be a coincidence. Or maybe she's heard Violet use it before.

See? That wasn't hard. There is an explanation for everything.

I yell to Vi, "Heads up!" The light-up frisbee leaves my hand and sails in a wide arch to Violet. She smiles and hops up to catch it. Then she tosses it to Presley, who though swift to get to it, fumbles and drops it in the sand. Soon, the boys, Sam, and Ivy are all in the game, and as we back up further and further, we have to use each other's voices as a guide for what direction to throw as the half-moon light is not enough to illuminate the beach.

Presley's voice seems to echo louder than everyone else's and I tell myself again, it's just my imagination. The frisbee careens against the blanket of stars, flickering its psychedelic light into the night. Everyone is laughing and running and diving. We tease each other and scream at lucky catches. I'm having a great time. And I'm relieved because if I can pull off an evening like this around Presley, than maybe she can be a part of our group. I swallow hard. Maybe she can be Reese's girl.

I chuck the frisbee toward Presley's voice. There's a clatter and then a scream followed by a splash. Confused, I run her way and realize that though everyone else had been playing on the sand, she had been playing from the dock. Or at least, had run down the dock to catch the frisbee. And she had fallen in.

Her gasping breath is tight and high, triggering a deep dread in me as I race down the dock toward her, Reese suddenly on my heels. His footsteps fall in time with mine, and as we run shoulder to shoulder, I tell myself I'm not really elbowing him to the side, I'm just trying to get to her. Reese gets there first.

He's immediately on his belly stretching his arm over the dock. He pulls Presley up in one quick movement, her body sprawling drenched and shivering on the planks. Then, Reese is on his feet, pulling her up. He yells for everyone to stay back and give her privacy and then I realize he's yelling at me.

"Turn away, Landon!"

"What, me? What about you?" Anger licks at the corners of my mind like flames.

Reese spits in exasperation and turns his back to Presley. "She needs to get those wet clothes off, Einstein. Pres, take everything off, nobody is looking." I turn my back to her as well and notice that the whole group except for Violet has gathered near the end of the dock, backs turned. Vi is marching down the dock toward Presley.

I'm surprised at how gentle Violet's voice sounds though.

"It's okay," Violet says. "We'll get you warm. Just get all of the wet stuff off. Nobody is looking," she reassures her again.

I hear the stuttered breaths of Presley as she shivers against the cold. Soon after, the sound of wet splats reach my ears as her coat and jeans hit the dock. Beside me, Reese is peeling off his Red Alpine hoodie and holding it out behind him to Presley without looking her way.

"Thanks," Violet says, speaking in soothing tones as she helps Presley put it on.

"I can't b-believe how fast my body stopped working in that freezing water. I couldn't even pull myself out," Presley says through what sound like clenched teeth.

"I know. I wasn't kidding when I got after those guys. It's a shock reaction to the cold water. People actually die sometimes because they can't help inhaling when their body is shocked by the cold." Violet tsks. "Oh, my. You're drowning in that hoodie. Let's get you back to my car. I have a bag of workout clothes and I know there are some joggers and a long sleeve thing."

Thinking it safe to look now, I turn around at the same time Reese does and see Presley's tiny frame shivering inside Reese's sweatshirt. It almost comes to her knees and she rubs her arms as Vi bends down to collect her wet clothes.

Reese and I look at one another as the girls walk past us and it's dark enough that I can't decipher the meaning in his eyes. But he looks away first and heads back down the dock. "I've got blankets in my car," is all he says.

Back at the fire, Reese hovers over Presley as he wraps her in two blankets. She's sitting in the sand closer to the flames and he gets down, positioning his body behind hers. He reaches down the back of the blankets and pulls the hood out, covering her wet curls with it. Then, he briskly rubs where her arms would be, smiling and joking, "You almost became a Presley-Pop."

Presley laughs, her face lit up by the fire, and I notice Reese scooting in closer and letting his arms settle around the bundle that is Presley. She blinks into the fire, her face now calm and serene.

Violet is on her phone, trying to look up the chords for that love song she's crazy about, and Garett has retrieved my black guitar from my car and is plucking out the few songs he knows. I know Vi's going to ask me to play, but I don't want to. Which is weird. I love playing at the beach. I look around for a distraction or an excuse before she can ask me and notice Sam and Ivy off in the shadows. Sam is hugging Ivy.

Uh-oh.

Sam catches my eye and somehow gestures with her face that I should come over. My feet are heavy as I make my way over to Ivy. Sam disengages from her and walks back to the fire leaving Ivy and me alone. From the little bit of light, I can see streaks of tears on Ivy's cheeks.

"Hey . . ." I use a soft voice, suddenly feeling surprised and guilty that Ivy is crying. "What's up?"

I can tell Ivy is trying to keep calm herself and to stop crying. And I respect her for that. I've been with a couple of girls who made me feel like they used their tears as a weapon to win arguments or to get their way. Ivy is never like that. She rarely cries, so when she does, I know something is really wrong. She lets out a couple of long, measured breaths and then meets my eyes.

She smiles and the rise of her cheeks makes a couple more tears fall, which she quickly wipes away. "It's stupid," she says.

I reach out and rub her arm. "It's not stupid. You're obviously upset." I keep rubbing her arm waiting for her to say something, but she doesn't. "What can I do?"

"That's the thing," she says, "I don't know. You haven't necessarily done anything wrong. It's just . . ."

"Just what?"

Ivy's face contorts, and she swallows back her emotion one more time.

"It just seems like your attention is split. And I don't know if it's the ski thing and all of the stress that's coming your way, or if you have something going on at home. It just seems like you're pulling away from me."

I take hold of her elbow. "No, Ivy. No. I'm not pulling away." I hear the words coming out of my mouth and I know they're a lie, but I want so badly for them to be true that I allow myself to say them anyway. Hoping that I can make them true.

"You are," she counters. "And I'm not saying that you're doing it on purpose. In fact, I don't think you can help it." Her eyes flicker to the fireside at Presley.

I feel a weight drop in my gut. The knot comes back and twists at my insides. I hate that whatever is going on in my head concerning Presley is affecting Ivy. She doesn't deserve it.

"I mean, I don't blame you. She is beautiful. She's mysterious. And I want to believe that the kiss you gave her at the race was out of pity like you said, but what if it wasn't? It's like that girl can cast spells, Landon. I mean, look at Reese."

I force my face to appear natural and glance their way. Garett is attempting Violet's song, and Reese is swaying with Presley between his arms. I can't tell exactly what her expression means, and I don't want to look too long, especially given what Ivy is sharing with me right now. I look away before my face betrays me.

"It's not a spell, Ivy. Reese is just . . . being Reese." I look at my feet and kick at the sand with the toe of my shoe.

"If Reese is just being Reese, then what are you being?" Ivy holds my eyes, searching.

"I'm being with you." I lean in and kiss her forehead. She closes her eyes, and I kiss the petal soft lids which are rimmed in lashes still moist from her tears. I make myself breathe her in, detecting all of the sugar-warm smells I've always loved. They're still there. My heart gives a feeble jerk and I encourage it by letting my kisses travel down her rounded cheekbones to the corners of her mouth. It's a game we always play. To kiss the corners of each other's smiles. I feel the corner of her mouth come up at my touch and let my lips linger there until she finds my mouth and returns a kiss that feels much less like someone slapping a stamp on a letter and more like someone sealing the envelope.

I feel her body melt into mine, releasing the tension it previously held. I'm deliberate to show her I care with my kiss. This isn't the time for a playful make out. This kiss needs to say, "I'm sorry." It needs to say, "I still want you."

We come together for a few more lingering moments and then come apart. Her eyes are dry and even in the firelight I can see the pink in her cheeks that has always driven me nuts. I take some of her raven hair in my fingers and let the silky strands trail through them. "See? You're the only one casting spells tonight."

She smiles back at me and nods.

"We definitely have a special sauce. You and me," Ivy says. Then her face smoothes out, swallowing up the contours that make up her smile. "But I feel like I need a little time to think. About us." Her eyes are clear and kind. "I appreciate you coming over here. I just need to find out what's best for me. I'm not saying don't call or come by. I'm just saying, I'm taking a little step back. Pushing pause."

Something tugs inside me. I can't tell if it's ego or disappointment. "Pushing pause."

Ivy's eyebrows come together. "Yeah. Just for a bit." She looks into my eyes. "If that's not going to work for you, I understand. It's asking a lot."

"No." I stop her there. "It's completely reasonable." And then I know I have to be honest with her. She deserves it. Even though I want to cling to her because she's one of the brightest spots in my world and one of the best distractions, I need to tell her the truth. "Maybe pushing pause will be good for both of us."

She closes her eyes and nods. "That's what I was thinking but didn't have the guts to say it. I'm glad you said it for me." She takes a step back from me, disconnecting all touch between our bodies. "I'm going to go." In what feels like a snap decision, she steps up and plants one more kiss on my cheek and then walks away.

Chapter Twenty

TWINTUITION

(LANDON)

28 Days Before

I rode to the bonfire with Ivy, but I'm riding home with Violet. The rest of our group piled into Garett and Reese's cars, so it's just the two of us. Violet is unusually quiet at the wheel, so I take advantage of the silence and recline my chair and close my eyes. She has the heater blasting, and I relax a bit as the air warms me.

I feel drained from the night's events: Presley falling in the lake, Ivy deciding she wants a break. Am I a villain for admitting that a small part of what I feel is relief? About Ivy? Things haven't been the same with us since Presley showed up. I still care for Ivy, but recently, she's mostly been a comfortable and safe distraction. If I'm honest, I've been forcing things with her. And it's not like I can just turn back time and make things the way they were before. What's done is done.

I let out a strong breath and try to push away all thoughts of Ivy and Presley. My body is as tired as my mind, so I try to sleep.

"I'm sorry about you and Ivy," Violet says. She must've mistaken my forced exhale as an invitation for conversation. So much for a catnap. I open my eyes a bit and glance at her from my peripheral.

Keeping her eyes on the road, she says, "I know how hard you worked to make things right with her and now this. Are you okay?"

"Honestly, Violet, I'm not sure why you care now." I shake my head. "That stunt you pulled by bringing Ivy to my room when Presley was there. Did you even consider how that might shake things up? You hurt a lot of people."

There's a long pause, then Violet says, "I'm sorry. You're right. That was inexcusable. And I should have apologized to you and Ivy a long time ago."

"And Presley," I say.

"Yes," she agrees.

I raise my seat and look out my window. The moon is only half full, but it's bright enough that it illuminates the pine trees that line the highway so that I can make out the individual branches. "I'm actually all right," I tell Vi. There's comfort in being honest with her, finally. A purging of all I've been holding. "It's been awkward with Ivy lately. Even without that bedroom incident, things would've been awkward." I rub at the back of my neck. "Would you think I'm a total jerk if I told you I'm kind of relieved?"

She shakes her head. "It's not like you planned for things to end up like this."

"I know," I acknowledge. "I guess I shouldn't be surprised it did though. Ivy's been through a lot since Presley moved here." I lay my head against the headrest. "If I put myself in her shoes, I'm not sure I would've hung in there as long as she did."

Violet giggles. "Uh, no. I don't think your ego would have been as tolerant."

"Oh, yeah? Look who's talking!" I can't help but laugh too. "It took you all of five minutes to dump Brian when you saw that he still had pictures of his ex on his Insta."

"That was totally inappropriate," Violet defends. "You don't keep pictures of your ex-girlfriend on your account when you're serious with someone else."

"I think the bro code is nothing like the chick code," I say. "It's not like we obsess over stuff like that. He probably forgot he even had those on there."

"Whatever," Violet says, closing the door on Brian with a flourish of her hand. Her face changes from dismissive to thoughtful.

"So, I need you to be straight with me," she says. "About Presley." She takes her eyes from the road for a moment and my stomach tightens at her expression.

"What about her?" I say, straining to keep my voice as disinterested as possible.

"That's just it. I don't *know*. I don't know what's up with the two of you. But something is."

Silence fills the car, but what can I say?

She taps her fingers on the steering wheel. "And this whole amnesia story. Maybe I *slightly* believe her because of her head injury. But the Landon I know does not simply kiss a stranger—in front of a huge crowd, mind you—and then forget where he knows her from. Honestly, Landon. You felt sorry for her? I don't buy it. And another thing, since when did you start hiding stuff from me?"

She's right. We don't keep things from each other. I trust her more than anyone. And it might actually be healthy to share with somebody. I hesitate. "Okay, but you have to promise that anything I tell you will never leave this car. Not Mom, not Dad, not Reese."

"Landon, I swear it. C'mon. You know better." There's a hint of nervousness in her voice.

"Okay." I exhale again and slide my palms down my cheeks. "I do remember Presley."

Violet eyes me for a moment and then turns back to the road.

"But not completely. It's more like déjà vu. Just bits and pieces."

"Like what?" Violet encourages. "What specifically have you remembered?"

"That day she showed up at our house? We were talking in my room. I don't know. Something about being alone with her. I had this . . . I'm not even sure what to call it . . . like this *vision* of her wearing my letterman's jacket. Then of her playing my piano. But that's impossible, right? Because before that day, she'd never been inside my room."

Violet says nothing. Instead, she pulls off the road and onto the shoulder. Once the car is in park, she drops her hands from the wheel, turns to me, and asks, "What else? Have there been more memories?"

"Yes," I admit. "Almost every time I'm near her, there's something. Like at Wild Cherries, when she made Mom's candy. Just the smells, watching her—everything. It all triggered a random memory of me and her in some kitchen I've never even seen."

Violet's nodding, like she totally gets it. I don't know what I expected from her, but not this.

"That *is* hard to explain," she says, "but I believe you. Even with me, there's something about her. Something familiar. I don't understand it and it scares me. And makes me mad."

I laugh out loud. "You're such a control freak." I squeeze her shoulder. "Is that why you've been so ticked off at her?"

"I've actually tried to stay mad at her." She purses her lips. "At first I told myself it was because she made a fool of all of us on live TV. Got you in trouble with the cops. And even after I heard about how serious her injuries were and you were cleared from any involvement, I was still furious with her." Violet closes her eyes and massages the area between her brows.

"Give yourself a break. Tonight you redeemed yourself. The way you went all mama bear and helped her with the wet clothes. Protecting her from all boys. I don't think I even realized how *off* you've been until I saw you back to yourself."

"It's hard to put into words," Violet says, chewing her lip. "I guess you're not the only one who's confused about Presley."

Chapter Twenty-One

RESCUED

(VIOLET)

27 Days Before

Seriously, Landon? Again?" Why my twin brother always steals my stuff is beyond me. This time it's my phone's car charger. Of course it's on the day I would get a flat tire *and* have a dead phone.

It's early on a Saturday morning and the tray full of coffee and hot chocolate I bought at Wild Cherries is steaming on the passenger seat. I'm bummed they will all be too cold to drink by the time I get to the school. *If* I get to the school. I guess the Honor Society will have to decorate without me.

I weigh my options. I didn't bother to wear super warm clothes because I just planned on running from my heated car into heated buildings. From the ice crystals on my windshield this morning, I estimate the temps to be just below freezing. The hoodie and leggings I threw on seem ill thought out now that I'm stranded on the side of Donner Pass Road. I know the school is less than a mile away, but I don't want to leave my car here or walk all that way carrying the bags of decorations.

Hoping to flag someone down, I get out and brave the chill. As I hold my arm up, a car with a paddleboard strapped to the roof slows to a stop and I'm shocked at my luck. That is, until I see who it is. Presley. It looks like she has her brother with her too. Unbuckling, she says something to him and then gets out. She's dressed more appropriately for early March in an all-weather jacket, boots, and a knitted beanie. A really cute beanie, actually.

She approaches, hands in her pockets. "You okay? Need a ride?"

The usual insta-bristle I feel when she's around is markedly weaker today. After she fell into the lake and my talk with Landon last night, I just don't have it in me to be mean to her. Plus, she's here trying help me.

"Thanks for stopping. I have a flat." I thumb toward the front driver's side to the deflated black rubber.

"Oh, I see that." Presley raises her eyebrows.

"Maybe if I could just use your phone," I begin. I roll my eyes thinking about how irritated my dad will be when I call him. It's the first weekend he's not been on call for Blackwood Ski Resort, and he and my mom were looking forward to sleeping in for once.

"What's the matter?" Presley asks.

"Nothing. Just that my dad won't be thrilled to have to come rescue me this early in the morning."

"What about Landon? Can you call him?"

For a moment I think that's not a bad idea until I realize he's long gone. Already on the slopes with his coach by now. Most Saturday mornings will be like this until the Olympics next winter.

"No. He's training." I let out a big breath. "I'll just call my dad. Or maybe Reese."

Presley leans down and inspects the tire. "You don't have to do that. I can fix this. I see you have your spare on the back. And I have a jack and tire iron."

"Are you serious?" I try to decipher if she's joking.

"Yeah. It doesn't take that long. I'd probably be done by the time your dad gets dressed and drives over here."

"Just do me a favor," Presley continues, "can you sit in my car with Chase? He gets nervous if I leave him alone and I don't want him bolting on the side of a busy road. He has autism, if you didn't know."

I knew something was up with her brother, Chase, but I didn't know it was specifically autism. I glance over at her car. The whole thing is rocking slightly and I see Chase inside moving his upper body forward and back with his arms raised, kind of jamming out to some indistinguishable music. He's a big kid, with a broad chest and giant hands. "Uh, sure. I can do that."

"Hope you like *Yo Gabba Gabba*." Presley smirks.

"Yo-Gabba what?"

She waves me off and laughs. "Nothing. Lock the doors, okay?"

"Okay." I'm kind of ashamed because I feel a little bit nervous to watch Chase for Presley. I'm not scared of him, I just have never been alone with someone with autism, and I'm not exactly sure what to say or how to talk to him. Before I get in her car, I grab the cup carrier from mine hoping to offer a hot drink to Presley for her trouble and thinking that maybe Chase would want something as well. As I slide into the driver's seat of Presley's car, I decide to treat him like I would anyone else.

He's humming and only takes the briefest look at me.

"Hi," I say.

He says hi back, but his voice is kind of strained, like it took some effort for him to speak to me.

"I'm Violet."

Chase smiles big, which surprises me, but then looks away. Presley is cranking away at the jack handle, raising the side of my car. She already has the spare removed from the back as well. I shake my head in astonishment. Suddenly, Chase grabs my hand and pulls it toward the radio. The obnoxious music is blaring away.

"Mu-zack," he says. Then he hands me Presley's phone. His brown eyes are wide and insistent. "Mu-zack."

As I try to juggle the phone and the cup carrier on my lap, Chase reaches over, snags a coffee, takes a big whiff through the sip hole in the lid, and then takes a long drink.

I laugh. "Coffee fan, I see."

He just responds with "Mu-zack," and takes another long pull on the coffee.

I scroll through songs on Presley's phone, having no idea what Chase would like. She has everything from Sesame Street to Metallica. I must be taking too long because he snatches the phone from me and deftly begins scrolling though the songs. One of Taylor Swift's sass-anthems fills the car and he takes another long drink of coffee, seeming satisfied.

With Chase happy and caffeinated, I casually take a look around Presley's car. There's a big bag of library books in the back filled with classic Gothic novels, Star Wars infographic books, easy readers for kids and some stuff on hypnosis, medical amnesia, and mediation. I shake my head, not knowing what to make of her choices. Truly, a mixed bag.

Besides the books, I see some paddles and duffle bags. I'm guessing from the paddleboard she had strapped to her roof that the bags probably have her wet suit, gloves, and booties. I'm surprised at her willingness to get back on the lake after her tumble at Kings Beach last night. Winter paddle boarding isn't really for beginners unless they are prepared to take a few dips in the frozen water while they learn.

As I watch Presley remove the flat tire and slide the spare into place, I think perhaps she can handle winter paddleboarding after all. The whole process took her less than twenty minutes.

Presley packs her tools back in her trunk, gives my spare a final kick, and then comes and knocks on her driver-side window. I roll it down, feeling silly that I'm sitting in her seat all warm and toasty and her cheeks are red with cold.

"You should be all set."

I pass a cup of hot chocolate through the window to her, smiling. She takes it and thanks me.

"It's just hot cocoa. I had coffee, but Chase drank it all."

She laughs at that. "Oh, boy. Yeah. He's a bean fiend for sure. We have to ration him or he'll be up buzzing all night. Won't you, bud?"

Chase smiles slyly.

"Hey, I noticed you have some paddleboarding gear. I didn't know you were into it."

Presley sighs. "I am now. I'm actually a runner, but my doctor hasn't cleared me for strenuous activity yet." Her face suddenly looks shy and I'm guessing she might feel weird reminding me about her stunt on the slopes the day of Landon's qualifying race.

I think back to that day. I hadn't been sure what to make of her. At first I thought it was a joke. Like she was some kind of halftime streaker or something. This random girl, half dressed running up to my brother with all of those cameras around—it was crazy. She seemed crazy. I was so angry at her that day. I'm not proud of it.

Looking at her now, so kind and capable—taking care of her brother like this. She's not the same person in my mind. I still don't know how to meld the two Presleys, but the girl standing before me now deserves a lot more credit. I gather my stuff, unplug my phone from her charger, and get out of the car. Presley and I make our way to the back of my Durango, and I notice she's put the flat tire in the back.

"What beach are you headed to?" I ask.

"Kings. I saw some boarders out there before. I'm hoping they'll call 9-1-1 if they happen to see me float by encased in a giant ice cube."

"Is Chase . . .?" I'm not sure why I don't finish my statement, but Presley cuts in.

"He loves the beach. Even when it's cold. He watches the water and listens to music. I'll stay close though, no worries. I was actually headed to grab him a coffee but I see that's no longer necessary. I guess I owe you." She's smiling wide, her eyes warm.

"Oh, please. You totally saved me." Without thinking, I reach over and hug her. My vision goes dark and before I can react with fear, it feels like I'm suddenly watching a glitchy movie. A flash of me and Presley sitting on a bed, cross-legged and knee to knee. I'm upset. I feel tears on my cheeks. Presley's face is concerned and she reaches for my hands. Then it's all gone.

Presley gives my back a couple of pats and steps away. I can only imagine the look on my face. I work to paint on a quick smile even though my mind is doing cartwheels from what just happened.

A line forms between her brows. "You okay?"

"Yeah, yeah," I say much too quickly.

Chase tries to open his door and Presley calls over my shoulder to him, saving me from my awkwardness. "No, no, buddy. Shut that door. It's not safe." She looks at me apologetically. "I'm sorry. I need to go. He's getting antsy. Will you be all right?"

"Of course," I lie. "Yes. You go. Thanks again."

She looks at me one last time as she gets in her car. "Vi, it was nothing."

I don't bristle at her use of my nickname. Even though that's a name only my family and close friends call me. Somehow when it rolls of her tongue it sounds, I don't know . . .

Exactly right.

Chapter
Twenty-Two

TOUCH AND GO

(PRESLEY)

25 Days Before

Chase and I had a lazy weekend as beach bums, spending most of Saturday and part of Sunday figuring out the logistics of paddleboarding. I got my gear for cheap from a sporting goods swap meet. Because most people are on the mountains and not the lake this time of year, I got great deals. On Sunday, I even picked up a board for Chase because he seemed so interested in mine all Saturday.

Some people might think a kid like Chase can't learn to do a sport like that, but I'm used to proving people wrong. Chase can rock climb, ride a bike, roller blade, and even zip-line. I wasn't surprised when he picked up the paddleboard as quickly as I did. I'm always reminding myself that he needs to try new things too. He needs to get outside and see the beauty of nature and exercise as much as anyone else. Maybe even more. It felt really good to see him happy on the water, following my lead. Being out there with him, having fun in that beautiful setting—it was almost like he didn't have autism for a little while.

Back at my afternoon shift at Wild Cherries, I wonder if I should feel guilty about taking that time over the weekend with Chase. I'm always feeling split between living the life I have now, with him and Gayle and working to save Landon. I know I need to be doing everything I can to stay in the loop with Landon and his friends and family.

I come out of the stock room with an armful of napkin packs. Monday is restock day, so I've spent the first chunk of my shift refilling paper towel, napkin, cup, condiment, sugar, and silverware dispensers and containers. Riveting stuff. I'm relieved when I see Erin sitting by the front window. She's become kind of a friend over the last couple of weeks and I can tell by the smile of greeting on her face that she feels the same about me.

"What's up?" I say it more like a WWF announcer than a sixteen-year-old girl.

Erin slides down in her seat, letting her legs splay out in front of her like two fallen trees. "Nothing. I'm bored."

"Me too." I stash the napkins in the cabinets under the counter and then make my way to the sink to wash up for veggie prep. "I'm going to be slicing some really interesting tomatoes if you want to visit me over here." She never leaves that window seat, so I'm surprised when she gets up and fills a stool at the counter opposite me.

She rests her chin in her palms. "Do you ever just think too much?"

I laugh as I slice through the first tomato. "Yes. Sometimes I feel like that's all I do. Like I'm not even really present in my life because I spend so much time obsessing over stuff."

"Exactly. And half the time it's pointless because once a decision is made, there's no going back on it, so why sit around and worry about whether or not you did the right thing? You know? It's not like you can change it anyway."

Erin rolls her eyes and slides her face into her palms. I get the impression that she's about to tear up and wants to hide it from me. I lay the knife down.

"Are you all right? It sounds like you have a lot on your mind," I say.

"I just feel so trapped sometimes."

"You can spill if you want, but no pressure. I would just say that sometimes things that feel impossible or hard to figure out can make us feel paralyzed. Fearful, you know?"

Erin nods, her face still in her hands.

"But at the same time, we always have our choices. Even if everyone is against you. We have to live our lives in the way that we think is best." I reach across the counter and lay a gentle hand on her shoulder. Her head jerks up, and I regret crossing the boundary. I pull my hand back and take up the knife and resume slicing. My instinct is to avoid her eyes. To give her space and privacy, but my gaze flickers to hers. Her face is harrowed.

"Tell me something you're afraid of," she says.

Her question takes me off guard, but because she's been open with me I feel compelled to return the effort. "Losing people I love." I drop my eyes and slice through the flesh of the tomato in long, slow motions. "I've lost someone before. I'm afraid it will happen again." My eyes sting with unshed tears, and I'm overwhelmed with how freeing it feels to speak these words to Erin. I hazard a glance at her and her face is smooth now, her eyes liquid and thoughtful.

I continue, "No matter how badly I want this person to be safe, I know I can't control him. He will make his own choices. But I will do everything I can to be there. I have to act, even though I'm afraid."

Erin nods once. "I hope you can help him."

I sniff back the urge to cry and force myself to smile. "Me too."

Just then Russell jumps against the door, scratching and whining. Erin and I look at each other and laugh; she seems as grateful for the funny distraction as I am.

"Your boyfriend's back," she says. "Better get some turkey."

I wipe my hands on a towel and retrieve the usual three slices of lunch meat. Erin follows me to the door and bends down to scratch his chin when he wiggles his way inside. He snarfs the food down, goes back to Erin for one more scratch, and then zips through the door and into the street.

"Presley!" Erin screams my name before I can react. A small car has hit Russell, throwing his body to the side of the road nearest the coffee shop. He lies on the pavement completely still.

I shove the door open and run to him, Erin behind me. I'm on the ground in seconds, but I'm afraid to touch his little body. Blood stains the fur near his mouth and is pooling on the road. I can't see any breathing motions coming from his rib cage.

"Oh, no. Poor little guy. Poor thing." I don't know what to do. I want to move him out of the street, but I'm still afraid to touch him in case I make it worse.

The driver, a guy in his twenties with shaggy hair and earbuds in his ears, gets out to see what happened. When he sees the tiny, still body on the ground, he just paces over me and Russell, cursing in between apologies. Traffic is beginning to pile up behind his vehicle and someone sounds a horn.

Shaggy hair guy turns and yells at the offender. "Chill, all right? Little dude just got killed. Let's give her a minute, okay?"

I have no idea who owns Russell and that makes me feel so bad for him that I reach down and pull his limp body into my arms. His little head flops heartbreakingly to one side, and I quickly reach to support it.

Erin is at my side apologizing too. "I'm so sorry, Presley. I'm so sorry."

A lump fills my throat because I can't block out the truth. Life can be snuffed out in an instant—like blowing out a candle.

What if I can't save Landon? What if James is right? What if Landon makes some idiotic snap decision that ends his life and I can't be there to prevent it? I don't want that to happen. It can't. I won't make it if he leaves me. I just can't face it.

The sobbing comes over me, and I don't even try to hold it back. Erin's hand is at my back and the shaggy hair guy starts cussing and apologizing. More people get out of their cars to see the spectacle, and I squeeze my eyes shut against them.

"Don't leave me," I say between sobs. "Please don't leave me." I can't tell if I'm talking to Russell or to Landon.

Then, Russell jerks in my arms, suddenly squirming against my body so forcibly that I can't keep a hold of him. He falls to the ground, his ribs hitting against the pavement causing a collective gasp to come from everyone watching, including me. But he's back on his feet again, barking at the guy who hit him with his car and then tearing off across the street that's still jammed with stopped cars. He darts between two parked cars and disappears again. I run after him calling his name, but he's gone.

Shaggy hair guy is whooping and pumping his fist into the air like some kind of rap concert hype-man. "Did you see that, y'all? Did you *freaking* see that?" He lets out another whoop and leaps into the air. He comes over and hugs me, but it does little to bring me out of my shocked state. "Freaking miracle pup, man. That was the wildest thing I've ever seen. I'm sorry I have to go. The pizza's getting cold."

I wonder at him for a moment, but then notice the lit Dominos sign on the roof of his car. He jogs back to his vehicle, tucks his long limbs inside, and honks as he drives away. The knot of traffic loosens, I back away and stand on the sidewalk as the pace of the cars resumes like nothing ever happened. I can still see the little puddle of blood on the street as cars pass over it.

I turn to Erin. Her face is unreadable. She's probably feeling as astonished as I am. "Erin," I say, "that dog was dead."

She looks at me, her face twisting into a look of utter disbelief. "I know."

Chapter Twenty-Three

SUMMONING

(ERIN)

23 Days Before

These last couple days have been the hardest I've endured since giving up my passage—since the day I became a Vigilum. I feel bad about how I've been avoiding Presley at Wild Cherries. But now that I know about her, I don't think I can pretend around her anymore. How can I act like quiet, bookish, people-watching Erin, when I know what she can do with departing spirits? I haven't even wrapped my head around it yet.

I keep playing it over and over in my mind. Russell lay dying on the road. Then he *was* dead. I've gotten good at knowing these things. Then Presley takes him in her arms and literally wills the life to stay in his body. Who does that? I guess I shouldn't have been as shocked as I was. After all, she can see, hear, and even touch the dead. I've heard of people who can do that—Vigilum call them "seers." But I've never heard of anyone who can do what she did with that dog. I keep trying to explain it away, but it had to have been something she did.

I've kept Presley's powers to myself. I know how dangerous her abilities can be to her *and* to me because I know about them. Even though I've only been a part of this world for six months, I've seen enough to know that there are certain Vigilum that would do just about anything to get hold of someone who can speak to the living on behalf of the dead. Anything to help them secure a passage. All I know is that if they find out about Presley, they'll never leave her alone. Ever.

Depending on how practiced a Vigilum is, some can make their voices heard inside people's thoughts, influence emotion, or the temperature in a room, and even sometimes manipulate solid objects. All of the creepy stories I'd heard as a kid at slumber parties and on ghost-hunter TV shows made much more sense after seeing what my kind can do.

As for me, I want passage. I knew days after deciding to give mine away, that it was a mistake. She was so convincing though. She knew exactly what to say to me. Somehow she knew how guilty I felt for sending that text while driving on the two-lane highway from Blue Diamond to Vegas. I had known better. The deaths of those people could have been avoided so easily.

She made me feel like I needed to pay a price. To suffer. Like I deserved it. And as I watched the departing spirits of the family say good-bye to their surviving loved ones trapped in that demolished car, I believed her. She didn't even have to ask me twice. I just gave it to her. She didn't bother telling me my decision is binding or that there's no changing my mind.

It took me a long time to discover what I am. But eventually I encountered others who are like me. It's lonely being a Vigilum. The only ones who have anyone to talk to are the ones who have decided to join forces. But I've already had enough guilt to last me the next umpteen eons, so I've never been eager to join any group knowing what they do.

The things they do.

I've never been willing to do any of it. But time passes slowly when you're a lone entity floating through existence without a purpose or people. I belong nowhere. I belong to no one. So when I heard about someone that can do the dirty work for me— acquiring passages to those seeking them— I have to admit, I was curious.

Of course these whisperings among us Vigilum may just be rumors. Some say he's the first Vigilum. Ancient. Someone whose purpose is purely rebellion—who refuses to accept the penalty of a Vigilum, so he offers his expertise to those of us who don't have a chance of taking a passage on our own.

Others say he does it for the power or the loyalty of his followers. Most call him "the Reaper" because nobody wants to use his real name, which after months of inquiring, I finally found out is "Apollo." The guy who told me his name didn't even speak it to me. He wrote it with his finger in the dust of a library shelf, then immediately wiped it away.

Vigilum who want his help are called seekers. But am I a seeker? I don't feel like I am. I'm just someone who wants more information. There's no name for that.

I don't know how to contact the Reaper. I'm not even sure I want to. I just want to know what my information would be worth to him. But it's not like I can go asking around. I wish I knew what kind of "person" the Reaper is. Is he reasonable? Can I trust him to compensate me for this information? I have this sick feeling that once I find him, I'll be committed in some way. That once he knows my secret, there won't be any turning back.

It's a risk to tell him what Presley can do. But I can't live like this any longer. I laugh bitterly to myself at the choice of words. "Live." Yeah, right.

I don't want to put her in any danger. But I also tell myself that it's just a matter of time before another Vigilum learns what she is and what she can do. If another one hasn't already. The way I see it, there's fifty-fifty chance that this will turn out badly for her. But at the same time, there's a 100 percent chance I will lose my mind if I have to stay trapped in this place alone for who knows how much longer. I've met Vigilim that have done this a lot longer than I have. I don't want to be like them.

So I'm going to do what I've wrestled with the last three days. I'm going to summon Apollo.

I choose Rainbow Bridge for the meeting place. The concrete arch spans the chasm of rock and is surrounded by mountain ranges and alpine lakes. Stunning beauty spans for miles around as the sun descends, setting the sky alight in orange and pink streaks.

I don't even know if my plan will work, but a bridge seems like the right place to try. Like it's neutral ground somehow. This connecting span of road is a place where he can come from his side and I can come from mine. We can talk and if we decide to part ways, we can leave the words here where nobody can hear them, and the Reaper can go his way and I can go mine.

At least that's the theory. It suddenly feels as flimsy as wet tissue paper.

I take one sweeping look at the horizon and force a breath in and out before I call his name.

"Apollo." My voice echoes in space and it startles me. "Apollo," I say again.

Nothing happens. Nothing at all. I'm half relieved and half disappointed. I close my eyes and laugh at my idiocy. I was so naive to believe all of that Vigilum gossip. After all, what else do a bunch of halted spirits have to do than make up stories for entertainment?

Then, suddenly the relief overpowers the disappointment. I'm glad I didn't expose Presley. My mind clears and I know that I'm not the kind of person who would give up a friend like that. At least, I think I know. There's a small part of me that still questions, but I inwardly hush it back.

I miss the ability to cry. If I were alive, I'd be crying right now. Because there's nothing worse than facing down an immeasurable stretch of time and knowing you'll be alone through the whole thing.

"You don't *have* to do this alone, you know."

My head whips around at the sound of the intruding voice and before me stands a tall man who appears to be in his early twenties. He's dressed in an impeccably fit charcoal jacket of an indeterminable era. Different than what is commonly worn in modern day, but not similar enough to a specific decade to give it a time stamp. His pale fingers are closed around a walking staff ornamented with a polished black horn. Unblinking, his eyes calmly take me in with their milky blue paleness.

Chapter Twenty-Four

Agreement

(Erin)

23 Days Before

Even though I already know who he is, I still ask, "Are you Apollo?"

His head tips slightly to one side and a hint of a smile appears on his lips. "I'm known by many names." His body is lean, but solid under his clothing, and his tall boots and hairstyle give the impression of some bygone era. "You are Erin Hupchert. Recently deceased."

I don't like that he knows my name. Also, I wonder at his use of the word "recent." But if he's as ancient as people say, I suppose six months would seem very recent.

All at once, the surrounding vistas and solid lines of the bridge begin to bleed into mottled colors of browns and grays, causing me to feel sick and disoriented. The ground under my feet is solid, but instead of the pebbled asphalt, it morphs into polished marble and silk rugs. Other shapes come into rapid focus like the sun has suddenly burned away the fog in some kind of solar flare.

Before me now are groupings of expensive furniture. Couches and tufted chairs bookended with rich wooden side tables and exotic looking plants. The ceiling is latticed with dark woods and hung with sparkling chandeliers. The overall effect of the sprawling room screams wealth and masculinity.

Apollo lowers himself into a chair and crosses his legs, revealing the flawless leather sole of his boot. He gestures for me to sit as well and without even checking to see if a chair exists behind me, I obey.

"You require something of me." It wasn't a question.

"I don't know yet." I expect his eyes to harden at my indecision, but they don't. In fact, they appear understanding—almost kind. This reaction encourages me. "I need to know more about what it is you do before I decide if I want to be a part of it."

His lips purse in amusement, and he dips his head in the smallest movement. "Continue."

My eyes scan the room again to ensure we're alone—we are. "I've heard that you can . . . that you know how to . . ." The words aren't coming to me.

"Assist those seeking passage." He finishes my thought for me.

I let out a breath. "Yes."

"It is true. Is this what you seek?"

"Yes. At least, I think so. Becoming a Vigilum, it's not what I thought it would be. It's lonely and I'm scared. I don't know what to do and there's nobody to help me and—"

"You regret forsaking your passage."

"Yes!" I'm so relieved that he understands how I feel. To have someone validate what I've been thinking since the day I made the decision to give it away.

His eyes close and again he nods in a slow controlled movement. "I can help you."

"Thank you." I'm gushing and all of the reservations I had before seem like distant echoes, fading into nothing.

It's almost like Apollo exudes an inebriating influence. It's powerful, like a blanket of well being so thick and padded it surrounds me and protects me from any discomfort. But something tells me if I'm not careful, this very same blanket could suffocate me.

I force myself to order my thoughts so that I can ask the right questions. "How does this work? If I decided to accept your help?"

Apollo raises his eyebrows and speaks in a tone as if we're sitting down to a picnic. He has a slight accent, but again, I can't place it with a specific origin or time period. "There is an order to these things. Those who have come before you will receive precedence."

"Of course." Again I find myself agreeing before I've even processed what he's said. The warning tugs at the edges of my mind again. *Be careful.*

He holds up one finger. "Unless you have something of value. Then arrangements can be made to expedite your position." His eyes seem to look inside me, scouring every hidden corner of my consciousness, and I'm expecting him to cross-examine me about Presley, but he doesn't.

"My assistance doesn't come without cost, you must know. Loyalties to the cause must be proven."

The air between us pulls tighter, like an invisible string being wound from each end. "How do I prove my loyalty?" It's an honest question, but I hope he doesn't take it as acceptance to some unspoken invitation.

He smiles, showing his row of gleaming teeth for the first time. "That is the question, isn't it? I'm sure you'll find a way. People often do when they want something badly enough."

Presley's abilities are bouncing, no thrashing around in my head, colliding with the sides of my skull and making the most obvious mental racket that I'm sure Apollo can hear my thoughts from miles away. I hold them back though. But why? This is why I'm here, isn't it? To know what my information is worth?

"I know something you might find useful." My voice is shaky and I curse my cowardice.

Apollo laces his fingers so smoothly they look like feathers sliding together.

"Something that you might find of value."

"Yet you hesitate to share it with me."

I swallow hard. "Yes."

"Then we are at an impasse. To receive my help in an expedited manner, you have to prove to me that you really want it. I don't have a cellar of preserved passages, you know. Rows and rows of jars just waiting for me to select one and break the seal so I can serve it to you fresh on a plate."

He chuckles briefly and clucks his tongue. His words conjure an image of my grandmother's cellar which was always stocked with shelves of preserved food in what seemed like endless jars. I wonder if Apollo knows I have this memory and used it to make me understand.

"These things take time," he says. "Certain events must be set in motion before a passage can be harvested."

Harvested. Another word that makes a soul's destiny sound like a tradable commodity. The truth of his words unsettles me, but I try not to show it. It's clear if I want his help, I'll have to give up something.

I draw in a shaky breath. "I know a living person who communicates with the dead," I say. The words hover between us like bait floating on the water's surface, waiting to be snatched. I'm testing him to see what he makes of this information. I'm not comfortable doing it.

Apollo's chin comes up. "A seer."

"Yes."

He considers me for a while. "You were right to think that this person would be of value to me. You'd be surprised at the variety of gifts that are useful for obtaining passages. Seership is among the most valuable because it links our world to the living with less effort."

I shift in my seat, suspecting he'd find Presley's other abilities equally valuable.

"I assume this person has spoken to you?"

"Yes, she has."

"I assume also that she does not know of your true nature?"

"That I'm dead?"

"Correct."

"No. She touched me and had no noticeable reaction." I instantly regret sharing that fact. I didn't have to. I could have easily proven my point another way. I make a note to be more careful.

Apollo's features subtly brighten. "She touched you. Well, then. That's something altogether different. I believe the young people these days would call that a level up." He enunciates the "p" in a way that makes a noise like a popping soap bubble. "I accept your offering. I find it of adequate value."

He stands like the deal is done and all that's left is to sign on the line and take the keys. I stand as well.

"You will observe this person and report to me when I ask you to. I want to know every detail of her life. Her family. Her history. Believe me when I say, there is no fragment of information too immaterial to take note of." His eyes sharpen and for a moment I detect a greedy hunger in them. But as quickly as it comes on, it passes and his expression smoothes into casual disinterest. "I will come for you."

Before I can respond, the walls melt into muddled swirls of dirty color. Apollo dissolves into a pillar of smoke and I'm left standing again on the bridge, alone. The sun is long set, and the sky a blanket of stars.

I didn't agree in so many words to do what he asked me to do—to spy on Presley and tell him everything I learn. But somehow, I feel like I have very little choice to do anything else.

Chapter
Twenty-Five

I TAKE IT BACK

(ERIN)

22 Days Before

When Presley pulls into the driveway, I will myself to look casual in the front porch rocker. I smile, though smiling is the last thing I feel like doing.

When she comes to a stop just feet from the front porch, I notice she's not alone. A teenage boy with dark hair and broad shoulders sits, no thrashes in the back seat. He struggles against his seat belt and takes several punches to his head—from his own fists. The entire car shakes, and husky and distressed screams come from inside the car.

Presley opens her door and the screeching, no longer muffled, is hard to listen to. Several decibels louder now, I sense that these aren't the screams of a bratty boy throwing a fit. I recognize pain . . . panic in his cries. Quickly, Presley walks around the front of the car to the back passenger side where the boy is seated. She doesn't even notice me.

I jump down the porch steps and call out, "Presley!"

She startles at my voice, then turns to me, relief washing over her distraught features. "Erin! Can you help me? I need to get Chase inside. He's so worked up I'm afraid he's going to break his buckle lock, and if he gets out on his own terms, I'm screwed."

Chase. She's told me a little about her brother before. He has autism. But that's all I know. By the looks of things, there's a lot more to it. The car continues to shake, then a sickening crack. Chase is pounding his head against the window.

"Please," Presley says. "We've got to get him out before he hurts himself. He's going to break the window."

"Tell me what to do," I say, though I'm not sure I can be much help.

"Just go stand by the entrance there." Presley points to the opening of the driveway, which has a fence on both sides. "We can't let him get through there.

He'll run toward the highway." She meets my eyes, and hers are determined. "Go, Erin! Please!"

No pressure.

I run to the entrance and stand in the middle of the opening, bracing my legs and stretching my arms on either side to make a larger barrier. Presley opens the car door and immediately an arm flies out and grabs her. Chase uses her arm to beat against his head. Presley's face contorts. I'm afraid he'll break her arm. But she twists free and speaks to him in soothing tones.

"Bud, you're okay. I know you're really, really upset, but you're okay now. And we can't go inside until you have safe hands."

Chase continues to cry and struggle, yanking at his seat belt, bet eventually his wails morph into something different. Sobs. Anguished, regretful cries.

The ability to absorb and magnify others' emotions is something most Vigilum use to manipulate the living. Sadness is amplified to grief. Jealousy becomes rage. It's their most powerful tool in taking passages. For me, this ability is a burden. I've never used it for selfish reasons. I've never used it at all. But I still absorb. Always.

I shouldn't be here. Not for Apollo. Not for me.

"I'm going to undo his seat belt now," Presley calls across the yard. "I think he'll come inside with me, but be ready just in case."

She bends her body into the car. After a moment, she takes Chase's hands and guides him from the back seat to standing. I can't make out what she's saying because she's talking to him in softer tones, caressing his face. Stroking his hair. I swallow around the knot in my throat.

Hand in hand, they walk toward the house, but just as Presley's about to open the front door, Chase wrenches his hand away and tears down the front steps toward me. Panic. Escape. Dread. Confusion. It consumes him. Fills him up. Radiates from his soul.

Reflexively, I block his emotions and with concentrated effort, project the opposites: calm, love, empathy, safety. I push these from inside me toward Chase. It's contradictory to the way Vigilum operate. Will it work? It's all I've got.

Chase slows. I work to maintain the emotions he needs right now, still pushing them into him: calm, safe, love. He takes a few steps more so that we're only an arm's length away, then stops. His warm brown eyes are so swollen and red. The angry splotches on his forehead are already deepening to a purple. This kid's got to have a monster headache.

He looks directly at me and says, "Chips."

I guess seeing dead people runs in the family.

I sense his panic is subsiding but not his confusion. And there's something else. Betrayal. Hurt. With the back of his free arm, he wipes at his nose. Presley joins us, breathing heavily. "What did he just say to you?" I feel her emotions too: sadness, anger . . .

"I think he said chips?" I start to doubt myself because his speech is a little unclear.

"Of course he did." Presley shakes her head. "Stupid, stupid." She grabs a handful of her own hair. "This could have been prevented completely."

As we walk back to the house, Presley explains to me why Chase was so upset. She'd gone to his classroom to pick him up for lunch and found an aid trying to pin his arms behind his back. Apparently he'd become frustrated and was hitting himself, so she thought it best to restrain him. She was a substitute and apparently had very little special needs training.

"Chase wouldn't finish a worksheet for her," Presley explains, "so she tried to punish him by not letting him have his snack. Can you guess what I sent for his snack today?" She raises one eyebrow.

"Chips?" I guess.

She laughs a humorless laugh. "I swear to you. I'm going to see to it that that chick never subs in this district again. First taking his food away, then pinning his arms? What did she expect from him? A formal apology?"

"Unbelievable. Poor guy," I say.

"Can you imagine a teacher withholding food from a general-ed kid for the same thing?"

"No. She'd probably get sued."

Presley keeps her eyes trained ahead as we make our way to the house. "Yeah. So why does Chase deserve any less respect? You know? He's a *human being*."

I've never seen Presley anything but pleasant, calm, kind. But seeing her now, the fire in her eyes and the way her mouth is pressed into a determined, angry line, I pity anyone who messes with Chase.

She shifts back to comforting Chase. "Poor buddy," she says, rubbing circles on his back as we walk. "Guess what? I'm going to let you eat the whole bag if you want to."

———

Chase is settled at the kitchen table with a full bag of salt and vinegar chips and a puzzle. He shoves handfuls in his mouth with one hand and works the puzzle with the other, occasionally hiccuping from the big cry earlier.

Presley's at the fridge with the door open. "Want a Diet Coke?" she calls over her shoulder.

"I'm good, but thanks," I say. What I wouldn't give for one right now, though.

She brings her soda to the table and sits next to Chase, helping him with the puzzle, though he looks like he's fine on his own. "So, what'd you come by for? And how did you know where I live?" Presley asks, struggling to make two puzzle pieces fit.

"I needed a change of scenery. You've told me about your little green cabin and how you love living so close to the library. This was the only green house on the street, so I took a guess."

"You are one brave girl." Presley laughs, shaking her head. "What if you'd been chillin' on some crazy person's porch?"

I give her a courtesy laugh because all I can think is that she's the brave one.

"So how often does this happen?" I know it's really none of my business, but I ask anyway. I did just form a human barricade for her, after all. "I mean, with Chase? Does he get upset like this a lot?"

Presley swallows down a sip of Coke and takes a deep breath. "Often enough." The way she makes direct eye contact when she speaks to me makes me slightly uncomfortable. I've grown so used to people looking straight through me the last six months.

Presley fiddles with the tab on the soda can. "If circumstances are ideal, he's stays pretty regulated. Today wasn't his fault. I can't imagine any kid, autism or not, would be happy to have his food yanked away when he's hungry." She closes her eyes and massages her lids, looking tired and sad. I feel helplessness radiating from her.

She opens her eyes and tells me, "And by things being ideal, I mean, when I'm in charge. This kid—if we wait too long to feed him, he gets frustrated. If he doesn't have enough variety in his day, he gets upset. It's not as big of a deal on school days, but weekends and summers are exhausting. I don't blame him. He's human. We all want experiences. He just relies on someone to provide them for him."

"That someone being you?"

"Most of the time, yes," Presley says. "Gayle helps a little, but she's the breadwinner. Work keeps her so busy. She actually hired a part time caregiver for Chase recently."

"That's good, right?" I encourage.

Presley doesn't look so sure. "The verdict's still out on that. Chase is having a hard time accepting her care, rather than mine. She's a good person at least, and it seems like she really wants to work with him."

"Well, there you go," I say. "Give it some time, and maybe Chase will warm up to her."

"He might," Presley says. "It's not like this is the first caregiver he's had. The problem is, we'll find a good one and Chase will get attached, but they don't stay forever. They find higher paying positions, go back to school, move away. There's always something. Then Chase waits by the window, not understanding why they don't come to see him anymore."

Presley's studying her Coke can like it's the most interesting thing she's ever seen. A few fat tears fall from her face and land on the table. She looks to me, her eyes wet and a brighter green because of it. "I can't be the one who never comes back, you know? I have to keep Chase with me always. And what if that means I'll be alone for the rest of my life?"

"What do you mean?" I ask.

"What if nobody wants me and all that comes with me?"

I summon hope, bright and clear. Optimism. Calm. I push it toward Presley. And Chase. They both need it right now. "I think you underestimate the human race, Presley. You're telling me that no one would ever want to commit to you because you have a brother with autism?"

"Not just because I have a brother with autism. Because I will be *taking care* of him until my dying day. His own father deserted him, Erin. And he was a good man." She wipes at a few more tears before they can fall from her face.

"Listen." I place my hand on hers. "You are the real deal. Chase is the real deal. Someone will come along that will be the perfect partner for you. For you, and Chase. Someone with a heart so big that there's room enough for you both."

"Do you really believe that?" Presley asks, a glimmer of hope in her eyes.

I'm honest when I answer. "I don't just believe it. I know it."

And there's another thing I know. I will not be feeding any information to Apollo.

———

Hours later, Apollo comes much in the same way he did before, quietly and just when I thought he wouldn't. The bridge, this time shrouded in darkness instead of the fiery light of sunset, feels lonely. Apollo doesn't bother to create the mirage of his opulent turf, but the way he stands so still and tall in his tailored coat, makes any place feel like his territory. And I, an uninvited visitor.

"Did I not say I would come for you?" There isn't any anger in his voice, but somehow the tone does nothing to comfort me.

"I'm sorry. I know that's what you said, but—"

"But?" His chin tips slightly to one side, his pale eyes expectant.

"But I've made a mistake. Presley's a good person and her family needs her. I don't feel right about—"

"Presley." As he says her name, I realize I've given him another piece of information that I shouldn't have. Another rookie mistake. Somehow his influence makes me word-vomit every stupid thing in my head. I privately recommit to hiding her other power from him. No matter what, I won't tell him what I think she can do. Command the body to reaccept it's vital life force. Make the body and the spirit one again.

I force myself to stop thinking about what she can do. Just in case Apollo can hear my thoughts. I wouldn't put it past him.

His long thin legs step toward me. "Am I to understand that you no longer desire passage?"

I back up. I can't help it. His lithe, towering frame drawing closer to me ignites a primal fear. I don't know exactly what I'm scared of, but the drumbeat in my chest and in my ears tells me to be. "I do want passage, but not like this. Not if it means hurting Presley."

A smile stretches his lips thin. "Do you expect me to forget what this person can do? Shall I sweep her gifts under the rug? Or bury them deep where none of our kind can benefit from them?" He makes a gentle clucking sound again. A sound a parent would make to a child who has just skinned a knee. A soothing sound. But it doesn't soothe, it feels like fingers of ice trailing up the back of my neck. "Surely you don't expect that."

"You said yourself that I would be surprised at how many gifts are found among the living. Why can't you move on to someone else? Leave her alone?"

"Because it would be a terrible waste. Gifts are abundant, it's true. But not gifts of this caliber. Presley's gifts are a superweapon."

"It's not a war," I say weakly.

"It is for me." His black pupils widen, making his irises shrink to an almost nonexistent halo of milky blue. "You would do well to remember where to place your loyalties. In war, you should always side with those who will serve you best. Think, what does this girl have to offer you?"

My eyes shift into a side-glance. I don't want to tell him what Presley means to me. How her friendship has kept me going—been a point of light in a never-ending stretch of darkness.

"Companionship? Dare I say friendship? Is that what you think you have?" he asks.

I hold my lips shut tight against what I really want to say to him.

"Erin, what you have is a master. And you are no better than a lapdog begging for scraps of her attention. Do you really want to center your existence around a being who could easily discard you?"

"It's not like that."

"Isn't it?"

He watches me, waiting for me to respond. I don't.

"Believe me when I say, I don't mean to be cruel."

I laugh humorlessly at that. "You don't?"

"No. I mean to be honest. Remember, I want to help you. I want to enable you to be free of this place. To move beyond this life of affliction to a place of meaning and purpose."

I narrow my eyes at him. "Why do *you* stay then?"

His expression brightens. "Freeing the convicted *is* my purpose. To turn the impossible into the possible. To break the chains—that fulfills me."

"I don't want her to be hurt. I can't live with myself if you hurt her."

"Do what I ask and that won't be any of your concern."

"I can't turn my back on her."

"There is no turning back the hands on the clock when you've already set them in motion. You will either be with me or you will be against me."

"Why can't I just be on my own?" My voice sounds childish. Why am I asking him for permission? I can walk away, can't I?

He ignores my question. "I will have Presley no matter what. Settle your mind on that fact. Now all that's left is for you to decide if you will be compensated for the prize."

Apollo's form begins to fade into roiling curls of smoke. "But choose wisely. You do not want me for an enemy."

The smoke expands into a tall pillar and then evaporates, leaving me alone with my wretched thoughts.

Chapter Twenty-Six

BUMP IN THE NIGHT

(PRESLEY)

21 Days Before

I'm just getting home from my Friday evening shift at Wild Cherries and I can already hear Chase's cries from outside the house. Both his caregiver, Janet, and Gayle's cars are in the driveway, and I brace myself for what's going down inside.

I hang my purse on a hook and call out, "I'm home." I follow the sounds of Chase's crying and find the three of them in the living room. Gayle bites at her nails and paces back and forth across the small room. She greets me briefly with her eyes but doesn't say anything.

Chase is on the couch wrapped tightly in a blanket that covers even his head. This isn't unusual. He cocoons to get to sleep most nights. But his cry raises the hair on the back of my neck. This is not an angry or post-meltdown cry. It's something I don't know. My eyes dart to Janet, but her face is awash with only concern and compassion. She stands to one side of Chase, rubbing his back and trying to soothe him.

"Hey, sweetie," she hushes. "Come out from there. Come on. Presley's home."

"What happened?" I ask, making my way to Chase. I sit next to him on the couch and wrap my arms around him.

Janet takes a step back, then says, "He's scared."

"Of what?" I ask, squeezing Chase tighter. "C'mon, bud. Come out from there. I'm home now." I feel like I need to see his face to help me unravel what's going on.

"Well, that's just it," Janet answers. "I have no idea." She rubs at her face. "According to his teacher, he had a great day a school. When we got home, we made a snack together and started to work on some flashcards at the kitchen table."

I nod at Janet, encouraging her to continue.

"So, he's labeling all the animals like the pro he is, but then gets distracted. Instead of looking at me, he won't stop looking *behind* me." Janet shudders and wraps her arms around herself.

Gayle pipes in. "I think maybe he's having those staring seizures again." She makes her way to the couch and plops down next to Chase on the other side.

"Staring seizures?" I say, confused.

"You might be too little to remember. It was after he was diagnosed with autism. Sometimes we'd be right in the middle of something—eating, doing a puzzle, anything really—and it was like some outside force pushed pause on him. He'd stop whatever he was doing, look around, and then start crying. The neurologist put him on some low-dose seizure meds for the next couple years. That seemed to take care of it. I haven't seen one since."

"Maybe they're back? Can we get him into the doctor?"

"I've already made a call. He has an appointment for next week," Gayle tells me.

I take a deep breath and let it out slowly. Like Chase needs a seizure disorder on top of everything he already deals with.

"That's not all though," Janet says. Apology mixed with resolve washes over her features. "I'm sorry to butt in. But that's not all."

"What's not all?" I ask.

"At the table. It wasn't just that one episode. He was scared of something all afternoon. Upstairs. Here in the living room."

"Okay." I stand and give Janet a pat on the back. "Thank you for helping him today," I say. "Why don't you go home early tonight? I've got Chase."

Janet nods and pats Chase's back. "Please let me know if you find out what's going on," she says and lets herself out.

—

No amount of prodding or bribing can convince Chase to come out from under his blanket. I offer a car ride to Starbucks, a trip to the movie theater, down the mountain to the skating rink. All of his favorites. Gayle has gone to the pharmacy to pick up some anti-seizure meds for him. Apparently the doctor on call was pretty convinced that was the issue and thought we should start meds right away. But because he didn't lose consciousness, it wasn't considered an emergency.

I leave Chase just long enough to grab my laptop from my bedroom. Once I'm back and settled next to him on the couch, I pull up some footage of staring seizures for reference. I don't remember ever seeing what Gayle described earlier.

Next, I open the nanny cam footage from Janet's shift. Twenty-four-hour surveillance was one of my conditions if we were to hire a caregiver for Chase. We have cameras mounted in every room. I fast forward through the footage of Janet and Chase making fruit salad together in the kitchen. Even in fast motion,

I can tell that Chase likes her. The way he sometimes touches her face or smiles when she acts goofy.

When I get to the part where they're doing flashcards at the table, I slow the speed. It happens exactly the way Janet described it. He's calm and happy one minute, but the next he's looking past her and growing agitated. There's nothing on the tape, but Chase *sees* something. Knots start to form in my stomach. His eyes, the way they rove and study the blank space. This is not a staring seizure.

I keep the footage at normal speed as I watch through several more minutes. After the kitchen incident, he bolts up the stairs, Janet close behind. I switch to his bedroom footage, where I watch him on his bed, backed against the headboard and hugging his knees to his chest. He points toward the wall across the room. Janet is at his side, soothing, rubbing his back, looking to where he points. She shakes her head and continues to comfort Chase.

The next scene makes me sick. Chase runs down the stairs, head craned over his shoulder as if something follows him. He bolts to the door and starts tugging on the handle. "Out," I hear him say to Janet.

"No, honey," she answers. "We can't leave right now." Her face is screwed up in worry and I catch her looking over her shoulder a time or two. She takes Chase's hand and guides him from the front door to the couch. Hesitantly he follows her and sits on the couch next to her. He seems to have calmed for a moment, but then his head darts to the left, then right, then left again. His eyes stay fixed for several seconds on whatever he sees, then he grabs for the blanket and wraps himself up.

I've seen enough. Enough to be certain about two things at least. One, Janet had nothing to do with this. Two, my brother does not have a seizure disorder.

I retrieve Chase's iPad from the coffee table. "Chase," I say. "I know you saw something scary today." Even as I say it, goose bumps raise the hair on my arms. "I believe you, buddy. I know there was something."

For the first time since I've been home, Chase emerges from the blanket. He keeps it wrapped around his body, but at least I can see his face, which is red and blotchy. His bottom lip trembles and he lays his head on my shoulder and cries.

"Bud—I need you to try and tell me what you saw." I hold his iPad up. I have it opened to his assistive communication app, which hold pictures of objects, emotions, places, food items, and all sorts of labels. I doubt he can accurately describe whatever scared him today, but it's all I've got.

Surprisingly, he wiggles his arms free from the blanket and grabs the iPad from me. He scrolls through rows of images until he finds the picture for "Tall." He presses the icon and the iPad verbalizes, "tall." I'm surprised because it's rare for Chase to use anything from the adjective row of images.

Next, he maneuvers to the row that has various people pictures like "mom," "teacher," "friend," and selects a generic icon of "man." He presses that icon and the iPad again verbalizes his selection, "man." My breath quickens.

Then he swipes down to an area he's never used—the emotion row. His next selection sends ice through my veins, "scared." I stay quiet and still because I can tell by the way Chase's eyes scan back and forth across the screen that he's got more to share, and I don't want to interrupt his thought.

He swipes to the very bottom row—pronouns. He scrolls through the images until he finds the one he wants: "me." The iPad again repeats his selection. I search Chase's eyes.

"Go ahead, bud." He's put the words together but I want to hear the whole phrase. Only then do I feel like Chase will know that I really understand what he's trying to tell me.

He wipes a straggler tear from his cheek, then taps the quotation bubble at the end of his sentence so that the app will string all of the words together.

With a robotic voice, the app reads Chase's sentence.

"Tall man scared me."

Chapter
Twenty-Seven

RUN FOR COVER

(PRESLEY)

20 Days Before

The next morning, Chase is in the passenger seat, one arm around Russell in his lap and his other hand closed around a to-go cup from Wild Cherries. I just needed to get him out of the house. I think he's scared to be there, so the only thing I could think to do was to give him both of his favorite things: car rides and coffee. I strapped the paddleboards on the roof too, just in case.

I was surprised to run into Russell again. I think somewhere in the back of my mind, I didn't expect him to make it. So when he hopped in my car at Wild Cherries, I decided if his owner wasn't going to keep an eye on him, I would. Plus, he jumped straight into Chase's lap, which proves he's a good judge of character. Hopefully Gayle will be on board with having a pet. I think when she sees the way he is with Chase, she'll cave.

I cruise around town, making the circuit again and again. Chase seems happy and I need to think. My mind is scrambled—completely blown away. Never before has Chase communicated with such complex thought on his iPad. Thus far he's only been able to convey simple needs and wants. Two word thoughts like "want movie." Or "want soda." That kind of breakthrough in his communication tells me he was extremely motivated—desperate.

I've heard of people with autism suddenly communicating with new words. But it's usually in a situation of fear or suffering. Like some non-verbal kid with a leaking appendix in excruciating pain, who out of nowhere, finds a way to say "hurt." I try to imagine what Chase must have been feeling to suddenly use three new methods of communication and I shudder.

I make the decision to believe him. I have that faith in him. I'm giving him that dignity.

He is scared of "tall man." From the video, it was obvious that the source of his fear was proximate—in the room with him. The more I think about it the more terrible I feel. Somehow, Chase can see Vigilum.

I've never felt so alone. Even if James knew I've been discovered, I don't know that he would help me. After all, he warned me that this could happen, didn't he? I tried to be so careful, though. Tried to speak only to people that seemed safe. I've wracked my brain trying to discover what I did that gave me away. I did something to cause this. But at some point, I have to give myself a little bit of a break because it could have been anything. The smallest mistake could have tipped off a Vigilum.

I could have accidentally made eye contact with someone who's never been looked at by the living. I could have walked around someone in the hall that's used to being invisible. Maybe somebody overheard me speaking to James. Or maybe it's something James never could have warned me about—a sixth sense the Vigilum have. Something I can't hide from.

I miss Landon so badly. I miss the way he made me feel safe against anything or anyone who wanted to hurt me. I think back to the way he and James put themselves between me and Liam's horde that day in the snowy meadow. Even though they were outnumbered, they didn't hesitate to protect me. What I wouldn't give for that feeling again. But Landon feels so far from me now.

I groan, thinking back to the way he kissed Ivy's eyes at the bonfire. Something about that gesture just broke my heart. Watching him show that kind of tenderness and love to somebody else. It's obvious he really cares about her. I know at some point, I'm going to have separate myself from him emotionally. I'll have to, because watching him with Ivy when I still feel like he should be with me is tearing me up.

I pass Blackwood Auto for the third time. Reese usually works for his dad on Saturday mornings and his truck parked on the side of the building is proof that he is there today. At the last minute, I crank the wheel and turn into the parking lot. The day is warmer and the ground is wet with melting ice. The dirty, plowed snow banks are porous and disintegrating on the edges of the lot. I squint against an insistent sun. Out here, on a nice day, with the sky so clean and bright, it's hard to imagine that I'm in any danger. But I know better. Acutely.

One of the bay doors automatically rolls up with a mechanical hum. Reese is standing with his finger on a wall-mounted button. His gray, long-sleeved thermal is smudged with grease as are the knees of his jeans. His dark hair, cropped close, matches the morning stubble growing along his jaw. Smiling, he meets Chase and me at the open door.

"This is a nice surprise." His teeth gleam in the sunlight and I can't tell if it's his presence or the actual sun that's warming me up. "What are you guys up to today?" He glances at the paddleboards on the roof and at Russell poking his black nose out of the crack in the window.

"Nothing. We were just in the neighborhood." I realize how stupid that sounds right after I say it, but Reese is totally cool about it.

"Come in." He nods toward the work bay. "I'll show you around."

But just as I take Chase's hand to lead him inside, he breaks free and runs over to Reese's black truck, tugging and jerking on the door handles. "I'm so sorry. He has a thing with other people's cars."

Reese smiles that knee-weakening smile and waves me off. "Let me pull inside and he can have at it." Pulling keys from his pocket, he aims the fob at the truck and a clicking noise cues Chase that the doors are unlocked. Chase hops in the driver side and immediately takes a big swig of whatever is in the cupholder.

"Chase!" I say through embarrassed laughter. "Manners, dude!"

Reese laughs it off and tells Chase to scoot over, which he does, looking happy to be in a new vehicle. Chase is already fiddling with the radio buttons, tuning to a Hispanic station. Reese parks the truck inside the garage and gives Chase a mock warning, "No drinking and driving, young man." Chase takes another deep swig of Reese's drink and switches the station again.

It strikes me how easy it seems for Reese to be happy. I know from experience that living without a parent is hard. His mom died when he was younger, but at least publicly, he never seems to let it bring him down, even though he must miss her. I can't help but admire him for his optimism, his humor, and his strength.

"I don't mean to interrupt your work," I say, inspecting an older vehicle that is up on a lift, its innards spread around the floor among pans of different colored liquids.

"Nah. It's slow today." Reese crosses over and stands next to me, admiring the car. "I'm actually just tinkering with this old Mustang my dad picked up the other day. The body is cherry, but it needs a new tranny."

"You call that tinkering?" I say, impressed that he can do such complicated repairs.

He shrugs and nudges me with his knee. "You'd be surprised at all of the things I can do. Basically a superhero."

I know he's just teasing, but his confidence affects me like medicine because I'm feeling anything but strong at the moment.

"I'm actually hiding from Aunt Afton. There's that big frou-frou gala at Vikingsholm Castle next month and I'm supposed to be going around town asking for donations for the silent auction. I'm procrastinating my part. The Blackwoods are big supporters of this thing every year and I somehow get roped into the begging for prizes part."

"It's because you're so charming." I compliment him and mean it. It's easy to see why Afton Blackwood would choose Reese to do any job that required convincing.

Reese stands a little taller and tugs at imaginary lapels.

I try to laugh, but even I can tell the humor is missing from it. Something's nagging at me. It's Vikingsholm. Vikingsholm happens the same day Landon is supposed to die. This revelation along with the events of yesterday darken my mood considerably.

Reese's face turns serious. "Pres, are you okay?" His voice is light, but careful. "You look like there's something bothering you." He glances over to Chase, who is humming contentedly in the truck and then back at me. "Is everything okay at home?"

I'm so struck at his perceptiveness that my answer must show in my eyes before I can hide it. I don't bother to lie. "Not really." I feel the sting of tears and know my eyes must be shining with them.

Reese pulls me into a hug, smoothing the hair down on the back of my head. The safety of his embrace and the sympathy he gives causes me to pull closer into him. Chase switches the station again and it lands on one of my favorite '80s alternative ballads. Reese begins to sway with me in his arms, at first in small motions and then picking me up so that my toes just graze the ground.

He holds me like that, completely supported for a few rotations and then lets me down, gently so that I stand on the tops of his shoes as we continue the slow dance. The closeness of our bodies fills me up with something that has been depleted in all of the stress and fear of the last day. Even if deep inside I know things aren't okay and maybe never will be, there's something about Reese that bandages up what's bleeding. I know it can't last forever, but for now it feels pretty near perfect.

He runs his hand down the back of my hair again, letting it come to rest between the blades of my shoulders. "I want you to know that I'm here for you, okay?" Searching, his eyes look into mine. "Whatever you need, I'm here."

I rest my face against his chest before he can see the moisture welling in my eyes again. "Thank you," I say. "I wish I could tell you everything, but I can't." I think how comforting it would be to have someone to confide in, and I debate for the smallest moment about telling Reese everything. But I shouldn't have. I'm learning that wishing and longing don't really help me.

"It's okay. Take your time. I'm not going anywhere."

I give him a little squeeze of thanks but say nothing. We finish the song that way, wordlessly communicating our feelings. Each reaching to be closer to the other.

Chase abruptly changes the station again to some cheesy, old party song. Reese and I break into laughter as "The Macarena" fills the garage. Reese turns me loose and jogs over to the truck, cranking the volume to absurd levels. Chase smiles widely and Reese leads him out of the truck and over toward me. He tries to teach the simple choreography to Chase, who is too busy free-styling his own moves. This makes us laugh even harder, and Reese finally gives up and takes a position behind me, covering my hands with his own as I slide them over my hips and swivel them back and forth before jumping to face Reese again.

I stumble in the execution of the spin-jump and tumble into Reese's arms, laughing. He pulls me into a hug again, my feet completely off the ground and shifts my helpless body back and forth to the music, making me laugh so hard I pinch his back before he makes me pee my pants.

"What's so funny in here?" The voice projects through the music and Reese puts me down. Landon is standing in the bay, silhouetted by the morning light.

Reese meets my eyes, seeming to be sorry the fun is interrupted, but then he flashes a friendly smile Landon's way.

"Dance party. Here, every Saturday. Didn't you get the memo?"

Landon raises one eyebrow. "Must have gone to spam."

Reese crosses over to the truck and lowers the volume. Chase follows him and turns it back up a little, then takes a seat behind the wheel.

Reese shrugs. "Well, now you know."

Chapter Twenty-Eight

LEANING IN

(LANDON)

20 Days Before

That was awkward. Really awkward. I felt like I was a cop breaking up the best party of the year. When did Reese become so close to her and her brother? It looked like they'd been friends their whole lives.

I'd originally gone by the garage to hang out with Reese. With my training done for the morning and Ivy out of the picture for now, I have little else to do unless I want to get pulled into the gala-palooza Mom and Violet are buried in. No thanks.

The garage has always been Reese's and my man cave. The place we can drink five Dr Peppers in a row, eat microwave burritos, and listen to our music way too loud without anyone having an opinion on our diet or our choice of punk bands. Reese's dad, Uncle Evan, never cares that I hang around while Reese works. That dude still sports his metal band T-shirts and lives on takeout. And since I usually lend a hand in whatever repair is going on, he considers it free labor.

So when I pulled up and found Presley there, with Reese's hands all over her, I was taken aback. First, I wasn't expecting to see her. And then I felt like I was intruding. Then I felt like *she* was intruding on *my* turf. So I'm sure through my stammering and interrupting and gawking, I basically looked like an idiot. I just didn't know what to say, so I left, but not before noticing the paddleboards on Presley's roof.

I went straight home to get my wetsuit.

Violet and Mom are at the dining table, papers spread out in front of them. Mom is scribbling something down with a smile on her face.

"Last year they only donated a weekend. This is fantastic. They've upped it to a whole week. No better resort than the Ritz-Carlton," Mom says.

"People better bid their butts off for that one," Violet responds. "None of this up-bidding in increments of ten dollars like some people did last year. Tacky jerks."

I clear my throat to get Violet's attention. She looks first at me and then zeros her eyes in on the wetsuit in my hands. "Avoiding the gala planning I see," she says.

"Obviously," I counter.

She flattens her hands on the table and changes her voice into a formal, but mocking tone. "Then how may I help you, sir?"

My eyes flit to my mom's for a moment, knowing she probably won't like what I'm about to ask, but I look back at Violet and do it anyway. "When you talked to Presley that day . . . when she helped you with your tire, what beach did she say she was going paddleboarding at?"

Violet's eyes glint mischievously, but I still see warmth in her features. "Why do you want to know?"

I narrow my eyes at her. "Come on, Vi."

I can tell my mom has figured out what's happening, but for some reason she doesn't protest even though she doesn't look thrilled that I'm about to go looking for Presley.

"Promise you'll take the first shift at the auction tables so I can make my grand entrance," Violet says.

"You are so vain, you know that right?" I say.

"Yes, I know. But the dress I'm wearing, well, it deserves to be appreciated."

"Diva."

"Promise, Landon. Or my lips shall remain sealed and you'll have to drive around the whole lake looking for her and she might be gone by then."

"Fine. Deal. Now spill."

Violet wags a finger at me. "Careful, or I'll make you promise to dance with Grandma too."

"I plan on doing that anyway."

She smiles at me because she knows I mean it. It softens her. "Kings Beach. That's where she was headed that day."

"Thanks." Our eyes meet and hers seem to be saying, "Be careful."

—

Presley's Civic is among a few other cars parked at Kings Beach. Even though it's one of the nicest days we've had this year, most people aren't quite ready for beach time. As I make my way down through the sand, I can see her on the water about fifty yards out, pulling her paddle through the blue current. Chase is standing near the water's edge, his board beached next to him. He's on his tiptoes, thrusting his arms forward and back and humming in a way that reads "happy" to me. The little dog with Chase takes a run at a cluster of blackbirds, scattering them.

Approaching from the side so I don't startle him, I lay my board on the sand. "Hey, Chase."

He immediately comes to me and wraps my head in a tight hug. He's much stronger than I expected. I laugh and wiggle free.

"Are you happy to see me, dude?" I ask. Chase is smiling so big his face might crack. I'm not ready for how much that affects me. "You happy to see me?" I say again.

Chase is still smiling, but now he's pointing to Presley, who has noticed my arrival. She's standing with her paddle suspended in one hand, her other hand shading her eyes. I wave and she waves back.

"I'm coming out," I shout and she gives me a thumbs-up. Chase is still pointing to Presley. "Yes, I see her. She's having fun, right?"

I realize then, that I've never tried to talk to Chase. In all of the times he's shared our table, I've ignored him and now I feel like a jerk. Especially given how nice he's being to me. Reese talks to him all of the time.

"I'm Landon. I'm Presley's friend."

Impossibly, he smiles even bigger and points again at Presley. He grabs one of my hands and pulls me toward the water, still pointing, almost frantically at Presley. He tries to tell me something, but I can only make out Presley's name. I think perhaps he might be trying to say my name too, but he doesn't seem to be able to pronounce the "L" sound.

"What's that, dude? What are you telling me?"

He jerks my hand toward the water again and then says clear enough that I'm almost sure I know what he said, "Presley loves Landon."

I freeze, a lump growing in my throat. I can't explain it and I don't fight it. "Presley loves Landon?" I repeat back to Chase.

"Yes," Chase replies. "Yes."

He pulls me into a hug again and I let him decide when to break free. When he finally does, I'm wiping my eyes. "I'm going to see Presley, okay?"

"Okay," Chase says.

She's smiling shyly as I paddle up next to her. The black Rip Curl wetsuit she's wearing hugs her body in a way I have to concentrate not to notice too much.

"Looks like you made a new friend." She nods toward the beach where Chase is still rocking happily on his toes.

Her eyes are bright and I find myself appreciating the sprinkle of freckles on her nose and cheeks.

"That was sweet of you to let him hug you like that," she says.

I shake my head. "Of course. Best bro hug I've had all week."

She laughs at that and I'm grateful she hasn't asked me about why I'm here or how I knew that she was.

"How long have you been paddleboarding?" she asks.

"Since I could walk. It became a thing around Tahoe when I was a baby, so naturally my dad had us kids doing it as much as possible." I cut my paddle through the water to orient myself toward her. "You want a few pointers?"

"Not if it's going to end up like your ski lift pointers. Bossy pants."

I feel my cheeks redden. "Look, I'm sorry about that. I should have let you go at your own speed. I butted in and I shouldn't have."

"Relax, I was just kidding. I needed the kick in the pants or I never would have gotten up the mountain. Seriously, don't feel bad."

I look her over and notice she's kind of a natural. Her feet are planted shoulder width apart, with a slight bend in her knees. Her board is nice and quiet in the water, and I noticed earlier that she kept her back straight as she paddled. "Well, you look like you know what you're doing. Pretty good for a beginner, actually. You seem kind of . . ." I try to find the right word. "Athletic."

"Runner." She shrugs with one shoulder. "Well, before I got hurt anyway." She sighs. "I miss my trail. There's this one little spot along my favorite one . . . it has a perfect clearing where you can see the snowy mountains all around you . . ."

"In Vegas?" I ask, confused. As far as I understood, that place wasn't big on precipitation of any kind. Every time I'd visited, I marveled at the naked mountains, how they were brown and treeless. They kind of reminded me of pictures of Mars—alien and barren.

"No, here." She smiles at me like I'm silly. "Do you know that one off of Glenshire that goes along the river? It's kind of easy to pass up because some geniuses shot up the sign so you can't read it. I don't even know what that trail is called, come to think of it."

I know the one she's talking about. It has to be the same one I went to the day I skipped school. Even though I feel an excitement over this shared experience, it doesn't seem like wise information to offer up. "I wouldn't have thought you've had much time to develop favorites since you were hurt so soon after moving here."

The smile on her face falls and she digs her paddle into the water, making her board glide along. "Right. It was just so pretty, I knew it *would* be a favorite, I guess."

"Maybe we can check it out, when you're feeling better. Together."

She lifts her eyes to mine. They're questioning.

"I'm not sure Ivy would be cool with that. I mean," she quickly tries to correct herself, "I know you're not asking me out or anything." She laughs and shakes her head of curls. I like the way her cheeks are more pink than before. "This is just getting more and more embarrassing." She laughs nervously again and blows a stray tendril out of her eyes with a puff of air. "I just meant I don't want to cause any trouble between you two. She seems really nice."

"She is nice." I pull the water behind me with my paddle in a long stroke. Presley mirrors my movements, but she's light on the water and passes me. "But we're kind of taking a break," I call after her.

"You are?" She turns back to me and for a moment I'm afraid she'll lose he balance, but her legs are steady. So are her eyes and I like the way they find me through her hair that swirls around her face. "Why?"

I paddle twice, keeping up with her and at the same time trying to avoid her question. But when I float up next to her, my board skimming the edge of hers, I find myself wanting to tell her even though it might be a bad idea to encourage her. Screw it. I'm going to be honest.

"I'm not going to say that you're the whole reason, but I'm not going to deny that you're a part of it."

She chews at her lip for a moment and I watch as it releases, more plump and pink than before. I make myself look away.

"I'm sorry. You guys seemed really close. I'm sure this isn't easy."

"Don't be sorry. It's not your fault. It needed to happen."

"Still." She balances her body as she folds down into a seated position on her board.

"Need a break?" I'm not sure how strong she really is. She's still on half days at school. Maybe she needs to rest.

"No. I've been meaning to test these booties. The lady at the swap talked me into the five millimeters and I've wondered if they were worth the extra money." She straddles the board and lets her feet slip into the water. A big smile splits her face. "Whoa. That's crazy. My feet are toasty and dry in these things."

My booties are three millimeters and more than adequate in the summer, but I haven't tested them in the winter. I find my way to a seated position too, but not as gracefully as Presley did. My feet are already cold, but gratefully when I put them in the water, they stay dry. I nod appreciatively. "The threes are holding up. But I wouldn't say I'm toasty."

"Money well spent then." She looks satisfied with herself and I find it adorable.

I know I'm not the only one who finds her adorable though. I think back to this morning at the garage.

"My turn for apologies," I say. "Sorry I interrupted you and Reese at the shop today."

She waves me off. "It was no big deal. I didn't even stay long." She smiles at me and I wonder if I'm stretching her expression in my own head to mean encouragement.

"Do you guys hang out there much?" I ask, trying to sound casual.

"That was the first time. I just had a really, rough day yesterday. Chase and me both. I needed a friend, I guess." She's nodding and forcing a swallow. I can't help but notice the shadow that passes over her face.

"I'm sorry. Is there anything I can do to help?"

She looks at me and I can see the glistening rim of tears building in her eyes. They seem like happy tears. She reaches out for my hand and I take it. We're both gloved, but I can still feel the connection between us. "You're doing it right now," she says. Then she lets go of my hand as quickly as she had taken it.

I'm anxious to keep the feeling of closeness and that makes me bolder than I normally would be with her. "Chase said something to me."

A crinkle appears between her brows. "He did?"

My heart picks up pace. "Yeah. He was trying really hard to tell me something and he finally got it out."

Presley's eyes drop. "He's been doing a lot of that lately. I think he just has so many important things to say right now, that the words are breaking through. What did he say to you?" She finds my eyes again and they seem worried.

I hesitate, wondering if this was such a good idea after all. But I'm in too deep now. "He said, 'Presley loves Landon.'"

Her face tightens and I see the slightest tremble visible below her bottom lip. "He said that?" she whispers. Her legs hang perfectly still, half submerged in the clear water.

"Yeah. Why do you think he did?" My voice is rough from trying to hold back emotion. *Where are these feelings coming from?* She smiles a sad smile and a tear finally falls, trailing over the dusting of freckles on her cheek.

She holds my eyes for a moment and I can tell she's debating about what to say. At last, she tips her chin up and answers, "Because he only knows how to tell the truth." I expect her to look away, but she doesn't and I don't feel the need to break our gaze either. She doesn't seem to need or want it.

A gentle swell lifts us on our boards and it feels like we are the only two people on the face of the planet.

"I'm sorry if what Chase said makes you uncomfortable. And I'm sorry if what I said upsets you," she says.

"It doesn't." My heart is in my throat and a part of me wants to take this girl in my arms. Just float away with her where nobody can judge us for what just passed between her lips. For what is taking root in me. Maybe I should be upset, but I'm not. "I can tell you're not lying. And that you're not crazy." I give a short laugh at that last part.

She laughs back, tears still shining in her eyes. "Well, thanks. I think."

"I'm sorry. I said that completely wrong. It's just that the way we met . . . on that slope. Me kissing a complete stranger. It *is* all a little crazy."

"I'll give you that." She gives my shin a little kick with her toe and I slide my lower leg next to hers and hook my heel around her ankle, anchoring us together and pulling our boards closer so that we're knee to knee.

We look into each other's eyes, each of us seeming to wonder what's next. "You did kiss me, you know. On that slope and later in your room. *You* kissed *me*."

"I did," I admit, thinking back to the tidal waves of emotion that drew me to her both of those times. The undeniable pull to be close to her. To comfort her and love her. To love her. That's what I wanted to do. I wanted to love her. "Would you hate me if I told you I don't understand why I did it?"

She smiles that sad little smile again and shakes her head. "Sometimes it's hard to understand why things are the way they are. I don't have all of the answers either. But there are a few things I do know. A few things that I hang on to. Because if I let go, I wouldn't know what to fight for anymore."

I touch my fingertips to her knee. "I believe you, Presley. That your feelings are real."

She closes her eyes and I can see she's struggling to keep her emotions reigned in. I am too. Then she meets my eyes, her gaze penetrating me. "Do you believe your feelings are real?"

I swallow hard. I'm tired of fighting what I feel for her. Even if I don't understand it, I can't fight it anymore. "Yes." It feels good to say it.

She hooks a gloved finger with mine, pulling us closer again, our knees touching, our legs tangled together in the water. "Then that's enough, for now."

Chapter Twenty-Nine

In Plain Sight

(Apollo)

20 Days Before

The waters of Lake Tahoe are famed for their crystal clarity. As early as the 1880s Mark Twain even called the clear blue water "the fairest picture the whole world affords." Experiments have been conducted on the cleanness of the water. A hundred years ago, one could see a white disc to the depth of 120 feet. Today, with modern development and a steady stream of motorized boat traffic, one can only see about 70 feet down.

It never ceases to surprise me though, how even a seer will not notice what is in plain sight. If she doesn't expect to see, she simply doesn't.

I glide mere feet beneath her and her male friend. The bubbling turbulence from their paddles distorts my form, but I know doesn't hide it entirely. Yet she does not see me. Not even when she dips her feet into the cold concealment, mere inches from my fingertips.

I could take her if I wanted to. It would be easy to catch her delicate ankle and pull her down to the bottom of the lake. I could watch the panic in her eyes soften to oblivion as the last bit of air in her lungs balloons to the surface in crystalline spheres. I smile at the thought.

But truly, how would that serve me? She's worth much more alive. Her gifts carry more power if she bridges the world of the dead with the world of the living. So, I'll let her be.

For now.

If she refuses my proposal, there will be time for such delights another day.

Chapter Thirty

BUMMED

(PRESLEY)

18 Days Before

Today at work, I dumped a bowl of sliced strawberries in with the tomatoes, gave a customer a side of mayo instead of cream cheese with his bagel, and accidentally threw a handful of banana peppers (instead of bananas) in the blender while making a smoothie. *Landon knows I love him.* He knows I love him and he didn't run.

Chase, that traitor. I still can't believe he spilled the beans. Where is all of this new and sophisticated communication stemming from? My heart thrills at the possibility that he may be on the path to sharing more and more. And I think for a moment, that this is probably exactly what he would've done if he didn't have autism. Just because he's limited verbally, doesn't mean he doesn't want to share. Or humiliate his sister. Most little brothers revel in that kind of thing, right?

My shift is over. I finish locking up, turn the open sign to "closed" and hit the lights on the way out. But I freeze halfway to my car. There's a man leaning against it. My heart thudding, I start to slowly back away. Before I get far though, he calls from the deserted lot. "Presley."

James. I want to punch him and hug him all at once. To say I've been watching my back since the "tall man" incident is an understatement.

I relax my fists and recover my breathing, meeting him at my car.

"Hey," I say.

"Hey yourself," James answers, and I laugh a little at his use of non-1800s language. A closer look and I realize something's wrong though. James's mouth turns down at the edges and he avoids meeting my eyes.

"James, what is it?" My heart picks up pace. *Oh, please. If anything's happened to Chase.*

James must sense my distress because he says, "Don't worry. Your family is fine. Landon is fine."

The tension that squeezes my chest loosens a bit. I let out a long breath and take a quick glance around the parking lot to ensure we're alone. "Why are you here?" I'm careful to keep my tone measured, as I try to reconcile exactly how I feel about seeing him. He basically deserted me after giving me the Vigilum warning. But I can't deny the relief that comes from seeing the only person in the world who understands the complexities of my life.

James rakes a hand through his hair and says, "I don't know."

"You don't know why you're here," I repeat, making sure I heard that right. With James, there's always a reason.

"Would you believe me if I told you that I'm tired of being alone?" He lifts his eyes to meet mine, and they're full of emotion. "That being stuck in this time just waiting for Landon to die all over again has worn me out?"

It's not like James to be so . . . human. "Yes," I say. "I believe you." I feel sorry for him. I ask, "Have you been alone this whole time? Haven't you been in touch with *anyone*?"

He shakes his head. "Completely alone. Nothing to do but think, remember, regret." He leans back against my car and closes his eyes. I've never seen him like this.

"You could change that, you know. There's plenty you *could* be doing."

"You mean help Landon."

"I know you care about him. Do you really want to just sit back while the clock continues to tick?"

"No." He shakes his head. "No, I don't.

My voice breaks in frustration. "Then *fix* it."

James rubs at his eyes with his palms. I've never seen him so defeated.

"If only it were that easy." He laughs a mirthless laugh. "I am not allowed to just fix things like that. I don't make the rules."

Even though he's worn thin, I can tell he's not budging. I'll have to do this alone. And I hate to add to James's load, but I have to tell him about the Vigilum. I'm not sure that it's the right moment to do it, but in times like these when everything can change in an instant, I don't have the luxury of delicacy.

"They found me. Someone came to my house a couple of days ago." I think of Chase and how terrified he was and my eyes well up.

James pales. "Vigilum? Did they say what they wanted?"

My mind spins at his questions. "I don't know. I wasn't there, but they scared Chase. Somehow I screwed up, but I don't know how." I wipe at my tears. "I saw it all on our security video footage. Someone was in the house." I swallow hard. "They were . . . *testing him*."

James's eyes darken, his face all hard lines. I feel the outrage radiating from his body. This is the James in the meadow when the Vigilum tortured me. The

James who offered himself as a sacrifice to Liam and his horde to give me a chance. "Tell me exactly what you saw," he orders.

I recount what I saw on the video footage. I tell him how scared and upset Chase was when I got home and how he communicated about "tall man" on his iPad.

"Chase sees dead people too," James says, matter-of-fact.

I nod. Poor Chase. As if he doesn't have enough demons in his life.

James paces. "Think, Presley. I know you've been careful in your interactions, but has there been anyone, *anyone* at all you can think of who could have discovered your ability?"

My heart swells with hope at James's apparent desire to help me. Because he's the only one who can. Before, I had James *and* Landon. But Landon doesn't remember and James has taken himself out of the picture. It's been scary living this alone.

"Believe me, I've been asking myself the same thing." I close my eyes and again rewind the interactions and conversations of the last while. "I haven't spoken to anyone other than in public places.

"At school, I'm sticking with my group and only acknowledging people who I see speaking to people I know. I haven't said anything to Landon to spark his memory." I shake my head. "I must've screwed up somewhere, but I can't figure out how."

"Don't be too hard on yourself. What I asked of you is nearly impossible. The Vigilum. They're good at what they do. Masters."

He's right. I have been as careful as I could possibly be and they found me. They found my house—and Chase.

James contemplates me for several long seconds, and I'm overcome by the determined expression he wears. He folds his arms across his chest and says, "What concerns me most now is your safety. Yours and your family's. Experience has shown us both that the power I believed I held over Vigilum isn't exactly what I thought it was."

I think back to the meadow and how the Vigilum scoffed at James's orders. They laughed at him and then they attacked him. We thought he was invincible against the Vigilum until that moment.

"But I believe I can still help," James says. Compassion softens his determined features. Then he straightens up a bit. "To be clear, I can't help you with Landon." He takes my hand and gives it a warm squeeze. "But with your permission I'd like to help you with your brother."

"Yes." I don't have to think about my answer for even a moment. "Yes, please." My well-being is one thing, but the nauseating reality that the Vigilum now have access to Chase makes me grateful for anything that James can offer.

He lays out a plan to stay near Chase, so that even though James can't fight "Tall Man" off, Chase will never have to face him alone.

Warmth and assurance envelope me like a favorite blanket, and I find myself smiling because of the passion with which James lays out his plan.

He must interpret my expression because he says, "Even the dead need purpose. That much doesn't change just because you die."

I take a moment to contemplate that. I think of Landon, when he was dead. No words have ever rung more true. But I'm done with the heaviness of this conversation and my heart feels lighter knowing that at least Chase will never again face "Tall Man" alone.

I lift an eyebrow. "How do you feel about jigsaw puzzles?"

James laughs out loud, looking a little perplexed. "I'm certainly not opposed to a good puzzle now and then."

"Good. I think it's time you meet Chase."

Chapter Thirty-One

PLANS

(PRESLEY)

16 Days Before

Chase and I are a little early to lunch today. He's been especially happy the last couple of days and I think I know why. It's been so long since he's had any consistent male influence in his life, and it seems like he's really taking to James. I think about my Dad, how he was forced out of mine and Chase's lives. He was a jerk for rolling over at Gayle's demands. But it will never be okay that he was *guilted* into leaving, and that Chase and I were cheated out of having a father all these years.

Watching James these past few days has deepened my affection for him. The way he marvels over the apps on Chase's iPad, and nudges at the correct piece when Chase is working a difficult puzzle. Chase has become quite territorial with James too, and pulls him by the hand out of the room whenever James and I try to have a conversation. I laugh at the memory, but my chest tightens as I think of their relationship, which will most likely be short-lived. Once I save Landon, James will surely leave—on to his next assignment. And Chase will sit at the front window once again wondering where his stand-in father has gone.

But I can't do this to myself right now. Chase is comfortable and happy, and I have to be grateful. If I'm going to stay focused on keeping Landon from harm, I can only take it day by day. Also, whoever harassed Chase last week has not shown up since James has been around. James is back. Chase is happy. Now I can stick to my plan, which based upon the other day at Kings Beach, seems to be going better and better.

I'm coaxing Chase to eat his carrots when Landon makes his way to the table and takes the seat across from me. This is new.

"Hey," he says.

"Hey," I say back.

"What's up, Chase?" Landon stretches his hand across the table and raises it to Chase for a high five.

The rest of the group, minus Reese, have arrived and are taking their seats when Landon says, "Pres, why do you make Chase eat rabbit food? Here."

He winks at me and tosses a bag of Doritos to Chase, who smiles like he's been handed a gold medal. Chase squeezes the bag until it opens with a pop.

"Hey, where's Reese?" Garett asks.

"Ms. Gebhart kept him late," Violet says, taking the seat next to me. "He didn't finish his test by the time the bell rang, so she's making him do it now," Violet continues. "Bless that woman." She places her hands together in mock prayer. "I swear, she's made it her mission to see him graduate."

"Pft. I'm like top of the class." I turn to see Reese approaching the table, wearing a backwards baseball hat. Without warning, he lifts Violet from her seat and plops her one seat away from me. "You took my spot, sista," he kids, then maneuvers himself between Violet and me.

She slugs his arm playfully. "Hey! I called dibs on Presley today." Since I changed Violet's tire that day, she's thawed considerably toward me—even adding me to the group's text thread.

Under the table, I wipe my clammy palms on my jeans, then risk a glance toward Landon who eyes Reese warily.

From the end of the table, Garett clears his throat like he's about to make an official announcement. "Okay, posse. We've put it off long enough. It's time to talk plans. After-party plans." His face has turned all conspiratorial and he rubs his hands together like a villain from a black and white movie.

"Agh. Garett. We're not going to be done at Vikingsholm until like midnight," Violet whines. Snickers and giggling ensue from all around the table.

The word "Vikingsholm" snaps me to attention. Anything having to do with the day Landon is supposed to die demands my diligence. My stomach is suddenly sick with anxiety.

"You act like a seventy-year-old retiree with a bedtime," Sam teases. "C'mon. After-Vikingsholm parties are tradition."

"I can bring my grandma's wheelchair for you," Garett cuts in.

"Funny." Violet rolls her eyes. "Ideas? What do you think, Presley? You never get to choose what we do."

I want to suggest that we all roll Landon up in a quilt like human sushi. Wrap him in duct tape, just to be sure. And then lock him in a padded room. Anything to keep him away from danger.

I must take too long to answer because Garett continues, "Let's head down to Reno and find a party. We'll take my dad's Suburban so we can all ride together," he finishes.

"Nah, dude," Reese dismisses Garett's idea. "Let's stay up here. We'll never get Grandma Violet on board if we pull an all-nighter in Reno."

"Go without me, then," Violet says and dismisses Reese with a wave of her hand.

"No," Sam says. "You can't leave Presley and me to fend for ourselves with these clowns."

I haven't said anything to Reese or Garrett yet, but I called up Violet and volunteered to help out at the gala. I was relieved when she agreed, making it so easy for me to stay near Landon that night. I'm doubly relieved that Sam just inadvertently invited me to be part of the after-party stuff as well.

"Clowns?" Garett chucks a grape at Sam, who barely dodges it. It sails past her to the next table and pegs another student on the back of his head. Everyone at our table suddenly pays the utmost attention to their lunches. "Why don't we just ditch Vikingsholm all together and go the river. I can swipe some booze from my parent's stash."

"No!" Several eyes are suddenly on me. "I mean, that would be rude to back out on Mrs. Blackwood." It's out of character for me to be so bossy with this group, so I do my best to backtrack. "You guys practically eat her out of house and home when you go over there. The least you can do is help her out for a couple of hours." I don't care how I sound, nobody is going to the river.

"Touché. Thanks, Presley." Violet gives the group a "shame on you" look. The boys groan in defeat.

I fight to hide the victorious smile pulling at my lips. I may have just knocked down a major obstacle to saving Landon.

Unexpectedly, Reese wraps an arm around me and pulls me sideways into him, interrupting my internal celebrations. "We could just do our own thing," he whispers. "I've been helping Landon and my uncle refurbish this awesome boat . . . vintage . . . gorgeous. The engine isn't bulletproof yet so we may get stranded for a bit . . ." He pumps his eyebrows suggestively.

"Let's just hang at my place," Landon says. His voice is cold, serious. Though I'm sure his suggestion is meant for the entire group, his eyes are locked on Reese, the muscles in his jaw working. Self-conscious, I shrug out of Reese's hold and open Chase's juice for him.

There's an awkward pause as everyone at the table looks from Landon to Reese, then back to Landon.

"I'm with Landon," Violet says. "Let's just hang out at our place. We always get dibs on the fancy leftovers. Let's just pig out and put on a movie. We just had a bigger screen installed in the theater."

Reese snorts and shakes his head. "Of course you did," he says under his breath.

Just in time the bell rings. "C'mon," Reese says, grabbing my hand and pulling me up. "I'll help you get Chase to class then walk you to your car."

Landon stands from the table. "Dude, you'll be tardy to Mr. Thorne's. Detention if you're late one more time."

Reese uses his free hand to nudge Chase up. He lifts his chin a bit when he speaks, "Thanks for keeping me in line, bro. I'm good." He steers Chase and me away from the table. I don't know what the rest of the group is doing, because when I glance over my shoulder my eyes only meet Landon's, which are hard.

Reese walks with me to Chase's classroom, and waits as I get him settled. I run my palms against my jeans for the second time today. Reese rests his hand on by back and we head for the exit.

"So, I think you need a proper date for Vikingsholm," he says as we walk to the parking lot.

"A date?" I wasn't expecting this. From what I'd heard of the Vikingsholm event, it seemed more like an old-fart, rich-people thing rather than a place for teenagers to show up with a date.

Reese's mouth turns up at the edges and he gives a short laugh. "Yes, a proper date wherein I'll wear a tux, you'll wear a fancy dress, and we will go *together.*" He lifts my arm and twirls me around. "Dance the night away."

We reach my car and I heft my bag onto the hood. "Oh man, Reese. I didn't know it was that kind of event. Violet asked me to help out with the silent auction table. From the sounds of it, I'm going to be pretty tied up with that for most of the night."

"That girl has no shame," Reese says, rolling his eyes. "She treats you like an outsider until she needs something . . ."

"No, it's not like that. We've kind of gotten to know each other a little," I explain. "She's been better."

Reese doesn't seem so convinced but takes my hand, twirls me again, then pulls me into his chest. "Save me a dance, then?"

"I'm sure I can do that."

While I'm not busy saving Landon's life.

Chapter Thirty-Two

ABANDON

(LANDON)

14 Days Before

The mountain spreads below me, white, groomed, and pristine in the afternoon sun. In my skis, I step up to the gate and calm my senses. Breathe in, breathe out. I visualize myself flying over the snow, my body centered over the skis, the edge angles just right. The ten-second beep commences. I plant my poles on the mat. Five seconds. I crouch, ready to push myself down the run. I still my breath and tense my muscles.

Then I see her. A flash of Presley's face that day on the slope. Her eyes begging me to come to her. I lean in and brush my lips against hers, whispering comfort to her as the tears leak from her eyes. I want to promise the world to her at that moment . . .

"Landon! Where is your focus?"

I jerk my thoughts back to the present. The countdown beep is silent. I've missed my launch. Coach Scheurer is at my side, his cheeks and nose red from the cold mountain air. His German accent comes out thick and that's how I know he's lost his patience. I don't blame him. This is the third stupid mistake I've made today.

On my first run, I missed the third panel completely and plowed through the fence. I could have been injured. I had to endure a string of German curse words from Coach while Ben, my equipment manager, re-waxed my skis, inspected my poles for damage, and eyed me with very little sympathy. If I keep making these kinds of mistakes, it will be the difference between first place and twentieth place at Calgary next year.

I steady myself on Ben as he kneels down and cleans the snow from my boots again. He checks my bindings and gives my calf a slap to signal I'm all set. Coach Scheurer approaches me, removing his gloves. Straddling my skis, he takes my face in his hands and bores his clear blue eyes into mine.

126

"You are not here. You are somewhere else. Am I right?"

I try to look away, but his hands gently direct my face back to his. I grit my teeth and nod. No matter how hard I try to focus, I keep thinking about Presley. Ever since that day on the paddleboards, she's constantly on my mind. She basically told me she loves me. And as insane as it seems, I believe her. It feels right. Somehow, I'm relieved—like an invisible pressure valve has been released and I can finally breathe again.

And though I'm happier than I've been in a long time, my rational self keeps questioning what I am doing with this girl.

I'm just tired. Tired of trying to argue away what is right in front of me. Burying my feelings is more distracting and disruptive to my life and to my sport than just accepting them. I feel like it would be better to simply abandon my skepticism and let my heart feel what it obviously wants to feel.

I just want to have a little faith in Presley for once.

Coach pats my cheek. "Forget the stopwatch, Landon. Forget the panels. I want you to take one last run today. I want you to ski this mountain for the pure pleasure of it. Let the expectations go. Just free yourself. We will start again tomorrow."

He gives me a half smile and I remind myself how lucky I am to have a coach like this. I owe him my best. And I will give it to him tomorrow. Today, I'm going to do what he said.

Let go.

He steps away and I launch myself onto the run, thrusting three strong pushes behind me. As I pick up speed and take the first panel, I feel the edge of my skis cut the perfect angle. I dip and bob my body in a smooth rhythm, not caring about my time, but only about the sound of the snow sliding under my skis, the glint of sun on the run like sparkling sugar and the joyful pound of my heart as I go faster and faster.

As I pass the finish line I hear the hooting and celebrating coming from the end coach's walkie. He informs me I shaved a quarter second off my best time. I guess Coach Scheurer *was* still timing me. I smile, knowing I should have expected as much.

Back in my jeans, down jacket, and boots, I sling my duffel over one shoulder and pick my way down the salted parking lot, aiming the clicker at my car. The sun dips behind the mountains, layering everything in a bluish hue and an immediate drop in temperature. As I approach my car, I see Ivy standing by the driver side door, shivering.

She's wearing a pink knitted beanie and matching scarf and mittens. Her silky black hair falls over her jacket and the tinge of color on the tip of her nose and cheeks make her look like a Korean doll. Feminine, beautiful.

She takes a few steps, meeting me before I get to her. She's smiling shyly and she wraps her small arms around my puffy coat in a brief hug. "Good to see you," she says, pulling back with her head tilted slightly to one side. She looks up at me from under her dark lashes and her eyes seem warm, but a bit uncertain.

"You too." I mean it. Since we decided to take a break, I have to admit I've missed her. Not being around her all day was like breaking a habit. It was uncomfortable at first. But, as the days passed, the nagging feeling did ease.

"I've been thinking." She swivels her shoulders slowly from side to side, making me think she's either trying to be cute or she's nervous. Maybe both. "I miss you." She chews on her bottom lip.

"I've missed you too, Iv." I drop my bag at my side.

A smile spreads across her face, lighting up her features. "So, if I miss you and you miss me, then I'm thinking maybe it's time we get back together. Push play again." She closes the distance between our bodies and nuzzles my chin with the tip of her nose. It's soft against my skin and her familiar smell triggers happy memories of us together. Of when I first fell for her.

I know she wants me to kiss her. And I'm not sure I don't want to. But it would just be a selfish kiss. A comforting walk down memory lane. And that's not really fair to her.

I take her softly by the shoulders and push her back a step. The smile slides off her face and a little crease appears between her brows. She blinks rapidly then looks away.

"Ivy, I'm sorry. I never wanted to hurt you. But it wouldn't be right for me to get back together with you right now."

She gives a truncated laugh and her mittened hand swipes at her cheeks. "It's her, right? Presley?"

I could lie. I could try to spare her feelings by making up some excuse about needing to focus on Alpine or something. But it feels disingenuous. It feels disloyal to myself and to Presley.

"Yeah, it's her."

Ivy's voice cracks. "I figured."

I let out a breath and try to touch Ivy's shoulder, but she pulls away.

She shakes her head and focuses on the distant horizon. "I don't get it, Landon. You barely know her. We've been together for months."

"And I've loved every second of it. I want you to know that. You've been good to me, Ivy. And I'm sorry that I'm hurting you this way. It's just how it has to be." I feel bad, but with every word I say, I also feel a growing sense of rightness. Like pulling away from Ivy is the correct course.

"So I guess we're not doing Vikingsholm then?"

I feel a sudden pang of guilt. Ivy was so excited about her dress. Her grandma had picked it up for her in Korea. She'd sent me a picture of herself in it and I'd made it my background photo for my phone. She looked beautiful in the cream lace . . . her bare shoulders and the bow cinched at her small waist.

"Can you save your dress for spring fling or prom? I'm so sorry. I know how excited you were to wear it. You can still come to Vikingsholm, of course—"

She shakes her head. "No. It would just be weird. I'll save it for prom." She raises her eyebrows and her voice cracks. "*If* I have a date."

"Of course you'll have a date, oh my gosh, Ivy. Every guy in this school is probably waiting in the wings for me to get out of the picture."

She shakes her head, but I see the ghost of a smile on her lips. "Whatever."

"You know it's true."

She shrugs. "I do catch Garett looking at me when you're not noticing."

I let out a laugh at that. I shouldn't be surprised, but I play along for her benefit. "What? I'll kill him! That jerk. He's one of my best friends."

Ivy laughs. "You will not kill him. I need him alive and well to take me to prom."

"Oh, I see how it is," I say, still laughing. "It takes you all of eleven seconds to get over me and move on?"

Our eyes meet and I see the kindness return to hers. We understand each other. She believes me that I care about her and I'm glad. "Thank you for everything," I say. "I won't forget you."

She smiles through a falling tear and I reach up to wipe it away. She catches my hand and I let her hold it in her soft mitten. Her lips find my palm leaving a warm print against my skin. "I'll see you around," she says, letting my hand drop.

"See you around."

She gets into her car, starts the engine, and drives away.

I take out my phone and turn it on. Ivy's face smiles at me from the screen. With a few taps, I remove the photo and replace it with a blue ocean wave—stock photography that comes with the phone, and then slide it back in my pocket.

I smile, a little sad. "It's done." I'll miss Ivy. I will. But a little part of me brightens. Walking away from Ivy just takes me that much closer to Presley.

And that's what I want.

Chapter Thirty-Three

MAN TO MAN

(LANDON)

12 Days Before

Reese jogs along beside me on our usual running trail. He elbows me so that I step in a puddle. I laugh and elbow him back. "Jerk," I say.

The afternoon tree shadows are long and stretch across the path in slashes.

"So how are things with you and Ivy?" Reese asks. "I haven't seen you together much since that night at the lake."

Maybe it's serendipitous that Reese asked me about Ivy right out of the gate. I planned on talking to him today about Presley anyway. I guess I was just hoping to have a mile or two behind us—to give me time to think about how to say it.

"We broke up for good a couple days ago," I say.

Reese makes a face at me. "What happened?"

I'm quiet for a few breaths. "I just don't feel the same about her as I used to."

"What?" Reese's voice comes up on the end. "Since when?"

"For a while now." Our footfalls keep in perfect rhythm.

"What changed?" he asks.

I push out a breath, steeling myself. "Look, I just need to be honest with you." The right words still aren't coming to me.

"Okay . . . sounds serious."

"Things got messed up with Ivy because of Presley."

Reese makes that face again, and his footsteps fall out of sync with mine. "Presley? What did she do? Is Ivy still all worked up about that kiss on the slope?"

"That started it, but there's some other stuff too."

"What stuff?" Reese's voice has an edge to it.

I've got to come out with it at some point, so I don't sugarcoat. "I don't feel the same for Ivy because I have feelings for Presley."

"Huh." Reese is quiet for a moment.

"What? I can tell you're thinking something."

"So what, a new girl comes to town and now Ivy's old news?"

I have to push a little harder to keep up with him. "Come on, man, you know it's not like that."

Reese keeps his eyes trained ahead. "It's just that you had a good thing going with Ivy. Why mess that up for someone you barely even know?"

How do I explain the feelings I have for Presley to Reese when I can't even explain them to myself? "You wouldn't get it."

Reese barks out a laugh. "No, I think I get it. Let me ask you something. Are you jealous that I've been hanging out with Presley? That she might have a thing for me?"

"What? No."

"Look me in the eye and tell me you're not jealous."

"I'm not jealous. Dude, more stuff has gone down with me and Presley that you don't even know about."

Reese shakes his head, and again, I have to run faster to keep up. My lungs are starting to feel it.

"Oh, okay," Reese says. "You and Presley have some secret love connection."

"I didn't say that."

"Well, maybe some stuff has gone down between Presley and me that you don't even know about," he says.

I grind my teeth, wondering if he's just trying to get under my skin.

"I just don't want things to be weird between us," I say. "I know you've hung out with her a little, but that's kind of how you roll with lots of girls."

"You're obviously going to do what you're going to do. But I give it a week."

I slow my steps and come to a stop, but Reese keeps going. I call after him, "You don't think I'm serious about this?"

Reese doesn't bother to look over his shoulder as he runs away. "Just do what you want."

Chapter Thirty-Four

T̶h̶e̶ New Rules

(LANDON)

10 Days Before

1. I will ~~not~~ initiate conversation with Presley. If she talks to me, I'll respond ~~as needed, but I won't start anything.~~ as much as I want to.
2. I will friend ~~not look for~~ her on social media.
3. I will ~~not try to~~ find out where she lives.
4. ~~If she comes to my house again, I will respect Ivy's wishes and ask her to leave.~~ I will invite her to my house.
5. If thoughts of Presley are bothering me, ~~I'll text or call Ivy.~~ I'll let them. I'll work through it.
6. From now on, I'll always tell the truth to ~~Ivy.~~ myself and others.
7. ~~I will burn the sheet music for~~ *Speed.* Who was I kidding? I know it by heart.
8. I will ~~not re-watch any of the news clips of our kiss on the slope or look for pictures of her in news stories.~~ do whatever feels right.
9. I will ~~never~~ be alone in a room with her.
10. ~~I will not ever kiss her again.~~ Never say never.

Chapter Thirty-Five

PROPOSITION

(PRESLEY)

7 Days Before

Friday nights are pretty slow at Wild Cherries. Most of the people my age in Truckee head down the mountain to go to the movies or some house party. I haven't minded the quiet nights until now. I guess I hadn't really thought about the great company Erin was until she quit coming. Maybe she went back to her family in Blue Diamond. Or maybe we weren't as close as I thought we were.

The dining room is empty, so I go ahead and flip the chairs up onto the tabletops. Nobody will be coming in the next ten minutes before closing time. It's first Friday and all of the participating restaurants and bars have their flags and sidewalk signs out, drawing in customers for cocktails, art shows, and live music. As I wipe down the counter one last time, the front door opens, bringing in a blast of cold air. Maybe Erin stuck around after all.

But it's not Erin. It's Landon. He stands at the entrance and pulls a black knitted beanie from his head, which rearranges his dark hair into a handsome pile of chaos. He combs his fingers through it once, giving himself the accidental look of a 1950s movie star. So unfair to be that cute without even trying.

"Hey," he says.

"Hey. We're still open. I was just getting a head start on closing."

He crosses the dining room, smiling. "I'm not here for coffee." He mounts a bar stool and plucks a peanut butter truffle from the pyramid of them on the cake stand by the register. "But I will take a couple of these. One for me and one for you." He sinks his teeth into his truffle and holds one out to me. I take it and make short work of it, smiling back at him.

"So you drove all the way to Wild Cherries to get a truffle? I mean, they are addicting, but maybe you should talk to someone about your problem," I kid.

He licks the traces of chocolate from his thumb and then crosses his arms on the counter, looking at me with a determined grin. "It's true. I do have a problem. I'm hoping you can help me with it."

I cock an eyebrow and lean a hip into the counter. "I'm listening."

He takes me in with his eyes, the pause growing more and more noticeable with each passing second. I feel the warmth in my cheeks rising under his scrutiny. His face is like he's seeing something lovely. I want to connect his expression to me, but still find it difficult.

A week ago, he admitted he has feelings for me, but we haven't talked about it since. Other than a few shy smiles at each other in class and at lunch, things have remained frustratingly the same. Of course, I want to make something happen. I want to bring our discussion up, but something tells me not to force him. Something tells me to let him come to me like he did that day at the lake. It's hard to play it that cool, especially when my hopes have been piqued, but I know it's the right thing to do. I wait for him to speak while he watches me from under those black lashes.

"Would you be open to an experiment?" His lips purse in a smile.

"An experiment?" The way he's grinning at me makes me smile back at him.

"Yeah. I know you feel something for me. You know I feel something for you. There's no point in ignoring it anymore. Don't you agree?" His teeth are gleaming and I love seeing him this happy.

"Sounds reasonable. So what's the experiment?"

He leans in, his weight resting on the counter. "Seven days. Seven dates."

I raise my eyebrows. "Sounds catchy." My heart is pounding and I'm trying to keep the excitement off my face.

"I figure we owe it to ourselves to find out what this is between us." His hand slides across the counter toward me. "Give ourselves a little time to get to know each other for real. No family or girlfriend drama. No rules. Just you and me."

"Ivy?" I enquire gently, because I know he cared for her. I'm glad that he's hinting she's out of the picture, but I'm also not a fool. Feelings like that don't just evaporate. I also feel bad for Ivy, because I know exactly what it feels like to love this boy.

"We're okay. We talked and it was the right thing."

"You're sure?" I can't believe I'm arguing with him about this, but I want to be sure he knows what he's doing. I want it to be his choice.

"Totally sure. I promise. With everything that's confusing right now, breaking it off with Ivy is actually one thing I *am* sure about."

I smile. I can't help it. "If you're sure."

He closes his eyes and gives a definitive nod. "I'm sure that I'm sure."

"Okay then. You were saying?"

"Right. You and me. No family or girlfriend drama. No rules."

"You had rules?" I waggle my eyebrows to tease him.

He holds back a smile, and digs his chin into the shoulder of his coat, avoiding my eyes. "Yeah, maybe."

I laugh at that, feeling flattered that he had been thinking enough about me to make rules. "Are you going to share these rules with me?"

His cheeks are glowing and I can tell I'm making him uncomfortable in the best way. "Uh, no." His voice comes up on the end. He's swiveling on the stool now and I love that he's being so cute and shy about his admission.

"Okay. I won't make you tell me. But I warn you, I have my ways of getting what I want."

He looks at me sideways, a Cheshire cat grin stretching deliciously across his face. "I believe you."

I waggle my eyebrows at him once more to drive my point home.

He finally stills his body and meets my eyes straight on. He does that thing again where he just stares and smiles and doesn't care how long he goes without speaking or how uncomfortable it makes me. I feel my cheeks starting to glow again.

"So, seven days . . . seven dates. You up for it?" He nudges his chin at me and I log that gesture away under "adorable."

"I'm up for it."

A smile spreads across his face and he blinks those dark lashes. "I think I might be in trouble, Miss Hale."

I warm at his use of my last name. I mean, I know he must know it, it's just that I've never heard him speak it. I love the sound of it on his lips. I log that away too. So many new things to experience with him. I want more time. It's already April.

A line from T. S. Eliot's *Wasteland* comes to mind, unbidden:

April is the cruellest month, breeding
Lilacs out of the dead land, mixing
Memory and desire, stirring
Dull roots with Spring rain.

I hope that we have a chance. I hope that Landon remembers us. Because it would be cruel indeed to stir up all of this memory and desire. To let the buds of our love sprout up, only to be stricken down by a snap of cold. To have him taken from me. To go through all of this again for nothing.

April is the cruellest month.

I force the words from my head.

"When do we start?" I say, so glad that he's invited me into his life and I don't have to watch from the sidelines, trying to keep him safe. With this proposal, I'll be with him every day. That has to be good. For the first time in a while, I actually feel hopeful. Less afraid.

He smiles and shrugs, shaking his head. "I don't know. Whenever you want. Now. This minute."

We're smiling at each other like crazy and it's all I can do to not leap over this counter and tackle him with kisses.

I laugh at his insistence. "I should probably go home and check on Chase. My mom's had a cold and I know she's worn out." These are the last words I want to say. I really just want to jump in the car with Landon and let him take me wherever he wants. But there's still time for us, and I love my brother and my mom. They need me.

"Walk you to your car then?" he says, and I can tell he's a little disappointed, which makes me even more glad.

I button up Wild Cherries, switching off lights, and double-checking the lock. I hit the fob, unlocking the door to my Civic, and Landon pulls it open and waits while I lower myself inside. I notice the lights on the ceiling aren't on and there's just dead silence when I insert the key instead of the usual cheerful dinging sound.

"Uh-oh," I say.

"Dead battery?"

"I guess."

"Yeah, it's pretty common for people's batteries to die up here if you're from the desert. The heat pretty much fries the battery and then when you put it in a cold climate, it's kind of the nail in the coffin. I'd give you a jump, but I'm betting you're going to need a new one. Why don't you let me drive you home tonight and we can swing by Uncle Evan's shop tomorrow and replace it? Your car will be fine here overnight." He kicks the tire like it's a hunk of junk.

"Hey, I'll have you know that Honda Civics are one of the most stolen cars because they are easily adaptable to trick out for street racers. You know those lowrider guys who put neon lights under the cars and pound their base and stuff?"

He's laughing at me now. "No. Not really. Truckee's not really a lowrider hub."

"Well, in Vegas? All of them are Hondas and other little import cars." I'm nodding my head to enforce my argument. "The Honda theft ring. It's a thing."

His smile gleams under the streetlight. "I'm sure it is. Your vehicle is obviously highly desirable on the black market. What was I thinking? We should post armed guards."

"You mock me."

"I absolutely do. Now will you please get in my car before you freeze to death?"

—

The whole way home I just keep pinching myself because I'm in Landon's car. Riding with him. While he's alive. Something so simple would probably seem dull to most people, but it's the little things like this that I've always wanted to do with him. He pulls into my driveway and kills the lights. His face is lit by the dash display. And I know at this moment I am not ready to say good night. Not by a long shot.

"Would you like to come in?"

He brightens and answers before I even finish my question. "Yes."

Gayle is under a quilt on the couch watching some crime show. Russell is under the blanket too, his bat ears and pointy nose poking out. She's surrounded in used Kleenex and is feeding him bites of what looks like cooked chicken.

"So, I see the no pets on the furniture and no table scraps rules are going well," I say as I hang my purse on the entryway hook and shed my coat. I gesture for Landon to do the same and I smile at the sight of his coat hanging next to mine. He follows me into the living room and Gayle answers me before she notices him.

"This little guy hasn't left my side since I got this cold," she says, scratching his ears while simultaneously feeding him bites of meat. "It's like he knows I'm feeling bad. I figure I owe him a little extra—" She turns and sees Landon by my side. "Oh, I didn't know we had company."

Gayle gathers up the used Kleenexes with one hand and pulls the blanket up around her chest.

Landon steps up to shake her hand but thinks better of it as her hands are full of Russell and tissues. "I'm sorry to intrude. I gave Presley a ride home from work because her car battery died."

Gayle's thin brows go up and I can see her scrutinizing Landon from head to toe. That's one of Gayle's weaknesses: she's the worst at shamelessly scouring people with her eyes, and I'm always elbowing her to knock it off.

"Well, that was nice of you," she says. Her eyes quit roving in that intrusive way and I let myself exhale. "I picked up a rotisserie chicken and some sides if you guys are hungry."

"Thanks," I say. "Where's Chase?" I ask because the house is unusually quiet.

Gayle looks puzzled. "He's upstairs. And it's really weird because he's been spending a lot more time up there than usual. He seems so happy lately. Super chilled out." She shakes her head. "I don't know what's different, but I'll take it."

"He *has* seemed super chill," I agree.

I smile to myself knowing exactly why Chase is happier. He has a new BFF in James. Those two have taken to each other over the last week. It's been melting my heart how seriously James is taking his responsibility to protect Chase. Even more touching is how Chase reaches out to James . . . doing stuff like demanding that James help him with puzzles. Asking for praise when he finishes one. They are an odd pair, but somehow it works and I can tell James has a renewed sense of purpose because of it.

I'm also happy for my mom. All our lives have been governed by whether or not Chase is having a good or a bad day. And when puberty hit, it just made things worse. Sometimes we feel like we live in a war zone. Those days feel like a battle, complete with injuries and fresh holes knocked in the wall. So when Chase has a good day, we don't take it for granted. I'm especially glad my mom is having a little time to rest and get better because that never happens.

I turn to Landon. "You hungry?"

"I could eat."

In the kitchen, I make us both a plate of chicken, mac and cheese, and potato salad. With plates and Diet Cokes in hand, we climb the stairs and I can hear a content hum coming from Chase's room. I poke my head in. The lights are off and Chase is wrapped in his favorite blanket on his bed, slightly bouncing on the mattress. James, kicked back in Chase's La-Z-Boy, is shaking his head and gesturing toward the TV.

"I don't understand children's programming these days, Chase. What ever happened to heroes and cowboys and Indians? You know, good guys and bad guys. What is this?" James points to the TV at the green striped hairy guy from *Yo Gabba Gabba!* who is waving his handless appendages around and babbling in some wordless language. I can't help laughing out loud, and James turns around and sees me with Landon.

James's face falls and he slowly gets out of his chair, taking in Landon with a concentrated stare. At that moment, I realize I hadn't planned for these two to meet. And that if the same rules that apply to me also apply to Landon, then he'll be able to see James since Landon too has crossed the barrier of death. Guilt is pounding in my chest because I shouldn't have sprung Landon on James like this. It was a stupid and thoughtless thing to do.

My eyes are apologizing as I force myself to make introductions. "This is my friend, Landon." Landon, his hands full of the food and drinks, nods and smiles at James.

James nods quickly, his hands hovering awkwardly over his pockets. "Pleased to meet you." His eyes look to mine, wounded.

"James is Chase's new tutor," I improvise.

Landon pauses a little longer than seems natural, seeming to study James, but at last addresses him. "Good to meet you, too. I've heard Chase is doing really well lately. I'm sure that's a compliment to you."

I smile at how polite Landon's comment was and I see a flicker of a smile cross James's face as well.

"Thank you. He's an incredible young man. And working with him doesn't feel like a job." James seems to have regained some composure and I'm relieved at that.

"We're lucky to have you, James." We exchange knowing glances, and I excuse Landon and myself to go to my room.

I pause at the door, remembering that I haven't tidied up in quite a while. My cheeks burn and I hesitate to open it.

Landon is smiling and trying not to laugh.

"What?" I say and then playfully nudge his foot with the toe of my shoe.

"It's a total disaster in there, isn't it?" He's biting his bottom lip, keeping the laughter at bay, and I can't tell if I want to smack him or kiss him.

"Why would you say that?" I ask, stalling. He's right, but I hate admitting that to him.

"Just a hunch."

"Oh, like you can talk, mister. Aren't you the one who has a whole landfill worth of Dr Pepper bottles on the floor of your car?"

"Relics of the nectar of the gods," he says seriously.

I snort at that. "Well, my room contains relics of . . . of . . ."

Suddenly, Landon comes in for a hug, arranging his plate and soda-bearing limbs around my body, leaving my arms pinned helpless at my sides. His soda can is cold against my lower back. As his broad chest presses into mine, he puts his lips to my ear causing a full-body flush to wash over me. "Stop worrying, Pres. I'm not over here to conduct a white glove inspection of your living quarters."

I close my eyes and soak in his smell and the sound of his voice running over my skin, filling my head with memories and a desire to be close to him like we used to be. "Okay," I say.

"Unless you're hiding old burritos or something in there. Then that's nasty and I'm gonna eat in the kitchen." He softly laughs against my neck, pecks a tiny kiss on my cheekbone, and steps back.

I want to have a snappy comeback of some sort, but stars are exploding behind my eyes at the brush of his lips on my skin and all I can say as I tuck my soda under one arm and turn the door knob is, "Come in."

And stay forever.

Chapter Thirty-Six

Déjà Vu

(PRESLEY)

6 Days Before

I'm pulling up the driveway to the Blackwood residence when I'm overcome with the most sickening déjà vu. Landon has invited me to "breakfast for dinner," a weekly Blackwood tradition, and though I'm thrilled at the chance to spend more time with him, I can't help but remember how that turned out last time. When Violet had invited me over for the same purpose, I'd found out that night that the boy I thought was Krew, was actually Landon Blackwood, Violet's brother who had recently drowned in the Truckee River.

I park my car between Landon and Violet's and make my way to the home. I shake my head as if to will all memories of that life-altering night from my head. Because nothing was the same after that. It was that night that I'd learned that the dead walk among the living. That I could see them, hear them, speak to them. Be deceived by them as I felt I'd been by Landon all that time ago. I can't rationalize why these feelings come on so strong when I've had months to wrap my brain around all of this, but they're here nonetheless.

At the front door, I straighten up and take a couple of deep breaths, reminding myself that tonight will be nothing like that night. Tonight Landon is alive, and it's my responsibility to keep him that way. To help him remember, or at the very least rekindle the feelings he once had for me. He's invited me here because he wants to spend time with me. We've come so far since that day on the slope. I keep these thoughts at the front of my mind, then knock on the door.

Landon opens it and meets me with a gleaming smile. His eyes are bright and warm. "Get in here, you." He grabs for my hands and pulls me across the threshold, taking my purse from me. My legs weaken at his gentleman-like behavior, the way his hands linger on my shoulders as he helps me out of my coat. Any reservations he had about me before seem to have vanished. Am I being too optimistic? It's never this easy, is it?

"Come and meet the rest of my family." The unsettling déjà vu threatens to consume me again, but I focus instead on pretending this is the first time I've met his older brother and sister and their families. Once we've gone through the procession of nieces and nephews, Landon walks me to the kitchen where his parents bustle around. "And you've met my mom, Afton, and my Dad, Frank."

"Everyone just calls me Mom," Afton says through a warm smile. She dries her hands on her apron and then gives my hands a quick squeeze. "We're so glad you could come tonight." Her warm greeting combined with the smell of bacon and French toast relaxes me a little.

"How's that noggin doin', kiddo?" Frank chimes in.

"Ummm, my doctor and I have different thoughts on it," I admit. "I'm feeling pretty good, but my neurologist still has me on half-days at school."

Landon playfully jabs my arm. "You're just ticked about the screen restriction."

Afton and Frank look puzzled, so I explain, "No TV, phone, screens of any kind." In truth I've been so busy with non-screen activities at Wild Cherries and paddle boarding that I'm a little grateful for the restriction, and the half-days. They've forced me into things I would have otherwise not considered. A job that gives me a little break from Chase and a new hobby that would have previously terrified me.

"Well, that seems like the worst kind of punishment for teens these days," Frank chortles. "We tried to take Violet's phone one time because she was getting a little too big for her britches. Sassing her mom and me." Frank scratches at the back of his neck and laughs again. "She acted like we asked for her right arm!"

"Seriously," Landon concurs.

"You're not much better in that regard," Afton teases.

Violet enters the kitchen and asks, "Can I help? The gremlins are about to tear the place down. They need food."

The same chubby toddler from last time streaks by, completely naked. Before Violet can say anything, I ask, "Potty training?"

"How'd you guess?" She laughs, rolling her eyes.

When Violet invited me for dinner last time, I remember being overcome with a sense of longing. As I'd watched the Blackwood family, I'd wished for a big one like theirs, with lots of siblings and brothers and sisters-in-law, cousins for my future kids. I'd thought how lucky they all were to have a mom who established fun traditions like "breakfast for dinner at our place, every Saturday!" I'd imagined my house like theirs—one full of jubilant chaos and home-cooked meals. I'd marveled at the way they supported one another and remember indulging a little in some selfish sadness that all I had was a preoccupied mother and a brother who required so much care.

But even more than my selfish envy, I'd grieved for the Blackwoods. I'd wished that they could unwind the tragedy that had so recently befallen them. That Violet could've had her twin back and Frank and Afton, their son. Because even more overpowering than the love, affection, and unity they had was a blanket of sadness so thick that it had dimmed even the brightest moments that night.

Tonight, I feel content. I squeeze the two-year-old who's found her way onto my lap at the dinner table and will only eat if I hand-feed her bite-sized pieces of bacon. I bury my nose in her messy toddler hair and soak in the nostalgic scent of baby shampoo. It's so easy to feel happy because nobody's missing Landon. Instead of the carved out emptiness that competed so strongly with the warmth of their home last time, the house now buzzes with his vitality and energy.

He's alive and I'm going to keep it that way.

I'm tearing up another piece of bacon when I hear a low chuckle from across the table. I look up to find Landon studying me. My cheeks warm and the warmth spreads down my neck and into my chest. I don't know how long he's been watching me but I guess by his smile that it's been a while. He winks and gives me a thumbs-up. I've been so caught up in undoing the past that it feels good for just a moment to contemplate the future. I envision it with Landon.

We could have everything. Things I was so willing to forsake before. How was I so quick to sacrifice a normal life? The answer is clear and strong. Because I loved him. I loved him in an intense, consuming, real but sometimes irrational way. I loved him so deeply that I was willing to sacrifice nearly everything for him.

"You're a real natural," Frank laughs, shaking me from my reverie. "Do you know the hoops we jump through to get this one to eat?" He shakes his head and laughs again. "Then you walk through the door and she's all but finished everything on her plate. You're going to make a great mother one day."

His comment warms me. I thank Frank for his vote of confidence and hazard a look at Landon. This time it's not just him smiling, but Violet too.

The front door opens then slams shut and a deep voice calls from the other room, "Did I make it in time?" Reese appears in the archway that leads from the living room to the kitchen. "C'mon," he kids, smirking at Violet. "Did you eat all the bacon again?"

"Yes," she plays along. "And I pigged down all the French toast and eggs too," she says, dabbing at her mouth with a napkin.

Reese must not have noticed me at first because when his eyes finally land on me, he looks surprised. "Hey, Pres," he says and smiles. "I didn't know you'd be here." He scoots around the table and toward the kitchen island where serving trays sit, piled with Afton-created yumminess. He grabs a few slices of bacon.

Landon calls over to him, "I thought you were working late today."

Reese squirts some syrup over his French toast and looks at Landon. "Nope." He shifts his gaze to me. "Since when did you and Vi become BFFs?"

I don't know what to say. I wasn't expecting this when Landon invited me over. I glance at Landon, then Violet, silently pleading for assistance.

Violet places her napkin on the table carefully, then says almost apologetically, "Actually, I wasn't the one who invited her."

"Really," Reese says. It's not a question. His eyes flicker from Vi to Landon, who rubs at the spot between his brows. Apparently the smears of maple syrup on his plate are fascinating because he studies them like they're a newly discovered species.

Finally, he lifts his chin and meets Reese's appraising stare. "I asked her over," he says casually. "Mom made peaches-and-cream French toast. Presley's new to town, and everyone's got to try it at least once."

I'm relieved that he's trying to downplay. The last thing I want is to come between these two.

"Hey guys, I'm going to take off," I say. "Thank you so much for dinner, Mrs. Blackwood. It was delicious." I rise from my chair but Reese makes his way from the kitchen to the table and softly presses on my shoulders, making me sit again.

"I just got here," he says. "Stay and hang for a bit."

Landon's eyes are fixed on Reese's hands, which haven't moved from my shoulders. He blinks, then forces a smile. "Reese is right. You haven't even stayed long enough for Ping-Pong. Come on," he gestures. "You and me. Best of five."

"Let's play doubles," Reese says. "You and Vi against me and Pres."

"You haven't even eaten yet, bro," Landon replies. "Come find us when you're done."

"I'll eat later," Reese says. His eyes stay fixed on Landon. "Save my plate, Aunt Afton?"

"Of course, honey." Her eyes are discerning as she glances from Reese to Landon.

"Let's go," Violet says. She motions to us. "But I think it should be Presley and me against you two."

Reese snorts. "Maybe if we start you with a 5-point handicap." He pulls my chair out, and I stand and follow Violet from the kitchen, keeping my eyes purposely trained on her back.

Upstairs in the game room, Reese and Landon refuse a girls-against-boys face-off. What they can't agree on is who will partner with me.

Finally, I speak up. "It's me and Reese against you guys," I say, pointing to Landon and Vi. They all gape at me. It's not like me to be so assertive with these guys.

"What? Someone had to call it," I say. "We'd be here all night . . ."

143

"If you're sure," Landon says. "I'm just warning you. Vi and I make a formidable team."

Reese rolls his eyes.

"What?" Violet says, pretending to be insulted. "You can't mess with the wonder twins. We've been doing this our whole lives."

I decide not to tell them that back in Vegas we had a Ping-Pong table set up in our garage and that Chase and I played almost every day. If he were here, he'd school us all.

"You guys, first," I say and bounce a ball to Landon.

I move my feet apart and bend my knees. Landon laughs as I crouch and ready myself for his serve. "You act like you've done this before," he teases before tossing the ball several inches above, then sending it my way with a forehand push.

The ball lands on my side of the table and I easily return it with an aggressive backhand drive. The ball ricochets off the table and between Landon and Vi. I jump to give Reese a high five.

"You've been keeping secrets," Landon teases.

"Beginners luck," I lie. I wager a sideways glance at Reese and notice how his jaw tightens. I serve next and we get a pretty good rally going. Landon and Violet shuffle their feet, each taking their turn without calling it. They really do have twin powers, though Reese and I hold our own. The next three points go to us and we celebrate with ridiculous handshakes and hip bumps. I haven't played in a while and it's fun to be so competitive.

We rally again and Landon crushes one with a forehand drive. The ball goes too high and pelts Reese on the jaw.

He rubs at the spot where the ball hit and eyes Landon incredulously. "What was that?"

"Sorry, dude. Accident," Landon says.

"Really?"

"Dude," Landon says. "How many times have we both been hit playing each other?"

The next time Reese serves, he sends it flying, barely missing Landon's head. It ricochets off the wall behind them. Landon's eyes narrow into skeptical slits. "And what was that?"

Reese shrugs. "Accident." He sets his paddle on the table, turns his back on all of us, and walks down the stairs and out of sight.

—

Later that night, back at home, I text Reese:

> Hey, I'm sorry how things went down tonight.

It's cool.

I feel like I'm part of the reason this keeps happening.

Maybe . . .

I'm sorry.

He doesn't text back.

Chapter
Thirty-Seven

FINDING HOME

(PRESLEY)

5 Days Before

So, does this count as our first date or our third?" I ask.

I'm in the passenger seat of Landon's Sequoia warming my hands in front of the heater vent while he navigates the car up a slow winding road edged with snow dusted pines. He's completely at ease and I love the way he looks in his classic black Ray-Bans. I flip the visor down to block the low hanging sun, which has set the frosty wonderland of the Sierra Nevada mountains in a fiery blaze of red and orange.

Landon smirks in a way that sends flutters through my middle. "Neither. It's our second date. Driving you home from work because your car wouldn't start doesn't count. But breakfast for dinner at my house does count because I specifically invited you to spend time with me." He looks at me and smiles, then turns his attention back to the road, the streaks of orange sky reflected in the lenses of his sunglasses.

My ears, which had been building pressure as we climbed in altitude, suddenly pop, prompting me to ask him where we're headed. We'd left the confines of town miles ago.

"It's a surprise," he says. "But don't worry, I know you're going to love it."

"How would you know that?"

He gives a quick shrug. "Because. I just know you." His lips press together and he's quiet for a moment. "I guess that sounds a little crazy, doesn't it? Given that we've literally spent less than three days together."

I kick my boots off and plant my fuzzy socks on the dashboard, wrapping my legs in my arms. Trying to hide my smile in the canyon of my knees, I say, "Not that crazy."

At last, the sun is swallowed up, but the mountains are still bathed in its pink light. Landon slows down and turns at a large stone sign that says "Blackwood

Lodge." I'd known that his family owned a ski resort, but I'd never seen it or imagined what it might be like.

This place is different than the hulking Craftsman lodge I visited a few weeks ago. The sleek modern lines of the roof slope skyward, mirroring the angles of the ski runs in the distance. The building is mostly wood, but includes a solid wall of windows looking out over the runs.

Landon bypasses the parking area and drives up a service road to park on the side of the lodge. The racks out front stand void of skis and snowboards and though the sign on the building bearing the lodge name is illuminated, the lights are off inside.

"Bundle up!" He reaches over and readjusts the furry hood of my parka to cover my head. I sit still, enjoying the fuss he's making over me. Even more, I appreciate his proximity, which allows me to count his dark lashes and trace the strong lines of his cheekbones and the bow of his lips. He meets my eyes. "Don't be scared, okay? I'm going to be with you the whole time."

It didn't occur to me until this moment that we would be skiing. My insides twist. It would be nice to spend some time with Landon in which I wasn't constantly fearful of death or dismemberment.

He must see the worry in my eyes because he tries to reassure me, "Don't worry. I'm going to show you around a little first. Come on."

I can tell he's excited to bring me to his family's place, so I concentrate on playing it cool. "Lead the way."

We pick our way across the icy walkway to the lodge. He pauses at the glass door. "Check this out," he says, pulling out his phone and tapping in a numerical code on an app. "My dad is such a tech nerd. He's got the whole place programmed." In an instant, the lights come on inside and a soft click sounds, unlocking the door. Landon gestures for me to lead, and my first glimpse up at Blackwood Lodge leaves me stunned.

Soaring ceilings, wooden beams, and gigantic hanging light fixtures greet me. A large dining area spans the windowed side, boasting heavy banquet tables and chairs arranged to capitalize on the incredible views outside. A gaping stone fireplace flickers to life near a sitting area and when I question Landon about this witchcraft, he just wiggles his phone at me.

"Told you he's a tech nerd." He takes my hand and leads me further to stand in the center of the room.

"I don't know what to say." I look around in amazement. "It's just so . . . beautiful." It wasn't as big as the other lodge, but every detail from the polished gleam of the wooden floors, to the mix of old world decor and modern lines made this place seem extra special. "Are you sure it's okay that we're here?"

Landon dismisses my concern with a cocked eyebrow and smart-aleck grin. "Totally." With the tips of his fingers on the small of my back, he guides me closer to the window where we take in the view for a few more minutes, commenting on the first star that pricks the emerging night sky.

Soon Landon is pointing out the stars he knows, and I'm matching him with every astronomical factoid I can recall. I tease him for making some stuff up, and he denies it with the most convincing deadpan.

"You don't have to lie to make me like you, you know," I say, digging a knuckle into his ribs. He lurches to the side, cluing me in that he is extremely ticklish. I dig back in without mercy, slipping my fingers under his jacket and under his arms to find the most sensitive spots. His voice cracks when he laughs, sending me into an even bigger fit of laughter as I worm my hands around his torso with no intention of letting up. "You are squealing like a little girl, you know that? Like a little girl in pigtails and a pink dress."

He attacks back, grabbing my wrists in one deft motion, pinning my hands together. I'm surprised at his strength and the way he can restrain both of my hands with only one of his. Something I could not have known before. I take an intentional moment to appreciate this new piece of Landon.

"Go ahead. I'm not ticklish." I challenge him with my eyes.

"Everybody is ticklish."

"I'm not."

He lowers his brows in that cocky way again. "I just have to find the right spot."

Still restraining my hands, he uses his free one to niggle a finger in my side and though it does tickle, I force myself to stay calm.

"Hmm. Maybe you're more of a horsey bite kind of ticklish." He pulls me over to a deep leather couch and playfully pushes me onto it, then takes a flying launch, landing next to me. He grabs my knee and squeezes, sending electric tickle shocks through my leg, but still I maintain my composure. He squeezes a little higher on my thigh, making it even harder not to laugh. "Oh, I think you might be ticklish after all, Presley."

Smiling, I defy him. "Nope."

"Time to take out the big guns, I guess." He pulls my hood to one side and gently pinches a spot between my shoulder and my neck.

I immediately trap his hand under my jaw. Anything to stop the uncontrollable giggle fit that is fighting to escape my throat.

"Ah! See? I knew you had a ticklish spot." He pinches and pokes me in all of my ticklish spots without pity until my eyes are watering and I'm begging him to stop before I have an embarrassing accident. The whole time I'm trying to wiggle out of his reach, but he's exceptionally good at restraining me without hurting me.

He finally relents and lets me catch my breath as the giggling subsides in both of us.

"Okay, so we both have our kryptonite tickle spots," he says. "I can *not* have anyone touch my armpits. Like, I was afraid I was going to accidentally elbow you in the face." He tucks his hands under his arms and holds himself to emphasize the point. "Worst second date ever if you went home with a black eye."

"And apparently I can't have anyone touch my neck. I seriously thought I was going to wet my pants." I collapse back and let my head rest against the plushness of the cushion. "Now *that* would be the worst second date ever."

"Truth." Landon lies back too and we turn to meet each other's eyes. "Okay, if your neck is so ticklish, I have the worst torture for you."

I nudge his leg with mine. "Like I'm going to sign up for that. Not unless you have a diaper around here in my size."

"Let's just test it," he says, already starting to giggle again. He leans closer to me. "It's a secret though. I have to whisper it in your ear." He reaches over and moves the hair back, exposing my ear.

The feel of his hands so close to my neck makes me ticklish again and I lift my shoulder up quickly, trapping his fingers against the side of my throat.

"I haven't even told you the secret yet!" He's laughing and I'm laughing, and it's obvious he knows I'm hypersensitive to every touch now that my tickle switch has been tripped. He capitalizes on my weakness, leaning in and whispering at my neck, "Presley, be still and let me tell you my secret."

I pull my knees up, my feet flexing against the uncontrollable laughter that's threatening to break free. I do my best to hold still while he again attempts to push my hair aside, exposing the sensitive spot. His lips hover at the lobe of my ear and his breath is making the mini hairs of my body stand up in a tingling wave.

"You ready?" he whispers.

My whole body is tense and shaking with the effort of trying not to laugh, and I'm fighting against the pull of my shoulders that can't help wanting to inch up. "Yes."

"Okay. Here it is . . ."

I want to hear the secret, but my ticklish body can't resist the little hiss of air that escapes through his teeth and I break into laughter.

Landon throws his head back and laughs too. "You are hopeless, girl." He pulls me up to a standing hug, taking a moment to settle his lips near my ear again. "And might I add very, very ticklish."

———

After making and devouring a couple of roast beef sandwiches, two cups of chocolate milk and sharing a frosted sugar cookie, we bundle back up and step outside. Landon kills the lights inside with a few taps of his phone. As my eyes adjust to the darkness, the sky begins to reveal the sweeping expanse of stardust.

Landon looks up at the celestial show with me. "Never gets old. Sometimes I come up here just to stargaze. Doesn't get any closer to heaven than this."

I feel his eyes on me and I have to agree with him.

"So, you ready for this?" He touches his phone again and suddenly the whole mountainside is bathed in bright, clean white light. "We've got the place to ourselves tonight. Let's get crazy." He walks toward the car and retrieves a couple of inflated snow tubes.

"We're going tubing?" A smile cracks my face and I'm so happy and relieved I want to hug him again.

We trudge up the side of the run, Landon explaining how he wants to take it slow since using the chair lifts would take us too high on the mountain. With the Olympics coming up and with his sensitivity to my anxiety about snow sports, he wanted to make sure nobody got hurt. I never knew tubing could be dangerous, but he told me a few funny stories about some bang ups he got with Reese when they were kids. I also learned Landon had a fake tooth and Reese a corresponding scar from one particular crash.

After a few crazy rides down the hill, sometimes catching air before skidding to a stop, I understand his decision to stay low on the run. All of the climbing and sledding works up a lot of body heat and soon Landon and I are shedding our coats at the bottom of the hill.

"One more run?" he asks.

We climb to the spot on the hill we'd been using. "Let's see if we can stay holding onto each other the whole time."

"I want to keep my teeth. I'm too young for dentures."

"A dent-*ure*, thank you very much. Just *one* denture."

"Still."

"Come on, what could go wrong?"

I roll my eyes and laugh.

We get situated in our tubes, linking our feet and ankles together so that we are facing one another.

Landon is so handsome it hurts. I just want to look at him this way forever. The flush of color on his skin, the gleam of mischief in his eyes. "On three. You with me?"

I smile back at him, trying to shake the love bugs free from buzzing around my brain. "I'm with you. One. Two. Three!"

We push off at the same time and slide down the hill, spinning in a spray of snow flecks and uncontrolled laughter. As we pick up speed, my laughter morphs to screaming, which makes Landon laugh harder. "Hold on, no matter what!"

"I'm trying!"

"We're almost there!" he encourages. And just as I'm sure I can't hang onto him anymore, the tubes veer to the side, catching a bump and sending us flying. We tumble a few times down the hill coming to a painful stop with tangled limbs and snow in the face. The tubes ditch us and roll to the bottom of the run.

Landon is pinned under me and has lost his beanie. Mine is so askew that one of my eyes is covered. We laugh at how ridiculous the other looks and Landon blows a blast of air on my face loosening the coating of snow. We roll apart, catching our breath and then limp to the bottom of the hill, Landon holding my hand the whole way.

He stows the tubes back in the car and then invites me back inside the lodge, only this time he doesn't turn on the inside lights, opting instead to turn on the fire. He gets me settled on the couch with a thick, soft blanket and promises to return with hot chocolates. While he's in the kitchen, I settle myself and watch the stars in perfect comfort and ease. It's the first time in a long time that I don't feel anxiety about saving Landon. Somehow in this peaceful moment, I feel like everything is going to be okay.

He comes back and hands me a hot mug. "You seem like a marshmallow girl." The warm liquid is piled up with mini marshmallows.

"My favorite."

"I knew it." He settles in beside me and we kick our feet up on the coffee table, both admiring the night sky outside. The glass is so clear it almost feels like no barrier exists.

Landon points to the North Star. "Polaris. The first star my dad ever showed me." A lazy smile appears on his lips. "Reese and I were always going on adventures when we were younger and after getting lost and our parents calling the cops, my dad taught me how to navigate with the North Star. Said it would always lead me home." He laughs softly. "It was pointless teaching a little kid something like that, I guess. Like I could ever actually find my way back using only a tiny flicker of light."

His words stir something in me. I've seen the tiny flickers of memory on his face. I believe in those times he truly knows me, but doesn't understand how to reconcile it. "I don't know. I think it shows how much he believed in you. That you really could do it. Find your way home."

Landon's leg slides next to mine, making one long line of warm contact. A small gesture, but I soak up the touch. He looks at me, his face all shadows and strong angles in the firelight. His eyes hold mine, warm and inviting. "Do *you* believe in me?" His voice is low and rough and I can tell there is a hidden layer of meaning behind his question.

I smile back at him, my heart swelling at the opportunity to share my feelings if only in part. "Can I tell you a secret now?" I lean over and rest my head against his chest and his arm enfolds me. I hear the steady pump of his life beneath my ear. The most reassuring sound I've ever heard. I never want it to quiet. "I'll never stop believing in you."

His arm tightens around me and we sit in companionable silence, watching the shadows dance on the wall and the sparkle of the stars outside against the inky sky.

I nest in closer to him.

"Best second date ever," I say.

Chapter Thirty-Eight

SUNRISE

(LANDON)

4 Days Before

I cut the engine as I roll up to Presley's driveway. The house is dark and quiet. She obviously thought I was joking when I told her I'd pick her up at 5:00 a.m. for breakfast. I send her a text.

> Wake up, cute stuff.

For a minute I wonder if her ringer is off because my phone stays silent. Then I see the three dots dancing on the text thread, informing me she's working on a reply. I can't help smiling. Last night at the lodge was pretty near perfect and seven hours apart feels like too long.

> Are you a crazy person?

> Yes.

> Do you know what happens to my hair after a night of tubing and then sleeping?

> No, but I'd like to.

You say that . . .

Is it more Chewbacca with a perm or a girl Will Ferrell?

Omg. Shut it.

Your mom shuts it.

lol. Ok. I warned you.

You didn't answer my question.

It's more Merida from Brave. If Merida had squirrels nesting in her hair for a week.

Okay, now I'm excited.

Give me a sec.

Like, two shakes of a squirrel's tail?

You're gonna get it.

Come at me.

Minutes later, she slips out the front door and closes it softly behind her. Her head is covered by her hood, but I can see coils of cinnamon hair escaping around the edges. When she gets in my car she smells like toothpaste and vanilla. I love how she still looks sleepy; it makes me want to pull her into a hug so I do.

"Good morning," I say, still holding her.

"Good morning." Her voice is a bit croaky from sleep.

I pull away and look at her eyes. "You really are tired, aren't you?"

She nods, pulling her hood back and releasing a wild tangle of curls. She couldn't be any cuter. "Chase was loco last night. I got like three hours of sleep."

I'm suddenly embarrassed. In all of my eagerness to see her, I didn't think about her having to take care of Chase at night. "We don't have to do this right now. Go back to bed. I'm an idiot."

Her face breaks into a smile. "No way. I wouldn't miss this." Her eyes are on mine and I'm instantly comforted by their eagerness and sincerity.

I reach up and run my thumb over her cheekbone. She closes her eyes and nudges her face against my hand. I slide my fingers around the back of her thin neck and pull her forehead to my lips, kissing her. I can't help wishing I was kissing her lips instead. But I know how I felt last time I did that and it's important that I keep my head about me if I want to truly get to know her.

"Let's go then," I say against her skin.

As I drive, Presley's toes are curled against the dashboard, and this time she's wearing socks with penguins and peppermint candies on them. It's probably a good idea to have two hands on the wheel as I navigate the highway between Truckee and Tahoe, but I can't seem to let go of her tiny hand in mine. She rubs my fingers with her thumb, and I marvel at how such a small thing can feel so good. Like holding hands with a girl is a brand-new experience.

"I thought you said we're going out for breakfast?" Presley says.

"Kind of."

"All the way in Tahoe?"

"Would you just . . . shush and let me dazzle you?"

She laughs at that. "You always dazzle me, but I'll never shoosh."

"I'm taking you somewhere you'll never forget. It's a Tahoe bucket list. I've been thinking about that, you know. There are so many things I want to show you—big and small. Like tomorrow we're ditching lunch and you're going to try the sweet potato fries at Burger Me."

"I'm down with that," she says, patting her stomach. "If it's food, I'm in. So is today a big or little bucket list item?"

"Big. Well, I think it's big. But I guess we'll have to see what you think."

Twenty minutes go by quickly as we take turns playing favorite songs for each other from our phones and talking about our first concerts. Our tastes in music have zero compatibility. Presley favors every pop princess out there and blames it on Chase and I stick with alternative, '80s punk bands and a handful of concert pianists. She teases me for being a closet emo, and I return a friendly jab or two of my own.

As I pull off at the familiar stone outcropping, Presley looks around at the remoteness and complains, "Hey, this place doesn't have bacon!"

"You get grumpy when you're hungry," I say, maneuvering my car into a position on the shoulder that's far enough from the traffic.

"You promised me bacon."

"No, I promised you breakfast and I will deliver." I reach back and pull out a paper sack from Sugar Pine Cakery and jiggle it in front of her. "Will sticky pecan rolls and OJ do?"

"Does Landon Blackwood sit in his dark room wearing guy-liner listening to depressing songs all day?"

"Hey, let's not make this personal," I laugh. "Someday I'm going to find a girl who appreciates my sensitivities."

"I appreciate your sensitivities," she says and then she sneaks her hand inside my jacket and tries to tickle me where she knows I can barely stand it.

I pull her into another hug and her arm slides around my back. I burrow my face into her hair and breathe her in as her body melts closer to mine. "Thank you for being willing to do this with me."

"You mean today?" Her voice is soft and thoughtful.

"I mean everything." I hold her a moment longer before we zip our jackets, lock the car, and then start up the narrow, overgrown trail toward the surprise I have planned for her.

We reach the swing with a few minutes to spare before sunrise. It's been a long time since I've come to this secret spot. A couple of years ago, my dad hung this wooden swing as an anniversary present for my mom. How he ever discovered this place is a mystery to me. He managed to find a sturdy pine, which seems to grow straight out of an offshoot of boulders. And the view of Lake Tahoe from up here is postcard worthy.

The horizon is catching fire with a tangerine glow. The growing presence of the sun reflects and spreads across the glassy blue of the lake like spilled light. The effect is gorgeous.

Presley is smiling, fingering the ropes of the swing. "This is incredible." She seats herself in the swing and gives herself a little push with her feet. "I can't believe how beautiful it is up here."

I step behind the swing and nudge her higher and higher until her hair is blowing in the breeze and she's laughing. I make myself paint this memory in my mind. It doesn't take a genius to know that this moment is special. I can feel the weight and importance of it. I never want to forget it.

Presley gasps and slows herself with a scrape of boots against pebbles. "Look!"

The sun is cresting the mountain like a blazing eye and suddenly the trees that were black silhouettes a moment ago are now tipped with light and texture. Presley's hair catches the sunrise, making it glow in a thousand strands of luminous copper and gold. I run my fingers softly over her curls, and she leans back against me while we watch the creation of a new day.

When the sun is fully risen, she reaches up to take my hand from its resting place on her shoulder and pulls it down to place a warm kiss on each of my knuckles. "Are you happy, Landon? Here. With me?" Her lips brush like silk against my fingers and the warmth of her breath travels through me, sparking a new warmth low in my belly.

"Completely happy," I say.

I pull her up to face me. Her eyes are calm and bottomless, like the serenity of the lake behind her. I want to touch her. Any excuse to feel her. So I capture a few tendrils of hair and slowly tuck them behind her ear, taking my time to relish the velvety softness of her skin. I run the backs of my fingers up and down her cheek until they are glowing pink and her breath deepens.

I calm my breath. "I hope you don't mind that I'm taking it slow with you. That I haven't kissed you again, since that day." The memory of the kiss curls through my mind like a tantalizing smoke, licking at the edges of my resolve. I push it back. I don't want to treat her like other girls. I want to be with Presley because of her. Because of who she is. Not because of what she does to me.

She closes her eyes and a hint of a smile passes her lips. "I think it's a good thing. I want both of us to be thinking as clearly as we can be."

"Exactly. Heads on straight."

She opens her eyes and straightens. "Totally straight."

I'm chewing my lip, hoping the pain will distract me from the pull I'm feeling to do the exact thing I know I shouldn't. I stifle a laugh. "This is really hard."

"But worth it," Presley says, her eyes still calm, but crinkled at the edges. Her voice and her gaze have a gravity that soothes me. "You're worth it."

"How do you do it?"

Her brow raises in a thin arch. "Do what?"

"Make me feel like I'm the most important thing in the world to you. How is it possible that someone I've only known for a couple of months and who I've dated for only a few days can make me feel like this?"

The serenity of her smile shifts gently, like a spent wave on the shore, approaching and then receding. Her eyes drop and I sense she has some hesitation about what she's going to say next. "I guess the truth has a way of making itself known. Even if it's unspoken." Her eyes meet mine again and they're shining.

Wanting to extinguish the space between us, I pull her into my arms and hold her there. I open myself to what she said. I let myself trust her. I want to believe her, so I do. I choose to be the most important thing to her. And whatever that means and for however long this feeling lasts, I'm going to embrace it. It feels so good to not be fighting against her. To just open the dam and let my feelings flow freely.

"Pres?" Her name on my lips sounds like home.

"Yes?"

"Does it freak you out that I think I'm falling for you?"

She gives a little laugh that almost sounds exhausted. "No." Her voice quavers. "That doesn't freak me out at all." She melts further into me and nuzzles her cheek against my chest.

My hand finds its way into her hair and my lips to the top of her head. I kiss her there. "Good."

Chapter Thirty-Nine

BLISS

(PRESLEY)

3 Days Before

I can't believe you didn't tell your coach it was a teacher workday. Avoiding a workout. Naughty, naughty Chauncy." My feet are on Landon's dash again, and he laughs at my ridiculous English accent I use to scold him. I can't stop smiling. One, because I love teasing him, and two, because I love that my feet on his dash is my thing. The fact that I have "a thing" I do when I'm with him makes me feel like everything is going perfectly. Better than I could have imagined a month ago.

The light flickers through the trees as we traverse the curvy mountain road. "I didn't see you calling up your boss to tell her you have a day off either, missy. So who's the naughty one now?"

I love this boy. I love him. I love the way his dark eyebrows playfully quirk at me when he's made his point. I love the way his hoodie lays open across his broad chest and how his hair is crazy, straight out of the shower without any product in it. It makes me feel like he couldn't wait to see me. Like he just ran out the door with one shoe on and a piece of toast in his mouth just to get to me sooner. I giggle inwardly at my fantasy.

Yesterday, we spent every second we could together. After our sunrise breakfast, Landon waited in my driveway, scribbling down some trig problems while I went inside my house and got ready, just so we could drive to school together. For lunch, we took Chase to Burger Me and devoured a mountain of sweet potato fries and fry sauce. Landon was right—they were a legit Tahoe bucket list item. And I love that I didn't even have to suggest that we bring Chase with us—Landon did.

After lunch, we zipped back to my house to get my car so I could go to work. I know the side trip made Landon late to class, but he didn't care. Not sure how my mom will feel about Chase being late though. Maybe she won't find out.

In the afternoon, I had work and Landon had training, but it didn't stop him from sending me a picture of himself on the slope. He filtered some pink hearts over his eyes and made a cute meme that said "When you're tryna train for the Olympics but you can't stop thinking 'bout your boo." I laughed so hard that my boss, Sara, made me put my phone in the office for the rest of my shift.

Long after Chase and Gayle were asleep, I stayed up half the night texting back and forth with Landon. Stupid stuff. Funny stuff. Stuff like him sending me a picture of a banana with sunglasses on and asking if I find him "a-peeling." And me declaring the hour between eleven p.m. and midnight a GIF only thread. Then that led to a funny GIF war, which led to us taking turns sending our favorite YouTube videos to each other. I slayed him with my "Goats That Scream Like Humans" compilation.

Then he sent me a text that said, "Have you seen this one?" The title of the video was, "The Most Romantic Thing You'll Ever See." It had 437 thousand views—the video of the day I almost died. I hadn't yet watched the footage of our kiss on the slope. I knew it was on the news. My mom even tried to show it to me to jog my memory. But I refused to watch it. It was too upsetting to see us together like that when I knew Landon didn't remember us before. But last night, I watched it.

It was hard at first. Especially when the cameras zoomed in and I could still see the burning intensity in Landon's eyes as he bent low to kiss me. What I hadn't seen back when it happened were the horrified expressions on other people's faces, especially Violet's.

After I watched it, I texted Landon and asked how the video made him feel. He told me it was comforting to him. That even though he doesn't know why he did it, it still makes sense because he feels something for me. He told me that he trusts me and he trusts himself.

Even if he never remembered us the way we were, he's falling for me now. And this Landon is better than no Landon. I love this Landon as much as ever and maybe he can love me back just as much.

That's good, isn't it?

Landon turns into Kings Beach and parks the Sequoia in one of several empty spots. Outside the car, he takes down our paddleboards and then shimmies into his wetsuit. I watch him in the side mirror. He's all browned muscle. Ripples and curves and hard angles. His dark hair falls in his eyes as he zips up and I cement this image of him in my mind forever.

I feel like I keep doing that—purposefully recording memories. Because if the experiences of this last while have taught me anything, it's that things can change in an instant. And life doesn't make any promises. So love while you can. Remember while you can.

After a lot of squirming and tugging in the front seat, I'm in my wetsuit too. I get out and both of us tuck our boards under an arm and traipse through the sand. The late morning sun is bright, bleaching the sky a powder blue. Landon chivalrously wades in and holds my board steady so I don't even have to get my feet in the water.

"My hero," I say as I steady myself and he hands me my paddle. The water, as usual, is freakishly clear—magnifying the round rocks below which look like some kind of prehistoric eggs.

Landon hops on his board in one swift movement. I thought I was mastering the sport, but when I see the lithe way his body commands the paddleboard, I think again.

"Wanna see some obscenely huge houses?" he says.

"You mean like yours?"

He narrows his eyes at me. "Ha ha."

"Seriously though, do you know what's it's like for a normal person to walk into your house?"

"No. And you won't be able to tell me because you're the last person I'd call normal."

I splash him with my paddle, which is a mistake because it makes me wobble perilously on my board. "What? I'm normal. Why would you say I'm not normal?"

The edges of his eyes crinkle and he smiles that smile that makes me want to kiss the curve of his upturned lip. "Normal girls eat the whole French fry. Not leave those little nubs on the plate."

"Hey! I like the squishy parts, not the crunchy parts."

He continues as he paddles. "Normal girls have okay feet, but you . . . you have ridiculously cute feet. Feet that should be in flip flops every day and never covered up."

I laugh at this because it's funny that he likes my feet of all things. Also, I remember him mentioning something similar when we met before. It comforts me somehow that he has similar thoughts now. With everything that's different between us, I love having a few anchors to our time before. Even tiny anchors.

"Okay, the French fry thing is a quirk, but I can't help my feet. They are what they are. I still wouldn't call myself *abnormal*."

His voice deepens and his expression does too. "You are though, Pres. In all of the best ways. Trust me on this."

We paddle parallel to the shore toward a place Landon calls Crystal Bay. I can begin to make out the homes he was talking about tucked away in the trees. He's right, they are incredible. Stone and wood and big windows. Multi-level decks built on the backs of boulders. One house even has a slide coming out of it that empties into the lake. "These are crazy!"

"Right? Quite the spectacle. But it's not the houses I like best about this place. Follow me."

Landon points the nose of his board toward shore and paddles hard, maneuvering around exposed rocks until we round a bend and a small sandy beach strewn with more boulders comes into view. The water beneath my board is an unreal aquamarine and I can make out the individual grains of sand on the lake floor. "This is gorgeous! How did you find this place?"

"Paddleboarding." He beaches himself and hops from his board. I hand him my paddle and he helps me to shore. The sun shines down on my head, warming my hair and the tips of my ears and nose. I always forget to wear sunblock because it's not hot, but the elevation takes no prisoners. My freckles have doubled on my nose and cheeks since I took up paddleboarding.

"It's like we're in our own little world out here," I say. "Private."

"Tahoe is full of these kinds of hidey-holes. If you know where to look. Come on."

He takes my hand and we explore the beach, reveling in the warmth of the sun and taking in the expansive views of the lake and the snowcapped mountains in the horizon.

"You know what would make this even better?" I say.

"What?" he says.

"Cookies. This day would be so much better if we had cookies. Or maybe chips."

Landon laughs and pulls me into a hug that feels more like an affectionate headlock. "You junkie. That's what you get for working in a coffee shop bakery."

"I'm sorry, what'd you say? I was thinking about cookies." He releases me and gives me another one of those looks that make me feel like a million bucks. Like I'm the cutest thing he's ever seen.

"Next time I'll bring cookies," he says. "In my cookie fanny pack."

"That is the best thing I've ever heard of. Marry me."

We laugh together and I follow him as we climb onto a flat boulder and leap from rock to rock until we are a couple dozen feet out into the water. The stones are dark and smooth and we lay out on them, soaking in their warmth as the water laps at the edges. Landon unzips his wetsuit down to the navel, exposing his chest. "Well, I think it's safe to say this will be the last few days of training. A couple more warm days like this and all of the runs will be closed for the season."

"Yay," I say. "More time with you." I'm immediately regretting the slip of the tongue. I merely said what I was thinking, but maybe I shouldn't have. Landon did say this was a seven-day experiment. And though I feel like our time together is going really well and I think he feels the same way, I wish I wouldn't have assumed out loud. Not yet.

But then he puts my fears to rest with one word, "Exactly. Although I will still be working out a ton, but you could do it with me. You'd love it. Tons of wall sits and deadlifts and box jumps."

"I'll just watch you and eat cookies."

We lay together with an arm draped over our eyes to block the sun. Landon reaches over and takes my free fingers in his hand. His thumb rubs soft circles on the back of my hand and I squeeze his fingers in response.

"Can I ask you a crazy question?" he says.

My stomach does a little flip because there's something in the tone of his voice that tells me he's serious. "Shoot."

"How do you think you'd know when you're in love? I mean really in love with someone? More than just infatuation, you know?"

If this were any other boy and I were any other girl I might read too much into his question. But since I had crossed the infatuation stage a while ago and have been living my life and making all of my decisions out of love for this boy, I feel like I have some true perspective to give. And rather than getting ahead of myself or getting too excited I just answer him honestly. "I think infatuation is all part of it. At least at first. It's fun to be so into someone that you can barely eat."

"Or sleep," he cuts in.

I laugh. "Or sleep. But the way I think about love is like this: It's one thing to feel a certain way for someone. But what would you do for that person? What would you sacrifice? What would you give to be with that person?"

Landon nods thoughtfully. "Love is more about what you *do*."

I go on, "When you know you'd do just about anything or give up anything to be with someone . . . then you know it's love."

He turns to me, his eyes still shaded from his arm. He rubs the circle on the back of my hand with a little more pressure now. "Are you speaking from experience?" His eyes pour into mine and I see the searching and the need to know.

"Yes." I match his gaze, wordlessly communicating the utmost truth of my words.

"I believe you." He pulls my hand to his lips and kisses the knuckle of my first finger, letting the warmth of his mouth linger on my skin. His eyes close and he presses his lips harder against my skin. "Be patient with me while I catch up to you." His eyes find mine again and my heart is swelling and pounding against my ribs. "I want to catch up to you." His eyes are pained but honest.

I want to tell him that I'll wait an eternity for him. But I know it won't take that long. He's coming back to me. Without his memories. Without the perspective I have, he's coming back to me. I place all of my faith in him because I can feel the rightness of what's happening. Somehow he knows what we have is real and he *will* find it again.

Right now I just want the pained look on his face to melt away so I roll toward him and prop myself up on an elbow so I can look down into his face. "We have all the time in the world." My heart pinches because I know that if my plans and protection don't go exactly right, we really only have days.

But I can't think that way.

The most powerful protection I can offer him at this point is my love. His breath deepens and I see the twitch of muscle in his jaw. His expression is one of painful restraint and I know that he's trying not to kiss me. When we kiss again I want it to be because he wants it, so I lean over and whisper in his ear, "I'm not going anywhere."

His arms come round my body and he holds me to him in a charged, tight embrace. I can feel the tension in his body as he wrestles with his emotions. In a further effort to soothe him, I trail my lips from his ear and place petal soft kisses on each of his closed eyes, whispering reassurances to him. "I'm here." Another kiss over his dark lashes. "I won't leave you." A warm tear leaks from the corner of his eye and I kiss that away too, realizing the depth of his emotions. Sympathy grows inside me as I realize how hard it must be for him to have such powerful feelings but not know why or how they came to be. It must be like trying to survive an avalanche that came out of nowhere.

The urge to touch my lips to his is too strong, so I lower myself into the crook of his arm and lay my head on his chest. I trail my fingers over his skin, letting my hand come to rest over is heart. The faint rhythm is palpable under my fingertips, the steady beat an anthem of his life. I close my eyes and smile.

The previous late night is catching up to us because I find myself drifting in and out of consciousness against his deep and unfluctuating breath. Though marriage is years away for both of us, I can easily envision how wonderful it would be to sleep next to him. Safe and protected.

Eventually hunger and the elements get the better of us and we paddle back to Kings Beach. But before we're out of sight of our private paradise, I look back and hope with everything in me that it won't be the last time we spend time there. I've been struggling with that feeling—wondering if everything we do will be the last time. It threatens to pull me under, but I have to fight it.

Landon takes me to a little café that looks like a log cabin. Our hunger drives us to order an excessive amount of food. We dig into a heaping plate of nachos topped with ice cream-sized scoops of guacamole and sour cream while we wait for the waffles and hash browns. When the plates arrive with waffles piled with sliced bananas and strawberries and the hash browns smothered in gravy, we look at each other and laugh.

"Who's idea was this?" Landon jokes.

"Well, if you would have brought the cookie fanny pack we wouldn't be in this mess." I lift a forkful of waffle to his mouth and he lets me feed him.

"So good," he says through a mouthful.

Even with all of the food, we still manage to share a giant waffle cone of ice cream. A scoop of pistachio for me, which Landon had never tried but liked, and a scoop of coconut almond for him.

We walk around town, ducking into shops and taking turns licking the ice cream cone. At one point Landon reaches over and wipes a bit of ice cream from my cheek, smiling. "You messy girl." He licks the sweetness from his thumb, trashes the rest of the cone, and takes my hand.

Relaxed and still full from our lunch, we wander back to his car and take a few moments to sit there and chat.

Finally, Landon looks at me. "I don't want to take you home. It feels like the worst idea ever."

I smile at him. "I know. But my mom needs to get some work done and Janet has the day off. She needs me."

"Why you gotta be so good all the time?"

I know he's joking, but still his words tempt me to play responsibility hooky. But I promised Chase I'd take him to Boom Town to play some arcade games. "You want to come with me and Chase today?"

"Can't. As much as I've tried to avoid it, my mom and Vi finally caught up to me and are making me haul all of the tables and chairs and stuff over to Vikingsholm. You know, they need the muscle." He playfully flexes his biceps, but I'm still caught by the hard roundness of the bulge under his skin. Even though he's joking around, I'm mesmerized by it.

"You're still coming, right? To the fund-raiser thing?" he says.

I nod. "Even if I caught pneumonia I'd be there. Violet practically made me sign a contract in blood. And your mom too, though her tactics were a little more gentle than Violet's."

"Where do you think Violet learned it all from?"

We drive back to my house and park in the driveway. The afternoon sun filters through the trees, lighting the motes of dust into flecks of gold. Landon turns to me and sighs.

"Can I just put you on my back and carry you around forever? Like an eternal piggyback ride?"

"I'm not sure that would work out. But you can give me a piggyback ride to the door."

He gets a mischievous look on his face and then races around to my side of the car, opening the door, and pulling me out before I can protest. He effortlessly hoists me up onto his back and carries me to the front step, setting me down gently on the bottom one so that I'm exactly the same height as he is.

"I like this," he says, running his hands over my shoulders and down my arms. His fingers trail back up over my elbows and the backs of my arms, sending my heart into a full flutter.

"I like it too." My voice has a little tremor in it from the electricity zinging through my veins.

He shakes his head slightly. "This isn't working anymore."

His choice of words should alarm me, but the starved look in his eyes tells me I have nothing to fear. I blink, waiting for him to explain himself.

His fingers vine through mine, pulling my body mere inches from his. "I'm so tired of fighting this." His eyes fall upon my lips. "Just a small kiss. Just one," he says, his eyes meeting mine briefly, but then finding my lips again.

I close my eyes and lean in slightly, our breath mingling before our lips meet. His lips brush against mine in a feather light touch. I force myself to hold still. To let him decide how much he wants. He comes back for another kiss, this time drinking a little more deeply, but then pulls away.

My knees are trembling, and I hold myself back as his hand slips into my hair and his lips brush against my cheek once, twice, and then against my lips again.

He steps back half a step and shakes his head at me again, his mouth turned up on one side. "You are . . . something else Presley Hale."

I give a little curtsy, which makes him chuckle.

He takes a big breath and lets it out. "Okay. I'm walking away now." He walks backward, his eyes still on me. "I'm leaving. I'm going to get into my car and drive to my house."

"Yes. Go home. Go directly home. Do not pass go. Do not collect two hundred dollars."

He growls and rolls his eyes, but finally turns and trots to his car. He calls over his shoulder, "Don't think I'm creepy if I text you two minutes from now."

"Never!" I call back.

The rest of the afternoon and evening crawls by. I want to be present for Chase as we hang out at the arcade, but my mind is a million miles away in "the love of my life just kissed me" land. I shake myself free of it the best I can and force myself to engage fully with my brother. He's so cute and eager as he shoots one Skee-Ball after another, looking for my approval.

I cheer for him and then encourage him to try some new games. He ends up loving the race car simulation, and I regret getting him hooked on it as each game takes eight tokens. But it's worth seeing him so happy. The place is pretty much dead on a weeknight, so we stay a little longer than usual. I buy Chase some fries and a Coke and then let myself scroll through the texts from Landon as Chase eats.

I smile and chew on my thumbnail as I read them.

> I can't stop thinking about you.

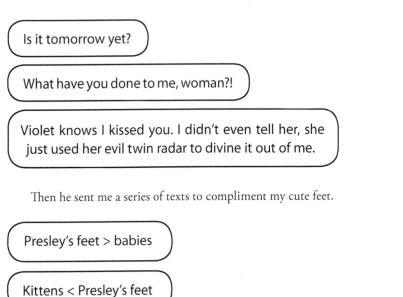

Is it tomorrow yet?

What have you done to me, woman?!

Violet knows I kissed you. I didn't even tell her, she just used her evil twin radar to divine it out of me.

Then he sent me a series of texts to compliment my cute feet.

Presley's feet > babies

Kittens < Presley's feet

Baby pandas < Presley's feet

I laugh at his unabashed affection. I could drink it up all day. I send a quick text back.

You are adorable.

Chase and I are having fun.
I'll text you when I get home.

He doesn't text back, which makes me think he must be busy toting tables and chairs for his mom.

Back at my house, Gayle is already tucked in bed fast asleep while the news drones on her TV. James greets Chase and me. "Have fun, you two?"

"Tons," I say softly, so as not to wake my mom. Chase runs up the stairs while I hang my coat and purse on the hook. "Looks like Chase is ready for puzzle time," I say, winking at James. "You two are quite the amigos now."

James nods, smiling. "We are. I would have never guessed it, but we have developed our own kind of rapport."

"It's called a bromance, James."

His face contorts at the term.

"It's like a super cute friendship between guys."

"Huh. Bro-mance," he repeats. "I like it."

"If you don't mind, I'm going to go take a shower. You have Chase?"

"Yes. I'll get him ready for bed."

I can't help myself. I reach out and hug James. "Thank you. Truly."

James, stiff at first, relaxes into my hug. "Of course."

As I head up the stairs toward the bathroom, I shiver a bit. "Why is it so freezing in here?"

James shrugs. "I didn't notice. I'll go around and check the windows."

After a long and luxurious shower, I take the extra time to dry my hair because even though the water was hot, I'm still chilled. I slip on a fuzzy pair of PJ bottoms, a long sleeve T-shirt, and then layer a UNLV hoodie over that. Chase's room is quiet, so I close my door and allow myself to unwind.

It's past ten now, and I know I should get to bed, but I relish these quiet moments when I have my brain all to myself. Tonight, I open up Landon's text thread and peruse his messages. He really is so cute. I shoot him a brief text:

> Just wanted to say I had the best day today. And good night.

The message feels so lame. Today was more than a good day. Today was everything to me. It was the day I knew Landon will come back to me. My heart squeezes because I want so badly for everything to work out. As the time draws nearer to his death date, James's words haunt me more and more.

Because what if he's right? What if there is nothing I can do to stop Landon's death? I have to keep my head about me. No matter how wonderful this time is between me and Landon, I have to remember what it is I'm here to do. To save him. No matter what. I need to keep that in the forefront of my mind even if all I want to do is be seventeen and in love.

In love. I am so in love.

I'm startled by a sound at my window. At least I think I heard something. It was a small chipping sound, like when a car on the highway kicks up a pebble that hits the windshield. I hear it again. It can't be an accident. I think briefly about going to get James to investigate, but either stupidity or morbid curiosity draws me to my window instead.

I push back the curtains and see Landon standing below holding a ladder under his arm. I laugh with relief and push up my bedroom window, startling a raven from the ledge. Heart still pounding from the bird, I lean out and whisper-call to him, "You better have cookies!"

He tries to laugh quietly. "I'm sorry if I scared you. I wanted to make sure this was your window before I climbed up." He sets the ladder against the house and nimbly climbs it, and then rests his elbows on my sill.

"You could have texted me to find out, you know." I rough up his hair, which is damp and crazy like it always is when he gets out of the shower without styling it. He's dressed in dark jeans and a stylish leather coat that has a soft hood. "Get in here before somebody sees you." I open the window all the way and Landon crawls in.

"I like what you've done with the place," he says, looking around with mock appreciation.

I take in my room through his eyes, noticing the days' worth of dirty clothes on the floor, the empty Amazon boxes that Chase's new puzzles came in, and the collection of water cups on the nightstand I've been too lazy to carry down to the sink. "Hey, love me, love my flaws. You knew what you were getting into."

He takes me by the hand and pulls me into a hug, murmuring in my ear, "I did know what I was getting into. And I do love you. Flaws and all."

My breath catches in my chest at his words. *Is he joking around? Or did he just say what I think he said?*

I pull away slightly to see his eyes. They're brooding and intense.

"I had to see you. I couldn't wait another second to tell you." His hand slides under my hair and cradles the back of my neck. "I love you, Pres."

I'm floating. My lips are tingling and my heart is winging around my chest like a trapped hummingbird. Tears prick at my eyes and my throat tightens. "You do? Are you sure?"

His brows lower almost like he's scolding me, but his soft caress on my neck tells me he's not. "I'm very sure. I'm only wishing I would have trusted my gut and let myself fall for you sooner. No matter how I fought it in the beginning, it was you. My heart was trying so hard to tell me that it's always been you. I don't need to understand why. And frankly I don't care why. I only care about you . . ." He leans in and kisses my forehead. A soft, loving kiss that leaves a lingering warmth on my skin. "And me. As long as we're together. That's all I care about."

My arms slide around his middle as I lay my ear against his chest and listen to the beat of his heart, which echoes the rhythm of my own. When he speaks, I revel in the sensation of the deepness of his voice that I can hear coming from inside him as well as outside.

"I've thought a lot about the things I can't explain, Presley. Like the feeling that I've known you longer than I have. Or that I have memories with you that never happened. And I *still* can't explain those things away." He's rubbing my back now and his mouth is near my ear. "But for some reason, those things don't bother me anymore. They're more of a confirmation that I should be with you. Not a distraction. Does that make any sense?"

I nod my head because I'm trying so hard not to cry. The relief at his declaration of love is still coursing through my body and threatening to manifest in an epic cry-fest that if I let it start, I'm not sure I can reign back in. Finally, I find my voice and I lift my face to his.

"There's time, baby," I say, using the name he used to call me. I didn't mean to, it just naturally rolled off my tongue. "There's time to figure out all of it." I say the words and I'm hoping, wishing and praying that they are true. That there will be time. And that someday, Landon will remember me from before.

He gently pushes my bangs back and smiles the most heart-exploding smile. "You called me 'baby.' Say it again."

"Why?" I say, feeling my cheeks warm. I'm suddenly embarrassed and regretting the lapse.

"Because it feels right. Say it, please."

He holds my eyes with his and somehow the sincerity and tenderness in his look melts away my insecurities and it's easy to say, "I love you too. *Baby.*"

He lets out a breath, pulling me to him and kissing me with a joyful urgency that I match. We're both smiling, which makes it harder to kiss one another, but somehow with his hands in my hair and mine cradling his jaw, we seal our declaration again and again until our lips soften and slow into a sweet give and take. A pure expression of honeyed promises and the new binding of hearts.

We share a last kiss, but hold one another tightly, not wanting even a molecule of air between us. Landon strokes my hair and in my dresser mirror I can see that his eyes are closed and there's a lazy smile on his lips.

"I'd say the seven day experiment was a success, wouldn't you?" he says.

"Smashing success," I reply.

"I can't wait for tomorrow. And the next day. And the next day after that."

I do the mental arithmetic. Tomorrow. The next day. And the next day after that. That will be the day James says Landon will die no matter what I do. My heart is lead in my chest.

Landon seems to sense something amiss because he pulls back and his eyes scour my face. "Hey . . . hey. Are you okay? Am I going too fast? If I'm freaking you out, I can totally dial it back." He squeezes my shoulders.

I pull him close again, doing my best to make my voice reassuring. "No, no. You're not doing any of those things—going too fast or pulling back. You're doing the exact right things. I think I'm just . . ." I choose my words carefully. "I'm just so relieved you feel the same way I do that it all seems too good to be true, maybe?"

Landon turns to my armchair, tosses my book bag to the floor, and pulls me down on his lap, looking into my eyes as he holds me. "Look, I know it's going to take time for this all to feel real. For you to completely trust me. But I want you to know that I'm going to do everything I can to show you how serious I am about you."

I reach up and run the tips of my fingers through his hair. "I do trust you already," I say. "I guess you're so important to me that I just want you close." I want to list the fifty things I wish he'd stay away from. Things that could turn all of my careful preparation on its head.

Things that could kill him.

But I don't. I know from experience, if I want Landon to stay close to me, he has to come on his own terms. I can invite, but I can't force. And I know scare tactics would only alienate him, not make him trust me. Friday is only three days away. And we have plans to be together almost the entire day. We'll be at school where I can keep an eye on him and then at Vikingsholm—dancing the night away and safe in each other's arms. I hesitate to think the words, but they emerge anyway: *What could go wrong?*

Landon touches his lips to mine, then to the tip of my nose, then to my forehead. "I have no other plans other than to stay *extremely* close to you."

I shiver at his words and his touch and nuzzle into him a little closer, burying my face in his neck. "Good."

He heaves a big sigh. "It's late. I don't want to go, but I need to."

I give him a pouty lip because I want him to stay forever, but I know he's right. His eyes zero in on my bottom lip and he takes it between his lips and kisses it, murmuring against my mouth.

"I."

Kiss.

"Love."

Another kiss.

"You."

The last kiss lingers longer than the first two and I feel myself falling into him, tempted to invite him to stay just a few more minutes but before I can, he's lifting me from his lap, standing, and smoothing down his clothes. He chuckles. "I better go now or I never will." He brushes a quick kiss on my lips again and whispers against my mouth, "'Night, baby."

"Good night," I say as he opens the window again and climbs out. I watch him leap to the ground from four or five rungs up, stash the ladder on the side of the house, where now that I think about it, it had been the whole time, and run down the driveway and out of sight where I assume his car is parked out of earshot.

I close the window and lean my forehead against the cold glass, shaking my head and smiling at the perfection of this boy.

"Touching," a voice says from my side. I whip around in terror to see a tall man sitting where Landon and I had just been. His eyes are icy and keen. His black hair parted and slicked back and his knee high boots polished to a sheen. He fondles a sleek horn, which tops his walking stick. A wan smile appears on his lips. "Young love. Gets me every time."

Chapter Forty

(PRESLEY)

3 Days Before

I quickly turn away from him, working to keep my face emotionless.

"There's no need to pretend you don't see me. I daresay it's much too late for that." His voice is light and unaffected, like I was just some side conversation and he was occupied with buttering his toast.

Still, I don't turn to him. I think about yelling for James and start to make for the door, but the man's voice stops me.

"Oh, yes. Do tell your great protector that Apollo sends his regards. Although, I'm not sure his services will be needed any further. As you see, I am in here and he is blissfully unaware in the very next room. So, truly. Is he much of a protector at all?"

I turn to him, slowly with a mixture of horror and searing anger boiling in my body. I take in his long legs, which clad in his tight black pants remind me of spider's legs. "It was you."

"Yes, I do apologize for frightening your brother, but you see I had to be sure he could see me."

My teeth are grinding together to the point of splintering. "Leave him alone." My voice quakes and quivers with fear for my sweet, sweet brother. An innocent soul who deserves none of this evil.

Apollo uncrosses his legs and lays his walking stick across the armrests of the chair. "Oh, I intend to. Though, in truth, that will be up to you." The veiled threat in his voice is not lost on me.

His neck lengthens and my skin crawls under his intensified scrutiny.

"You know, I had thought that you were a mere anomaly. A random person with *the sight* that I was lucky enough to stumble across. When I came to investigate further though, imagine my shock when I discovered your brother bears the same gift." His slender white fingers trail down the length of his walking stick. "It leaves me to wonder if it's an incredible coincidence or if it runs in the family."

He continues, "Of course, I have seen other cases like your brother. Of those whose minds are confined through no fault of their own. There is an innocence to them. A lack of guile. You see, most people spend an inordinate amount of time in the act of misleading. Hiding their true thoughts about themselves and others. Putting on a mask. Dodging, diverting, lying. So when I discover someone like Chase who only lives in truth, I find it hard to hide myself from him. He sees all. Even if I try to conceal myself from him. His lens to the world is pure."

"What do you want from us?"

"I wasn't finished. Permit me to continue?"

His manner and elegance are beguiling. If he were any normal person on any normal day, I might think him beautiful. But it's the kind of beauty that carries a poison. Like the sumptuous curve of a black widow abdomen. Polished, sleek. But deadly. I nod to him to continue because I have little choice. And I need to know as much about him as possible.

"The other fact that causes me pause is that you house the dead here. And not just any dead. A guide." His eyes pierce mine. "And what would a random seer be doing housing a guide under her very roof? I asked myself this and can come to only one conclusion. You, my girl, have dealings with the dead." He levels his eyes on me again and it's almost like I can feel him reading my mind. I try to hide my fear, but the twitch at the corner of his mouth tells me he's pleased with my reaction. "In this thing, we are alike."

"I'm nothing like you." Bile roils in my stomach, burning the back of my throat.

"Tell me then, what exactly has been your experience with my kind?" His head cocks to the side like he's merely curious, but I know better.

"I drowned. As a child. That's why I can see the dead."

"Did you!" He slaps at his thigh like he just cracked a party riddle among friends. His glee at finding out this new information disgusts me. "Well, then. There you have it. Mystery solved."

The muscles holding up my spine begin to relax to the smallest degree.

"Except—" Apollo holds up one finger. His fingernail is somewhat long and shaped into an oval at the tip. He wags the finger at me and flashes a wicked smile. "Except that doesn't explain why you have a guide here. Or why your dear Landon seems to have memories of things he never lived." Apollo's tongue clicks gently inside his mouth. "Surely you'll admit it's all very curious."

My insides freeze. Like someone has hollowed out my chest and packed it with ice. I don't like Apollo making connections with Landon. Not at all.

I block and counter. "James was my guide when I drowned. We've kept in touch, I guess you could say," I lie. "He found out that you had terrorized Chase and offered to help." I will my eyes to remain steady, my posture erect. "As for Landon, I didn't realize you'd been eavesdropping."

Apollo raises his eyebrows in mock innocence. "I couldn't help but overhear."

I do nothing to hide the vitriol in my voice. "Not that you'd understand, but it's not uncommon when you make a connection with someone to feel like you've known them your whole life. Love 101."

His eyes narrow at me and a wry smile twists his mouth. "Thank you for the education. I will consider your explanations." Apollo then stands, placing the tip of his staff into my carpet. "Now then, let me tell you why I'm really here."

Now my eyes narrow and a growing dread fills my stomach like it's plumbed to a flowing faucet of filthy water.

He continues, "Simply put, I want you."

My skin crawls at the idea of being associated with him in any way. "Dream on, freak." Perhaps I should have chosen different words, but a few minutes ago I was in the arms of the most loving person I've known. The sheer contrast of this scheming evil Vigilum cracks my judgment and causes me to not guard my speech.

He gives a brief chuckle, which perforates his reply. "Dear child. If you could be so lucky."

I furrow my brows at everything he is saying and doing, but choose to question one thing. "Why do you call me child? You don't look much older than I am."

He lifts one brow and an ethereal quality comes over his expression, drenching his voice in a far away tone. "I am older than you can imagine. As ancient as mankind itself. I am the first. I will be the last."

"The first and the last what?"

"I thought it would be obvious. I am the first to remain on this earth after death. The first to forsake my crossing."

"The first Vigilum."

He nods appreciatively. "Very good. You know more than I thought."

"I know someone," I say, referring to James.

His face takes on a devilish expression. "You may know more of us than you think."

Something breaks inside of me because I know he's right. James had warned me again and again to be careful. That I might attract Vigilum attention simply from having the ability to see them, or as Apollo would call it, having *the sight*.

"Comes with the territory, I guess," I say.

"Indeed." He takes a step closer to me. "Now for my proposition. I deal in passages, Presley. They are my currency. I am a benevolent lord, you see, and I dispense them to the deserving. I assume you are familiar with the concept of passage?"

I nod, remembering my first education from James and Landon. I'd learned that passages are like a ticket to the afterlife. Transferrable and with an expiration date.

"Good. I want you to work for me. Someone with your . . . abilities could be very valuable."

"I don't see how," I say already having my mind made up to have nothing to do with this man, but still genuinely curious as to what he thought I *could* do for him.

"Don't you? You are a link to the living world. You could be my hands, my voice, my servant."

"Are you insane?"

His eyes harden and I know I've insulted him. That could be dangerous, but I don't see how I can respond in a way that won't offend him. It's not like I can say something like, "Thank you for the generous offer, but I'm on a coffee shop career path right now, so I'm good. Thanks, but no thanks." Plus, I'm still so angry that he hurt Chase that I want to unleash on this demon. I want to leap on him and scratch his eyes out.

He ignores my response. "Imagine our collaboration. I, having an army at my disposal, all with the incomparable ability to sense the sick, the despondent, the volatile or suicidal, and you, who can speak to the living—cajole and encourage any behavior I tell you to. The possibilities, Presley. Think of it. We would be a powerful force, you and I."

His words, though purposefully ambiguous to make his suggestions somewhat palatable, are clear. And I'm simultaneously in despair, shock, and sickened so much by his idea that I can barely stand. My voice is a strained whisper, "You want me to help you kill people so that you can collect passages?"

His teeth gleam. "Exactly."

"No." I say the word, but I know it won't be that simple. I've had enough dealings with Vigilum to know they'll try to get their way no matter what. I brace myself to endure the kind of torture Liam imposed a couple of months ago. I resign myself to the fact that my refusal could cost me my sanity or my life.

But Apollo doesn't behave like Liam. Instead, his voice is like warm cream and honey. And I'm aware that he's using a different kind of mental manipulation. Even though I know he's using his power to numb me against his proposal, I still can't help feeling somewhat soothed and relaxed. My body accepts his intrusion and is grateful for it. I claw at my wits, willing myself to keep my thoughts straight.

He steps even closer and runs a single finger down my cheek. I'm helpless. Frozen. I can't even flinch at his touch let alone turn away from it. I start to get a sense of his power.

"I expected that my proposal may seem distasteful to you. But let me assure you, the kinds of passages we would be harvesting . . . well, they will come available with or without our encouragement. It's only a matter of time. Why not make use of them? Why not control the circumstances so that we can give them to people who are truly deserving?"

Though my body is frozen, he allows me to speak because my words flow unfettered. "What makes you think you should be the judge of who is and who isn't deserving of a passage?"

"I'm no judge. They come to me. They know I can help them. And as I said, I am a benevolent lord over the wandering, the lost, the hopeless. Can you see that it is a kindness I perform? That we could perform together? Presley, we would offer relief to the suffering."

The candy sweet words pour over and through me, but something in my core knows he lies. No matter how much artificial persuasion he pours over me, I know he's a deceiver. "I won't do it. I cannot be a part of this."

Apollo stares at me for several seconds. The seconds stretch into what feels like a long space of time. I can feel the smoke and mirrors of his persuasion fading away, leaving me cold and shaking against my control. It's the same cold I felt when I first walked into the house tonight. I realize with horror that Apollo has been here all evening, I just didn't know it.

"I had hoped you'd be more cooperative." His face morphs into a pained sympathy. "I had hoped I wouldn't have to . . . persuade you further. But you leave me little choice."

He steps even closer so that I can feel his icy breath on my face. I also feel a tightening around my neck, not so much that I can't breathe, but enough that I can't swallow. My heart begins to gallop, remembering the panic I felt at Liam's touch those months ago.

"I want you to know that I can and I will follow you and your family to the ends of the Earth. I have nothing but time. Time is nothing to me. I may give you peace for a season. Just enough that you may begin to wonder if I've lost interest . . . to wonder if you are truly released. But then I will come in the night. I will leave you entirely untouched. But for everyone you love or have ever loved, I will manifest their darkest fears. I know you don't know what Chase is afraid of . . ." His mouth widens in a wicked, wicked grin. "But I do."

Tears well in my eyes at the thought of this . . . *thing* hurting my brother. Apollo looks over my face, mere inches from his own like I'm a priceless work of art.

"Tell me, my dear, in all of your vast experience of seventeen years, have you ever heard the screams of someone trying to make the whisperings stop? Have you ever known anyone to claw out their own eyes to make the visions go away?"

Apollo cradles one side of my face and closes his eyes. In the faintest whisper, he says, "Let's hope you'll never have to."

The light flickers once and he's gone. My neck throbs as the arteries usher blood back through the pinched highways.

I don't know how he found me. I don't know how to escape him. But two things I do know.

Even though he's a deceiver, his threats were truth.

And he'll never stop.

Chapter Forty-One

MORE THAN YOU KNOW

(JAMES)

3 Days Before

Chase is asleep before midnight for once. The western-frontier puzzle we worked on made me sentimental, so as we sorted through pieces, I told him everything I could remember about my life with Lucy and our son, Michael. Not a day passes that I don't think of them, but sharing stories out loud made my memories come alive even more. I'm not sure how long I let myself get wrapped up in reminiscing before I noticed that Chase's head was tipped forward and his eyes closed.

He snores softly and I laugh as it occurs to me that I bored him to sleep. I'll have to share that pointer with Presley. I rise from my seat to help him to his bed but pause when I hear footsteps in the hall.

"James?" Presley appears in the doorway, and even though the room is lit only by a small lamp, I can see that her face is drained of color. She grasps at the doorjamb with both hands as if to steady herself. An icy stream of air trickles from the hallway behind her and into the bedroom.

Quickly, I drape Chase's arm around my neck and lift him from his chair. "Come in. Shut the door." I lower Chase onto his bed and cover him with an extra quilt.

Presley is frozen in the doorway, so I go to her. "Come in," I encourage once more, but I have to pry her hands from the doorframe. She falls into me and wraps her arms around my neck, crying into my chest. Hot tears soak my shirt as I rub her heaving back. She holds me for several moments, then takes a step back and meets my gaze, her eyes wild with fear.

"He was here," she whispers.

I don't have to ask. I'm surprised the Vigilum have kept their distance this long.

"It was only a matter of time," I say. Dread punches through my chest and choke-holds my heart. I've grown complacent the last few weeks as the Vigilum have stayed in the shadows, but I knew they'd be back. Somehow they've learned Presley can see the dead and that's far too great a prize to ignore.

Presley makes her way to Chase's table and collapses into a chair. I lower myself into the chair opposite her and take her hands in mine. They're ice cold and trembling.

How I lament the day she spotted Landon in the parking lot all those months ago. For a moment I engage in a make-believe "I told you so" argument with Landon. Had he let her go from the beginning as I'd instructed, Presley and her family would be free from Vigilum threat.

She takes her hands back and rubs at her face. "There was just one," she says and her face crumples into a terrified mess. "He wasn't here for Landon's passage. He doesn't even know that Landon died. All he seemed to care about is that I can see the dead. And he wants me to join him. To help him do terrible things." She covers her face with her hands. "But I could never."

"Did he identify himself?" I ask.

"He called himself Apollo." She worries her bottom lip, then eyes me skeptically. "He told me to give you his regards."

My stomach tightens. As far as I knew, Apollo was nothing more than Vigilum legend. I've heard whisperings that describe a ruthless and powerful monster with an uncanny ability to assemble followers. Rumors allege that even guides desert their assignments if Apollo challenges them. But in all my years as a guide, I'd never even met someone who'd crossed paths with him. So to accept him as nothing more than myth was easy.

Presley studies me and her eyes are full of questions.

"I don't know Apollo," I tell her truthfully. "I've heard of him, but I've never met him." I decide to share as little as possible. "I didn't believe he was real. Like your legend of Bigfoot. Everyone's heard it, but no one believes it." My explanation seems to placate her and she nods.

"He was different than Liam," she says. "Calmer, more in control of himself."

A storm of emotion hangs heavy between us as she recounts Apollo's visit and his terms. Conflicting expressions wash over her face, and I can sense the internal war waging inside of her. The decision that lies before her is anything but cut and dry, right or wrong.

She's silent for a moment, and I can only assume, like me, Presley is assimilating to this new and impossible reality. When I learned Vigilum had discovered her, I imagined they'd be intrigued by her ability, I just never expected someone with Apollo's power. Proof of his existence changes everything.

Eventually Presley rises from the table and makes her way across the room to Chase. At his bedside, she kneels and caresses his face with her fingertips. "James, he's going to hurt Chase. He's going to hurt Gayle."

As if to shield him, Presley covers Chase with her upper body and wraps her arms tightly around him. Her cheek lies against his broad chest. "I have to save Landon, then I have to join Apollo." She seems to be convincing herself more than talking to me. "I'm almost there. In three days, Landon will be safe. I'll prevent his death, then I will do what Apollo says."

She straightens then and rocks back and forth. "I am so screwed, James. I'll give up my soul, but at least everyone I care about will be safe." Slowly and deliberately she nods her head as if she's cementing her choice. "In those terms it doesn't sound so bad, does it? Because it won't end with Chase and Gayle. He made that perfectly clear. Anyone in my life is a target."

"Yes. That is typical of Vigilum," I say.

"I have to do it."

I join her at Chase's bedside and place my hand on her back. "Please consider a different way."

"There is no other way," she argues.

"There may be. Let me continue to watch over things here. My instinct tells me that although he's threatened to harm Chase and Gayle, he will avoid that while I'm here. At least for now.

"Remember," I continue, "his end game is to convince you to join him, but I believe he understands the magnitude of what he asks of you. If you tell him you need time to set things in order, it will seem reasonable to him."

"I don't see how that solves anything," Presley says.

"It doesn't. It's not a permanent solution. But it gives me time."

"We don't have any time." The distress in her face tugs at my sympathies.

"I'll see what I can find out about Apollo. Everyone has an Achilles' heel. Let's see if we can find his."

Chapter Forty-Two

Choices

(PRESLEY)

2 Days Before

I lay on my side, curled into Chase's back. Even with two heavy quilts covering us, ice, thick and unbreakable, has taken up residence in my core. I move closer to Chase and wrap my arms around him, trying to absorb some of his heat. I will be sleeping with him every night from now on.

James paces across the room, his hands clasped behind his back like a soldier keeping watch. I'm grateful for his presence and try to imagine sorting through this without him. My heart quickens though, as it dawns on me that in just days I *will* be on my own. Once Landon's death date passes, James will surely be released from this time. Despite what James believes, I will save Landon. And he will not be needed here to guide.

James will be gone.

But Apollo will stay.

Though I know Apollo can't be trusted, I do believe him on one account. He *will* torture everyone I care about if that's what it takes to convince me to join him.

James has always preached about free will and choice. Agency, he called it. The right to make my own choices, even if they come with unappealing consequences. It was something I didn't understand as well as I should have. That we shape our destinies choice by choice.

And ever since I've landed here, I've been so thoughtful with all of my decisions. I've endured rejection and indifference from Landon and Violet, so that I could stay near him and prevent his death from happening all over again. My choices have been anything but easy, but at least they were mine.

But now my hands are tied. I don't *get* to decide whether or not I will submit to Apollo's demands. I don't get to decide to stay with Landon. I'm not allowed to love him anymore, at least not outwardly.

I can't help but believe that Apollo waited for the perfect moment to approach me. Like he bided his time waiting for Landon to admit that he loved me. He wanted to be sure of our feelings for each other. More ammunition. More leverage. Now, Landon is as big a target as Chase and Gayle.

And if Apollo ever finds out that Landon also has *the sight* because he too has crossed the veil of death? Ice trickles through my veins as I contemplate the disastrous consequences. Apollo hurting Violet, Frank, Afton, or Reese just so he can manipulate Landon.

I just feel so . . . violated. That I've been studied, watched. The hairs on my arms and neck rise as I contemplate how often Apollo or perhaps one of his followers may have observed me with Landon. I had no idea he was here tonight before he revealed himself. James didn't either. How could I have grown so comfortable and relaxed this last week, knowing that Vigilum had found me? Reckless.

Nausea rolls in my stomach as I admit to myself what I must do. The only way to protect the people I care about is to sever ties. Acid climbs up my throat.

I could never convince Apollo that I've grown distant from Gayle and Chase. They are my family. But couples my age break up all the time.

Landon and Ivy.

Landon and me.

I shut my eyes against the erupting hot tears. But they pour down my cheeks anyway, drenching the pillow.

Teenagers can be fickle, right? Surely Apollo has learned that much in his centuries of observing the human race. So, I will do as James suggested. Tell Apollo I need a few days. Enough time to get me past Landon's death date. I will save him and then I will convince Apollo that Landon was nothing more than a fling. Eventually, when I move away from Truckee, maybe he'll believe me.

But before that, I'll have to convince Landon that I don't love him. Sobs catch in my throat as the words I would say float through my mind.

I bite down on my cheek, the taste of metal turning my stomach even more. No matter how many deep breaths I try to govern in and out of my lungs, my heart still pounds. Because everything is so unfair. We've only just begun. This time with the chance at a real future. We've overcome death, and lost memories. We've built it all again, which tells me that Landon loves me for me. Not just because I was the only human who could see him before. In so many ways, it's even better this time.

But what did I just tell Landon about love? The way you differentiate infatuation from love is by how much you'd sacrifice. I have no choice but to sacrifice our love to keep him safe from Apollo. Safe from *me* and what I will surely become as one of Apollo's servants. Landon will deserve better than me.

Despite what I told James, I have decided. I will join Apollo. I don't believe that he has an Achilles' heel as James suggested. I sensed no weakness tonight. If he is indeed the first Vigilum, he's as good as immortal.

Invincible.

And I don't dare cross him.

—

Miraculously, fatigue won out, and I fell into a dreamless sleep last night. This morning I find Gayle and Chase seated at the kitchen table sipping from two steaming mugs, tea for her—coffee for Chase. He stops slurping now and then, pausing to spoon more sugar into his cup. The familiar smells somehow comfort me. Real, routine, warm. As if reading my thoughts, Gayle rises from her seat, takes another cup from the cupboard and then pours hot water from the kettle over a fresh tea bag.

She hands me the mug and says, "You look awful. Are you feeling all right?" She places the back of her hand to my forehead.

"Actually, no," I answer truthfully. "I feel like I might be coming down with something. I'm thinking of staying home today."

"Influenza is wreaking havoc at the high school," she says, taking her seat again. "I hope you're not going down too. Maybe you should stay home and rest up."

I join them at the table and say, "Do you think you could get your Las Vegas job back?"

If we could leave Truckee, it would be so much easier to cut ties with Landon and my group of friends. I know I will never be free of Apollo but at least I could place some distance between the Blackwoods and the others.

Gayle studies me over the rim of her mug before setting it on the table. "What's going on?" she asks.

"Nothing. I . . . it's just that we left right in the middle of my junior year and I miss Vegas. My friends."

"I thought you'd made even better friends here." Her mouth twists into a wry smile. "Especially that dark-haired guy with the huge biceps."

I roll my eyes. "Don't be gross, Mom," I scold. "I'm being serious."

She holds her hands up in a peace-making gesture.

"So is it possible, you think? To get your old job back?" I ask again.

Gayle raises her eyebrows. "You hate it here that much? I thought you loved your job, and having Janet's help . . ."

"Just yes or no, Mom? Is it possible to get back to Vegas?"

"You're serious." It wasn't a question this time. She eyes me skeptically. "Did you have a falling out with Landon?"

"No."

"Because we can't just pick up and leave over some teenage drama, Pres. This is our livelihood and our future we're talking about."

Emotions well within me, pressing against the dam, threatening to burst. If only I *was* entangled in some teenage drama-fest.

I don't blame Gayle for asking questions. She's completely in the dark. But it's not like I can be truthful with her about any of this.

I am in love with a boy who was once dead. Miraculously, he is now alive, and though his second chance at life came with no memories of me, we've built new ones. And he's fallen for me again. My heart squeezes.

When I try to remember my life without him, I mostly remember the bleak and empty parts. An indifferent mother, an absent dad, and little but attending to Chase's needs to fill my time. My love for Landon fills in all the cracks and crevices of aching and longing, plus some.

But now I must abandon it.

It's impossible to separate myself from Landon but remain in Truckee. Seeing him at school, around town. It would break me. And until I'm old enough to be on my own, I'm going to need Gayle's help on this. I choose my words carefully.

"I need to leave here, Mom. I need to go."

Her eyes narrow into slits. "What's that supposed to mean?"

I lift my chin. "I can go to Dad's." Though I can't imagine going through with it, he has offered as much in his letters. Since my hospital stay, he's been trying make amends. And though living with my dad is something I never would have chosen before, as things are now, it would be better than staying here.

Gayle's eyes are wide and filled with shock and hurt. She sets her tea on the table and takes my face in both of her hands, forcing me to look at her. "What is really going on?"

I look down, because I know she will see the lie in my eyes. "I told you. I miss Las Vegas. I miss my friends." Then I utter the ugliest lie. "I have no one here. I hate this place."

Gayle doesn't release my face. "Look at me, Presley. Look at me."

I lift my eyes to her, hoping the deceit doesn't show in them.

"We have to stick it out the rest of the school year. Okay? They've filled my position in Vegas and it's almost impossible to transfer anywhere this late in the year." She quirks one eyebrow and studies me for a long moment. "But, if you're still feeling homesick in a couple of weeks, I'll see what's available. It may suck for my career, but if you're miserable here, I'll do my best."

This brings me no real comfort, only a sickening and twisted relief. I remind myself that separation will make it easier for Landon too. And hopefully, if I'm no longer around Landon, Apollo will never find out that he has *the sight* as well.

After Chase and Gayle leave for school, I find James in Chase's room, looking out the window.

"I'm sorry," he says quietly.

"For what?" I ask.

"I've allowed myself to become so immersed in my relationship with Chase and with you, that I failed at the one thing I was meant to do."

I join him at the window and place my hand on his shoulder. He continues to stare out the window at nothing in particular.

"I wasn't there for you when Apollo came." He rubs at his face and laughs a humorless laugh. "I didn't even know he was here. I'm not sure how useful I would have been, but you shouldn't have had to face him alone." He shakes his head. "There's just no excuse."

I lay a hand on James's back. "Your time with Chase has been the most meaningful gift anyone has given to me."

I didn't know guides could cry.

Neither of us have anything else to say, so I go back to bed and wrap myself in my quilt.

Shortly after nine, when Landon must realize I'm not coming to school, I get a text.

> Ditching without me? ;)

I take a deep breath before texting back. He can't know that it's over between us until he's safe.

> Never! I'm sick. :(

My heart is sick, my brain is sick, my *life* is sick.

> I will bring you chicken noodle soup at lunch. And a sticky pecan roll. If you're good.

I deliberate on the wisdom of allowing Landon in my house when Apollo could be near. Could be watching. But honestly, how much more damage can we do in the next few days? He already knows how we feel about each other. And I need him. Even if our hours are numbered. Selfishly, I want to have as many together as we can. Apollo never showed himself to Landon before. I'm hoping he won't today.

> I'll split it with you. If YOU'RE good.

> No way. I'm getting my own.

> Is that any way for a future Olympian to eat?

I meant to have a shower before Landon arrived, but it didn't happen. It's amazing how fast time goes by when you stare at the wall, contemplating the last normal days of your entire life.

I type in the code on the keypad and open the front door. Then focus on behaving naturally, for Landon's sake. "What? No bedroom window delivery?"

Landon stands on the doormat, his arm piled with crinkly white paper bags. A delicious aroma wafts over. Cinnamon and butter and herbed broth. He nods to his bundles. "Sorry. Hands full."

I make a tsk noise, "Excuses."

Without warning he crosses the threshold and kisses me warmly. I kiss him back, soaking in the medicine of his touch, and for the briefest moment, I can almost forget the nightmare of reality. I pull back.

"Yeah," he says. "I'm not going back to school today."

"I'm going to get you sick." I lie because as much as I want to lose myself in him, I also feel like it would be a cruel thing to do. For him and for me.

"Does it look like I care?" he says, kissing me once more and my resolve crumbles a bit. This time he pulls back. "You look cute."

I know he has to be joking. I'm dressed in my mom's old UNLV basketball championship T-shirt from the nineties and some baggy PJ bottoms. My hair is pulled up in a messy knot on top of my head. "I try," I say, laughing off the obvious.

He shakes his head and smiles crookedly, "Seriously. I dig this slumber party look." He gestures toward the living room with his chin. "Now come on, let's get you laid back down. I'm going to feed you and take such good care of you that you'll have no choice but to come back to school tomorrow."

He's being so sweet and I wish more than anything that it all were that simple. He must see the crack of dismay on my face, because he tenderly wraps his free arm around me and guides me toward the couch. I settle in and Landon tucks a quilt over me and then heads to the kitchen. I hear him rummaging around in the drawers and cabinets. Soon, he's back with a mug of soup and a pecan roll atop a folded paper towel.

"Such service," I say as I take the offered food from him and sip at the soup.

Landon sits at the opposite end of the couch and pulls my feet on top of his lap. "This is so much better than Trig. Remind me to sign up for Snuggling 101 in college. In fact, I want to major in it."

"With an emphasis in pecan roll eating?"

He nods deeply. "Yes."

"Deal," I say. But my stomach is sick suddenly as I think of him going off to college without me.

It's not something I'd thought about yet, but obviously I won't be going to college. Inwardly, I laugh bitterly. *Not with the night job I'll be holding down, anyway.* Most college kids deliver pizzas or pick up a gig waiting tables at night to get through school. None of them will be clocking in to trick passages out of the dying. Nobody would have a boss like I'll have.

"Seriously, though, what do you want to study?" His eyes are bright, and he licks sugary glaze from his finger like it's the only thing he'll have to worry about today. I'm glad he doesn't know anything. I'm glad he can be happy for now.

"Law," I answer, even though every word from here will be pointless because my life is decided for me. "There are so many kids like Chase who don't get the help and services they need because their families don't have the resources to fight for them. I want to help them."

Landon nods, a little crease appearing on his brow. "That's awesome. I should have known you would do something like that. You're always helping people."

"What about you? How will school fit in if you're all busy winning gold medals and posing for cereal boxes?" I wink and force a bite of roll.

He shifts on the couch and settles into the cushions a little deeper. "I plan on studying as much as I can. Business, probably. I'd like to do something similar to what my dad's doing. I love this town. I love the mountains and the lake. I want to make a living helping others enjoy it."

"I can see that."

Landon heaves a big breath. "SATs are next month. Stuff's already starting to get real. Is your mailbox filling up with college pamphlets like mine is?"

I give a little laugh. "Not yet. We mostly get AARP stuff and Senior Living magazines. I think there may have been some older people living here before us."

"I'm pretty sure no matter what I'll be going to UNR. It's my family's alma mater. Wolfpack all the way, baby. There are a lot of other schools with Alpine teams that I'll apply to just to appease Violet and my mom, but I know deep down my dad will die if I don't go to Reno." His face turns mischievous. "Hey, you better not go back to Vegas and become my arch enemy. No Runnin' Rebels allowed in the Blackwood house. My dad would have a stroke. You should see him during football season." He laughs and shakes his head.

I laugh along with him, imagining Frank getting all worked up over a tense game.

After our laughter settles down, I brave a topic I don't want to think about, but know I need to. "We might not end up in the same place, you know. You and me." The warm mood that had glowed in the room is suddenly doused, like a bucket of water on a fire.

Landon's face falls and a hurt expression comes over his features. "Why would you say that?"

"Because, Landon. Stuff happens. Roads fork. We might end up taking different paths."

He swallows. "Okay . . . but that's like ages away."

"It might be closer than you think," I say, my voice breaking on the last word.

That statement was a mistake. And though I meant to soften the blow for our inevitable separation, I realize now that was a stupid move. I feel Landon's body tighten under my legs. This isn't the way to keep him close to me. Not if I want to protect him. I have to make a choice between warning him and protecting him. And I can't do both.

I can see Landon's confidence chipping away right before me. Distrust and hurt surface in his eyes. I can't let him go there.

"I'm sorry," I say, freeing myself from the blanket and climbing over to him and into his lap. "You're right. It's all ages away. It's stupid to think that way."

Gratefully, he accepts me into his arms and I feel his muscles relaxing as he pulls me closer to him, speaking softly into my hair. "I just found you, Presley. I'm nowhere near ready to let you go. You scare me when you talk like that."

I hide my face, burying it in his neck so he can't see the tears that are wetting my eyes. I want to prepare him. I know what it feels like to wake up one day and your whole heart has been ripped from your chest without warning. I have a whole new understanding for how Landon must have felt before, on the last night we spent together before the Vigilum came for us. How he must have agonized over our last moments. Our last kiss.

I agonize over every moment now.

I lift my face and touch my cheek against his, soaking in the warmth, like sunlight. My fingers find their way into his hair and I run them over his head and down the back of his neck, memorizing every curve and contour. My lips find his ear. "Promise me that no matter what happens, you'll always know how much I love you. Here. Right now."

He embraces my body and our foreheads find each other, touching and connecting us in a sweet intimacy. "Promise me," I say.

His voice is low and soft, "I promise."

He pulls me into a kiss that I don't fight against. Instead, I let my lips and my breath and my embrace show him the depth of my love. I can give him that.

I'd kissed boys before whose kisses were all taking. But Landon's kiss somehow gave more than it took. And though I could feel the heat between us building, he never felt selfish. And that generosity, that sweetness made me love him even more.

Loving him like that hurt so much.

Eventually we curled up in each other's arms and dozed off for an hour or so. Later, I excused myself to go take a shower and Landon offered to tidy up the remnants of our lunch.

I let the hot water stream over me, disguising the tears that I let fall freely. I resigned myself to the fact that there was going to be a lot of crying in the next couple of days. And there was no purpose in fighting it. When the hot water finally begins to run out, I turn off the shower and throw the curtain aside, reaching for a towel.

On my fogged mirror, letters, clear and defined in the steam, spell a message.

Tick Tock

I know instantly it was Apollo, and I tear the towel from the hook and wrap it around me, feeling even more violated than before. "I know you can hear me," I say, my voice a strained whisper. "I need time. Surely you can understand that giving my whole life away to serve you is going to require me to tie up a few loose ends. Two days. That's all I ask."

No matter what happens to me, I have to have enough time to save Landon. In my mind, it's non-negotiable.

A cold trickle of air snakes over the back of my neck, like a frozen sheath of silk. The hairs of my body rise in alarm. Before my eyes, letters begin to trace across the mirror. They spell one word.

Granted

Chapter Forty-Three

TRUE COLORS

(PRESLEY)

1 Day Before

Erin is waiting for me on the front porch when I get home from my shift. It's been so long since she's stopped by Wild Cherries, I'd begun to worry about her. It occurs to me that we need to exchange numbers so we can keep in touch from now on. Or maybe we don't. Of course we don't. No friend of mine is safe. In that regard, I guess it's fortunate that Erin's been MIA the last few weeks.

She rises from the rocking chair as I make my way to the steps.

"Hey, stranger!" I say and even though I feel like wrapping her in a hug, I stop myself. Erin has never been touchy-feely and I don't want to catch her off guard. Or send signals to Apollo that I care too much. Because even though he promised me two days to put things in order, he could be watching.

"Hey yourself." She smiles. "How have you been?"

"You want the truth or the standard, 'Great. And you?'"

"That doesn't sound good," Erin says, and her smile slides into a frown, amber eyes serious. "What's going on?"

I purse my lips and close my eyes. There's nothing. Literally nothing of truth I can share. I open my eyes and force a smile. "I'm just tired. Chase has been sleeping like crap. Same ole, same ole." I punch in the combination and push the door open, inviting Erin to follow. "What about you? I thought you'd moved to China or something."

Erin doesn't answer my question or follow me inside. Instead she's on tip-toes peeking over my shoulder and asks, "Where's Chase?"

"Gayle took him out for pizza tonight. It's Janet's day off, so she's keeping him out late."

Erin's shoulders visibly relax and she steps across the threshold.

In the kitchen I offer her a soda, but she declines.

"You never eat, woman," I laugh. "Trust me though," I say, popping the top of a cold Diet Coke, "you're going to love what I'm about to make."

Earlier today, I decided I would busy myself and make Landon a batch of his family's peanut butter truffles. In just hours, I will save his life, break his heart, and give my soul to the devil. If I allow myself any free time, my mind takes over and I can barely breathe. Plus, these will make Landon happy. One last gesture.

Erin and I make small talk as I mix the butter, Rice Krispies, powdered sugar, and peanut butter in a large bowl. A few globs of the mixture fall from the counter and onto the floor. Before I can clean it up, Russell runs into the kitchen and does it for me.

"Still scrounging, I see," Erin laughs.

"It's like he's got built-in radar. Whenever any piece of food drops, he's here within seconds," I say.

"Come here, buddy." Erin pats her legs and coaxes Russell to her side of the kitchen. She leans forward in her chair and scratches his back and rubs his ears. "Did you miss me? Did you miss me? I missed you. Yes, I did."

Unexpectedly the front door opens and both Erin and I startle. "Pres? We're home," Gayle calls from the entry. "I brought pizza."

"In the kitchen," I call back.

"You can meet my mom," I say to Erin. But something is wrong. Her already pale face has gone completely white, making her dark eyes stand out like shiny black jewels.

Gayle walks into the kitchen, Chase following closely behind, plucking pieces of pepperoni from his pizza slice and shoving them in his mouth. "I'm glad to see you out of your room," Gayle says. "You must be feeling better. How was work?"

"Long," I say, leaning into the counter.

"I'll tell you what," she says, placing her purse right on the chair where Erin sits. Right *through* Erin. My eyes fly to Erin's. Her eyes are wide and our gazes are locked in an unspoken tension.

Gayle prattles on but her voice sounds far away, "Since it's just the three of us here tonight, let's see if Chase will watch some TV in his room and you and I will put on a chick flick and pig out on ice cream . . ." I tune her out but I can't take my eyes off Erin.

Revelation.

Erin is the first to look away. Her eyes dart to the left, then to the right as if she's assessing a way to escape.

Betrayal, poisonous and thick, swirls in my stomach.

Maybe the shock shows on my face because Gayle asks, "What's the matter?" She takes my arm and leads me from the counter to the table. She moves her purse to the tabletop and tries to lower me into the chair where Erin sits.

"I don't know," I say, brushing her away. Then more for Erin's benefit than hers, I say, "I just feel really, really sick all of a sudden."

"Let me help you to your room," Gayle says.

"No, I'm just going to sit for a minute," I say, lowering myself into the chair next to Erin. "Would you mind grabbing me a wastebasket just in case?" I ask.

Gayle flies from the room and I shoot Erin a weighted glare. Then quietly so Gayle won't hear, I hiss, "Don't leave." My breaths grow rapid and my face hot. "Don't even think of it."

When Gayle returns with a wastebasket, I tell her that I'm feeling a little better and that I think I will go to my room after all. I rise from my seat and subtly motion for Erin to follow. Once Gayle has me settled in bed, she tells me she's going to make me some soup, and Erin and I are left alone.

My eyes begin to sting with unshed tears, so I clench my jaw and take deep, measured breaths through my nose. I will not cry for Erin. She's not worth any of my tears.

"I know what you are," I say. I shake my head but more at myself than her. "You pretended to be my friend." How could I have been so stupid? I assumed because we were always together in a public setting, that she was safe. But when I recall all of our time together, there was never anyone at the coffee shop when she was there. As soon as a group would come in, she bolted. I should've known better.

Erin hovers near my door and stares at the floor. She makes no attempt to deny it.

Rising from my bed, I say, "So, you're one of Apollo's little slaves then?" I keep my voice low, not wanting to alert Gayle.

"No, it's not like that. I don't answer to him."

"But you don't deny you told him about me? That I can see dead people."

"I'm sorry, Presley . . ."

"What's in it for you, huh? Did he promise you a passage?"

"No, he didn't promise me anything. I was just curious . . ."

"Nice. You were curious. Do you know what your *curiosity* has caused?"

"If you would just listen to me for a minute. Let me explain."

"No. You listen to me." I walk across the room and jab a finger inches from her face. "Let's see if your curiosity about Apollo was worth it. He came to my house when I wasn't here and tormented Chase, Erin. I have the video footage. Would you like to see what it looks like when a kid with autism is chased around the house by a demon?"

Erin's face crumples and she shakes her head. "After I met Chase, I went back to Apollo. I told him about your situation. I thought maybe he would leave you alone if he understood everything you had on your plate."

"No, Erin. He did not leave me alone." I clench my fists. "He was very intrigued by my *gift*. And thrilled by Chase's ability to see the dead too." I press my palms against the wall to steady myself.

"And now he requires my service or he will torture Chase forever. He will taunt my mother." I straighten. "And do you know what he means by *service*?" I finger quote the last word. "He wants me to help him manipulate people out of their passages. I serve him, or my family and everyone I love suffers."

Erin looks like she'll cry. "I thought I was helping, telling him about Chase," she says.

"You just made it worse. He promised he would hunt me and my family forever. Do you see what you've done? He will never stop."

Saying it out loud really does make me sick. I run to my bathroom and am grateful that Diet Coke was all I had in my stomach. On my knees, I hug the toilet and cry. I've lost everything. Landon, my freedom, my soul. I may keep Chase and Gayle safe, but what will they think of me? Surely my presence as one of Apollo's army would cause them more harm than good. Chances are, I will have to leave them as well.

"I'm sorry. I didn't know he would hurt you," Erin says from behind.

I don't have the strength to even lift my head, so I just say, "If you were so curious, you could have just asked me. You're not the first dead person I've met."

"Presley, please, I'm so sorry."

"Just go, Erin. Go."

Chapter Forty-Four

ALLIANCE

(JAMES)

1 Day Before

I wait for Erin in the front yard. I overheard the entire showdown. So the mystery of Presley's discovery is solved.

My heart beats with raw compassion for both girls. In her mind, Presley was betrayed by a friend. Another cross to bear at a time when she carries more than anyone should. Erin realizes the magnitude of her mistake and is undoubtedly filled with regret for inadvertently betraying her only friend.

Erin emerges through the front door, as I thought she would. There's still so much human in her. She stops on the porch when she sees me.

"It's okay," I say. "I'm a friend."

She swallows hard but doesn't move.

"Please, Erin." I take one cautious step toward the porch.

She tenses away from me. She's a flight risk and I can't have her bolt because she's my only link to Apollo. "My name is James." Another step. "I overheard your conversation with Presley, and I know you didn't mean to hurt her. I believe that."

Her stance loosens a bit but she asks, "Did Apollo send you? I told him I don't want to work with him."

"I have no dealings with Apollo," I say, but discontinue my steps because she still looks ready to bolt. "I'm a friend of Presley and Chase. I've been helping them. And I'd like to help you too."

She eyes me skeptically. "Why would you want to help me? You don't even know me." Her bottom lip quivers. "I don't deserve anyone's help."

"But you do. We all make mistakes."

She laughs but there's no humor in it. "You have no idea."

"You may be surprised," I say.

Her eyes narrow. "How are you friends with Presley?"

I take a deep breath as I contemplate how much I should share. I believe Erin's loyalties lie with Presley. That she has truly forsaken Apollo. I make my way to the porch and sit down on one of the rockers.

Emotions radiate from her spirit and I feel affection, regret, and helplessness. Deceit and manipulation are absent in the realm of her consciousness. She must take in some of my emotion as well because she lowers herself into the chair next to me.

I choose my words carefully. "Presley had a friend who died not so long ago. I was his Guide."

Erin's face registers something I can't interpret.

"Surely you had your own," I probe.

She shakes her head. "I can't remember." A line forms between her brows.

"Then you were deceived very quickly."

"Yes," she says but her eyes are far away now. "Yes, I think I was."

For several minutes we sit as silent companions. I can only imagine our conversation has unearthed trauma. Her demeanor changes and despair, thick and palpable, lingers between us.

Finally she says, "I still don't understand how you are Presley's friend."

"It was at the time of her friend's death that Presley discovered her gift. Though her friend died, she could still see him. And me. We developed a friendship through the process." I'm withholding important details, but I can't risk exposing Landon. I don't know Erin well enough.

"And you know Chase because seeing the dead, what? Runs in the family?" she asks, a slight edge to her voice.

"Something like that." It would only add to her guilt if she knew I was protecting him from Apollo.

She studies me, struggling to make sense of this new information. "And you're still here *because?*"

I answer as truthfully as I can. "Because her friend still lingers. He has not transitioned yet." My throat is thick with emotion as I contemplate Landon dying all over again.

Erin swears. "That's great. So on top of everything else, she's got a death to grieve. No closure 'til he moves on, right?"

I nod.

"Awesome," Erin says.

"She carries quite a burden," I agree.

"Correct me if I'm wrong, but it seems like your cup runneth over with Guidely to-dos. Why would you want to help me?"

"You care for Presley," I say.

Her eyes close and she purses her lips. "I do."

"So do I. She has a long life ahead of her, and I can't stomach that she live it in Apollo's service."

"I know. I know," Erin moans, pressing her palms against her forehead. "I screwed things up for her."

"You have experience with Apollo," I hedge.

She drops her hands to her lap and appraises me with wide, incredulous eyes. "I wouldn't exactly call it *experience*. I've spoken with him twice."

"Yet that's twice more than I have. Do you agree that Apollo lies when he presents himself as a benevolent master? As one who dispenses passages to the deserving?"

Erin snorts with disgust. "That guy is pure evil."

"I need you to help me discover his weakness," I say. "If we can determine where it lies, we may be able to help Presley."

"You've never met him, James." Erin bites her lower lip. "I have the feeling he's more dangerous than he lets on."

"I don't doubt it. I once believed that Vigilum could do nothing to harm the dead. I was wrong. Following his tracks will be risky."

"Any information is better than no information," she says.

"Exactly. Currently we know nothing other than who he claims to be and what he claims he can do. Let's start by seeing if there's any truth around his claim to dispense passages."

"Did you ever think you'd see the day you'd align yourself with a Vigilum?" Erin asks sarcastically.

"And yet, I don't see you as such," I say. "Have you ever attempted to deceive a passage from a recently deceased?" I ask.

Erin looks horrified at the question. "No!"

"Therein lies the very definition of Vigilum. They are watchers whose only remaining purpose is to lie and deceive."

"I went to Apollo for help. I told him about Presley."

"Your curiosity got the best of you. You are human."

At my last word, Erin wipes at her face and I realize that her eyes well with emotion. "It's been so long since I've thought of myself as anything even close to human."

"Will you let your mistakes of the past stay there?" I ask. "Can you move forward with me to help your friend?"

She shakes her head. "I will never forgive myself for the things I've done, both alive and dead." Then her eyes shift from sorrowful to determined. She lifts her chin and says, "But yes. I can put them in the past for now if there's even a small chance that I can help Presley."

"You will need to be brave," I say.

"What have I got to lose?" she asks.

Chapter Forty-Five

Turning Tables

(Erin)

1 Day Before

From the roof of the adjacent parking structure, James and I look down upon Renown Regional Medical Center. It's a gray day and the din of traffic and smell of car exhaust reveal we're no longer in Truckee.

I stare at the hospital, taking in its cement and glass facade. "Why aren't we checking the hospital in Truckee first? Seems like geographically, it's more relevant."

James shakes his head. "No. We need a more urban area. I know this sounds bad, but the patients in the Truckee hospital are mostly affluent. Affluency suggests stability. Apollo will be looking for the unstable. People who because of their circumstances have made choices that have led to their situations." He crosses his arms over his chest, seeming to think. "There's more to work with emotionally with those kinds of people. More guilt and despair."

A police siren activates and wails as the cruiser streaks down the street below. "Trust me. We'll have better luck here," he says.

Luck seems like the wrong word to use in a case like this, but I know what he means. James reaches over and says, "Take my hand."

In a quiet blink, we're standing next to a vending machine outside the access doors to the ICU. The sound of daytime TV percolates from the waiting area nearby. I assume James didn't take us inside the actual unit yet, because if Apollo is here, we have to be careful to not be seen.

I realize I'm still holding James's hand and it's trembling. I'm too scared to be embarrassed about it.

"It's going to be all right," he says. "You're doing the right thing by trying to help Presley. And when you're doing the right thing, there's never cause for true fear."

I give him a smile that I'm sure looks weak. "I'm ready."

We phase through the door and suddenly we're surrounded in a hive of activity. The thing that surprises me most is that more of the individuals around us are otherworldly than mortal. My eyes flash to James's.

196

"I know. It's startling at first. To see so many of us in one place."

"Yes," I whisper. I watch them. Some of them are pacing the halls. Some are curled up in a corner looking dejected, their eyes dark and rimmed in shadows. One woman is leaning over the charge nurse station, seeming to scan the computer screens and open files for information. James notices her too.

"She's been here a while. Knows what she's doing." To my dismay, James crosses the room to where the woman is standing. Fearful of being left alone, I follow him.

The woman sees him approaching and immediately backs away from the station, but not before she issues a hiss at James. The sound makes every inch of my skin ripple in repulsion. As I look around more, I discern that most of the otherworldlies are like her. And only a few are like James. I can't pin down the exact difference. It's more of an instinctive feeling. Or a reflex. When I look in the eyes of James, I feel peace. When I look in the eyes of the others, I don't.

I put my hand on James's arm. "You help the dying. I know you do, but how?"

His hazel eyes are clear. "I guide them home. I show them there's nothing to fear."

"You guide them."

If I think very hard, I may remember having a guide. The person I'm thinking of was a woman, but older than the Vigilum who snaked my passage. In fact, her hair was silver. She stood in the distance, almost seeming frozen. At the time I was annoyed that she didn't try to help the other injured. I don't remember much else other than her eyes were profoundly sad. So sad, I looked away from her.

"I did have a guide. I just didn't know that's what she was at the time. I wish I wouldn't have given up so quickly," I say with some shame in my voice.

James shakes his head. "That seems to be happening more often these days. I'm sorry it happened to you."

His words comfort me. The fact that he doesn't blame me for giving away my passage makes me hope that in some future day I can forgive myself too.

James rounds the nurse's station and leans over the attendant's shoulder.

"What are you looking for?" I ask.

James's eyes scan the multiple sources of information in front of him. "Because I don't have an assignment here, I can't feel who is nearest death." He cocks an eyebrow. "I have to do it the old-fashioned way."

After seeming satisfied, he heads down the hall, looking from side to side. I know he's looking for Apollo. "What did you find?" I ask.

"Maybe nothing. But when a patient has had multiple organ failures over the last few days, that's usually not a good sign."

My heart feels heavy. Even though I'm here to help Presley, I'm acutely aware that these are real people who are losing their lives. They have loved ones and friends who are mourning this transition. My feet are lead as I follow James to a room a few doors down from the end of the hall.

Inside, there are several beds. But they don't look like beds. Beds are comfortable. Beds provide rest. These people, hooked to miles of clear tubing and machines—taped with every kind of sensor—look anything but restful. It's more like they are suspended in a silent torture. I hadn't spent much time around hospitals in life, so I don't have much to compare to, but I'm blown away at the sheer amount of equipment it takes to keep these people alive. It crowds and clutters the space to the point I can't imagine how the doctors and nurses keep it all straight.

James pauses and gives me an inquiring look, "You all right?"

"Yes," I lie.

James makes his way down the line seeming to feel something from each patient. After each apparently intuitive "inspection," which he performs entirely with his eyes closed, he opens his eyes and moves on to the next.

Finally we reach the last patient. Though his eyes and face are swollen under the breathing mask, I can tell he can't be older than his early twenties. His face and arms are mottled with angry looking sores. This is the first patient James touches. He runs his fingers over the man's lower arms in a way that looks respectful and kind.

"What's happened to him?"

James shakes his head slightly, inspecting the man further. "My guess would be an overdose."

I look at the man again wondering how James could be right. Even though I'm no doctor, his swollen body and open wounds make him seem like he has some kind of disease. "What are all of the sores?"

James answers me, his voice sober. "Some drugs slow the blood supply, causing the collapse of circulation." He winces. "But more likely, he did a drug that makes users feel like there are bugs crawling under their skin. Sometimes they even hallucinate insects crawling on them. So they pick at themselves, trying to relieve the creeping sensation."

Looking at this man, helpless to move, I wonder if he's still feeling the invisible bugs in his skin. I feel nothing but sympathy for whatever led him to this.

James does another closed-eye inspection. "It won't be long," he says, laying a tender hand on the man's chest. When he turns to me, his eyes are serious. "You're sure you want to do this?"

My insides chill at his expression. "Yes. It's like you said, we'll never know what Apollo does with the passages if we don't see him in action. But are you sure he will come?"

"No. But there's a shadow over this place. Can you feel it? A hopelessness?"

I wasn't surprised at his comment. After all, we were basically standing in the middle of an institution of death. "Is that so out of the ordinary?"

James nods and scans the room again. His shiftiness makes me nervous. "Death doesn't always equate with despair. But this place, it has a dark presence."

Suddenly, the machine monitoring the man's heartbeat begins to chirp in a fast, but irregular rhythm. The hallway is peppered with the sounds of footfall and a team of doctors and nurses pour into the room, barking out orders and working on the man in a practiced form of chaos.

James turns to me, takes me by the shoulders in a hold that makes the surface of my skin buzz like there's a gentle electric current going through it. Before I can protest, he's guiding me backward. He nods in encouragement and bids me to remain silent with his eyes. The current is now running down my spine and the backs of my legs, and I realize I'm fading into the wall.

I'm inside it.

James smoothly follows and soon he's standing beside me. "It's okay," he whispers.

My eyes must be wide as I take in the tangle of wiring and building supports that fill the space between the hospital walls. I can still see the hospital room and the people working on the man, but it's like I'm viewing it through a very thin film. Slightly blurred, yet still discernible. "I've never done this."

"It's an old guide trick. I use it when I don't want Vigilum to know I'm watching them. The material world can shield us from anyone who has the power to see us."

"You said 'can.' Why do I feel like there's a catch?"

"I said 'can' because most beings don't think to look inside walls. Not unless they have a good reason. But if they were to try, they'd see us. So, yes, we can be seen by the dead if someone were to look hard enough. But I'm gambling that nobody will."

At that moment, a man enters the room. He's younger than most guides I've seen but he calmly positions himself at the foot of the bed. He waits as the minutes pass. The doctors try again and again to restore the heart rhythm, but the poor man on the bed looks so fragile. I can't help hoping that he'll be saved somehow. But I know it's like reading a book about the Titanic and hoping the ship won't sink at the end. His guide is here. He's going to die.

James puts a careful arm around my shoulders. "You don't have to watch. I can tell you when it's over."

"No. No, I feel like I should watch. It feels like I give him more dignity if I don't look away."

"You know, even after all this time, even I want to look away sometimes," James says. He gives my arm a squeeze and I wonder how he can do it. Witness the pain over and over again. My respect for him expands.

The movements of the room slow and a couple members of the team peel away. One woman checks the clock on the wall. "I'm calling it," she says. "Time of death, 3:04."

I don't know how I expect it to look when a spirit leaves a body. I don't remember leaving mine exactly. All I remember was I was driving and then I wasn't. I became a bystander to the scene. I have no memory of the transition—if there was one. So when the last nurse covers the body with a sheet, and shuts down the monitors like she's locking up for the night, I'm dismayed. I don't see any luminous figure ascend from the body. No shaft of light. Nothing.

Confused, I turn to James and he quietly motions with his chin for me to look again. When I turn back this time, I see the man standing off to the side of his bed looking over his lifeless shell. His new form looks younger and healthy, and his blonde hair is shorter and has a rich sheen that his mortal hair lacked. But for all of the renewal his spirit now reflects, his expression is as pained as his old body.

"It finally happened. I finally pushed it too far," he says. He looks around the room, this time addressing the guide. "Who are you?"

"A friend. I'm here to help." His face is kind.

The man laughs shortly. A bitter laugh. "A friend. Right." He motions around the room with a lazy gesture. "I don't see any of my real friends here. Not even my mom." He shakes his head like he can't believe it. "I guess I can't blame them though. Not after everything I put them through."

"It's all over now," the guide says, taking a step toward the man. "It's time to move on. I can help you with what comes next. Come with me."

I like the guide immediately. His face is warm and his voice soothing. Unlike the other dead who roam these halls, he carries a sense of dignified purpose. I envy him. He extends his hand and just as the skeptical man's face begins to soften, they are interrupted.

By Apollo.

He enters the room with a smile on his face that could almost be friendly. I grasp James's hand. Now that the moment has come, I doubt the wisdom of our plan. And even though James explained that Apollo would most likely not see us through the shield of the wall, I feel naked and exposed. James squeezes my hand reassuringly.

"You're excused." Apollo's voice is sunny and casual as he addresses the guide.

But the guide doesn't move from his spot. "You can't keep doing this. This man is my charge."

Apollo raises his eyebrows and leans his walking staff against his hip. The movement is swift and delicate like he's done it a thousand times. Then he removes two black leather gloves and tucks them into an inner pocket of his charcoal jacket. "Not anymore. As I said, you're excused."

Almost imperceptibly, Apollo's eyes begin to darken, like a spot of black ink is bleeding into his irises, spreading like liquid night until no icy blue remains.

The guide suddenly hunches over, holding an arm across his stomach and steadying himself against the safety rails of the bed.

"What are you doing to him?" The man moves forward to help the struggling guide, but Apollo smirks and shakes his head in a tight, controlled motion.

"Trust me," Apollo says. "He's of no use to you."

Whatever power Apollo exerts over the guide must dissipate because the guide straightens, slows his breath, and without looking back at his charge even once, makes for the doorway. As he steps through it though, he turns back to Apollo. "Someone will stop you. Eventually."

Apollo's face morphs into mocking sympathy. "I'm sure you're right." The door slams, startling both James and me. Too late, I cover my mouth to stifle the whimper of fear. James stares at me, a finger over his lips and urgency burning in his eyes. He shakes his head slowly.

Message received.

Apollo approaches the man like nothing ever happened. "It's good to be bad sometimes, isn't it?" He says it like it's a private joke between the two.

Surprisingly, the man gives a laugh in return. This makes Apollo nod and smile in a way that turns my stomach. It's been less than sixty seconds, and he already has this guy eating out of the palm of his hand.

Apollo crosses his arms casually and leans into the bed like there's not a corpse under the sheet. "Tell me, Seth. What is it you really want?"

At first, I'm surprised that he knows his name, but then realize I shouldn't be. There's plenty of information to be had around a hospital if one is invisible to the living.

Seth shrugs, his smile fading. "I just wanted to play music, man. To hear the people calling my name. I got close a couple of times. But I got sick, you know?"

It amazes me that Seth has the gall to lie about how he died. How much he must want to impress Apollo.

Apollo is nodding his head and smiling again. "Ah, yes. Nothing quite like the thrill of thousands of people screaming just because you walked in the room." There's a gleam of understanding in his eyes that pulls Seth in even further.

"Yeah, man. It's crazy." He says it like he's experienced it even though I know he hasn't. At least not firsthand.

Apollo's voice is a whisper now and it chills my bones. "I want to help you, Seth. I want to give you everything you've ever wished for."

Apollo's eyes bleed to black again and my stomach tightens. Seth is smiling through the tears, his eyes gazing around the room like he's staring into a distance that doesn't exist within the confines of the space.

"Where did all these people come from?" Seth says, amazement dripping from his voice.

Apollo rises and takes a step closer, gesturing with his arm in a wide arch. "They're all here for you. They want to hear you play your music."

James looks at me, shock in his features. I want so badly to explain that I know what Apollo is doing to Seth, because he did it to me. He is creating a dreamscape that doesn't exist. Whatever he thinks will manipulate the victim the most. He probably gave me the vision of wealth and opulence to intimidate me. Maybe somehow he knew I grew up in a trailer in the Nevada desert.

He obviously knows exactly what will influence Seth.

Admiration. Glory. Power.

"Listen to them, Seth. They can't get enough of you," Apollo says, zeal in his voice.

Seth covers his ears, laughing. "It's so loud!" he shouts. "I can't believe they're all here for me."

Apollo reaches out and takes him by the shoulder, shaking Seth's body in a chummy way. "Give them what they want, my friend. They'll be here every night if you let me give it all to you. Will you let me?"

Seth is still covering his ears, but he's smiling and nodding his head. "Of course! Yeah. This is what I've always wanted."

"No!" I want to scream, lunging myself toward Seth. But before the sound even escapes my lips, James has his hand over my mouth, holding my body still with a strong arm around my waist.

"I know you want to help him," James whispers in my ear. "But right now is *not* the time."

James is right. Neither of us are any match against Apollo. My teeth grind together thinking of how he tortured Seth's guide.

"Then it's yours," Apollo continues, eyes vibrant and greedy. "I only require one thing."

"The crowd! It's too loud, bro!"

Apollo steps nearer to the man. It's a quick, greedy step and if Seth were in his right frame of mind, he might be scared by it. But he's not in his right frame of mind. And when Apollo puts his mouth to Seth's ear and whispers words I can't hear, Seth nods and says, "Yes. It's yours. Take it."

Apollo slowly backs away, just a step, and the expression on his face can only be described as pleasure. It reminds me of my dad. Of when he'd shower after work, plant himself in his chair to light a cigarette, and then take that first deep drag. The soothing satisfaction, the relaxed smile. The relief.

Effortlessly, Apollo takes up his staff, which was leaning against the bed. With a flick of his thumb, the polished ebony horn flips open as if it were on a hinge. He takes the horn in his hand like a cup and disconnects it from the staff, extending it toward Seth who is still reveling in the ecstasy of faux admiration.

Seth doesn't notice when a fine gold dust begins to slowly curl out from his mouth and nostrils. Apollo motions with his slender fingers, coaxing the shimmering smoke toward the horn with the grace of a dancer. The passage floats in the air between them, seeming to be a living thing that responds to Apollo's beckoning gestures. He captures the current of gold like a magician performing a vanishing handkerchief trick and manipulates it into the horn. When every bit of dust is swallowed up, he replaces the horn on top of the staff. Tucking the staff under one arm and with a few quick motions, he puts his gloves back on, straightens his coat, and walks out leaving Seth alone.

James and I look to each other and his face mirrors what I feel. Astonishment. Complete horrified astonishment. "He *can* store passages," I say.

We turn our attention back to Seth. He must be coming out of the dreamscape because his face is now fallen and he looks like he's about to be sick. His eyes bounce around the room, taking in the only company—near-death patients of the ICU. "Hello?" His voice is wobbly. "Hello?" he says again, but this time his voice is a high, strained whisper. Panicked. He runs from the room and we hear him continue to call out. He doesn't even know his betrayer's name and that angers me.

"Apollo just wants the power." James interrupts my thoughts but his statement echoes my own conclusion. "If he really wanted to help the deserving . . . if he really were 'benevolent,' he wouldn't have interfered with Seth's crossing in the first place. He's in it for the passages and the power they give him."

"When I first went to him for help, he told me he doesn't have access to a lot of passages. He made it sound like he dealt with a limited number that had an expiration date."

James gives a short, disgusted laugh. "He lies. He's managed to create some kind of powerful artifact—the horn. Passages, as far as I've ever known, were only kept within the holder until the holders chose to use them." He shakes his head. "But he's figured out some kind of alternate containment. Unbelievable."

"And who knows how many he's got in there?" I say.

"Exactly. You saw how many Vigilum there are within this hospital alone. Imagine the possibilities if he's been working like this for . . . centuries? Millennia?" James phases through the wall and back into the ICU room, looking exhausted.

I follow him.

"I need you to think, Erin. Has Apollo ever told you his name?"

I sift through my interactions with him to the best of my memory, which in this case is pretty sharp. Terrifying experiences tend to stick with you. "No. He never did. When I asked him directly, he deflected by saying he's known by many names. But I did summon him by his name."

James pauses, seeming to digest what I told him. "But he made a point to use his name with Presley. Even asking her specifically to tell me."

"So?" I say, not following.

"So that tells me he prefers to remain anonymous with a certain demographic." James's jaw tightens.

"What are you saying?"

Apollo doesn't want his Vigilum followers or seekers to know that in many cases, he's the one who caused their misery. It would cut his power off at the knees. Can you think of the consequences for him if he were to be exposed?"

"How do you know that Vigilum don't already know that he steals passages? I mean, if we are right and he's done it thousands of times, then wouldn't there be whole legions of people who know his secret?"

James blinks and looks at me sideways. "You of all people should know how powerful his guises are. How do we know that he doesn't cloak his identity from his victims? Something like that would be nothing to him."

"True. So, to the people he offers passage to, which now we know he probably only does if they can give him something he wants, he appears as the benevolent Lord Apollo."

"But to his victims," James picks up where I left off, "he could appear as . . . anyone."

"Sly," I say, shaking my head in disgust.

"Very sly."

"The sick thing is the same people he victimizes will likely look to him for help later. Looking to the very person who destroyed them, to save them." My teeth are set on edge from the thought. "If only there were a way to expose him, like you said."

"Yes," James says. "It would take a Vigilum to do it." He looks at me meaningfully and I shrink back.

"I don't have any power against him. Why couldn't a guide bring him down? Someone like you?"

James raises an eyebrow. "Because Vigilum are distrustful of guides. We are viewed as enemies. Even if I could get anyone to listen, the progress would be slow going and likely ineffectual." He runs a hand down his face, resting it over his mouth for a couple moments before letting it fall off his chin. "What we're talking about here—exposing him for what he really is to his followers? That would have to be an inside job. And you're the only friend I have on the inside."

He gives me a sad smile. One that seems to communicate he doesn't think there's much hope even if I agreed.

"James, it's not like I'm some überpopular Vigilum that knows everybody. In case you haven't noticed, we're kind of a bunch of loners. We're competing for passages. There's no point in making friends." I curse and I notice James narrow his eyes at me. "I wouldn't even know where to start."

"If you want to have any hope of helping the one friend you do have, you'd better start somewhere."

Chapter Forty-Six

Good-bye, Again

(James)

Today, Landon will die.

Again.

In just hours. Already, the familiar tingle that a death is imminent, feathers up and down my spine. The wheels are in motion.

All I can think about is how cruel it is.

For Landon.

And Presley.

I wonder how she will survive it. All that keeps her moving now is the hope that, at least, Landon will be saved.

"It's not fair," I say to Chase. "Sometimes things are just *not* fair." We sit together at the kitchen table. He's finishing up dinner while Gayle bustles at the sink, rinsing dishes. He looks up from his plate of spaghetti and studies me. He doesn't have the words to ask, but I know my comment has him curious. His large eyes are full of questions, so I afford him the dignity of an explanation.

"You see, someone I care very deeply for is going away. And I wish he didn't have to leave."

Chase blinks and ponders me longer than usual. It's so easy to smile when I'm with him that he must wonder why my smile is absent today. Eventually though, he goes back to his spaghetti, slurping noodles and making a marinara mess. I hand him a napkin for the sauce on his chin.

Gayle calls over her shoulder, "More noodles, kiddo?"

Chase says, "No," instead licking the sauce from his plate, then hightailing it up the stairs. In his room, he pulls me to the television.

"Video," he says.

"How about Memory first?" I suggest, pulling his Disney Memory game from the shelf above the TV.

Ever the cheater at this game, and always the winner, he seems happy to oblige. We sit at his table and spread the pieces out upside down.

On his turn, Chase flips three pieces up and, jokingly, I call him out for cheating. He smiles slyly and places a match on his side of the table.

As we continue to flip pieces, I contemplate what I could've done differently these last several months. If only I could've convinced Landon to take his passage before. If he wasn't so stubborn. Had he only listened to me, then he would have never met Presley.

Until Landon, my role as a guide had been pretty cut and dry. Helping people make the natural transition from one stage of life to another has always carried with it meaningful satisfaction. Supporting those in their time of greatest need fills me. But not this time. There will be no fulfillment in guiding Landon again.

I spent eight months with him when he was a spirit. More than enough time to form protective and almost fatherly feelings for him. And I've been privileged to watch him live the last few months.

I don't want him to die.

The tingle in my spine grows stronger and stretches its fingers through my back and into my core, where it begins tugging—a guide's beckoning that their services will soon be needed. But I have no desire to witness the events leading up to Landon's death. Events I have no power to change. I will arrive in time to guide him, but not before.

Chase and I finish our game and he slides all of the pieces back into their box with one swoop of his arm. Apparently, our game of Memory has taken his mind off of television, because he retrieves his tracing book and dry erase markers from his cubbies.

With difficulty, I swallow around the lump that has formed in my throat. What started as a favor to Presley has become one of the most treasured periods of my life. Spending time with someone as unjaded and innocent as Chase has changed me. His purity has carved me out and left me raw. I didn't intend to form such a deep attachment, but to know this boy is to love him. What surprises me even more is the affection he has developed for me. I will miss him. I hate to think of how he will miss me.

I wish I had more time. To leave Presley and Chase completely vulnerable to Apollo's whims seems the worst sort of treachery. Parting may be easier if Erin hadn't essentially gone missing. I've not heard anything from her since she left in search of more information about Apollo. I can only hope that she's still trying and hasn't let her fear get the best of her. Still, how can I justify leaving Presley and Chase unprotected?

Because I am not a protector of the living. That was never meant to be my role. The pull inside me sickeningly reminds of that, and I know my time with Chase is nearly up.

"Chase," I say. "Will you put the marker down for a bit?"

He finishes a row of J's and replaces the cap on his purple marker, looking at me expectantly.

"I need to tell you something, kiddo."

He smiles and hums contentedly as he rocks back and forth in his chair. My chest tightens and I take a moment to steady myself. Surely he's not expecting to hear what I must say.

"I have to go, Chase. Pretty soon I have to leave your house."

Chase grabs my wrist as if to keep me here.

Other than my field trip to the hospital with Erin, I've spent nearly every minute of Chase's waking hours with him. His sleeping hours as well, though he doesn't know that. I give myself a moment then attempt to clear the emotion from my throat. I have to make Chase understand that I'm not just leaving for a while.

That this is good-bye forever.

"I feel sad, Chase. Because I have to leave your house for a long time. I won't be able to watch *Yo Gabba Gabba!* with you anymore. Or put puzzles together. I can't be here when you get home from school anymore, buddy."

Chase's grip on my wrist tightens and a crease forms between his brows. My eyes sting, and with my free hand, I swipe at the hot tears that trickle down my cheeks.

Unexpectedly, he releases my wrist and crosses the room to his dresser. He returns with his iPad. Inside his assistive communication app, he starts scrolling through the icons. Since Apollo's visit, Chase has been more motivated to communicate with his iPad.

He pulls up the first picture. It's a question mark with the word "when" beneath it. Scrolling down to the pronoun row, his eyes scan the options, then he taps the "you" icon. Next, he finds the action row and presses on a green arrow that is the symbol for "go." And last, he presses the conversation bubble that strings his words together in a sentence. In a rote voice, the iPad says, "When you go."

"I have to leave right now, Chase. James has to go right now." I regret waiting until the last minute to tell him this. I could've prepared him the last several days. I considered it, but ultimately decided it would be unkind to worry him prematurely. Now, I believe I made the wrong call.

"No," Chase says. Frantically he taps at his iPad again. He holds it up so I can see and taps the conversation bubble. "I like you," the iPad recites.

I let my head fall into my hands. Through blurry eyes, I make myself look at him. "I like you too, Chase. I don't *want* to go. I want to stay here with you. But I have to go."

Now it's Chase wiping tears. His bottom lip trembles as he scrolls through his iPad once more. "Please," his iPad says.

I take Chase's hands in mine and help him to stand. Then I pull him into me and wrap my arms around him. He rests his head on my shoulder and returns my embrace. As I speak, I cradle the back of his head in my hand.

In his ear, I say, "I love you, buddy. I have loved every single minute with you. Do you know how smart you are? Don't ever let anyone tell you differently.

"Thank you for helping me become a better man. I feel so lucky to be your friend."

Chase trembles in my arms and I realize he's sobbing. But he's trying to be discrete because he's still quiet.

"Be good for your mama and Presley. You stay strong, okay?"

I release him then, take a step back, and soak in one last look of this boy who could be my own. Then phase from his room to Vikingsholm Castle.

Chapter Forty-Seven

VIKINGSHOLM

(PRESLEY)

Vikingsholm is magical. The perfect mix of castle and cottage, it lies hidden in a forest of pine trees and overlooks the lake. The only way to access it is by boat ride to Emerald Bay, or by a steep and narrow path that winds from the highway above and down the mountain behind the estate. It's private, exclusive, and enchanting.

Under different circumstances, I might have let myself get caught up in the dreaminess of this place.

Tonight though, my only focus is keeping Landon alive. In just hours, his life will be safe and his future secure. Then I will tell him it's over between us.

Even now, Apollo could be lurking. If he were to discover that Landon has *the sight*, he would be better off dead. I won't let that happen.

In the library, I sip on a glass of sparkling cider. It's one of thirty-eight rooms in this place, looks out over the bay, and is beautifully decorated with Scandinavian antiques and artwork. The sound of champagne glasses tinkling and the revelry among party guests almost distract me from the reason I'm here.

From across the room, I spot Landon and Reese, both dressed in fitted black tuxes, shaking hands and chatting with people who are also dressed to the nines. They're quite the duo with their matching dark hair, defined features, and broad shoulders.

A twinge of something pulls at my heart. I feel badly that I let Reese down. At the same time, I'm relieved that he won't be on Apollo's radar. The further he stays away, the safer he is.

Landon catches me staring and a wide smile breaks across his face. He whispers something into the ear of an older man next to him, then excuses himself from the group and makes his way over to me.

"Look at you," he says, taking me in from my head to my silver strappy heels. "Yellow is your color. Do you know that?"

Even with the weight of this evening's agenda monopolizing my thoughts, I feel my cheeks flame under his scrutiny. He lifts my hand and twirls me around. My gown is fitted on top, but from the waist down it's light and billows out as I turn.

I relish the warmth of his hand and soak him in as his lips touch mine, light as a feather.

Against my lips he whispers, "By far the most beautiful girl here."

Giggling, I reply, "Yeah, because everyone here is old."

"No." His eyes are serious, deep. "You take my breath away, Presley. I was such an idiot for fighting it for so long." He pulls me in close and whispers in my ear, "All I want now is to make up for lost time."

And for just this moment, I immerse myself in his love. What we have isn't some teenage infatuation. It's enduring and selfless. I let it wash over and warm me.

One last time.

"I love you, Landon Blackwood."

He takes a step back and studies me with eyes the color of the lake. They glint mischievously, matching the crooked grin on his face.

"Dance with me," he says, grabbing both my hands and leading me to the living room, which tonight doubles as a dance floor. He takes me into his arms and looking down into my eyes says, "I love you too."

I wrap my arms around his neck and rest my cheek against his chest. His hands rest on my lower back as we rock back and forth for several unspoken moments.

"This is one of my favorite places," he tells me.

"Mmmm," I say. "It's easy to see why. I feel like I've been transported back in time right in the middle of a fairy tale."

"In a castle, with your prince . . .""

"Something like that," I say. The beat of his heart pulses against my cheek and I smile knowing that after tonight, it will continue to beat.

"Lora Knight, the lady that built this place, actually spent a ton of time in Europe visiting old castles so that everything here would be totally authentic."

"It shows," I say.

He motions with his head out the front window. "See that little island?"

I nod.

"It's the only island on the lake. Fannette Island. And that tower? She had that built just so she could take guests out there for tea parties."

"Really?"

"Chick was crazy rich. She bought this whole bay. Why not build a place on your very own island just for tea?" Landon pretends to sip from a cup, holding his pinkie finger just so.

I can't help but laugh. "What's that island used for now?" I ask.

"It's my personal hideout," he says, winking.

"Right. Your own little tower. Must be nice."

"It's my thinking spot," he says seriously. "The skiing, my training schedule, sponsors. Sometimes I just need to be where I know no one will come looking. In the summer, people swim out there all the time. But no sane person goes out there in the winter. Luckily, sanity's not my strength—hence my very own thinking tower."

"Your secret's out. Now I'll always know where to find you." I say that without thinking and it nearly knocks the air from my lungs. I've grown so used to picturing a future with Landon that it's too easy to slip up.

"I will always want *you* to find me," he says, his voice husky.

Despair and anger mix to form a toxic blend in my chest. Tonight I lose Landon and give myself to Apollo. I try to disguise the emotions that snake through my body, but I've never had the best poker face.

"Babe, what's the matter?" Landon asks, concern painted over his features.

"Nothing," I say through a forced smile, brushing a few traitorous tears from my face.

Landon's eyebrows push down and his mouth forms a hard line. I cringe as I notice the muscles in his jaw tighten.

"It's not *nothing*, Presley. You've been off the last several days." His voice is kind but serious. "I feel like there's something you're not telling me." With his thumbs he wipes new tears from my cheeks.

I don't mean to, but I laugh a mirthless laugh and shake my head. "Please, Landon. I swear I'm okay. Can we just dance?"

He says nothing, but pulls me to him and we rock slowly. I let the warmth of his body envelope me and memorize what it feels like to be wrapped in his embrace.

It's the last time he will hold me like this. Our first dance—our last.

When the song is over, I excuse myself to the powder room. I'm grateful that the room is empty and take a moment to steady my breathing. When I return to the party it's quite a bit more crowded, new guests streaming in.

Landon's busy now at the entrance, greeting the new arrivals, Frank at his side taking coats and purses. I wait until Landon notices me and raise my hand in a timid wave. He winks at me and I take a deep breath, relieved that he doesn't seem upset.

Violet, looking stunning in a little red number, bustles around the silent auction table and waves me over. After gushing over my dress and complimenting me on my hair, she gives me a list with detailed instructions and tells me she'll be around if I have any questions. She's almost back to the Violet from before. Too bad we won't be able to pick up where we left off. I'll miss her too.

"You've got this," she tells me, then hustles from the table and out of the room.

I study the list for a moment, familiarizing myself with silent auction do's and don'ts. It's pretty straightforward, so I take advantage of the moments that I'm not assisting bidders to keep track of Landon. He's still near the entrance, visiting with a small group of guests.

"Presley," a voice calls from behind. Reese ambles towards the table. "We're partners tonight," he says through a smile.

"Partners?"

"Afton puts me at the silent auction table every year." He rolls his eyes then finger quotes. "She says my *charisma* influences the guests to bid higher."

"That makes perfect sense," and I can't help but smile at him. "I can't imagine why she put *me* here then."

Reese's eyes turn serious. "How do you do it?" he asks.

"What?" I laugh nervously.

"How do you manage to be the most striking person in the room, in *any* room, and not know it?"

"Whatever," I say and punch playfully at his arm, but my cheeks flame. I wasn't expecting him to act like this after the last couple weeks of avoidance.

There's a break in the music and over the speakers the DJ says, "This one's by request. A beautiful song for a beautiful girl."

Guitar chords, soulful and familiar, fill the room. It's the opening to my favorite Coldplay song.

"You promised me a dance," Reese says, offering his hand to me.

"Yellow," I say.

Reese smiles.

"Wait," I say. "Did you ask them to play this?"

"Perfect dress. Perfect girl. Perfect song," he says, his voice low and velvety. Then he places a gentle hand on my back and guides me to the dance floor.

I glance nervously at Landon. Thankfully he's still engrossed in conversation. I did promise Reese a dance, but things have changed between Landon and me since then, and I don't want to risk either boy getting the wrong idea.

I think it's too late.

He twirls me away then back into him, running his hand up the bare skin of my back. It doesn't feel right.

"What's this?" Landon has left his spot near the entrance and now stands just feet from us on the dance floor, his face all serious lines, eyes narrow and questioning. His hands are shoved into his pockets, and I can tell by his posture that he's holding back.

Reese rolls his eyes, but instead of letting me go, leads me away from Landon. He calls over his shoulder, "This is me and Presley dancing, bro. We're just dancing."

Landon follows. "It didn't look like just dancing."

The couples around us are starting to stare. "C'mon, you guys. This is stupid." I shrug out of Reese's arms and leave the dance floor, hoping they will follow.

They don't. So I march back onto the floor and try to usher them away from the guests, but both boys remain firmly planted.

"So what? You have exclusive rights to Presley now?" Reese challenges.

Landon lets out a disgusted laugh. "She's my girlfriend, Reese. I don't care if you dance with her, but that was more than dancing. I saw the way you touched her. The way you've been looking at her all night."

"You guys," I say, wedging myself in the middle of them. The tension between the two of them is charged. "Please don't fight," I say, trying to control the emotion in my voice. "There's no issue here. This is stupid."

"I'll tell you what's stupid," Reese seethes. "Throwing a fit unless everything goes your way."

"What's that supposed to mean?" Landon spits.

"Forget it," Reese says, shaking his head. He starts to leave the dance floor when Landon catches his arm and yanks him back.

"Where's all this coming from?" Landon asks. "What is your problem?"

"Okay. You really want it?" Reese says, yanking free from Landon's grip.

Landon opens his arms and cocks his head. "Bring it."

"Reese, please." I take his arm and try to pull him from the floor, but he shrugs away from me. "Landon, c'mon. Stop it," I plead. "You guys are making people uncomfortable." I gesture to the increasing number of guests who've either stopped dancing to gawk, or who keep glancing this way, but are trying to be inconspicuous.

"Here it is," Reese says. "You're a spoiled little rich boy, who melts down unless he gets everything he wants. You don't have to work for anything you have. It's all just handed to you on a silver platter."

Landon rolls his eyes. "I work my tail off seven days a—"

Reese holds his hand up and cuts Landon off. "I wasn't done. You're headed to the Olympics, have a free ride to any school of your choice, and stand to inherit a multi-million dollar business."

"So you all of a sudden hate me because my family has money? And because I'm going to the Olympics?"

"I don't hate *you*. I hate that you have to have *everything* or you throw a temper tantrum. Why can't you let me have this one thing?" Reese takes my shoulder and moves me to his side.

I want to cry. *Oh, Reese.*

"She chose me," Landon says, matter of fact.

"No. She chose me *first* and you couldn't stomach it. You had a girlfriend. You saw that Presley and I were hanging out, and you couldn't stand that I had something you didn't. It's been that way our whole lives. Only this time, I'm actually saying something about it."

Landon's eyes move to mine, which are overflowing with tears. "Is this why you've been so off this week?" A dawn of recognition spreads across Landon's face. "You're into Reese and you've been hiding it from me. That's why you've been acting so weird."

"No," I whisper. "I'm not into Reese."

Reese blinks. Shakes his head and walks away. I feel horrible. I know what I said sounded worse than I meant it. Another night, I'd follow him to explain, but I can't leave Landon right now. I turn to him.

"I can't believe you would think that," I say.

"It's not what I *think*, Presley. It's what I *saw*. All cozied up to him, his hands all over you. Even my dad asked what was going on between you two."

"Landon, you can't actually believe I'm choosing Reese over you. It's you. I'm with *you*." Tears stream down my face and I let them. I grab his arms and try to pull him to me but he steps back and pries my hands from him.

"I don't know what to believe right now," he says flatly. "You've clearly been hiding something from me, and I can't help but believe it's this. You obviously still have feelings for Reese. I just wish you would've told me sooner." Then he shakes his head, turns his back to me, and leaves me standing on the dance floor.

I run after him as he goes out the front door, but someone grabs my arm. It's Violet, and she doesn't look nearly as upset as I would expect her to. "Let them go," she says. "I know I told you these two never fight, but they do. Just give them some time to cool off."

Time. If only. It's less than an hour to Landon's death time and he's gone.

I start to protest, but Afton Blackwood has woven herself through the tangle of guests and now stands between me and the exit.

"What's up with those two?" she asks. I feel my face and neck get hot, and I look out the window, at the ceiling, anywhere to avoid meeting her eyes. "No time to worry about it now," she tsks. "If they're going to act like punks, I'd rather them not be here anyway. I'm just so embarrassed. And now we're down two people."

Violet places a reassuring hand on her mom's shoulder, then takes the clipboard from her hands. "They're pretty worthless in the help department anyway," she says, scanning the paper on the clipboard. "Here, I can run the silent auction solo. Presley, I need you at the entrance. We'll have some stragglers showing up late and someone needs to be there to greet them."

"There," Violet says, handing the clipboard back to Afton. "Problem solved. Go do what you do, Mom. We've got this."

Afton plants a quick kiss on Vi's cheek and shoots me an appreciative look. "Thanks, girls. I've got to run."

With Violet distracted at the silent auction table, I weave my way towards the entrance, but instead of stopping to greet guests, I bolt straight through. I know Landon arrived by boat, so I run to the beach, hoping to find him there.

Relief mixed with anxiety fills me up when I spot Landon inside his family's vintage boat, messing with the starter. The engine spurts and spits, but won't turn over.

"Landon!" I call. "Landon, wait!" I kick my heels off, bundle my dress above my knees, and struggle to run through the cool sand. "Wait!" I yell again, waving my arm.

I'm only feet away. He just needs to stop this foolishness and listen to me. "Stop, please." I send up a silent prayer of gratitude that his boat is giving him trouble.

"I trusted you, Presley," he calls. "I knew you had a thing for Reese before us, but you told me that was over."

"You can trust me. I swear. It is over with Reese. I'm with you!"

For a moment he stops trying to start the engine and rests his arms on the steering wheel, letting his head hang between them. "I was letting myself fall hard for you." He shakes his head. "So hard."

It feels sick and wrong to tell him how much I love him when in just minutes, I will have to leave him. But right now, it's all I can do to prevent his death.

"I fell hard for you too. Please just stop," I beg.

"We can talk about it later," he says. "Right now, I just need to be alone." He tries the starter one more time and the engine turns over. Without giving me another look, he backs up and turns the boat around, leaving nothing but a white wake in the water behind him.

I run to the boat tied down next to where Landon's was docked. No keys. I try boat after boat, but every ignition is empty. I squint into the waning sun to see if I can still spot Landon. He's docking his boat at Fannette Island. Good. At least I know where he is. But there's no way for me to get there without a boat. My heart picks up pace, reminding me that I can't just let the minutes count down to his death.

My board. It's on my car in the parking lot at the top of the mountain. It's all I've got. I ditch my shoes in the sand and run barefoot to the courtyard where guests arrived earlier via golf cart. Two carts are parked there. Empty, with keys hanging from the ignition.

Leaping into the cart, I crank the key, shove it in reverse, and back out of the driveway. The cart travels up the forested path faster than I could ever run, but I'm conscious of every second that ticks by.

At the top, I run to my car and unfasten my board from the rack. My duffle with my gear and wetsuit lay inside on the back seat, but I don't have my keys to unlock the car. And even if I did, I can't afford the time it would take to change. With my board and paddle balanced precariously in the back of the golf cart, I press the gas pedal to the floor. Speeding down the curvy, narrow path, I just keep praying that I'm not too late.

At the beach, I hurl my board in the water, climb on, and thrust my paddle in the lake. My skirt is instantly drenched, sticking to my legs. The wind kicks up whitecaps, making it hard to balance.

I fight the waves with my paddle, but the wind is so strong. My chest heaves and my shoulders burn but even with the physical exertion, I'm freezing without my wetsuit. In the distance, beyond the mountains, angry gray clouds churn, illuminated sporadically by jagged flashes of light.

The island isn't that far, but I've been paddling forever and it doesn't seem like I'm making progress.

I can't quit now though. I won't.

But my hands are frozen; my fingers ache and I'm struggling to keep my grip on the paddle. "Don't quit!" I scream into the wind.

My hands have gone from frozen to numb. A rogue wave slaps against me, almost knocking me off the board. In the effort to keep my balance, I drop the paddle and the wind carries it out of reach. I'll never make it in time.

Chapter
Forty-Eight

REGRET

(LANDON)

I climb the steps to the teahouse tower, which is nothing more than a stone stairway leading to four crumbling walls and a corner fireplace on the upper level. The roof is gone, so there's an open view to the sky, which today is an unsettling shade of green. Lightning arcs through heavy black clouds, but the storm must be far away because the sound of thunder doesn't follow.

While this place usually brings me peace, I feel nothing but guilt. I screwed up tonight. I wasn't upset with Presley. I was unjustifiably jealous. The way Reese held her. Touched her.

I snapped. And there's no excuse. I only hope she will forgive me. I hope Reese will too. He's my best friend and I didn't even contemplate his feelings when I followed my heart and asked Presley to give us a chance. It was obvious how he felt about her, and I ignored it.

When I make it to the top, I lean into the frame of what used to be a window. It looks back at Vikingsholm. In the fading twilight, lights glow from the house, and the remnants of music and laughter float across the wind.

I should be there. I should be there right now, down on my knees asking for Presley's forgiveness. I know that she loves me. The look on her face as I accused her of loving Reese will haunt me forever. I can tell her that I'm sorry but that image will never leave me.

I turn from the window and jog down the staircase. I'm going to find Presley and beg her to give me another chance. What can I say to her that will fix this? I'm torn from my thoughts by a panicked scream.

I jump down the last few stairs. Clearing the bottom step, I lunge myself from the old building and onto the rocky ground.

My breath stops. Presley wavers precariously on a paddleboard, struggling to pull her paddle through the water. A wave pummels her and though she manages to keep her balance, she drops the paddle.

"Get low!" I yell. "Just try and sit down. I'm coming to get you!" I pick my way down the boulder-strewn path to the beach where my boat is tied.

The wind is ice and even in my tux jacket, I shiver. I swear at myself, imagining how frozen Presley must be in her thin gown.

I make it to the boat and hurdle myself inside.

"Landon!" she screams. The wind is too strong and knocks her from her board into the lake.

"Presley!" I shout. "Hold on, I'm coming! Hold on, baby!"

I watch in horror as she struggles to keep her head above water, clawing at the board. I jam the starter but the engine won't catch. I curse myself for convincing my dad to bring this boat tonight. He tried to tell me it wasn't ready.

"Say something, Presley. I need to know you're still with me. Say something, baby!"

The silence that follows is deafening.

Chapter Forty-Nine

Blindside

(Presley)

It's not the brain-cracking cold of the water that scares me, it's that no matter how hard I try, my lungs will not pull air in and out the way I'm telling them to. It's like my ribs have instituted some kind of lockdown and will only allow the tiniest gasps to come and go. They aren't enough.

And my hands, already stiff and numb from the spray and the wind, claw for the edge of the paddleboard. I find purchase, but the freezing waves are hitting me in the face and jerking the board from my grasp. Each time I kick up to grab the board, I'm weaker. Less and less of my body leaves the water each time, making a mental alarm scream warnings that I'm in more trouble than I thought.

Over the sound of the water and my own hammering heart, Landon's calling out instructions to hold on. That he's coming. But I don't hear the motor and I'm terrified he'll try to swim to me. He can't. He just can't. Not after everything I've been through to keep him safe.

I kick and kick, trying to gain enough height to throw my torso over the board. But my limbs are sluggish and increasingly unresponsive, like the blood in my veins has congealed. With a great clumsy kick, I manage to get my upper chest onto the board and hold on to the other side, but the balance is tricky. The board wants to flip over and I don't have the coordination and sensation to keep it steady.

I close my eyes and pray, even though I'm not the praying type. "Please," I whisper. "Please."

I open my eyes and James is standing ankle deep in the waves. The water splashes at his pants, soaking him to the knee. His face is the image of complete distress. Choking out my name, he immediately kneels to pull me up, but when our hands stretch to make contact, they slide past each other like two magnets with opposite polarity. We try again, but James stops just inches from my fingers. The tendons and veins in his arms and hands stand out against his effort, but he can't get to me.

My hands slip down the board a few more inches, submerging my body further. The muscles in my back contract with painful, spine rattling tremors. My teeth clatter, preventing me from speaking clearly, but I try, "James, what's happening?"

He holds his helpless hands in front of him and cries like a child. "I can't help you."

I'm crying because he's crying and because I'm confused and terrified at what he's saying. "I don't understand. James, please. Please."

Tears are streaming down James's face and his voice is strangled, "The anchor I told you about. The slash in time that marks the moment Landon died . . . it's here. It's going to happen."

"I know," I cry. "You can't let me fail, James! I tried so hard. I was so close to saving him. There has to be enough time left." James is sobbing and clamping his hand over his mouth. I've never seen him this undone and it makes any hope I had for Landon and me flicker and then wink out. Extinguish into blackness.

"Landon is safe." James coughs out another sob, his eyes bulging and still streaming with tears. "He's safe."

Landon is safe. I believe James. But I still don't understand why he's so upset. Why he can't just reach out and pull me up. My mind feels like a thick fog is rolling in, smothering my thoughts, robbing me of speech.

I stop kicking because kicking and thinking at the same time are too much. Holding on to the board is too much. Breathing is too much. I think I'm still holding on, but it's hard to know for sure.

"I'm *your* guide now, Presley. The death will be yours, not Landon's. I'm here to take you on," James's voice calls through the fog.

The words splinter inside my skull. Understanding snaps like a finely spun string of glass—clear and true. Clearer than anything else in my mind.

It's my time to die. Somehow I have taken Landon's place and James is here to guide me. This is what James is trying to tell me. I don't want to believe it.

My words manage to escape in a tremulous string, "How . . . do you know?"

"I feel it, Presley. The pull. It's clear. The compass inside me points to you now. Not Landon. It's you, sweetheart. I'm so sorry. It's you."

I believe him. As awful as the words are, they feel true. I know they are true. If guides are given a signal to know who they must guide, maybe the dying are also given a kind of sign to know when it's their time. Because as much as I don't want it to be my time, I feel it coming for me.

"I'm tired," I say. I want to close my eyes, but James is so sad. I can't leave him.

In the distance, the boat engine sputters to life, but then quits. This should bring me hope, but strangely it doesn't. I hear Landon's voice, which is now more panicked, calling to me, "Hold on, baby, I'm coming." More engine sounds. "Presley! I can't hear you honey! Talk to me."

I want to call to him. Tell him that I love him. But the amount of air required for such a feat isn't available. I can't raise my voice above a whisper.

My eyes turn to James again. He's calmer now. He's not sobbing, but there are great furrows across his brow, shadows on his face and the tears still leak from his eyes. "I would save you if I could. I swear to you," he says. And the look in his eyes confirms his promise.

I can't feel my body. I can't feel my hands. My brain is commanding them to hold on, but the only proof I have that I'm still holding on is that I haven't slid from the board. Yet.

James is still kneeling in front of me. I don't know if I'm losing my mind or if he is . . . shining. Like the edges of his body are lined in a luminous thread. The thread glows enough to light him against the darkening sky. I reach for him with my eyes. I don't want to be alone. "James—"

"I'll stay with you until the very end," he says. "Don't be afraid. I won't leave you." James is looking at me like I'm the most pitiful tragedy he's ever seen. Maybe I am.

These are my last moments. Several thoughts compete for space on the stage. My dad. I'm sorry I never was able to reconnect with him like I wanted to.

Chase. How I'll miss him. How he'll miss me. It breaks my heart to hurt him.

My mom. I hope her strength will carry her through and that she will continue to be there for Chase. I take comfort in the fact that Apollo will likely abandon my family once I'm gone. I'm just so sorry for all of the pain. So sorry.

"I'm sorry," I whisper. It's all I can manage. It's meant for Chase. For my mom. For James. For Landon.

"You acted in love." James seems to understand my heart. "You acted in love," he says again and I let his words wash over me, giving me the only warmth I can feel.

Landon. I acted in love for him. With me gone, I hope Apollo will never discover that Landon also has *the sight*. I hope I've done enough to protect everyone I love.

I love.

I love.

At the end of it all, I can say that I loved.

My arms feel light and I know the board is no longer under them. I'm floating weightlessly under a sky that's churning. It's the strangest shade of green. James leans forward, his hands on the board where mine used to be. I focus on his face as the waves overtake me again.

"Don't be afraid," he says.

And I'm not. I'm done fighting. James's eyes are the only thing I can see. They are my only tether to life.

And then I don't see them.

I close my eyes and let myself sink into blackness.

Chapter Fifty

Too Little

(Landon)

If this boat wasn't the only hope I have of saving Presley, I'd burn it right now. Cover it in gas and throw the match. I ram the starter button with my finger again and again, but nothing will catch. The engine complains and groans for more gas. My best guess is that there's still air in the system from when my dad changed the fuel filter, and the only thing I can do is force it out by cranking the engine.

Presley has stopped calling out and that scares me. I don't have time to mess around with this. She won't last long in this cold of water. I'll have to jump in and swim to her if I can't get it started in the next few tries. How are there no life jackets in this boat?

"Come on!" I slam the steering wheel again as I jam the starter button down. I hold it longer this time and the engine grunts to life. At last I have a steady rumble, so I jerk the shifter in reverse, pull away from the shore and crank it into gear. At first glance it appears that Presley is standing, waiting for me, but as I look closer I can tell it's not her. The figure is bigger and dressed in dark pants.

What is happening? Where is she?

As I speed closer all I can see of Presley is a trace of her yellow gown floating near the surface.

Horror.

Panic.

"Help her! Pull her up!" I shout to the man standing . . . on the water. The man is standing *on the water* as Presley's board drifts toward land. He just stares at me like I'm speaking another language. How is this happening? And how can he let her drown?

Closer now, I can see her floating just below the surface, her yellow dress fanned out in the swells like spring petals. Misjudging my speed, I can't slow the boat in time. I'm forced to circle back as I beg the man to help Presley, but he continues to ignore my screams. I glide up next to them and throw the boat in neutral, not wanting to risk the engine dying again when I'll need to get her to help. It dies anyway. I hate to waste one more second, but I chuck the anchor.

Once I jump, with all this wind and waves, the boat could skirt along the surface and out of reach in seconds.

The next instant, I'm diving in and tearing through the waves toward Presley. The water is a freight train to my senses and I gasp against the shock. At last, my fingers reach her dress and I tear at the fabric in an effort to pull her toward me. When her face emerges, her eyes are closed and her lips part peacefully like she's just sleeping. If her lips weren't gray, she could just be sleeping.

"Presley! I got you, baby. Stay with me. Stay with me." I swim to the step at the back of the boat, towing her limp form behind me. She's so still. She doesn't flinch or stir as I drag her up onto the stern. I lay her on her back and the sight of the clear water running out of her mouth and nose takes the ground from beneath my feet. I am petrified. Completely unable to act in any useful way. Her hair is matted to one side of her pale face and her poor little body is trapped inside that soaked gown. She was so beautiful in that gown. The tears coming down my face burn against my skin.

"It's all right, Landon. She's at peace."

I whip around to find the man standing inside my boat. James. How do I know his name? "James?" My voice is hoarse, disbelieving that I'm speaking it, but I don't have time to wonder why.

"She's gone," he says.

Every muscle in my body protests those two words and I rage against their speaker. "No!" I snatch Presley up into my arms and hold her against me. I want to make her stay. I want to fix her. Suddenly, sense is returned to me. I lay her back down and begin compressions on her chest, clearing her lungs of more water. It trickles out the side of her mouth and the sight of it makes me weep.

"Landon." Her soft voice floats from behind me and when I turn and see her standing next to James, I can't believe it. She's still in her yellow gown and it billows around her legs just like her hair, which is now dry and carried in the wind. "Don't. It's okay. I'm okay."

I turn back to the cold, still body I'm trying to awaken and I can see that she's lifeless. The Presley I know is now standing next to James, looking at me and her dead body.

Falling, spinning, drowning.

I'm drowning. I'm in the river, tearing against the current that is too strong. The last air I ever will breathe leaves my lungs in a parade of bubbles toward the surface. At least, I think it's the surface. I'm not sure. I'm not sure which way is up or why I'm suddenly looking down at my body lying on a rocky shore.

The visions flicker and race through my head, each an image—just a slice of memory, but each carrying minutes, hours, and days of depth. Meeting James for the first time on the bank of the river. My funeral. Violet sobbing on her bed. The months of isolation and arguing with James about my reasons for staying.

The decision to take my passage, but then I don't. I don't because I meet Presley that day in the parking lot. I linger on that memory, savor it like I can taste it on my tongue. Savor the moment everything changed for me.

Now the memories are flying by too fast. Central to all of them though, is Presley. Our feet on the trails, running side by side, the sun in her hair. Her laugh. The first kiss we ever share when her spirit breaks through the bounds of her body and connects with mine. The thrill of touching her. The ache of falling in love with her day by day. The torment of leaving her in the meadow.

I remember now. Liam. The other Vigilum. They're closing in and the only choice is to hide her, so I do. My love encircles her and I bring her as far back as I can. To the mountain.

And then I forgot her. How could I have forgotten her?

Every memory from that day on the slope until now is painted with guilt for letting myself forget the time before. I can't hold back my tears. Presley was so patient with me. Watching me with Ivy even after I kissed her and then sent her away. Sitting just a seat away from me in class, knowing all we'd been through but keeping her silence. Why didn't she tell me? Why did she hide it from me?

I wouldn't have believed her. She knew I wouldn't see so she brought my memories back—her way. She made me love her again. I do love her again. I can't be without her.

I don't know who to cling to. The Presley that I'm holding, or the Presley standing next to James. I can't give up on her, so I rock her body in my arms and hold her protectively. James. *He* should have protected her.

"How could you let this happen to her?" I shout, my voice raw. "It was supposed to be me, not her! Never her." I can't keep the sobs from racking through me and I hold Presley to me, trying to make her feel my love. Maybe if she feels how much I need her she will wake up. Maybe it will all be over if she can just see how much I need her.

"I'm so sorry, Landon," the luminous Presley says. She tries to step closer to me, but James puts a hand on her arm and she stops.

"No," James says. I can hear the distress in his voice, and anger builds in me for him trying to take away this moment. It could be my last with her. Can he not give that to me?

But then there's another voice. "Two days," it says.

I turn to the source. A Vigilum stands across from me on the stern. I know he's a Vigilum because I can feel it. There's no denying the dark vibes these things throw off. His tall black boots step down into the boat as he steadies himself with some kind of walking stick. He takes his position next to James, who is visibly livid.

"I gave you two days," the intruder speaks to Presley. "A generous offering in my mind. And then you have the nerve to die on me?" He makes a tsking sound. "Not a very nice way to repay my generosity, is it?"

"Shut your mouth!" I can't stand the way he's talking to her. Addressing her death like it was some minor oversight or mistake. I don't know what his dealings are with Presley and James, but he will not talk to her that way.

His gaze lands on me. I forgot how unsettling the whitish-blue eyes of the watchers can be. Especially when they smile.

"Well, this is unanticipated," he says. "It's remarkable how unpredictable life can be. For instance, I'm sure you didn't expect to bid farewell to your love in such a tragic way." His expression of mock empathy taunts me. "And I didn't expect to find a consolation prize." He touches a bony finger to his chin. "I must know, Landon. How is it that you, too, have *the sight?*"

Chapter Fifty-One

WASTED

(PRESLEY)

It was all for nothing. Apollo knows Landon has *the sight* and he will never leave him and his family alone now. Everything I did to protect him was in vain. Living a life in Apollo's shadow is even worse than death. I didn't think it was possible for my heart to break any more than it already had in the last few moments, but now I know. There is no end to pain.

There is no cure for evil.

There is no hope for any of us now.

James steps between me and Apollo. "As you can see, Presley is no longer available for your purposes."

Apollo, in his restrained way, rounds on James, but his voice is sharp. A sound that turns my blood cold. "Don't try to distract me from the prize before me now. I'm not a fool. And I'm not leaving here without taking what I came for. It makes no difference to me who carries what I'm owed."

Apollo's eyes are lethal when Landon protests. "Just leave. Nobody owes you anything. You're all the same. You take. You lie. You threaten. We've already lost everything, don't you see? There's nothing you can take from us now."

Landon curls over my old body and sobs, his face buried in my hair.

"Not so, my friend," Apollo says. "There is plenty to lose. There's always *plenty* to lose." Apollo's eyes are poisoned with an inky blackness that spreads until his entire eyes are dark. My insides curdle at the sight.

Landon is still quietly crying, but now he stares off at something I can't see. My body slips lifelessly down onto his lap. "No," his broken voice whispers. "Leave them. It's me you want."

I know what Apollo is doing. James told me what he and Erin saw that night at the hospital. How Apollo can make his victims see visions. Anything he wants. Because I know how Vigilim work, I know that Apollo is giving Landon a vision now. Like a wakeful nightmare.

"Please," I call out. "Leave him alone."

After everything, he deserves to live his life in peace. I know it does no good to appeal to Apollo's mercy because it's clear he has none. But what else can I do?

I'm no match for him. I look to James for guidance. For something I can say or do that will make Apollo change his mind.

James looks as bleak as I feel.

"You don't need him," James says. "It's obvious your power is great without his assistance."

It seems James is appealing to Apollo's sense of pride. But I'm afraid Apollo will want Landon no matter what. Because with Landon's feet in the world of the living and the dead, he would be a very useful soldier to Apollo. Just like I would have been.

The sky broods and seethes overhead, the greenish hue darkening in places to a bruised purple. In the distance, a rushing sound roars toward us and then around us. I see the moment that a crack appears in Apollo's expression as the sound takes his attention away from James and Landon and he slowly cranes his head toward the disturbance in the sky.

Heading straight for us is a shape-shifting cloud. An undulating mass that's liquid and unpredictable. As it draws closer, piercing screeches tear through the air. They're birds. Black birds by the thousands, all flocked together, twisting in a strange but beautiful aerial ballet. Apollo takes in the spectacle with apparent fascination.

James grabs my arm and I can tell from the zeal in his eyes, this is no natural phenomenon.

As I look closer, I can see the birds are ravens. A memory from my childhood surfaces. A group of ravens isn't called a flock.

It's called a murder.

"She's coming," James says, not bothering to whisper. The roar of the ravens draws closer, and the sounds of wingbeats assaults our ears as they circle above us in a living cyclone.

"Who?" I ask.

He doesn't answer so I follow his eyes. A single raven flitters around Apollo's head, dashing in to peck at his face, scratch at his eyes. He swipes it away, but not before the bird leaves an angry slash across his cheek. The raven beats her wings, hovering just in front of him and then dissolves into black smoke. The smoke forms the rough outline of a body and then solidifies—revealing Erin. The wind from the birds tosses her red hair around her face and through the tangle I can see her eyes. Fierce and bright.

"It's over for you," she says to Apollo.

Apollo wipes at his cheek and chuckles low in his throat. "Pity," he says, "I was quite enjoying your little parlor trick."

"You would know about tricks," she says. "It's impressive, I'll give you that. How you so benevolently give passages to the very people you stole them from. *If* you give them at all."

227

Apollo's eyes narrow and a muscle tightens along his jaw.

"Oh, yes," Erin continues as her eyes aim skyward toward the cloud of wingbeats and screeches. "They know. And soon, all Vigilum will know. Word has traveled fast since I told them about your little ruse. How you're like a robber that comes in the night, steals the food, and then sells it back to them the next day."

Apollo's pale lips part.

"Nothing more than a common thief. I suppose you think you're special, but you're not. You're just a really good liar."

There's a hardness to Apollo's brow. "Your filthy mouth is not fit to speak my name." His impossibly black eyes darken, carrying a fiendish shadow across his entire face. "Let me shut it for you."

Erin stiffens against Apollo's mental attack. At my side, James lunges to support Landon, who can barely hold his head up now that he's released from Apollo's influence. James gets to Landon just in time to prevent him from slumping to the side and falling overboard.

I rush to Erin's side, but my touch has no effect on her. Her body is tight, trying to survive whatever horrors Apollo inflicts on her.

"It doesn't matter what you do, Apollo," Erin says, though her eyes are a million miles away. "I know your weakness. And they know your weakness." She groans against a new wave of anguish, but persists. "This isn't real. It's just another one of your lies."

Apollo's teeth are gnashing. "This is my dominion. I was the first and I *will* be the last." He targets Erin with a new intensity, twisting his face into a grisly expression.

In turn, Erin's face contorts as a scream tears from her throat. The scream must signal the birds because they stop their ceaseless circling and fall from the sky like arrows raining down. I glimpse the storm of silken feathers, claws, and jeweled black eyes. Just before they hit the water, though, they materialize first into smoke as Erin did and then into human forms. The boat is surrounded for what seems like miles with Vigilum. They stand as James did, ankle deep, watching and waiting. A single raven lands softly on Erin's shoulder.

This spectacle breaks the hold Apollo has on Erin and as she regains her breath, the spark returns to her eyes. "You're outnumbered," she says. "Admit it." She lifts an eyebrow, waiting for Apollo to respond.

He backs away from her, then slowly climbs onto the bow of the ship, not taking his eyes from her. Then he glances furtively at the legions of Vigilum surrounding the boat. "I did it to serve all of you. I have forsaken my own passage for *centuries* so that I could be your defender. To give help to the hopeless." His voice is so confident. So sure.

The raven on Erin's shoulder alights with a few flutters of its wing and hovers before Apollo, who flinches at the intrusion. The raven transfigures into smoke and then into a man. A young man with golden hair that curls up at the ears, wearing an old concert T-shirt.

Apollo swallows hard. "Seth." He blinks rapidly and there's a break in his voice.

Seth half turns and surveys the watching Vigilum and then calmly returns his gaze to Apollo. "Yeah, it's me. I never got a chance to thank you, man. For leaving me that day in the hospital. Friendless, lost, and—oh yeah, without any way out. That was pretty slick, dude. The way you snaked my passage right out from under me."

Apollo backs up half a step and lets out a truncated laugh. But it's all air and no substance. Just like him. "I did no such—"

"Liar!" Seth roars. Then he gestures to the watchers on the water, his face darkening and his mouth curling up on one side into a snarl. "At least have the decency to admit what you did!" His hands clench into fists and a tremble shows along the muscles in his arms.

Apollo's mouth gapes open and then shut. "I—I did it to help the deserving." He appeals to the watching Vigilum now. "This man *wasted* his existence. Squandered his life on drugs and every other kind of filth you could imagine." His eyes are zealous, bulging from his face. "Why should someone like him get to move to the next world when there are so many more deserving? People such as the rest of you?"

Seth's lips pull back, exposing his teeth. The fracturing of his features and the fresh shine of tears in his eyes break my heart. Who knows what this kid has been through that landed him in that kind of life?

He steps forward, lunging a finger into Apollo's chest. Apollo swipes Seth's hand away, but Seth just jabs his finger back in the exact spot. "Who goes and who stays is not up to you. That's up to us. You do not take our will from us." He jabs again powerfully, making Apollo take another half-step back toward the tip of the bow. Seth's voice is louder now. "You are going to pay for what you've done."

A murmur ripples over the Vigilum, and is it my imagination or have they moved in closer? Less space between them, less space between us and them. As I'm trying to confirm my perception, a single raven streaks past me and settles onto Apollo's shoulder. In a frenzied movement, he slaps it away. It lands again, this time on his head. When he tries to grab it, his fingers only cut through smoke. But another raven dives in and takes a peck of flesh from his face as it passes. Soon, it's joined by a handful of more birds, each darting and nipping away flesh from Apollo's ears, face, and hands. I realize then that Seth is gone and I wonder if one of the birds is him.

"Stop it. Call them off!"

"They're your followers, aren't they? *You* call them off." Erin's teeth gleam as a stream of ravens swarm him, covering his body in a fluttering cyclone of clipping sounds, trills, and squawks. He stumbles back and Erin takes the split second to leap onto the bow, charge him, and rip the staff from his hand. Apollo fights against the barrage of beaks and claws.

In a few swift movements she disconnects the ornament on top, which releases a gushing fountain of golden dust. Though I've never seen one, I know they are passages.

Erin holds the staff aloft and swings it in a wide circle, stretching the dust into a swirl of golden strands. The shimmering filaments spread out in a lustrous layer over the boat and then extend, enlarging the reach and scope until the entire army of Vigilum are under its shadow.

Apollo slashes his arms through the air in screams of terror and anger. Erin holds her palm up and the birds relent, scattering skyward with a departing screech. His eyes take us in. James, Landon, me, Erin, and the Vigilum that are left. His face, which before held so much dignity and grace, is now pocked with holes and missing strips of flesh. Cowering, he inches backward like a cornered dog.

"Your turn," Erin says to him, manipulating a passage from the golden film overhead. It trails down like a glimmering rivulet and responds to her motions. She sends it toward Apollo, and it curls and writhes above and behind him . . . almost as if it were eager. Hungry. "I'm not leaving until you take a passage of your own. You will never harm anyone again."

Apollo hisses and turns from her, closing the distance to the tip of the bow as though he's about to leap.

"You'll never rebuild, Apollo. Your dreamscapes won't work. I'll make sure of that. Everyone knows magic tricks lose all their wonder when the methods are revealed. You're a hack. Nobody will ever follow you again. And nobody will ever need you because, let's face it, I've raided your cellar. The shelves are empty."

Apollo's shoulders slump at her words.

She continues, "And I will make it my mission to hunt you to the ends of the earth and to expose you to every lost soul you try to exploit. It won't be hard to find you. Not now."

"Leave me." Apollo wavers on his feet. His eyes meet Erin's and they are two iced pools of bitterness.

Erin steps closer to him. "That will never, ever happen." Apollo sways on his feet, his eyes roving around at the remaining Vigilum.

A chorus of voices rises from the ranks. From the cacophony I'm able to pick out a few words and phrases, "Leave . . . you're not wanted . . . pathetic . . . we'll find you . . ."

Erin's face holds no malice now. Just clear, piercing truth. "I think you may be the most hated Vigilum in history."

The glimmering layer of passages begins to fall away, drifting down like tiny flecks of golden snow.

"Take them!" James calls out to the Vigilum. "They're yours, take them!"

One by one, the Vigilum stretch open their arms and reach skyward. It's as if they call down the passages because strands separate from the cloud and snake down to the callers. They absorb into the brilliant dust, rapture on their faces as they flash into a pillar of light and then are gone. Some linger though, not yet taking a passage, and I wonder at that.

The transference to the next life has a vibration to it. A kind of music I could feel inside me but could never put into words. It brings tears to my eyes—watching them take their freedom at last. I look to Landon and he's watching the scene with awe.

Erin captures the few remaining strands of passages with a flourish of her fingers, and coaxes them back into the staff, but leaves the hovering dust around Apollo. "Your followers are gone. There's nothing left for you. You're worthless."

Apollo's eyes are two empty pits of hate. Something comes over his face that alarms every nerve in my body. He gnashes his teeth and lets out a scream that whitewashes my senses in terror. Then he claws at the golden dust with both hands.

The music isn't the same. It's a single vibration of discord that I feel in the pit of my stomach.

He vanishes in a pillar of dirty smoke.

Chapter Fifty-Two

Dissolution

(Landon)

In the distance, a handful of Vigilum still congregate on the now calm water, waiting and watching. I'm guessing from what I just witnessed that Erin is a friend of James or Presley. Staff in hand, she smoothes her free hand over the black horn, taking in those that chose to linger with an urgency in her eyes.

For a few moments, nobody seems to know what to say. The monster is gone. Relief overpowers me, but not for long. My eyes drop, to the beautiful girl lying motionless in my arms. I beg her body to stir. To take a breath. But her stillness is unrelenting. Water laps at the side of the boat like an insensitive bystander.

"Presley, we should go," James says. "The both of you know this isn't going to get any easier." James's face is pained and as much as I don't want to admit it, I can tell he's trying to protect Presley and me from further anguish. But Presley defies James by detaching from him and sitting next to me on the stern. Her eyes briefly sweep over her body and then her hand cradles my face. I can feel her love infusing through my skin and filling my being.

"I never meant for this to happen. I was only trying to save you—to keep you safe," she says.

My hand closes around her wrist, refusing to let her touch leave my skin. "I remember everything, Presley. Every single thing. Meeting you, our runs on the trail, watching you sleep, falling in love more every day." I'm bridging the gap between her spirit and her body. One hand connected to each, begging them to reunite. I can't turn loose of her body because that would be abandoning hope and if I do that, I'll come undone. Presley's eyes are still green, but look brilliant somehow. I gaze into them, pleading for her to stay.

"Please," I say, squeezing her wrist tighter. "I can't do this without you. I've had the chance to love you twice and it wasn't enough. I want to be with you always." The pain clenches around my throat, making my voice break. "Don't leave me. Please—"

Presley's eyes close against the emotion brewing in them. A tear trails down her cheek. I take her hand from my face and hold it against my heart. Then James infringes on us.

"You know that you can't ask that of her, Landon. You of all people should understand that it's not a half-life you want for her. Not for someone you love so much."

My eyes flash to James's. "Not a half-life. I want her to live! To not give up on us." The venom in my tone forces him back a step and the rising volume of my voice rasps against the rawness in my throat. "I want you . . . to do whatever it takes to save her. There has to be something. Things you thought were hopeless weren't. Look at me. You have to know a way." My lips are trembling and I refuse to let go of Presley's hand.

James's mournful eyes glisten. "You know I can't do that."

I feel my insides breaking. Snapping and splintering, cutting and bleeding. Sinking into a blackness that scares me. Presley's arms come around me and we're sobbing into each other's necks, each not able to let go.

Her voice is at my ear and I swallow down the pain of how beautiful it sounds. Now that I know her. Now that I remember. Now that I understand how much she loved me all along.

"I'll always love you, Landon. I promise you that with time it will get better. And when it does, I want you to be happy. Do you hear me? Do what makes you happy. That's what I want for you more than anything."

"I can't do this, Presley. I can't. Not after I just got you back."

"I know, baby. I wish we had more time. I would stay if I could, but I can't do that to you. You can't get better if I'm still here."

"There has to be another way." I say the words, but I know there isn't. I'm just delaying the inevitable.

Erin steps down from the bow into the boat, momentarily drawing my attention away from Presley. Her eyes are on mine and there's some kind of purpose in them as she sidles past James. I can't decipher her intention as she sits near Presley's body. She pushes the wet skirts of the yellow gown up to Presley's knees and then lays her own hands on top of Presley's lower legs.

Erin closes her eyes for a few beats of time that stretch out into what feels like minutes. She breathes evenly and a look of serenity smoothes the space between her brows, making the little crease that was there, disappear. When she again opens her eyes, she looks to James. "Her body is still vital."

I don't know what this otherworldly vocabulary means, but it sparks a jolt of hope in my heart. "What does that mean?" I ask. But nobody is answering me. Neither James nor Erin.

James shakes his head, dejectedly. "It won't be for long. There's not time to get her to any help. Even if we could, it wouldn't matter. I can *feel* it."

I cut in, "Someone tell me what that means—the body is still vital." Every millisecond that ticks by without an answer turns my insides hard.

Bewildered, Presley looks between Erin and James for answers. "Erin?" Presley's voice is tiny, trepidatious.

Erin speaks to James. "I didn't tell you because I wasn't one hundred percent sure I could trust you with the information. And Apollo, he had watchers everywhere. You have no idea—"

"What? What?" Everything in me is threatening to explode into pieces. My hand closes even tighter around Presley's and she squeezes back in turn.

Finally Erin talks over me. "Presley called a spirit back into a body that had died but that was still vital."

James's eyes widen and his jaw hangs slack. A few beats of agonizing silence pass. "What are you saying? She—"

"She called a spirit back, James. And it obeyed." Both James and Erin are now looking at Presley, but each face wears a completely different expression. James—shock. Erin—something akin to admiration or pride.

Now I'm looking to Presley, but her breath is coming fast and dismay paints her features. "Russell?" she says.

Erin nods her head. "Yes."

Presley stands, her hand disconnecting from mine. She's backed against the edge of the boat like a scared rabbit. "That . . . that was just an accident. A fluke."

Erin's eyes flash an intensity. "No it wasn't. You did that. I was there. I saw it."

I'm sick over the letdown. "The dog?" What are they talking about? Presley saved a dog? "How does that even matter right now?"

"Even if I did what you say, it was just an animal. And I couldn't do it again. I don't even know what I did."

"Maybe that's not true," James interrupts. "You have come back before. When you were a child. Maybe you caused that to happen as well." James brings a fist to his lips and shakes his head. "It's worth trying. At this point, nothing would surprise me." His eyes shine with tears.

"But I can't." Presley's voice and hands are trembling. She looks to me, heartbroken apologies in her eyes. "I don't know how."

"Yes, you do," I say. "Yes you *do*." I reach for her, but she doesn't extend her hand in return.

Instead, she looks to James, her face crumpling in despair. "Help me. Please." She holds out a shaking hand to James and with the tenderness of a father, he goes to her, closes his large hand around her small one, and guides her to me.

"Go to him. Let your love for him call you home," James says.

The blackness in the pit of my stomach flees and I'm suddenly filled with light, a hope that rushes and expands through my body so that I expect to see it pour from my fingertips at any second. My eyes meet Presley's and I thrill at the determination that is banishing the fear in hers. I reach for her and she takes my hand.

"I love you, Presley. Come back to me. Come back." I gently pull her toward me, allowing her to lay herself exactly over her body. To once again fill the empty shell.

I witness the melding of flesh and spirit as the light of her being melts into her cold form, warming the skin on her breast with a pink flush. The life bleeds into her cheeks, thawing the stone-like features of her face into the youthful beauty I once knew. Her lips bloom with color and I'm drawn to her, closing my mouth over hers, which begins to warm under my kiss. Everything about this kiss feels right and whole. I know she feels it because I can feel her. The real her.

Taking my lips from hers, I pull back to witness the miracle of her chest rising in its first full breath.

Chapter Fifty-Three

FINISHED

(PRESLEY)

I must be dreaming. Or I'm in heaven. Because I know I'm in Landon's arms and his lips are on mine. This is the only bliss I want. I have to be dreaming, because I want to kiss him back, but I have to do something else. Something important.

I need to breathe.

I'm not used to telling my body to pull air into my lungs, but for this instance it's a necessary command. A choice. So I do it. I tell myself to breathe and the air fills my chest in a delicious rush of life. The newfound vitality travels through my body making the tips of my fingers, my scalp, every inch of my skin tingle with . . . joy. I open my eyes and see that I'm not dreaming. I am in fact, in the arms of the love of my life. His hair is blowing in the breeze and I can feel the rise and fall of the swells beneath us. Landon's smiling through tears and that ignites a stinging in my own eyes.

"I knew it couldn't all be for nothing. I knew you'd come back to me," Landon says. He pulls me up against his chest and holds me, but then pulls back with a look of concern. "Presley, you do remember us, don't you?"

I laugh through a sob as I pull him into a kiss. And then another one. Between the kisses I reassure him, "I remember us. Every single second." His lips smile against mine and I can't tell if I'm shivering because of the wet dress I'm wearing or because my body can't contain all of this feeling.

Landon reluctantly pulls away from my kiss, peppering my lips with a few parting ones of his own. He moves to the middle of the boat and tears a seat cushion from a seat, pulling out a heavy wool blanket. He's back in seconds, wrapping me in it and then his arms. "I am never letting you go. Ever."

With one arm around me, he reaches to James and Erin. I do the same and they come to us and each take a hand. "Thank you," Landon says. "For not giving up on her. She wouldn't be here with me if it weren't for you, Erin."

"And you," he says to James, "you showed her the way." Landon's voice is thick, but he's smiling. "I know that kind of thing isn't your normal gig."

James is shaking his head, smiling. His eyes shine with unshed tears. "No, it isn't. Not my usual gig at all." He turns to Erin. "What will I do with myself now that these two aren't wreaking all kinds of havoc in the universe?"

Erin laughs. "I don't know what you're going to do, but I know what I'll be doing." She takes up Apollo's walking staff and lays a hand over the polished horn. "I'll be returning these to the people who need them."

For the first time, I notice that the lingering Vigilum who surrounded the boat are now gone. It saddens me to think that they left without a passage. Perhaps they felt undeserving or were too scared to move on for one reason or another. I hope Erin can help them.

"It will be good to have a purpose again," Erin says, and James nods in understanding.

"Make sure to save one for yourself." James smiles crookedly.

"I will," she promises. Then her face turns serious. "But really, James. Where will you go?"

James shrugs. "Something will come up, I'm sure. It always does." Just as he says the words, two figures emerge from the trees on the rocky shore of the island. The light is fading, and I can't see them perfectly. Somehow I know they aren't of this world, but it doesn't scare me.

"James," I say. And something in my tone causes him to follow my gaze to the two people on the shore who, looking closer, I can see are a woman and a young boy. The woman hails us with an uplifted hand.

"Lucy!" James's voice comes out in a gush of breath. "And Michael. Oh, my sweet boy, Michael." James's face is streaked with tears as he turns back to us with elation on his face. "It's finally time."

I only heard James speak of his family once before. Back when Landon and I were fighting to justify our love to him. I remember the feeling in his eyes when he spoke of his wife and son. How heartbroken he was when he lost them over a century ago. I don't know how long he's been separated from them, but it seems his assignment has come to a close and his family is here to bring him home.

James lays a fist to his lips again, obviously struggling against the emotion. Then he takes a large step, pulling Landon loose from our embrace and into his. Landon hugs him back with mirrored intensity. They exchange words without letting go of one another.

"I wish I had more time with you, boy," James says. "I'm so proud of you." His voice breaks on the end. "You take good care of this girl, you hear me? It was obviously meant to be. I didn't understand it at the time, but it was always meant to be," James says.

"Thank you," Landon says, clearing the emotion from his throat. "I'm sorry I gave you such a hard time. I know you always wanted what was best for us."

They part and take each other into a firm handshake. "I don't know how to repay you for everything you've done for us."

James closes his other hand around their handshake. "You just take good care of Presley and Chase. They're a package deal." James's comment brings tears to my eyes because I know how much he loves Chase. And I love him for understanding that whoever loves me will also need to love him. I notice Erin wiping a tear from her cheek as she smiles at James.

"I will. I promise." Landon speaks the words to James, but my heart swells with his pledge. The two pull each other into a last hug and much back slapping ensues as they each blink away tears.

James turns to me now and takes my hands into his. "Thank you," he says. "For teaching me a thing or two about belief." He shakes his head. "I don't pretend to understand the reasons behind what was allowed to happen here. It's incredible—you two finding each other through the obstacles of time and death. Most people, even people like me, would think it was impossible. But somehow you two came back to one another. It's an incredibly unique miracle. And trust me, I've seen my share."

"We couldn't have done it without you," I say. "Or you, Erin." I turn my eyes to hers and the warmth and friendship pours back to me. "I wish you both could stay forever. I really do."

Then James takes me tenderly in his arms and strokes the back of my hair. "Oh, sweetheart. You have far too much life to live to have any time for an old man like me." His voice catches and a lump rises in my throat. "Go and live it now. Be happy." I hug him tighter and he hugs me back. I'm not sure how to let go, but James does it for me.

James nods to Erin. "I'll see you around." The way he said it makes me think it is true.

Erin plants a kiss on her fingertips and sends it his way. "See you around. Thanks for seeing something good in me."

James shakes his head and smiles back at her. "So much good."

And then he's gone. My eyes fly to the shore where he's running toward his family. When he reaches them, they all three hold one another in an embrace I'll never forget. Soon after, they all three fade from view.

Landon's arm comes around me as we watch our friend leave with his family at last. Erin straightens and we know her time is nearing as well.

"Come find us before you take your passage, Erin. Please. We'll want to say good-bye," Landon says.

"I will," she says. "When my work is done here, I will."

"And you don't have to do this alone, you know. We're your friends. Come to us when you need to," I add.

"I'll be okay, I think. There are still so many lost souls. And they need me. Helping them will bring me a lot of peace."

Erin comes in and hugs Landon and me in turn. "Good-bye, my friends. Thanks for being freaky little weirdos with *the sight*. Not sure where I'd be if I hadn't met you."

We both laugh at that and Landon shoots her a two-finger salute, his arm still holding me to his side. "Any time."

Erin climbs onto the bow for the last time and walks off the tip and into thin air. Scenes like that never cease to impress me. "Wow," I say.

"Yeah. Wow." Landon's voice is soft and velvety so I turn. He's looking down on me. His fingers trail into my hair, guiding it away from my face in the softest movement. My skin sings at his touch.

This is the first moment we've had alone since his memory came back to him. The first time it's just us with all of our combined memories and experiences.

From now and from before.

Looking into his eyes, I can't imagine loving someone more than I do right now. I unwrap my blanket and fold him into it. This tight circle of space containing our bodies feels like the only world I'll ever need.

"It's about time you took me for a ride on this old boat. I've been waiting for what seems like forever," I tease. He smiles at me, recognition glinting in his eyes. My mind travels the swift roads back to the time before when Landon was only spirit, but I didn't know yet. Of when he took me to the boathouse for the first time.

"I remember that," he croons. "I wanted to kiss you so badly. So, so badly." His lips curl into an irresistible smile.

"I wanted to kiss you too," I say, marveling at the way he makes my heart leap with a single look.

"I have good news for you," he says, leaning in so that our noses nearly touch. "I'm going to be kissing you forever." His lips brush briefly against mine, only making me want to kiss him more.

"And ever," I say. Grateful I don't have to wait long to feel his lips on mine again. He kisses me sweetly, lovingly. A kiss that sings with promise.

His voice is silk against my lips. "And ever."

Epilogue

(PRESLEY)

In the clear light of midsummer, Vikingsholm Castle barely seems like the same place. The troubling events of four years ago have melted away like winter's snow—the memories, faded. From the upper round room's window, I survey the shimmering water of Emerald Bay, its center ornamented with Fannette Island. I think of James and his family and wonder what he's doing now. I haven't seen him since that night, and though I miss him, I know it's the right thing.

I saw Erin twice before she took her passage. She was happy when she went. At peace. I'd long since forgiven her for the events those years ago, and she'd forgiven herself, so our parting was affectionate and emotional. I've felt her absence acutely. I think we would have been lifelong friends had the circumstances been different. Thankfully, I have Violet. Though now, she's more of a sister than a friend. She lays a hand on my shoulder.

"Are you ready to go down?" she asks. I turn from the window and take in Violet. She's beautiful in her bridesmaid dress. The peachy lace drapes from her tall form in light, feminine layers, complimenting the sage and peony bouquet perfectly. She hands me my matching bouquet, and together we take the stairs down to the entry and out to the beach.

Though Reese and Zoey were happy to accept the generous gift of a Vikingsholm wedding from Frank and Afton, Reese respected the wishes of his free-spirited bride and conceded to waterfront nuptials instead of a stuffy court-yard affair. Afton, thrilled to take part in the first Blackwood wedding in years, agreed if the reception could be held in the courtyard. So with banquet tables set on the stone-floored courtyard, and a simple ceremonial area staged right in the sand, everyone was happy.

Zoey opted for a single guitarist to play music of his own creation at her ceremony. He sits casually on a stool, his sleeves rolled to the elbow and smiles at me as I follow Violet down the aisle. My eyes catch Landon's who stands behind Reese. He's smiling in that way that weakens me in the knees. It's hard to walk so near him without a touch, and take my position in the line.

These boys make my heart swell. Reese, handsome and nervous in his suit and bowtie. Are those suspenders I see peeking out under his jacket? Landon, almost his double with the same near-black hair and broad shoulders. And behind him, Chase, looking quite dapper in his own bowtie and suspenders. Chase keeps glancing at Landon for reassurance and my heart melts as I see Landon reach over and squeeze his hand. Landon and I practiced with Chase for this day and he's doing beautifully.

I find Frank Blackwood in the front row and give him a warm smile. He's already blubbering, bless him. He holds the hand of his brother, Evan, who looks like he could belong in a rock band, with his slicked back peppered hair and his tailored leather jacket. He brought a date, too. I haven't met her yet, but that's so Uncle Evan. Leave it to him to bring a beautiful mystery woman to his own son's wedding. I stifle a giggle and shake my head.

My mom sits on Afton's right. Each of them are looking a bit misty as well. Reese and Zoey's wedding is kind of like a preview. I feel for the diamond solitaire on my left hand and circle it around my finger. I still can't believe it's real. In another month, I'll be walking down the aisle too. Two Blackwood weddings in one summer.

Frank Blackwood sniffs loudly and takes out a handkerchief. Uncle Evan chuckles and pats Frank's leg. I think Frank is the most excited out of everyone. He already bought tiny skis and gave them to Reese and Landon. "For when the kids are ready," he said. I glow inside when I think of what a great grandpa he will be to our kids someday even though babies are quite a ways down the road.

Frank is such a teddy bear. He even gave Chase a job at the lodge. With the help of a fantastic occupational therapist, Chase now helps out at the rental and waxing counters. He runs a very tight ship and the other employees are happy to fall in line with his excellent abilities to keep the place organized. He has a summer gig too.

Landon is in the middle of his second summer of operating Blackwood Paddleboard Company, and Chase is his right hand man. The last couple of summer breaks have been busy with learning how to start and run a business together, planning our wedding and all of the kissing. Lots and lots of kissing. I'm amazed either of us passed our classes. But Landon's a year away from graduating with his business degree, and I've been accepted to UNR's School of Law.

I was heartbroken when Landon injured himself months before the Calgary Olympics, but we got through it. I was more upset than he was. I finally let it go the night he looked into my eyes and said, "I'm really okay. My dreams aren't what they were a year ago. I have new dreams now." And then he slipped the ring on my finger.

Trying to be discreet, I touch the cool cut stone to my lips, letting my mind linger on the memory of that perfect night. Landon catches my eye and I smile shyly at him. I can't believe this man will be mine forever.

Zoey makes her way down the aisle in an off-white lace slip dress. Her strawberry hair is crowned with a wreath of peonies. I smile at the way her freckled skin warms in the afternoon sun and the way Reese's eyes light as she approaches. I never thought of him pairing up with someone like Zoey. But they are perfect for each other. She plays her music for him while he makes his beautiful boats in the side bay of Blackwood Auto. They're happy and that makes me happy.

Zoey doesn't even wait for permission. When she reaches Reese, she wraps her arms around his neck and kisses him soundly, eliciting laughter and some whooping from the audience. Once they part and the officiator takes his place, I look out over the people here to celebrate their love. Each face is a dear friend. Or a future family member. I reach up and squeeze Violet's elbow, barely able to contain my happiness. These people are my life now and I couldn't be more grateful.

As Reese and Zoey exchange their vows, Landon and I can't take our eyes off each other. The words float between us . . . *forever, to be yours, pledge to love, cherish, forsaking all others.* I see the promises shining in his eyes and I return them a hundred fold.

When Zoey and Reese seal their marriage with another kiss and make their way down the sandy path to start their lives together, Landon and I meet at the top of the aisle. He takes my hand and kisses it, letting his lips linger on my skin, his eyes teasing, but full of love. "So are you ready to become Mrs. Blackwood?"

I slip my hand under his jacket and give him a playful pinch to the ribs. "Depends, what does this position entail?"

He slides his hand around my waist, pulling me closer. "Oh, the usual, I suppose. Lifelong devotion, breakfast for dinner every Sunday, an entire extended family who loves you more than they even love me . . ." He leans in and kisses the skin between my neck and my shoulder. "And some other things."

"Cookies?" I say, trying not to laugh out loud at how much his lips tickle on that sensitive spot.

"If you're good, I suppose. But they'll cost you," he says, pulling back slightly, his eyes crinkling on the edges.

I smile back at him, my heart bursting with how lucky I am to have this man. "Oh?" I say.

He gives me a little squeeze on my hip. "Can't get something for nothing, you know."

"How's this then," I say. "If I promise to love you every day for the rest of my life in the best way I know how, will you promise to always give me cookies?"

"I'm liking where this is going," he says, stroking his chin. "But I hesitate to commit until I know you're good for it." He draws back a little further, his eyes passing over my expression like he's trying to judge my character.

"Oh, I'm good for it," I say, laughing at how deadpan he can be at the drop of a hat. He laughs back, but then his gaze deepens as does his voice.

"Prove it," he says. He pulls me by the small of my back, closer to him again.

My gaze matches his, and I'm lost in the blue of his eyes. "I plan to. For the rest of my life."

He takes one last fervent look at me before his eyes close and his lips meet mine. "I'll love you forever," he says, our lips still touching. I kiss him back, wordlessly communicating the same. It's almost impossible to pull ourselves away, but we do have a reception to attend. Toasts to give, cake to eat.

Finally separating my lips from his, I take one last look around. "Then meet me here next month. Same place. August 6th. I'll be the one in the white dress standing right in this spot waiting for you."

A wide smile breaks across his face. A smile so joyful, I know my life with him will be the dream I always hoped for. The life *we* always hoped for but never thought possible. "It's a date," he says.

He takes my hand and leads me back down the aisle, through the soft music, into the waning afternoon light and into the rest of our lives.

The End

Acknowledgments

Together we'd like to thank the team at Cedar Fort: Kaitlin Barwick, Briana Farr, Hali Bird, and Melissa Caldwell. Thank you to Shawnda Craig for capturing the essence of *Before* with your beautiful cover design. Vikki Butler—you rock. You always have our back.

A special thanks to Brock Shinen for your time and expertise.

Kendall Tenney and the team at Las Vegas Now—thank you for sharing our story with Las Vegas!

Thank you to our beta readers: Sarah Swindel, Jaune Curtis, Sara Cecchini, Brookie Cowles, Emily Taylor, and Lisa Jurvelin. Your enthusiasm and input made *Before* a better story.

So much gratitude to Kim Larkin, Holly Feland, Michelle and Brent Larkin, Frank and Sandy Cecchini, Christene Houston, Steph Budoff, and Sara Cecchini for the launch party of a lifetime! Thank you to Craig Bergonzoni for capturing it all on film.

Thank you to the network of book bloggers who read and shared reviews for Beyond.

Huge hugs to Terry and Charlie Cecchini, Danielle Skiles, The Peavine Pickers and the team at Wishes and Wild Flowers. We'll never forget that hoe down!

Thank you to the teams at Barnes and Noble Las Vegas, Barnes and Noble Temecula, and the Round Mountain library. Those first book signings will always be cherished. Thank you for welcoming us.

Catina Haverlock

A huge thank you to our readers! Your excitement for *Beyond* is the reason for this sequel. I hope you will love this story as much as we enjoyed telling it. Much gratitude to every person who showered us with love and support through your messages, reviews, attendance at book signings and parties, etc. You made me feel like a rock star and I'll never forget it!

Thank you to the autism community. Many of you shared how Chase and his story resonated with you and how you were grateful to see autism portrayed in a real and raw way. Your encouragement filled me with confidence to continue Chase's story in *Before*. The autism prevalence is now 1 in 37 boys and 1 in 59 children—an entire generation of precious individuals without a voice. Thank you for inspiring me to speak up for them.

Sarah Swindel—I can't tell you in words how much your selfless friendship and fierce loyalty means to me. Thank you for your love for me, and your love for this story and its characters.

To my coauthor and sister, Angela—thank you for a wild ride filled with belly-hurting laughter, creative collaboration and for your confidence in me.

Finally, thank you to my family. To my husband, Scott—your sacrifice of free time without one complaint during deadline season makes me want to be better. Adam—my real life inspiration for Chase—thank you for carrying what you carry and allowing me to share a little of you with the world. Zac—you've grown from my little boy to a faithful partner. Thank you for your patience, love and support. Elle Belle—thank you for celebrating every success of this journey with me. Your excitement keeps me excited. Crew—I love that you recently asked me when the movie for *Beyond* would hit theaters! Way to believe, little man, way to believe. Zac, Ellie, and Crew—you carry a lot too, and much of how Presley loves and cares for her brother comes straight from you. You are awesome.

ANGELA LARKIN

I'd like to acknowledge the community of people who've supported me in the joyful pursuit of creating stories.

First, to my husband, Nic and my children. I recognize and appreciate the sacrifice of time you've given so that I can write. You five are my biggest cheerleaders. You celebrate every piece of good news, you compliment me and even brag about me! Y'all know how to make a mama feel like a million bucks. Thank you for making my dreams important in your lives.

Coauthoring my first book, *Beyond*, was an unforgettable experience because of the amount of excitement and well wishes from my friends, family and communities I've been a part of. That enthusiasm for the first book carried me through the writing of the second one. I want to give special thanks to my people, the people of Round Mountain, Tonopah, and Las Vegas, Nevada. I was showered with your love and support. To every person who came to a book signing, launch party or book club, thank you. After the book tour for *Beyond*, I was physically and emotionally spent because I didn't know how to take in so much love. I never anticipated the sheer tidal wave of backing we would receive. I don't know how to repay it. So, I just offer my deepest thanks.

Thanks to my coauthor and sister, Catina, for your special way of getting me through those valleys of writing-self-doubt. You are generous in spirit in all you do.

Aside from the happiness I get from creating, I started writing romance to solve a problem. I couldn't find enough books that were intensely romantic without crossing my lines. It all began with writing a story I would love to read. Thank you to all of the readers who have shared your experiences with me about how the Beyond series has affected you. Your stories touch my heart. To those of you who have shared how meaningful it was to relive those feelings of first love and loss—your words stay with me and give me the push to keep writing.

Thank you to Kiki Comin for always encouraging me and letting me call you my best friend even though I upped and moved to North Carolina!

Lastly, I give thanks to God for making my dreams possible. I see His hand in the smallest details.

About Catina Haverlock

Catina Haverlock is a #1 best-selling coauthor of *Beyond*, a Whitney Award Finalist. She worked her way through college as a TV reporter and a dating game show host. A sucker for young adult romance stories (both real and make-believe), she has a panache for matchmaking and loves that many of her "setups" have resulted in marriages.

After spending most of her adult life in Las Vegas, Catina traded in tumbleweeds for earthquakes and now lives with her husband and four children near San Diego, California. If she's not home, chances are you can find her at the beach, Disneyland, or In-N-Out.

Scan to Visit

www.beyondthenovel.com

About Angela Larkin

Photo Credit: Kiki Comin

Angela Larkin is a #1 best-selling coauthor of *Beyond*, a Whitney Award Finalist. She spent much of her childhood under a blanket with a flashlight, secretly reading past bedtime. She's been a gold miner, a pool cleaner, a mannequin dresser, and a teacher. She's lived a true romance: meeting her husband in a case of mistaken identity. They recently moved with their four children from the sparkling city of Las Vegas to the shade of the North Carolina pines.

Scan to Visit

www.beyondthenovel.com